<u>Praise</u>

"This book was a wild ride from beginning to end. There were so many fun twists that I didn't see coming, and the chemistry between the two main characters? Absolutely magical."

—Angela Montoya, author of *Sinner's Isle*

"Come for the magic and twisty action; stay for the incredible cast of characters. Octavia, Leif, and their found family have captured my heart! Full of lovable and complex characters, jaw-dropping twists, and a wonderful magic system, *Cursed Coven* is an unputdownable witchy read."

—Allyson S. Barkley, author of the
Until the Stars are Dead series

"A deliciously dark, yet heartwarming debut. Destructive, sexy, and witchy, *Cursed Coven* beautifully blends tragedy, self-destruction, found family, and forbidden romance into a story that pulls you in from page one!"

—Emily Blackwood, bestselling author of
the Fae of Rewyth series

"A refreshingly adult take on the magical dark academia genre, *Cursed Coven* grips its readers from the first page and doesn't let go."

—Jamie Zaccaria, author of *Lavender Speculation*

"Cursed Coven is an action-packed coming-of-age story that has it all: romance, a diverse found family, a bold heroine that grabs your heart, and more. Octavia's journey is so relatable, and I'm rooting for her all the way. I can't wait for the next installment!"

—CK Fullerton, author of *Blood and Brujeria*

CURSED

KARA BADALAMENTI

COVEN

WILDLING PRESS

ISBN: 978-1-957833-06-4
LCCN: 2023905905

Designed by Michael Hardison
Production managed by Christina Kann
Proofread by Mary-Peyton Crook

Printed in the United States of America

Published by

 **WILDLING PRESS**

www.wildlingpress.com

To those who fear their darkness is unworthy of love.
All of you is worthy.

And to the band, Paramore—for teaching me this lesson
& inspiring the words on these pages.

PROLOGUE:
DECEMBER 30TH, 2003

The chill of the night penetrated the walls of the house despite the fires crackling in the hearths. All the adults were cramped into the large sitting room, engaging in "grown-up talk," but Octavia paid them no mind as she raced up the stairs to find her next victim. She had already eliminated two of her friends in their game of tag.

She was halfway up the staircase when she felt a gust of cold air blow across her face. Unperturbed, she continued up and came across an open window in the third-floor hallway. The night was frigid and still outside.

Why would this be open on such a cold night? Octavia wondered.

She reached up to close the window when the sounds of rapid gunshots and screams froze her in place. Before her, the snowy scene was tranquil; the deadly barrage was coming from inside the house, stories below. Hairs prickled on the back of her neck as a shiver ran down her spine. She turned toward the staircase, her hand dropping to her side, and walked to the railing. She looked over the banister as more screams pierced the cool air.

The front door banged open, the sharp *crack!* of splintering wood making Octavia flinch and the walls shudder. Several people dressed in black charged into the house, heading straight down the long hallway, toward the sitting room. Octavia's grip tightened around the wooden rail as her stomach dropped. Terror twisted its way through her chest, so cold it burned.

But the urge to protect her parents quickly overcame her fear. She didn't know what she would do, but she needed to do something. As Octavia moved to the top of the staircase, a pervasive thought stalled her mid-step. After a moment's hesitation, she whipped in the opposite direction and continued down the hallway.

In the first room on the left, Octavia found June hiding in a corner. Her flaming red hair shone in the moonlight, and her eyes were wide with fear.

"Come here," Octavia whispered. "We need to find the others."

"No!" June whispered back, her voice quivering as misty clouds of breath swirled around her words. "I—I'm scared."

Octavia grabbed her trembling friend by the wrist and yanked her up from her hiding place. Pulling June along behind her, she jogged down the hallway, peering into every room. Endless, disorienting screams assailed their senses as the hallway wrapped back around to the giant staircase, spitting them out where Octavia had started.

None of the others are on this floor. Where do we go next? Up or down?

Panic crushed Octavia's chest as her gaze locked with June's. Wide green eyes brimming with tears mirrored the fear Octavia felt. In the next breath, she decided to go farther up the staircase, away from the intruders, dragging June along with her. They'd reached the fifth step when June let out a high-pitched scream. Nausea upended Octavia's stomach as June's wrist was ripped from her grasp.

Breath burst from Octavia's lungs as two large arms gripped her around the middle and yanked her off her feet. The stairwell faded into a single fuzzy brown smudge until her chest expanded, air flooding every corner of her body, snapping her vision back into focus. A heavy weight pinned her against something solid—someone solid.

Her captor was big and tall, so Octavia did the only things she could think of. She kicked, thrashed, bit, and scratched. Anything to make the person drop her. But every blow she landed only made the grip around her tighten.

My tummy hurts! Let me go! I want to go home! she wanted to scream.

But she was already home. And this wasn't a nightmare. Mom would not be waking her up with soft words and warm hugs. This was real.

June continued to scream as they descended the two and a half flights of stairs to the foyer. Octavia's captor muttered several bad words under his breath in response. They passed the front door, which was still hanging ajar, and rounded the corner into the sitting room.

Octavia's mouth filled with sour bile, and she gagged as dread clawed up her throat.

The fire in the hearth had been doused and was now smoking heavily. Crimson blood splattered the walls. Several bodies lay motionless on the floor. The remainder of Octavia's friends were huddled in the corner of the room, surrounded by several people dressed in black.

The adults, her friends' parents, were grouped together in the opposite corner. The intruders all held firearms or big knives in their hands, each weapon aimed toward a member of Octavia's family. Instinctively, she scanned the room for her parents, but her eyes were overflowing with tears, and everything was blurry.

"Found these two up on the third floor," her captor grunted as he dropped her next to her friends. They immediately pulled her into their embrace, each one of them trembling like a leaf. June joined the huddle a moment later.

One, two, three, four, five, six, seven, eight, Octavia counted her friends frantically. *All here.* The head count was a force of habit that had been hammered into her head by Elder Thaddeus. The coiled knots in her stomach relaxed just a fraction.

A tall man spoke first, his glossy black gun pointed at the adults and his voice full of hatred. "You thought you could hide from us forever? Pitiful." An uneasy silence, interrupted by sporadic sobs and moans of pain, followed his question. "Cooperate, and we will leave the children unharmed. Fail to do so, and we will be forced to use more ... draconian methods."

A woman Octavia recognized snarled, "I know your kind are ruthless, but would you really stoop so low as to murder defenseless children?" She had long, platinum blonde hair, and her body was visibly shaking with rage. Octavia recognized her from holidays and family meetings but wasn't sure exactly who she was. The woman raised an empty hand toward the man as if she were preparing to slap him, but she was too far away to do so. Her face was full of an emotion Octavia had never witnessed before—her eyebrows were pinched tightly together, just like her lips, but her eyes were sad, as if she knew what was going to happen next.

"We'll do whatever it takes to restore balance," the stranger replied calmly, lowering his gun. "If the sacrifice of satanic youths serves His divine plan, so be it."

"Your lot should know by now that's not where our magic comes from," the woman hissed through clenched teeth. "Our craft might be spiritual in nature, but we aren't religious people. We don't worship gods—or fallen angels, for that matter. Our magic comes from the essence of nature."

Magic? Are they here because of our family's magic? Octavia wondered. *But how do they know about it? We aren't allowed to practice outside the walls of this house. It's forbidden.*

"Of course, that's what you'd have us believe. But we know

the truth. Lucifer doesn't want to lose his followers after all, his *accursed* army." The man spat the words as he tightened his hold on the firearm, readjusting his aim.

A deep exhale swept through the woman's lips as she lowered her head in defeat. Octavia's heart thrashed uncontrollably in her chest, and her head felt light and dizzy. The pounding of her pulse in her ears almost drowned out the words the woman spoke next.

"We will never give up our way of life." The woman raised her face to meet the man's, her chin inching higher and higher until she was glaring down her nose at him. "You'll have to kill us all."

The man's face split into a grim smile. "Very well."

He pulled the trigger, and the room exploded into a cacophony of noise. Octavia's eyes narrowed against the flashes of gunfire. She could barely process the scene unveiling before her. Bullets sliced through the air, and bodies started falling. Octavia watched in horror as Uncle Adam hit the ground, clutching his chest; Aunt Tamara's lifeless body slumped face-first into an armchair.

Bursts of magic flared in every color, exploding like fireworks across the room. The acrid smell of burning hair and flesh permeated the room as flames erupted from nowhere and consumed one of the enemies. The children wailed, clutching each other for dear life.

A burst of vibrant purple magic flashed in the far corner of the room. A woman with dark brown hair, dressed in a simple green sweater and blue jeans, turned away from a stranger in black lying on the floor. Slowly, the purple light dissipated. A heartbeat later, the woman's eyes found Octavia's, and a small, sad smile stretched across her lips.

The frantic rhythm in Octavia's chest skipped a beat, and for a fleeting moment, despite the danger and chaos, she felt safe.

Mom.

But her mother's smile faded as quickly as it had appeared, replaced by an open-mouthed gasp. Her gaze was unblinking. The green sweater was slowly turning red. Octavia watched as the crimson stain grew, the liquid dripping to the floor, creating a puddle beneath her mother's feet. She watched in horror as the light faded from her mother's eyes, replaced by a clouded, glassy film.

Octavia knew her mother was dead before her body hit the floor. She knew it because she felt it. She felt it in her blood, in her bones, and in her very soul.

Octavia threw her arms out wide, pushing her friends back behind her. She took one step forward as loss consumed her and hatred boiled her blood.

Grief tore from her in one tortured, feral shriek.

And then, everything went dark.

CHAPTER 1
OCTAVIA
Eighteen years later

*N*on est umbra sine lumine.

The familiar words echoed through Octavia's mind as she came to. She lifted a hand to shield her eyes from the oppressive fluorescent lights of the subway car.

"You dozed off and started dreaming," Quintin said as he nudged Octavia into an upright position. "We wouldn't want you making a scene on the T."

Octavia shook the last wisps of sleep away as she took in her surroundings, orienting herself. It was late, and the train car was almost empty. Apart from Octavia and Quintin, there were only two other people, a few seats away. They all swayed in rhythm with the movement of the T.

"Thanks for that." Octavia sighed. "Those poor normans would've thought I was crazy if I started screaming."

"Don't worry about it," Quintin replied. "We all get them . . . the nightmares."

"I know," she murmured. She hadn't needed his clarification. It was a rare occurrence when a night passed in the loft without one of their terrified screams fracturing the silence.

Octavia shifted uncomfortably in her seat, suddenly aware of the cool, damp clothes sticking to her skin. She'd been working out with her personal trainer, Dante, earlier that evening. The session had been particularly grueling, so it was no wonder Octavia was covered almost head to toe in sweat. She was sure she smelled terrible. Quintin was either very kind or very stupid to be sitting so close to her.

She stole a glance up at him through her lashes. His attention had already drifted back to the book he had open in front of him. Quintin looked the same tonight as he always did: enviously nonchalant—his posture, in direct contrast to hers, all smooth, rounded edges—and disarmingly handsome in his academic slacks and loafers. The strong curve of his jaw complimented the seriousness in his dark brown eyes as they bounced along with the words on the page. Soft yellow light danced across his umber skin as streetlamps passed them by.

The book he was reading was old and tattered. The title read, *A History of Hex Signs*.

"Hey, you don't need to be reading that, you know," she insisted as she reached for the book.

Quintin quickly moved it just out of her reach. He smiled when he saw the annoyance flash across her face. "You're honestly not going to accept my help here? You've been researching so much lately. It's borderline obsessive."

"You're being dramatic," Octavia snapped as she averted her eyes. "I'm researching the same amount I always have."

They both knew that was a bald-faced lie. Octavia had been running herself ragged the past few months. Between researching ways to break hexes, training with Dante, and attempting to attend classes, she'd barely had time to even talk to Quintin.

"We miss you," Quintin murmured softly, as if worried he might spook her away.

"I miss you all too," Octavia admitted. "Maybe if I had a friend who could save me the trouble of commuting home with a little portal magic, I'd have more free time."

Quintin flashed his signature smirk. "You know all too well

it'd take me at least half a day to conjure a portal strong enough to travel that distance. Do you want me to die trying?"

"No, I guess not," Octavia chuckled.

Their banter was interrupted by the T's automated voice system: "Next stop, Porter." Quintin shoved the book into his backpack as Octavia grabbed her exercise bag. They stood and walked to the doors.

When the car slowed to a stop, they hopped off the train and onto the platform, into the dark December night. Immediately assailed by the abrasive cold, Octavia burrowed her hands deeper into the pockets of her parka, while Quintin nuzzled his chin into his scarf. They crossed the street and began their silent trek home.

One of her favorite things about Quintin was that he was comfortable with silence. He never forced Octavia into conversation when he knew she'd rather be lost in her thoughts, like now. Cold, starless evenings like these always brought her back to that terrible night eighteen years ago.

When Octavia awoke to the distant sound of sirens, she was cold to her very core. A thin layer of snow coated the room around her. She pushed her weary body up off the ground. Black soot stained the floor beneath her. Her head pounded, and her throat was as scratchy as sandpaper from breathing in the smoke around her. It took her a moment to remember where she was and what had happened.

Why is it so cold? Mom would never let me get this cold. Like a key sliding into place, the thought of her mother brought the memories flooding back—the horrific, gut-wrenching memories. *That's right. Mom is . . . dead.* Her sorrow twisted into a painful knot at the center of her throat that sent tears pricking her eyes.

But Dad. Where's Dad?

Swallowing against the pain, she stood and whirled around, taking in the wreckage that surrounded her. Why was there snow at her feet? She looked up and realized she was no longer sheltered from the outside. The walls of the house had crumbled down to the studs. The upper floors, roof, and entire left side of the building were simply gone. She was enveloped in the cold winter night.

To her right lay the many soot-covered bodies. She started trying to count them, but it was pointless. So many members of her family had come to the house earlier that evening for the meeting.

Could every last one of them be lying here dead? Including Dad? Am I the only one left?

As new tears welled in her eyes, she heard a high-pitched voice yell, "Faster, you two! We have to get back to Tavi!"

She recognized that voice. It was Quintin! She turned toward the sound and ran, through the hallway, into the kitchen, and out the back door. The snow burned painfully against her bare feet, but she ran anyway. At the edge of the forest behind the house, she saw Quintin, June, and Sage break through the line of trees. A relieved sob tore from her chest as they ran to her.

A few heartbeats later, they were wrapped in each other's arms, shaking and breathing heavily as they pulled in close.

"We ran to Mr. Winston's house through the forest," Sage panted between breaths. "The man with the big, mean dog. He called the police for us. He said they should be here soon."

"And when we woke up, the house and some of the bodies were on fire," Quintin said. "Sage's dad cast a fire spell at an intruder during the fight. The fire probably spread from there. We tried to get to you, Tavi, but you were closest to the flames. They were too hot, and the smoke was too thick. We were choking on it. We couldn't get you out. I'm sorry."

Octavia's heart ached at the haunted look in Quintin's gaze. She was grateful her friends had tried to help her, but she was happier they'd left her behind to save themselves.

"It's okay," she reassured him as she rubbed her nose with ice cold fingers. The cloying scent of burning embers hung in a dense cloud around them. "I'm fine. But what do we tell the police?"

As if on cue, the sirens got louder as they began their descent down the long, winding driveway to the house. Octavia spied the red and blue lights through the barren trees. A fresh wave of fear doused the relief she'd felt just moments before.

"What do you mean?" June asked. "The bad people came into the house, and our parents used magic to protect us; that's what we tell—"

"We can't tell them the truth," Quintin cut her off. "No one outside of the coven can know we practice witchcraft."

June closed her mouth slowly and nodded.

Quintin's eyes drifted from face to face, urging them to agree with his plan. "If they ask how we survived, we say we escaped and hid out in the forest."

"What about the other kids?" Octavia asked, worried she already knew the answer.

"I don't know." Quintin shook his head. "They aren't in the house. All of the bodies on the floor are too big to be any of them."

A spark of hope ignited in Octavia's chest. *Maybe they ran into the forest as well. Maybe they'll come back safe and sound, just like Sage, June, and Quintin.* Her thoughts were interrupted by the sound of a police officer yelling from the front of the house. As Octavia turned to look, her head exploded with pain, the world around her dissolving into an endless sea of bright white as a string of loud, thundering words reverberated through her mind.

Non est umbra sine lumine!

She screamed and instinctively clutched her hands to her ears, falling to her knees. The heavy crunching of snow under boots approached.

"What's wrong?" Sage cried, crouching down next to her.

"Are any of you hurt?" a police officer asked, dropping to her knees. "Jesus, you're all half frozen to death. Rick, come quick! Tell the EMTs to bring four blankets stat."

"I'm fine," Octavia murmured thickly as the voice continued to echo in her mind. She was grateful when the darkness came for her again. The strange voice didn't speak to her there.

Octavia sighed, lifting her head to the velvet night sky. That voice had haunted her for eighteen years. She couldn't recall a single day those words hadn't made themselves known. *Non est umbra sine lumine.* When she was old enough, she'd looked up what the Latin words meant: there is no shadow without light.

After that night, Octavia could no longer access her magic, and although she couldn't prove it yet, she felt certain the echoing phrase, in all its cryptic glory, was connected.

Thankfully, the coven elders hadn't attended the meeting on the night of the attack. Octavia's maternal grandmother and matriarch of their coven, Jocasta, had been able to determine why Octavia's magic had left her.

She'd been hexed; the thread between her and her magic indefinitely severed.

Eighteen years later, Jocasta still had no idea who could've cast the hex or why. And so, Octavia was a magicless witch from a broken coven—a coven comprised of the last living descendants of the resilient Salem witches. Just one reason why their coven was such a prize to the witch hunter cult. Cutting down the last of the Salem witches must've been quite the accomplishment within their organization.

Octavia scoffed thinking about it. *Good thing we took all the witch hunters down with us.*

As the county police had told Jocasta after their investigation, they suspected the attackers had all perished in the resulting fire, either from burns or suffocation, just as the remainder of their family had. In total, sixteen lives had been lost that night: ten coven members, including Octavia's soft-spoken mother and kind-hearted father, and six witch hunters.

The other children who'd been present during the attack were never found like Octavia had hoped they would be. The police searched the crime scene, the forests, and inquired at the local hospitals for weeks afterward. The children had seemingly vanished into thin air and were still listed as missing persons in Vermont.

Octavia's pain had dulled over the years, no longer quite as sharp or piercing, but it was still there. Every waking second of every day. From what she'd learned in bereavement therapy, that was normal. Her therapist had made a habit of reminding Octavia, time and again, that grief never really got smaller or easier, but eventually, people grew and had more room to live around it.

Octavia was grateful when her morose thoughts were cut short as they walked up the steps to the entrance of their apartment building. Excited by the prospect of a warm shower and a drink, Octavia grinned sidelong at Quintin. "Race ya up."

Chapter 2
OCTAVIA

Octavia took the steps two at a time, racing up to the fifth floor.

"That's not fair!" Quintin huffed, out of breath. "You're in way better shape than I am. And we're not ten anymore." Octavia reached their apartment door first, then turned to watch as his eyebrows knitted together in mock frustration.

"Such a stick in the mud," she retorted as she slid the key into the lock and opened the door. The air in the loft was saturated with the sweet, floral scent of lavender. *June must be concocting some kind of potion.*

Quintin and Octavia hung their winter gear on the hooks in the entryway before drifting into the living room. As suspected, June was sitting cross-legged on the floor next to a small pewter cauldron. A diverse array of herbs and flowers were arranged in neat rows on the coffee table. Her long red hair was piled atop her head in a messy bun, while her bright green eyes roved over the pages of an old, tattered grimoire on the floor in front of her. A light sheen had formed on her brow, likely from the warm steam of the cauldron.

Potions were June's magical specialty. She infused her magic into each of her concoctions, so even though she often followed recipes written by previous generations of witches, the products were unique to June. It was a highly individualized practice. Another witch could never duplicate her work perfectly, no matter how hard they tried.

"What are you working on this time?" Octavia inquired as she walked to the kitchen.

June glanced up. "Just a little something for one of my coworkers. She gets terrible migraines."

"You're an angel," Octavia praised, and she meant it. June was the kindest person she'd ever met. The flip side to that coin, however, was that June tended to put everyone else's needs, emotions, and desires above her own. So, Octavia had made a vow to herself years ago to be the one to take care of June, while June was busy caring for everyone else.

"Has anyone eaten yet?" Quintin asked as he opened the refrigerator.

Octavia reached around him to grab a beer. She twisted the cap off as she shook her head. June also shook her head as she studied the grimoire intently.

"Nope!" a call came from one of the bedrooms beyond the kitchen. Seconds later Sage entered, dressed to the nines like they were ready to go out.

"Wait a minute. Didn't you have a date tonight, Sage?" Octavia checked the clock on the wall behind her. It was already 10:30 p.m. "Are you just now getting ready to go?"

"No, it was just so terrible that I'm already back. I couldn't even make it through our first round of drinks," they replied.

"I think I need the full details of that story." Octavia smirked as she lifted the beer to her lips.

"You'll get an especially good kick out of it, Tavi," June called from her place on the floor.

Of course, June already knows. Jealousy burned hot and sharp in her stomach. It had become such a familiar sensation, she wouldn't be surprised if she came down with an ulcer one of these days.

Calm down. It's just because you hadn't come home yet. Stop giving yourself a complex.

"Well, let's hear it," Quintin urged as he pulled a diverse array of vegetables from the refrigerator.

Sage jumped to sit on the kitchen counter and began the story, which Octavia noted was very similar to every other story Sage had shared with them regarding their experiences with dating apps. The common thread was that none of these dates ever ended well. Sage was intimidating, strong-willed, and ridiculously sarcastic. Needless to say, they were an acquired taste.

But above all, Sage was powerful, in every sense of the word. They performed elemental magic, meaning they could harness fire, water, earth, and wind, and bend them to their will. Their affinity for the elements had come as no surprise to anyone, since Sage was a Wardwell. For generations, the Wardwells had practiced exclusively elemental magic, one of the strongest magical specialties from the Salem bloodline.

Octavia questioned whether it was Sage's power that ignited so much jealousy in her or their close relationship with June. Since June's specialty was potions, she wasn't particularly skilled at protecting herself, which is likely why Sage was so protective of her.

Or perhaps they're just better friends with each other than they are with you.

The thought sent an acidic taste sliding down the back of Octavia's throat, but she chased it away with a long swig of beer and shifted her attention back to Sage's story.

"So, long story short, they were a complete ass," Sage said in exasperation. "I mean, come on! Who in their right mind doesn't believe in climate change at this point? Especially the type of person who goes on a date with a nonbinary person. It just doesn't add up!"

"Well, regardless of their opinions, they really missed out,

Sage," Quintin said as he chopped the freshly washed vegetables. "You look great tonight."

"Thank you, Quin! If you weren't like a brother to me, I'd be on you like butter on toast," Sage replied with a mischievous wink.

They were joking, of course, but as Sage continued their story, reminiscing on the failed date, Octavia thought there had to be a bit of truth behind the statement. Quintin was basically perfect. *Perfect Sage and perfect Quin would make the most perfect of perfect matches, wouldn't they?*

Quintin was right though, per usual. Sage looked amazing tonight. They'd recently dyed their close-cropped dirty blond hair pink. Their arms, chest, and shoulders were covered in beautiful tattoos, most of which were colorful depictions of the elements, barely visible through their dark blue, loose-knit sweater. Sage's hazel eyes were framed by their favorite hexagonal gold-rimmed eyeglasses.

Octavia replenished her beer from the fridge as Sage continued their story, occasionally handing requested spices to Quintin as he cooked their pad thai on the stovetop. She choked on her drink as Sage described their date's opinion on intimacy after a first date.

"They literally said, 'Sex is required.' I stood up right there and then, downed my drink, and left. Didn't even say goodbye. Just paid the waiter on the way out and apologized for the trouble they were likely going to cause when they realized I only paid for my own." Sage chuckled, clearly impressed with themself.

"Savage," Octavia complimented as the spiced aroma of their meal wafted her way. She inhaled deeply, suddenly much hungrier than she'd been moments ago.

Quintin plated the food, and Octavia's stomach growled at the sight. But her attention was stolen a moment later as two small, shimmering silver portals soundlessly ripped open, hovering in space. The first portal hovered four feet in the air in the middle of the kitchen, near Quintin's elbow, while the second appeared next to June, levitating just off the floor.

Quintin grabbed a plate and fork and stuck his hand into the portal. The hand, plate, and fork appeared next to June a moment later.

June finally looked up from her potion and smiled brightly at the steaming plate of rice noodles and vegetables. "Thank you!" She took the food from Quintin, and the portal disappeared silently, as if it had never been there.

Quintin's magical specialty was portal magic, Octavia's personal favorite. It might not give him a huge advantage in combat, but damn, it was cool. The downside to portal magic was that it took a great deal of energy and concentration, so he rarely conjured portals that were farther apart than a couple of yards.

Octavia, Sage, and Quintin brought their plates into the living room. They sat on the couches and chatted about their days as they ate. While Quintin, June, and Sage had all graduated from their respective colleges and gotten day jobs, Octavia was still in school, or at least she was supposed to be. She was still technically a graduate student at Boston College, but her attendance record and participation level over the past few months had put her academic standing in serious jeopardy. She knew she should've cared that she was only a few missed lectures away from being kicked out of the program, but she just couldn't bring herself to.

Instead, her mind was consumed with the echoing voices of evil hexes. In an effort to drown the voices out, she'd been pushing her body to its limits during her training sessions. Not to mention that all the while, she'd been trying to tame her rising jealousy and resentment toward Sage, June—and quite frankly, everyone.

Octavia knew she was in a bad place, just as she knew her behavior was making the others worry. But she also knew that what she was doing was helping by keeping her mind quiet and calm. Her friends may not have approved of her coping mechanisms, but they weren't inside her mind, so they couldn't understand.

Once she finished her dinner and beer, Octavia rose from the couch and put her empty plate in the sink. "I'm going to shower, then go out for a bit. I'll be late, so no one wait up for me." She braced herself for an onslaught of protests.

"It's already eleven o'clock," Quintin objected. "Why don't you just stay in and drink with us?"

"It's Wednesday, and you have work at eight," Octavia countered. "I'm not going to be the reason you feel like the walking dead tomorrow." She continued through the kitchen, making her way toward the bathroom, when Sage's voice, dripping with judgment, stopped her in her tracks.

"Why do you even try, Quin?" Sage grumbled over their empty plate. "She's obviously decided that self-destructing is better than hanging out with us." They were facing the opposite way from Octavia, so she couldn't read their face.

June had already returned to her potion, but she took a moment to look up and scope out the entrance to the hallway as if she'd fully expected to find Octavia there, silently listening in. Pinned under June's sympathetic gaze, Octavia couldn't even pretend she hadn't been eavesdropping.

Before embarrassment could scald her cheeks, June smiled ruefully at Octavia, the bend of her lips so slight it was barely perceptible. But it was there.

Octavia flinched.

She knew they all looked down on her. *Poor Tavi, magicless and parentless. No wonder she can't deal.* Their pity made her want to puke.

Octavia made her escape from the hallway by slipping into the bathroom. Immediately, she hopped in the shower. The hot water reinvigorated her senses, previously dampened by the cold weather and her sore, overexerted muscles. She cleansed herself with several pleasant, citrus-scented soaps and conditioners, courtesy of June. When she stepped out of the shower, she ran a hand across the fogged mirror.

The reflection that looked back at her was a disappointment. Long, stick-straight, chestnut brown hair fell in wet tendrils around her shoulders. Dull brown eyes looked back at her, shadowed by dark circles. Her pale, translucent skin revealed a weaving network of light blue veins in her forearms under the harsh fluorescent light of the vanity.

Octavia banished her reflection by opening and reaching into the medicine cabinet. She grabbed an orange prescription bottle with her name on it. Little did the others know, she had run out of the appropriately prescribed antibiotics months ago. Now she used the bottle to store . . . *less* appropriately prescribed prescriptions—specifically Vicodin. Thankfully, she knew a student at Boston College who was able to keep her supply stocked for nights like these. She popped a large white pill into her mouth and swallowed.

Wrapped in a towel, she walked out of the steam-filled bathroom, through the kitchen, and into the now vacant living room. She grabbed the small wooden chest that June used to store her herbs from its hiding spot under one of the end tables. A small glass vial was sitting neatly inside the box that contained the mixture she was looking for. She took an empty water bottle from the kitchen and filled it to the brim from the tap, then sprinkled a pinch of the herbal mixture into the bottle and shook it up.

Walking back to her room, Octavia drank deeply from the bottle. She'd recently learned that, when taken with the right drugs, June's magical herbal mixture calmed and quieted her mind like nothing else ever had, providing pure, unadulterated contentment.

Octavia knew the others were starting to suspect she was doing these sorts of things, but they'd yet to prove it. She tried to convince herself to care what they thought of her while she got ready in her room, dressing in a cropped gray sweater, black jeans, and scuffed Doc Martens, but again, she found that she couldn't make herself give a shit . . . especially not after the mixture took effect.

Her mind thrummed with the buzz of the herb and drug cocktail as she reached for her keys and parka in the entryway.

"Why won't you accept my help?" Quintin asked softly.

Octavia gasped, clutching her chest as she whirled around. She hadn't heard him walk up behind her. The disappointment in his eyes sent her startled heart racing even faster. "What?"

Quintin sighed. "Magic isn't everything, so why do you act like it is?"

Octavia stared at him; her parted mouth motionless, unable to find the right words. She could try to explain it until she was blue in the face, but she knew he would never really understand why, to Octavia, magic *was* everything.

"Just be safe, Tavi."

She cleared her throat before responding, "Always am."

Another lie.

She had no intention of being safe tonight.

CHAPTER 3
LEIF

The pub was quiet tonight. That was ideal, since Leif's target had evaded him the night before thanks to the Bruins game. There was no guarantee that the target would return to the same pub two nights in a row, but Leif had figured it was worth a try. If he evaded him again, Leif could always ask Jiro to do some recon. He was confident he'd find the dude eventually.

Leif was positioned in the corner of the pub, his back to the wall. He raised his vivid blue eyes over the top of his book and took a quick inventory. Two men in matching leather jackets had vacated a pool table to his right and now sat in a booth to his left. Three sports fans were exiting the bar, signaling the end of the game being aired on the television above the old, chipped wooden bar top. The bartender was wiping down clean glasses fresh out of the washer.

Nothing suspicious.

Just as his eyes began to drift back to the page, a young woman entered the bar and hopped onto the stool closest to the cash register. Leif was far enough away that he couldn't hear their conversation over the sound of the music, but she looked like a regular. Her body language was relaxed, clearly comfortable. She crossed her legs, tossed her coat onto the stool next to her, and grinned widely at the bartender.

Yeah, definitely a regular.

The bartender didn't ask for her drink order; he just began making it—a whiskey sour, by the looks of it. When he handed her the glass, she drank deeply, downing half the cocktail in one gulp. She engaged in casual conversation with the bartender until her drink was empty, and he began making her a second one.

At this point, Leif had decided that she was of no concern to him. The dagger strapped to his right calf under his jeans remained cool against his skin. If she was a threat, the dagger would've warmed to an uncomfortable temperature.

But even as he tried forcing his attention back to his book, his eyes kept wandering back to her, causing himself to reread the same sentence over and over. She was beautiful, yes, but Leif had seen many beautiful women while on patrol—and yet none of them had ever been a distraction before.

Frustrated, Leif checked his wristwatch. It was 12:30 a.m. The pub was closing in thirty minutes. At this point, his target was unlikely to show, so he decided to head out. He drank the rest of his lukewarm beer and placed a bookmark in his book.

When he looked up again, she was standing in front of him, half a whiskey sour in her hand.

"Let me guess. You're a . . ." —she cocked her head to the side to better read the title of his book— "history buff with a particular interest in the Salem witch trials, right?" She waited for his response.

Leif's heart hammered, but he refused to give himself away. He schooled his features into an impenetrable mask of mild confusion: gaze locked, eyebrow cocked, jaw relaxed. He wasn't about to mess this up. "I'm sorry?"

"Your book there. It's about seventeenth-century Massachusetts. Most historians interested in this region in that time period are interested in the Salem witch trials." She sized him up, her gaze raking over him in one slow, lazy sweep.

Fuck.

"Actually, no. This is just something to pass the time." The corner of his lips lifted in a half smile, the lie rolling easily off his tongue. "It kinda sucks, actually."

"Ah, that's a bummer. I'm usually good at sniffing out fellow historians. Guess I was wrong. Sorry for bothering you." Her gaze lingered on his face for several moments. Then, as quickly as she came, she turned to go.

"Are *you* interested in the witch trials?" he heard himself ask, the cool steel of the dagger soothing his raw nerves.

The woman pivoted back toward him. "Not particularly. But my grandmother used to be on the Archives Committee in Salem, so I've learned a lot over the years. I just figured I'd help you out if you were interested. But I see my help isn't needed." She turned again toward the bar.

Instinct took over. "I was just about to leave, but I think I'd like to stay. Can I buy you another drink? After all, what kind of historian would I be if I didn't take advantage of your offer?" Leif asked.

The woman turned back to him, eyes darting over his face, reading him again. It was slightly eerie, but also strangely familiar. Her eyes, their movement, their suspicion of him . . . all familiar. Not déjà vu. Not a memory. Just familiar. But he couldn't figure out why.

"I thought you weren't a historian?" she teased.

"I used to be."

"Interesting." Several seconds passed in palpable silence. "Sure," she finally relented. "I'll have another drink."

Leif stood and gestured for her to take the seat across from him. "I'm Michael. It's nice to meet you. What's your name?"

"Back 'atcha. I'm Octavia." She sat, downed the rest of her drink, and handed the empty glass over to Leif.

"Cool name. Whiskey sour, right?"

She nodded easily, but he caught the flicker of surprise that flashed across her face.

"I'll be right back," he said.

At the bar, while he waited for the bartender to prepare their drinks, he looked back over his shoulder at Octavia. She'd picked his book up off the table, and he watched as she flipped through the pages, finally stopping to read a passage he'd highlighted just that morning. It was about the colonization of Massachusetts; dry, depressing, and more than a little maddening. *Nothing to be proud of, that's for sure, but at least it doesn't give anything away.* He wouldn't be so careless as to bring evidence of his identity with him on patrol.

"Damn, you were right. This book *is* awful," she said when he returned to the table. A curtain of dark brown hair fell over her shoulder.

He handed over her drink and took his seat. "Hey, I warned you, didn't I?"

"Fair enough." She took a sip, a half-hearted smile pulling at her lips.

"So, you're a historian too, are you?" Leif inquired.

"Yep. I'm getting my master's in American studies from Boston College. You?"

Leif sipped his beer slowly. "I studied history in college, but I'm taking a gap year to do some research and pursue other interests."

"That explains the weeknight drinking." She smirked.

"Then what's your excuse?" he challenged.

"I have none," she replied breezily, then took a long drink.

Leif could only blink back at that.

"So, what interests are you pursuing during your gap year?" she asked.

"A bit of this and a bit of that. They're mostly sociological interests, but they're pretty niche."

The best lies are always rooted in the truth.

"So, is this," she asked, gesturing to the book by tossing it back onto the table, "part of your research?"

"Unfortunately, yes."

"I see. Personally, I find the domination of colonialism revolting." Her eyebrows furrowed in disgust as she eyed the book.

"I completely agree." Leif slid the book to the side of the table. He wanted her full attention back on him.

Her gaze returned to his as she tapped her nails against the side of her glass. "And where did you study? Before your gap year?"

Leif kept a straight face, refusing the smile that threatened to curve his lips. This was his favorite lie to tell. "Harvard."

"Ah, a Harvard man? How posh." Her small smile returned.

Leif laughed, rubbing a hand against his jaw. "Not at the moment, no. But you are at a pub in Cambridge. Are you really surprised?"

"To happen upon yet another Harvard student? No. To meet one like you? Yeah," she answered matter-of-factly as she tucked thick strands of hair behind her ear.

Leif shifted uneasily in his seat. "Why?"

"Because I've been surrounded by Harvard men for years. They're often so self-absorbed they don't even bother to ask for your name before droning on about themselves. It only took you a minute to ask for mine. But it's more than that. I—"

Leif leaned forward. "What do you mean?"

"I don't know," she said quickly, averting her gaze. "Never mind."

"Yeah . . . okay." He leaned back again, giving her space. They had just met, after all.

But then Octavia's deep brown eyes flitted back to Leif's, and he felt heat flush his cheeks. The intensity of her stare ignited a familiar ache in his chest that quickly traveled lower.

This is not how I planned for this night to go.

Despite his growing discomfort, Octavia appeared cool and collected. Her cheeks had pinked, but that was likely due to the alcohol. Her piercing eyes never left his face. She really was beautiful with her strong jawline, full lips, and bright skin.

Who is this woman?

Leif cleared his throat. "You know, I'd like to take you up on your offer to assist a fellow history buff, but a pub at one in the morning probably isn't the best place for a lesson. Rain check?"

"Sure," Octavia agreed, pulling her phone from her pocket.

She eyed him for a second longer before she finally lowered hers to her phone. The break in eye contact was welcome, so he didn't understand why his chest tightened as he waited for her gaze to meet his again.

"You know," she said, looking up from her phone and into his eyes, "I usually go to another spot after this, but I think I'm in the mood for a change in plans."

Leif's heart beat erratically under his ribs.

Dropping the volume of her voice, Octavia asked coyly, "Would you like to come back to my place?"

He thought of a hundred reasons he should say no.

I'm on patrol tonight. I have a literal dagger strapped to my leg, which would be hard, if not impossible, to hide in the heat of the moment. I just laid eyes on this woman not thirty minutes ago. And to top it all off, she's had three drinks within that span of time. This should be a no-brainer.

Leif swallowed hard against his nerves. "You've had more to drink than I have. Are you sure?"

"I have a pretty high tolerance, but if you're worried about my ability to consent, feel free to decline. You know what?" she said, suddenly standing. "Think about it for a sec while I go settle up. Follow me out if you're up for it."

Octavia walked gracefully over to the bar. She seemed perfectly sober, apart from the pink in her cheeks.

This is definitely a bad idea, and I know I'll get shit for it tomorrow.

But Octavia glanced back at him then, her dark eyes playful and daring.

Leif chugged the rest of his drink, threw on his coat, grabbed the book, and followed her out into the cold.

CHAPTER 4
OCTAVIA

The man from the bar—Michael—caught up to her about half a block from the pub. The crisp air soothed her flushed cheeks. Even though she was both tipsy and high, she knew the heat in her cheeks was due to something else entirely—or rather, some*one* else. Her entire body felt tender and sensitive, like she'd spent the day lying out at the beach, baking in the sun.

This—the bar, the drinks, the man—wasn't a new experience for her. In fact, ever since she'd discovered just how much the pleasure of sex added to her drug and alcohol-induced euphoria, Octavia had been pursuing a string of one-night stands. With the previous people, she had felt sexual attraction and curiosity, yes, but this . . . what she was feeling right now was *tension*. The urge to dispel it immediate and imperative. Every molecule in her body stood at a heightened state of attention, ready for anything and everything. *This* was true desire.

The realization quickened her pace.

Michael easily stepped into stride next to her, seemingly as eager as she was to reach their destination. Luckily, the loft was only five blocks from the pub.

Octavia glanced up nervously at Michael. His face was shrouded in shadows, but his jaw twitched determinedly. He looked down at her then, as if he had sensed her staring, and the corner of his mouth tugged into another charming half-smile.

There was no denying it: he was *devastatingly* handsome. His cerulean eyes were utterly mesmerizing. The light blue irises were interrupted by slivers of gray, so light they almost looked white, framed by thick, dark lashes. The sight of them reminded her of a flashbulb going off.

She hadn't been able to look away at the pub. His eyes had left her completely transfixed. They seemed to look directly at her—*through* her, even, to her very core. It was a bit disconcerting, but she couldn't shake that feeling of familiarity.

His ash-blond hair fell into those eyes as they rounded the corner to her apartment building. She resisted the urge to push the strands back as she fumbled in her pocket for her keys. *Get a hold of yourself, damn it.* She took a deep breath before she opened the door of the building. Michael followed close behind as she climbed the many flights of stairs.

Octavia had texted her friends from the bar to warn them that she was having a visitor over, like she usually did, but now she thought it might've been a better idea not to tell them. The desire to keep him all to herself—a secret only the two of them shared—hit her swift and hard, like a punch to the gut. If her friends saw these feelings on her face tomorrow morning, they'd be insufferable. Like dogs with a bone, they'd never let it go. She'd die a slow, agonizing death at the hands of their impossible expectations and endless, nosy questions.

Outside the apartment door, she reached to place the key into the lock when strong hands guided her firmly back against the wall. Her stomach fluttered when she looked into those hypnotic eyes.

His words stumbled out gracelessly. "Before we go in, I need to make sure that this is something you still want to do. You don't know me. I don't know you. I can walk away right now. Are you sure about this?"

Octavia swallowed hard. The skin on her shoulders burned feverishly beneath his touch, despite the layers of clothing between them. She took a shallow breath. "Are *you?*"

"Definitely."

"Then I am too."

Her body reacted immediately, a delicious ache curling tight in her lower abdomen. Michael moved his hands from her shoulders to the wall behind her as he closed the distance between them. Her chin tilted up in reply. This close, she could smell his scent of snow and pine, like a fresh winter breeze.

The first brush of their lips was tender and gentle. She leaned into it, closing her eyes. His full lips were warm against her own, despite the cold they had just walked through. It was not the type of kiss she'd been expecting based on their blood alcohol levels, but surprisingly, the tenderness of it only made her want him more.

When Michael pulled back, she could tell he felt the same by the hungry look in his eyes. Their second kiss would not be tender or gentle. As soon as she opened that door, there would be no going back. The only option would be to fall over the edge.

And then the door was open. Their coats were on the floor. Sweaters were removed and left to litter the path from the entryway to her room. The bedroom door slammed closed behind them; their lips were greedy, never separating from each other. Her back was against the door, legs wrapped around his waist, as his mouth ravaged her neck, her skin sensitive and tingling in its wake.

Lean muscles feathered under his skin as he pinned her against the door. Her black fingernails dug into the skin of his shoulders as he nipped at her ear. Eager, she lowered herself to the ground and reached for his belt.

Her breath caught in her chest as she was twirled around,

finding herself suddenly face to face with the door, her hands pinned above her head. His mouth continued exploring her neck and shoulders. She felt the firm brush of him against her backside and shivered.

"No need for you to do the hard work," said Michael, his voice husky and laced with amusement.

She heard his pants hit the floor behind her. The ache in her lower abdomen tightened and impatience sparked, just as he spun her back around to face him. One of his hands lowered to cup her breast, while the other slid around her waist and pulled her close.

"I know I said it before, but it is really, *really* nice to meet you." She laughed freely as he pulled her toward the bed.

That night, her mind was clear, calm, and focused for the first time in months. The echoing voice of the hex was nothing but a memory.

Chapter 5
LEIF

Leif woke from a deep sleep early the next morning, the unfamiliar room around him blanketed in near darkness. Octavia slept soundly next to him, her hair splayed out across the pillows. He took a deep breath, reveling in the sweet, citrusy scent that lingered in the space.

As he lay there in the dark, memories from the night before seized his mind. Dark eyes flashing mischievously; porcelain skin, soft as velvet, against his. His desire sparked anew at the memory of the soft whimpers she'd breathed in his ear.

The sex had been so intimate . . . *especially* for a one-night stand. Leif had never experienced anything like it before. Octavia had been so shrouded in mystery at the pub that he hadn't expected her to be so vulnerable with him. Had she felt the same strange sense of familiarity he had?

Shaking the thought from his mind, Leif rose out of bed quickly and quietly, trying not to wake her. He retrieved his pants from the floor; his dagger and its holster were still hidden in one of the legs. He fastened the holster to his calf and sheathed the dagger before dressing.

Remembering his sweater that lay discarded on the kitchen floor, he checked the time on his wristwatch. It was early, 6:30 a.m., but not so early that he couldn't venture out to retrieve his sweater and get a glass of water.

As he walked to the door, his attention snagged on a cluster of polaroid photographs on the wall as they reflected the weak morning light creeping in through the window. In the dark, he couldn't make out the images, so he removed his phone from his pocket as he strode to the wall. Using the dim screen light, he studied the photos. A black dog running in a park; a cheerful older couple smiling in a bright kitchen; a man swinging fiercely at a punching bag in a gym. When Leif reached the group photos, he locked his phone and forced himself to look away, the shame of snooping creeping up his neck.

But as he continued to the door, he smiled to himself. She enjoyed photography too. He was reluctant to admit, even to himself, just how happy that made him.

He left the bedroom, careful to close the door silently behind him. He winced at the shock of his bare feet against the cold kitchen tiles as he grabbed his red sweater off the floor and pulled it on over his head. Then he turned to the cabinets and quietly searched for a glass.

"Farthest to the left," a deep voice said behind him.

Leif noticed the sudden heat of the dagger a split second before he spun around. A young man stood in front of him. He was squinting at Leif—either in distrust or disgust, Leif couldn't tell. The dagger seared against his calf, the skin there prickling against the heat. It was uncomfortable, but not hot enough to burn. Another person might have felt nervous, scared, or uneasy, but Leif didn't. Instead, adrenaline flooded his veins.

All his focus homed in on the man before him, for nothing else mattered. The man—currently glaring at Leif with his arms crossed and nostrils flaring as if he'd like nothing more than to kill him—was Leif's target from the night before.

Fate is a tricky little bastard.

Leif forced his muscles to relax. The last thing he needed was to spook his target by appearing aggressive.

"Right. Thanks," he whispered as he walked over to the cabinet in question. He grabbed a glass and turned on the faucet, his back to his enemy. He took a long drink from the glass and slowly set it down on the counter.

Leif broke the silence as he turned to face the man once more. "Sorry for the invasion. I'll head out as soon as Octavia wakes up. I don't want her thinking I ran off."

"That's kind of you," the man murmured, even though the look in his eyes said otherwise. "I'm Quintin, Tavi's friend and roommate."

"Good to meet you." Leif retrieved his glass from the counter and briefly raised it toward Quintin in a subtle toast. "Is Tavi her nickname?"

"To some," was all the response Quintin gave. He started for the living room, his scowl set firmly in place.

Eager to gather as much intel as he could in light of his beyond lucky circumstances, Leif pushed on, knowing all too well how risky it was. After all, this spawn of Satan was living with an oblivious, innocent woman. Leif had her safety to consider as well, not just his own.

Quintin began gathering the books that were scattered all over the living room and organizing them into a backpack. To anyone else, it would've appeared as if an average bookworm was getting ready to go to work. But Leif knew the contents of those books without even having to look at them, and he was absolutely certain that there was nothing average about those grimoires . . . or that man.

"Have you been friends for a long time?" Leif probed as he sipped his water, leaning against the counter.

"Yeah," Quintin answered, his voice tainted with irritation and something else—anger for sure, but maybe even something stronger than that—hatred perhaps.

Ah, I see. He loves her. Maybe that's why he's kept her close, as she's clearly not one of them.

"She seems great."

Quintin clenched his jaw, the muscles straining.

Shit, maybe he heard us last night. Change topics. Immediately.

"You know, now that I think about it, you look a bit familiar," Leif ventured. "Were you at Tucker's earlier this week for the Bruins game?"

Will he lie or confess? Either way, I'll get vital information.

"I was just there to pick up Tavi." Quintin set the backpack by the door and stalked into the kitchen to start making coffee.

"Oh shit, she was there too? Small world, huh?" Glass empty, Leif skirted around Quintin as he moved toward the sink to refill it, carefully avoiding getting too close. They didn't need yet another reason to be uncomfortable around each other.

How did I miss her then? And how did I not notice them leaving together? Am I losing my edge?

Again, Quintin offered no response. Just as Leif was about to pry further, he heard a door creak, and Octavia stepped into the kitchen.

She looked stunning, even with bedhead and remnants of sleep clouding her eyes. She wore an oversized sweater and socks, no bottoms. In his peripheral vision, Leif noticed Quintin's gaze sweep over her bare legs as she walked past him.

This man's got it bad. But my gut's telling me she only sees him as a friend. A selfishly vengeful thought lifted the corners of Leif's mouth into a genuine smile. *All the better for me.*

Octavia noticed his smile and lifted an eyebrow. "What in the hell are you two talking about?" Without waiting for a response, she eyed Leif's glass of water and asked, "Can I have a sip of that?"

"Nothing much." Leif handed over the water. "Quintin and I just discovered that I could've met you a night earlier if Tucker's hadn't been so packed on Tuesday night." He had to be careful here. He didn't want to further provoke his target when Quintin was so clearly already angry.

Like last night, Octavia drained the glass in one gulp. She wiped her mouth with her sleeve before asking, "What? You were there Tuesday night too? How'd you two figure that out?"

"He recognized me, apparently." Quintin's voice was tight and controlled, the hatred carefully stripped.

"Crazy coincidence. What a small world," Octavia murmured.

"That's exactly what I said."

The bittersweet smell of freshly brewed coffee quickly filled the loft. Octavia took a deep breath and grabbed a mug from the cabinet. The sound of two more doors whining open reached the kitchen.

"Yes! Coffee!" a feminine person with an androgenous buzz cut squealed upon entering the kitchen. The dagger burned even hotter against Leif's leg. Despite his efforts, he stiffened.

A third roommate, smaller than the others, followed closely behind. "Mm, thank you, Quin," she whispered as she took a hot mug from Quintin.

Leif swallowed the hiss of pain that pressed against the inside of his lips. His leg felt as if it was on fire.

Fucking hell. She's living with three of them.

Even in his shocked state, Leif went through the motions well enough. He accepted a cup of coffee, sipped it quietly, and introduced himself to Octavia's other two roommates, Sage and June. But Leif knew these weren't normal roommates—not normal *humans*, for that matter. Three out of the four people standing in front of him practiced witchcraft, and thus, they were his mortal enemies.

He wasn't taking a year off from school to pursue other scholarly passions. He was taking time off to hunt down and hopefully eradicate the last of the witches in Massachusetts. Leif had been trained in witch hunting for most of his life, but before Tuesday, he'd never met a witch in the flesh before. He'd heard and read about them, and seen photos, of course, but the gravity of standing before not just one, but an entire coven, had his spine sagging. These people were evil, vicious killers, and he was just sitting there, drinking coffee like everything about this situation was perfectly normal. It wasn't. The coffee curdled in his stomach.

Two days ago, Leif had thought he'd hit the jackpot when his dagger had seared against his skin as a young man had crossed his path downtown. Finding even a single witch these days was like finding a needle in a haystack. Leif had trailed him the rest of the day and ended up at Tucker's, only to let him slip through the cracks.

Then last night, he'd made the rash—and arguably irresponsible—decision to hook up with a complete stranger, only to wind up in the lions' den. The loft of an actual coven.

How could Octavia not know who these people really are? How dangerous they can be? I mean, for fuck's sake, there's a literal cauldron sitting in the corner of the living room!

Perhaps they weren't hiding the truth from her at all. Leif thought this could be the most likely explanation, especially since the witchy aesthetic, with all the crystals, herbs, and tarot cards, had become so trendy. That would allow them to practice in their home without divulging their true magic to Octavia. After all, normal humans couldn't sense magic on their own. That's why Leif needed the dagger: its metal blazed red-hot whenever magic was in close vicinity.

The roommate named Sage offered to make them all breakfast, but everyone politely declined. Quintin and June had to jet to work, while Octavia said she'd grab something on her way to the gym. Leif smiled internally at her dedication to physical fitness. It might've been the only method of protection she had against these vile creatures. At the very least, hopefully she'd be able to outrun them. He was pretty confident she could, given the impressive strength and stamina he'd witnessed from her last night.

Leif cleared his throat and shooed the thought away as he stood from the couch to make his exit as well. "It was really nice to meet you all. Thanks for the coffee and hospitality. I hope to see you all again soon." He wasn't lying. He would like to see them again soon . . . as long as he could plunge his dagger through their hearts.

The roommates responded with various niceties as Octavia stood to walk him to the door. She followed him out into the hallway and closed the apartment door behind her. "I'm sorry about them. I wish I could say they aren't always this nosy, but they are. We've been friends for a long time, so we're close—probably a little too close."

With the apartment door separating Leif from the coven, the dagger began to cool. "No worries. They all seem cool. No one gave me a hard time."

"Good, I'm glad . . ." Octavia drifted off, seeming uncertain of how to proceed, as she fidgeted with the hem of her sweater. Leif knew he had a unique opportunity here—an in. And he needed to make sure he kept it intact. The knowledge of what he had to do—who he'd have to betray—sent icy guilt slithering through his veins, raising goosebumps on his arms.

He bent forward, leaving but a few inches between her face and his own. Her cheeks flushed in response, and he smiled genuinely, glad to know he still had that effect on her. "I had fun last night. I'd like to ask if we could do it again, but I think I'd like to take you on a proper date next time. Can I have your number?"

Her long, dark eyelashes fluttered as she blinked. "Um, no. I mean, yeah, sure. I think I'd like that too. Here, give me your phone and I'll put in my number."

"Great." Leif handed over the phone and watched her enter her number. He laughed as she typed her name into the contact form: *Octavia (best night of my life) Martin*, followed by a winky face emoji. Of course, she just *had* to be funny on top of everything else.

When she handed the phone back, he made sure his fingers grazed over hers and lingered a moment too long. He pocketed the phone and started down the stairs.

Leif was in deep shit, and his heart knew it; it clenched like a fist in his chest. She would never want to be with him after ... after he'd done his job, so what the hell? He might as well take advantage of what little time he had left with her.

"Wait, I almost forgot." Leif climbed back up the stairs and kissed her, slow and greedy, as if he was committing her mouth to memory. Her smile was a bright flash of white as he pulled away.

"See you soon, Octavia."

Chapter 6
LEIF

It was a long commute back home, but Leif was grateful for the time to think. As the subway raced south, he strategized. It wasn't a perfect plan, but help from the crew would make it doable.

Despite the fact that this once-in-a-lifetime opportunity had fallen into his lap, Leif didn't like the situation he now found himself in. It didn't matter how cool Octavia was, how much he liked her, or how amazing last night had been; his loyalty to his family—to their mission—overcame everything. So, he was going to exploit his new acquaintance with this mysterious, bewitching woman—the woman he wished he could have a real, honest chance with. But that wasn't the reality he lived in.

Octavia was his way in, his opportunity to infiltrate the coven; then, if he was lucky, he'd dismantle it from the inside. But first, he needed to figure out a way to ensure her safety. A typical human couldn't survive being caught in the middle of a battle like that. Even though witch hunters had no magic, they were anything but typical. They trained from childhood in the necessary skills: hand-to-hand combat, weapons, reconnaissance, as well as the art of espionage.

Leif wished he could ask his adoptive father, Garren, about all this—this plan, this woman, these conflicting emotions. Realistically, he could. Garren was always a call away, even now, when he was away on a hunt. He was helping a crew of witch hunters on the west coast take down a particularly powerful coven that had evaded them for far too long.

That was his father's current role in the organization: to swoop in like a superhero and save the day whenever and wherever he was needed. Simply saying Garren was good at his job would've been an understatement. Over the years, Leif had lost count of how many witches Garren had single-handedly taken out. Everything Leif knew, each of the deadly skills he'd acquired, were all thanks to his father.

But Leif wouldn't call Garren, not this time. He likely wouldn't be home until the end of the month, and the longer they waited to act, the greater the likelihood of failure, so this operation would have to go on without him. They'd do this on their own. The realization didn't deter Leif at all. He knew his crew was a force to be reckoned with in their own right. They'd make Garren proud, Leif had no doubt.

The T crawled to a stop, drawing Leif from his thoughts. He exited the train car as the doors slid open. It was windy and overcast, and the streets were packed with people commuting to work. Leif threaded through the throngs of people on the subway platform, then slowly made his way home.

The crew's house, which they'd affectionately deemed their "headquarters," was only a few blocks from the Andrew subway station in Southie. It'd been an old, small, piece-of-crap apartment building when Garren had first bought it, but thankfully, he'd had the inside completely renovated, including private suites for each of them, before they moved in. But the outside remained an eyesore, and for all intents and purposes, the building was invisible to passersby, creating the perfect hideout—exactly as Garren had intended.

Leif hurried as he looked up at the worn red brick building—

home. Apprehension stirred in his chest at the thought of sharing the story of his good fortune with the others. He took the front steps two at a time and whipped out his keys. As he put the key in the lock, he placed his left thumb on the discreet fingerprint scanner, cleverly disguised as a doorbell. Three internal locks clicked, and Leif entered the building.

Immediately, his ears were assaulted by the pounding bass of EDM music and high-pitched screaming. Laughing to himself, Leif climbed the staircase.

"What the literal fuck, Jiro?" Delta yelled over the railing on the third floor, her black bob a tangled mess, still dressed in her pajamas. "It's eight in the goddamn morning!"

The only response was a slight increase in the volume of the music.

Leif grimaced, the sound scratching against his eardrums like metal on metal. "You know it's no use!" he yelled over the noise. "He's a morning person."

"Yeah, well, morning people can go fuck themselves!" Delta shrieked, slamming the door to her apartment behind her.

Leif peeled off the staircase at the second floor and opened the door to Jiro's apartment without announcing himself. Jiro wouldn't have been able to hear over the music anyways.

Jiro was in his living room, which he'd lovingly converted into a techie's wet dream. An enormous, sleek black desk lined three of the four walls in the room, and almost every inch of desk space was covered by monitors, blueprints, or computer parts. Jiro's back was facing Leif as his fingers danced across a keyboard, writing code like the goddamn Matrix.

Leif walked over to the large stereo speakers and twisted the volume dial down. "Delta's actually going to kill you one of these days."

Jiro spun around in his chair, arms raised in welcome. "Well, would ya look at that! The prodigal son returns!" His easy grin was mirrored in his warm, dark eyes.

At the sight of his bright and unfailingly devoted brother, Leif knew he'd have to bury his apprehension somewhere deep down. He'd protect that smile with his life.

"And you're not going to believe the intel I got while I was out."

Jiro's eyebrows perked up in interest.

"Come on, let's get everyone up and moving. It's time for a briefing."

"Oh, hell yeah!" Jiro wheeled his chair to the speakers and cranked the volume all the way up.

An hour later, the crew had convened at the dining table in Leif's first-floor apartment. With coffee in their mugs and breakfast on their plates, they were finally ready to hear what Leif had to share.

"Come on," Jiro mumbled after scarfing down a mouthful of eggs. "Don't make us wait all day. Let's hear it."

"All right, all right." Leif paused a moment for dramatic effect. "I found a coven."

The table erupted into chaos.

"You're lying." Tripp scoffed, running a hand through his chestnut curls.

"Do you seriously think we'd believe that?" Delta snorted, rolling her eyes. "There's no way a coven would've let you walk away unscathed."

"How in the hell did that happen?" Jiro asked.

"I'm getting there," Leif said, palms raised against their impatience, encouraging the three of them to quiet down. "On Tuesday, I was waiting to cross the street when a witch walked right in front of me, going the opposite direction. My dagger burned hotter the closer I got to him, so I followed him all the way to a pub in Cambridge, but somehow, he shook me."

Tripp *tsked*. "Amateur."

Ignoring the slight, Leif continued. "So, I went back to that same pub last night, hoping he was a regular or something, but he never showed. Instead, I met a woman."

Delta rolled her eyes again as Jiro chuckled under his breath.

"Long story short, this morning I woke up in her loft to find not one, not two, but *three* witches living there—a goddamn coven! And one of them was the guy I ran into on the street, my target from the day before."

"But this woman you met, she would have to be a witch then too, right?" Tripp's eyebrows rose as the corners of his lips tugged into a frown. "What other reason would she have for living with a bunch of freaks?"

"No way. My dagger never heated around her, so she definitely doesn't have magic," Leif explained as he absentmindedly swirled the lukewarm coffee left in his mug. "But she did say they'd been friends for a long time. Maybe they just got really good at hiding it? But then again, I did see witchcraft paraphernalia all over the place, so they could be practicing while keeping the true power of their magic hidden from her somehow."

"So, how did you get out of there alive?" Delta asked tartly, jealousy ebbing off her in waves.

"Well, I'm obviously not dumb enough to reveal myself in the home of a coven, D. I stuck to my alias, kept my emotions in check, and got the hell out of there as quickly as I could. Plus, I had her as a buffer."

"So, what's our play then?" Jiro urged. One of his heels was tapping rapidly under the table, causing their plates and cups to jiggle.

"I'm going to infiltrate the coven by pretending to date the woman I met last night, and you all are going to help me take them down. It's not perfect, but I think I have a plan." Leif flashed an exultant grin.

"You just have an answer for everything don't you, golden boy?" Delta rose from the table, irritation staining her voice.

"Wake up on the wrong side of the bed this morning, D?" Jiro called after her as she slinked off to the kitchen. "Come on, this is a huge breakthrough for all of us, the whole crew. Garren will be so fucking proud when he hears we took down an entire coven on our own."

"Jiro's right," Leif called through the doorway after Delta. "The only way my plan will work is with your help. You know me. I'm not great with people. I'm going to need your help getting Octavia to trust me, and I'll also need your help getting intel from her roommates. We need to create the perfect opportunity to strike."

Leif paused, listening to the sound of cabinets opening and closing in the kitchen.

"Compliment her more," Tripp whispered.

"We all know you're the best at manipulation and espionage, D," Leif called. "You're the foundation of our crew. We need you on board if we're going to do this."

Delta returned carrying four shot glasses and a bottle of tequila. "Fine. But if we do this, we do it my way. All right?" Leif nodded, but his annoyed expression had Delta scowling. "I'm not agreeing to a half-cocked plan, so tell me everything you know about these four, and do not leave out a single detail."

Delta placed the shot glasses on the table and uncorked the bottle. Amber liquid splashed over the sides of the glasses, spilling onto the table as she filled them to the brim, not bothering to clean up the mess she left behind. Thick, wet trails followed the overfull glasses as she slid them across the table.

"You know it's not even ten o'clock, right?" Tripp exclaimed through pursed lips, feigning judgment while he eyed the shot glass between his fingers.

"Shut up. You know a buzz helps me focus," Delta snapped, holding her dripping shot glass out in front of her expectantly. "And it looks like we have a day full of strategizing ahead of us, so drink up. Let's get to work."

Leif raised his own shot to meet the others', then downed the contents of the glass. The liquor burned on the way down, the sting just strong enough to mask the lingering guilt that flared every time his thoughts drifted back to Octavia.

"Okay." He coughed, then took one deep, steadying breath. "So, here's what I was thinking . . ."

CHAPTER 7
OCTAVIA

Sweat dripped over Octavia's brow, salt stinging her eyes. Her breath came in shallow pants, the air rushing out before she could take in enough oxygen. Hands against her knees, muscles shaking, she bowed her head in exhaustion.

Octavia was especially grateful for the distraction today—her training. Against her better judgment, her mind kept wandering back to memories of strong hands, light eyes, and ragged breaths. Her cheeks burned. She refused to let those thoughts wander any further. She never got like this over one-night stands, and she wasn't about to let herself start now.

Instead, she focused on the fact that only a year ago, she would've fainted by this point. Thankfully, her body had grown accustomed to pushing its limits.

Standing, she wiped the sweat from her brow with the back of her hand. Her trainer, Dante, handed her a water bottle, which she accepted eagerly. Her mouth was as dry as the protein powder she'd added to her pre-workout shake, but she forced herself to sip the water slowly, not wanting to shock her system. The cool feeling on her parched throat was a godsend.

"You're getting there," Dante said, then drank from his own bottle. "But you're still too focused on the technicalities. You've got the steps down; now you just have to get into a rhythm and watch your opponent, anticipate their movements. You're close, but you're not there yet."

"Gotcha. I need to get out of my head. Okay, let's try it." Octavia tossed her water bottle on the floor and readjusted the tape on her hands.

"Okay, but this is our last spar of the day. You're almost tapped out." Dante slipped into a fighting stance: feet wide, fists raised, hips angled toward his target. "Ready? Go!"

Octavia's body moved instinctively, dipping low to avoid Dante's aggressive right hook.

Too predictable.

She popped up, throwing a three-punch combo, two jabs to his chin and one to his stomach. *Thwack—thwack—thwack.* With muscled forearms as good as any shield, he blocked her attacks with ease.

She took a half a step back, feigning an opening. He whirled, kicking out his leg, aiming for her abdomen. She grabbed his ankle with both hands and twisted hard. Dante spun to the ground, trying to control his fall in midair by shifting his weight so his free leg was underneath him.

Octavia pulled up on his ankle, changing the way he fell, making it harder for him to orient himself. He crashed to the ground chest-first, and she was on top of him in an instant, leaping over his lower body to restrain him with a grappling hold. Her grip confined his neck and one of his arms while her legs caged his abdomen.

"Nice," Dante coughed out over the pressure of her forearm against his windpipe, a mischievous glimmer in his eye.

Before she could respond, he twisted in her grip, fully freeing his legs and forcing Octavia to the side. Countering, Octavia flipped over him, her legs landing on either side of his hips, her weight and strength pinning Dante to the mat.

Another second passed, and his left leg lifted to trap her right shin against the floor, while he used his other knee to push away her hips. His elbow swung out, forcing Octavia into a closed guard position with his powerful legs wrapped around her middle. She gasped as his legs tossed her body to the right, her back slamming against the mat.

He was up and off her in an instant. She was a fraction of a second too slow in rising off the floor and paid the price, groaning as pain blossomed under her ribs. *His kicks are so fast.*

The pain was already fading as she stumbled back, giving herself a moment to recover. She'd only been working on this new kickboxing combination for a few days, but she felt confident she'd already gotten the hang of it. Rallying, Octavia struck at Dante, jabbing left, crossing right, and then swinging hard with a left hook.

Dante blocked it all skillfully.

She finished off the combination by dropping low to deliver a swift kick to the ankles. Using the momentum of her kick to control his fall again, she went in for the kill. Dante fell to the mat with a *thud.* Octavia twisted him into a chokehold, this time using the last of her strength to secure him.

Dante tapped her forearm, and she released him. Dropping to the mat, she threw her arms wide while she tried to control her breathing. A victorious grin slicked across her face.

Dante sat up a few feet away, smiling in return. "Good job. I just taught you that combo on Monday. I definitely wasn't expecting you to use it so quickly, and with such precision."

"You're damn hard to surprise, so thanks," Octavia panted. She closed her eyes and focused on bringing her body back to homeostasis.

Dante had been training with Octavia for a couple of years, but they'd been working almost exclusively on hand-to-hand combat for a year now. Dante was the only person in her life, apart from the members of her coven, who knew that her parents had been killed in front of her. She'd told Dante that they had died due to gun violence, which was half true. Her mother's official cause of death was documented as a gunshot to the chest, but her father's was suffocation from smoke inhalation.

Because Dante knew Octavia's story, he understood her desperate desire to be able to protect herself and her loved ones. She was sure that was the only reason he agreed to train her like this, as his other clients only trained in self-defense.

But what he didn't know was that her desire was also fueled by the loss of her magic, like a black hole in her soul, slowly sucking her self-worth away. The combat training . . . it helped, even if just a little bit.

The one caveat of their training was that they'd never trained with weapons. They'd used props to run disarming drills on occasion, but that was the closest she'd ever knowingly gotten to a firearm since the night of the attack. With little to no education in that arena, if she ever came face-to-face with a witch hunter again, she'd just have to wing it.

She had faith in her abilities, though. In their years of training, Dante had made sure she wasn't lacking confidence, not that she needed much help in that department. Her rigorous training and love for the movement easily compounded her dauntless spirit.

"A few more months of this, and you'll be a serious force to be reckoned with. A total badass," Dante said mirthfully. "I might not be able to keep up."

Octavia grinned as the mix of praise and endorphins made her heart feel light as air.

He reached out for her hand and pulled her upright again. "Now, take the rest of the week to rest up, and I'll see you first thing Monday morning. We'll start with jiu-jitsu, and then review those kickboxing combos again."

"Sounds good. Thanks, Dante. Have a good week."

Octavia collected her belongings from the side of the mat and started toward the locker room. She took a deep drink from her water bottle as several himbos noticed her walking past the weight-lifting room. None of them had the decency to avert their gaze after she caught them looking. Rolling her eyes, she threw her over-sized sweatshirt on and flashed a not-so-subtle middle finger their way. She wasn't training this hard, pushing her body almost to the breaking point, for anyone but herself—especially not for a room full of insecure jocks.

CHAPTER 8
OCTAVIA

O ctavia's grandmother, Jocasta, lived in Brookline, a small town that bordered Boston proper. Since Octavia's gym was only a couple T stops east from her grandmother's house, she decided to stop by for a visit. Hopefully, Jocasta had found a new lead for Octavia to pursue in her research by now.

But that shouldn't be my primary motivation for visiting my grandmother. I'm such a selfish asshole.

Shame heated her face. Unfortunately, the endorphins only kept her self-loathing at bay for so long.

At the St. Paul Street station, she exited the car, hopping onto the platform. She loved walking through the streets of Brookline on the way to her grandmother's house. It was truly a beautiful little town. It emanated the vibe of a quiet suburban neighborhood, despite being in a noisy, bustling city. Every couple of blocks, she passed a small, quaint neighborhood park, and while this time of year they were often vacant and barren, she still thought they were beautiful. Octavia admired nature's ability to endure through the harsh northeastern winters, year after year.

Maybe I can endure as well.

She rounded on her grandmother's house, a beautiful, tall, brick building originally constructed in the nineteenth century. She hadn't even finished climbing the porch steps when the front door opened before her.

"My girl," Jocasta cooed. Delicate lines framed the corners of her eyes as she smiled. Today, Jocasta's straight hair was pulled back into a neat bun at the base of her neck, each expertly dyed dark brown strand perfectly in place. She wore an all-black outfit consisting of a thin sweater, straight-legged slacks, and ballet flats—her signature style.

The weight in Octavia's chest lessened slightly at the mere sight of her. "How are you, Grandma?" Octavia asked, pulling her petite grandmother into a tight hug. She breathed in the familiar scents of mint and Earl Grey tea, the tension in her exhausted muscles unfurling in response. This was where she felt safest, here in her grandmother's arms.

"I'm doing just fine. The more important question is: How are you? Just look at you." Jocasta broke free from Octavia's embrace and held her at arm's length. "You look exhausted. That won't do. Come inside, out of the cold."

Octavia followed her grandmother gladly, a shiver running down her spine as the welcoming warmth of the house enveloped her. Jocasta ushered her into the dining room, taking her coat and gesturing for her to sit at the large mahogany dining table. An array of sandwiches, fruits, and deserts awaited her arrival on the table.

Of course, she knew I was coming.

Octavia glanced at her grandmother, one eyebrow raised.

Casually, Jocasta said, "I saw your visit in the cards this morning."

"You're going to have to teach me that little tarot trick when I get my magic back," Octavia said as a tinge of jealousy slithered through her gut. She quickly shooed the feeling away.

"Yes, of course, but before we do anything, you'll eat," Jocasta commanded, pulling out a chair at the table.

Octavia nodded, sitting down in front of the smorgasbord

of food. She took a plate and began piling food on it, suddenly realizing how hungry she was.

Jocasta smiled as Octavia sipped her tea and nibbled on a sandwich. She asked about Octavia's studies; Octavia lied through her teeth. She was in fact missing a lecture at that very moment, but her grandmother didn't need to know that—not today, at least. Instead, Octavia updated Jocasta about her friends and bragged about winning against Dante.

Jocasta watched Octavia with sharp, attentive eyes. She'd always had an intimidating presence, a trait that Octavia had gotten over quickly as a child. It hadn't taken Octavia long to discover that the pressure others felt around Jocasta was due to the magnitude of her magic, not her personality. She was, and had been for decades, the strongest member of their coven.

Jocasta's face softened as she appreciated the empty plate in front of Octavia, finally satisfied that her granddaughter had eaten enough. "Now, what to do about your fatigue? It's a quarter moon tonight, so I won't be able to make a very potent elixir, but I could make *something*." Jocasta rose gracefully from her chair and wandered toward the kitchen.

"Grandma, please," Octavia whined. "I don't need anything right now. I'm fine."

"My house, my rules, darling," was the only response her grandmother offered, effectively ending the conversation as she disappeared beyond an arched doorway.

Jocasta specialized in lunar magic. Lunar witches were exceptionally skilled in almost every facet of witchcraft; however, the effectiveness of their spells, conjuring, or potions depended completely upon the moon's cycle. For example, Jocasta's potions were most potent when brewed during a full moon, whereas her portals were most stable during a crescent moon.

A big black Labrador retriever jaunted into the dining room.

The dog trotted over to Octavia, tail wagging enthusiastically.

"Well, hi there, Luna. How are you today?"

The big dog barked affirmatively.

"I'm glad to hear it. I see you've been taking good care of Grandma for me. Thanks for that." Octavia bent at the waist and rested her forehead against Luna's. A large wet tongue grazed her cheek as she pulled away. Octavia laughed as she wiped at the saliva with her sleeve, and then the dog was off, trotting toward the kitchen to find Jocasta.

As is common in the world of witchcraft, there was more to her grandmother's dog than met the eye. Luna wasn't a run-of-the-mill, domestic pup; she was a familiar, a supernatural entity in the form of an animal that protected and served a witch—specifically, a powerful witch. Because they bonded magically with their witches, they were often cherished companions as well. Luna had bonded with Jocasta when Jocasta became matriarch of the coven, which meant the familiar was close to thirty years old.

Octavia rose from the dining table and followed Luna into the kitchen. The dog was on her hind legs with her front paws on the counter and nose in the air, sniffing at the contents of the cauldron. Jocasta was chopping up a mixture of dried herbs and flowers at the opposite counter.

"Would you mind asking Thaddeus for some more dried vanilla beans? I think he has some extra in the greenhouse out back." Jocasta's eyes never wandered from her task.

"Sure." Octavia grabbed a chunky wool wrap from the row of hooks by the back door and ventured into the backyard. Pulling the wrap tight around her shoulders, she walked to the greenhouse at the far corner of the lawn. When the door swung open, she inhaled a breath of dense, humid petrichor.

Thaddeus stood at a workbench, repotting a large tropical plant. His hands were coated in dirt, and a soft smile adorned his handsome, aging face. Thaddeus was Quintin's grandfather and the coven's only remaining elder besides her grandmother.

"Octavia, to what do I owe the pleasure?" Thaddeus asked as he wiped his hands on an already soiled rag at his hip.

"Just stopping by for a visit. How've you been?"

"Can't complain, can't complain. How's my grandson? Are you keeping him in line?"

"You know he's the one who keeps the rest of us in line," Octavia chuckled, the moisture of the warm air beading on her upper lip.

"Well, that's good to hear. I'm glad he's keeping his head on straight. Now, I'm sure you trekked out here through the cold for a reason. What can I help you with?"

"Grandma ran out of vanilla beans and thought you might have some extra out here." Octavia eyed the array of dried flowers and herbs stored in containers on the shelves above the workbench.

"Well, that I do." Thaddeus grabbed a glass jar full of dried brown vanilla beans from the topmost shelf and handed it to Octavia.

"What's that plant you're repotting?" she asked.

Thaddeus gestured to a long, spindly plant with a tiny bud. "This here is tropical hibiscus. June likes to add the petals to her potions on occasion," he explained. "Would you like to watch it bloom?"

"Yes, please."

Thaddeus turned back to the plant, packing down the soil in the new pot before he dug the tips of his fingers into the dirt and closed his eyes. The air in the greenhouse shifted slightly, raising the hairs on Octavia's arms. As she watched, the plant evolved, growing several new, glossy leaves and sprouting a single blossom that swelled and then unfurled five large, brilliant red petals with a prominent, orange-tipped stamen.

Thaddeus's specialty was green magic. He could use magic to control plants' growth and development. He'd even majored in botany in college, enabling him to use his magic to the best of his abilities. In truth, June's potions wouldn't have been half as powerful if not for Thaddeus's quality ingredients.

Octavia stared at the flower as Thaddeus removed his hands from the soil.

"It's beautiful," she murmured. "When does it bloom naturally?"

"In the summer or autumn in tropical regions. Without this greenhouse here, it'd never bloom in this cold climate, whether I used my magic to help it along or not." Thaddeus placed the hibiscus shrub on a shelf behind him. "Come on, let's get that vanilla over to Jo."

Thaddeus opened the greenhouse door and followed Octavia across the yard and into the kitchen, kicking his boots against the back stairs before entering.

"Here you go." Octavia passed the container to Jocasta as she slid the wool wrap from her shoulders.

"Thank you." Jocasta's gaze swept to Thaddeus. "There's lunch on the table, Thad. Please help yourself."

"Thanks," Thaddeus replied as he went into the dining room, leaving Octavia and Jocasta alone in the kitchen.

Jocasta and Thaddeus lived together, and to the best of Octavia's knowledge, they'd never been lovers, just the best of friends. Both had lost their non-magical spouses to illness before the attack, and they'd decided to move in together when the coven relocated to Boston. Octavia figured the decision had been partly influenced by the attack, but she also believed they wanted to stave off loneliness. No matter the reason, Octavia was grateful they had each other.

"Now, do you really think I don't know what instigated your

surprise visit today?" Jocasta asked in a sharp tone, finally turning to face her granddaughter.

"That's not the only reason," Octavia said quickly, guilt pinking her cheeks. "I missed you."

Jocasta's mouth pressed thin. "Mhm."

"But yes, I did want to ask whether you've gotten any new leads on where to focus my research efforts," Octavia admitted, dropping her eyes to the floor.

"I wish you hadn't inherited that stubbornness from your mother and me. It's terribly frustrating." Jocasta sighed deeply. "If only you were more laid back, like your father." A moment passed between them in silence. "Of course, that means I fully understand why you can't stop searching, even if it causes you nothing but pain and disappointment. It's the same thing I would do . . . your mother as well."

Emotion clenched like a fist in Octavia's throat at the mention of her parents, but she pressed on. "So, *have* you made any new discoveries?"

"Actually, I have," Jocasta began with a small smile. "A childhood friend of mine, Patricia, recently relocated back to Salem. She was getting bored in retirement, so she started working part-time at the Archives Library a couple of weeks ago, organizing the archives. She complained to me that it's been a bear of a task, but she discovered some interesting documents in the process. I'm assuming she's stumbled upon some of our old coven records and possibly even grimoires. I asked Patricia to keep these documents stored safely out of sight until one of us has the opportunity to go investigate, which she's graciously agreed to do."

"Wait, I thought you picked through Salem's Archives Library years ago," Octavia said.

"Yes, I thought so too, but that was weeks after the attack, and if my memory serves, the library was in a terrible state of disarray.

It's very possible I missed something back then." Jocasta turned her face toward the kitchen window, the gray light throwing shadows across her angular features. "You won't remember this, but it's difficult to go there now. To Salem. Our home mourns our losses with us, amplifying them in a way."

Octavia's stomach twisted into knots.

"If you go to Salem in search of these documents, you must emotionally prepare yourself," her grandmother warned.

"I understand." Octavia nodded.

Jocasta turned back to the cauldron and stirred the mixture several times. Once satisfied, she ladled some liquid into a teacup, which she handed to Octavia. "Drink."

The concoction was clear as water and smelled pleasantly of vanilla. It was surprisingly viscous as it trickled down her throat, leaving a warm, tingling sensation in its wake. Moments later, every cell in her body began to stir, suddenly rejuvenated.

Octavia felt energized, as if she'd just spent a weekend away at one of those fancy wellness spas in the mountains of Vermont. Jocasta smiled at her, glad to see that the elixir had had the desired effect. "That's better."

Octavia opened her mouth to respond, but her phone dinged in the dining room. She went to retrieve it, stepping carefully over Luna lying comfortably on the floor. Thaddeus was eating his lunch at the table, happily scratching Luna's neck with his foot.

Octavia grabbed her phone from her gym bag and frowned when she saw a text notification from an unknown number. She gasped as she opened and read the text. Her entire body warmed. She knew immediately who it was from.

Is your offer from last night still good? I'm ready for that history lesson.

CHAPTER 9
LEIF

"Will you all calm down? The text was fine. Let's move on!" Delta narrowed her eyes as she turned back to one of Jiro's many monitors. They'd moved upstairs to Jiro's living room, as they needed his computers to formulate their plan. The monitor in front of Delta displayed multiple blueprints of the coven's apartment building, which Jiro had hacked his way into accessing earlier that evening.

"Then why's it taking her so long to respond?" Jiro spun his desk chair in a circle. "It's been hours."

"Look, we need to determine the best point of entry into the loft," Tripp said as he leaned against the desk. "It can't be facing the street. We don't need passersby calling the police."

Jiro let out a muffled whine, Leif supposed because he realized he was being ignored.

"There's a window in Octavia's room that faces the alley," Leif explained. "You'd have to scale the side of the building to access it, though."

Everyone glanced up at Tripp; he was the only one of them capable of doing it thanks to his superior strength and flexibility. His years of experimenting with every sport known to humankind had primed him for physically demanding jobs like this. Gymnastics, skate boarding, rock climbing, tennis; if a person could name a physical activity, Tripp had likely tried it *and* excelled at it.

"That's not a problem," Tripp said firmly, flicking a fidget spinner in his hand. "Plus, we know that room will be unoccupied, which makes it the ideal choice."

"Is there a way we can confirm the loft won't be protected or booby-trapped with spells?" Jiro asked, his dark eyebrows furrowing in concern. "We can't risk losing the element of surprise by triggering traps."

"Magic of that caliber would be costly, and likely not sustainable long term, even if this particular coven is powerful," Delta said, crossing her arms over her chest. "It's a gamble, yes, but I'd say the odds are in our favor."

"What about familiars?" Jiro looked to Leif.

"I honestly have no idea," Leif replied, shaking his head. "I didn't see any animals when I was there, but that doesn't mean there weren't any in the other bedrooms." His stomach sank. He should've taken the initiative to snoop around more when he'd been there.

"Another gamble," Delta murmured.

"Keeping the element of surprise until the last possible moment will help us neutralize as much of the risk as we can, given the unknown variables," Tripp reasoned.

"Okay, so Tripp enters through Octavia's bedroom window," Delta explained as her finger traced the route over the schematics displayed on the monitor, "then sneaks through the kitchen to let the rest of us in through the front door. Now, we don't know which witch will be in which room, so unfortunately, we can't plan match-ups in any meaningful way. The three of us are just going to have to be on top of our game."

"I still strongly disagree with that part of the plan," Leif said, his hands clenching at his sides.

Leif had originally envisioned he'd be able to help his group gain access to the loft from the inside and be able to fight with them. But Delta had shut that idea down completely. She wanted Leif to make sure Octavia was out of the loft before the confrontation went down, which meant he wouldn't be able to take part in the battle at all. Leif's chest had tightened at how easy it'd been for them to remove his chess piece from the board, forcing him to watch from the sidelines. He tried to ignore the unfamiliar sensation of jealousy simmering in his stomach as Delta's frustrated gaze swung to his.

"Well, you're just going to have to get over it, aren't you?" Delta retorted, her mounting irritation obvious by the increasingly rapid tapping of her index finger.

As Leif opened his mouth to argue, his phone buzzed in his pocket. Everyone's attention shifted to him as he retrieved it.

"Read it out loud," Jiro requested, so Leif did:

Definitely, but the lesson involves a field trip. Are you down for a trip to Salem?

"Reply, 'Sure. Sounds fun. What's in Salem?'" Tripp instructed.

Leif typed out the text as the others nodded in agreement.

Octavia's response came through immediately.

Salem's Archives Library. Library access is restricted to authorized personnel only, but I have a family friend who's willing to sneak us in tomorrow. I know it's short notice, so I understand if you can't make it, but I hope you can.

Leif cringed against the blush rising in his cheeks as he read the text aloud. *I hope you can.*

Jiro shot to his feet, pacing back and forth in excitement. "No way! Can you imagine the kind of information you could find in that library? Coven records, family trees, maybe even grimoires!"

"See, Leif?" Delta exclaimed. "This is perfect. Now your job will be just as important as ours. Use the time in that library to gather as much intel as you can on other witches or covens that might be in the area."

"Respond to her," Tripp directed, pushing off the desk to read over Leif's shoulder. "We need to figure out the timing."

Leif: I'm in. What time?

Octavia: Great! Say around 11am?

Leif: Sounds good. I have a car. Are you cool with me driving us there?

Octavia: Sure. Pick me up at my place?

Octavia: I know we'll be in a stuffy old library most of the day, but here's to hoping we can find a way to make it as fun as last time...

Leif swallowed hard as his pink cheeks turned red. He couldn't believe his siblings were reading this over his shoulder right now.

Leif: I don't doubt it! See you then. Goodnight, Octavia.

Octavia: Night!

"Eleven is too early," Delta barked. "You're going to have to find an excuse to keep her in Salem overnight." Her gaze flicked to Leif's phone screen. "But luckily, I don't think that'll be very difficult given that text." Delta sneered, suppressing a chuckle.

"D's got a point," said Tripp as he flashed Leif an apologetic glance. "We don't want her coming back to the loft early and discovering the carnage."

"All right, I got it," Leif said, embarrassment stilting his voice. He pushed on, "Now all that's left is to figure out how we're going to lure all of the other tenants in the building out of their apartments for the night."

Thankfully, this was Jiro's and Delta's area of expertise. Delta was a master manipulator, and Jiro was a tech genius. Between the two of them, they could easily devise a plan to rid the apartment building of the rest of its occupants, ensuring safety for everyone *but* the coven.

Before they could jump back into planning, a loud, lengthy yawn erupted from Leif's mouth, causing each of his siblings to turn his way. He attempted to stifle the noise behind his hand, but it was no use. He was too tired to even try to control it. "Sorry," Leif murmured after his jaw had closed.

"Leif, you're exhausted," Jiro said flatly as he sat and swiveled his chair back toward the monitors. "Go get some sleep. Leave the rest up to us."

Leif nodded, even though Jiro couldn't see him. He was right. If Leif was going to be of any use tomorrow, he needed to rest.

He excused himself as the others continued scheming, exhaustion crashing over him in waves. He exited Jiro's apartment and drifted down to his own, his bed calling to him.

Leif walked through his bare-bones living room to his similarly unadorned bathroom. He'd never had the inclination to decorate or make the space his own. The life of a witch hunter was often nomadic, as they typically went wherever the work demanded. The home they inhabited now only existed because Garren had wanted to let them grow up in an environment with some semblance of stability. But stability had never appealed to Leif.

In the bathroom, Leif shed his clothes and showered. The warm water and steam soothed his tense muscles as he reviewed the plan once more, calculating an estimated risk-to-reward ratio. Rinsing himself, he determined that their plan was a solid one. It was all thanks to Garren that their crew had been able to come up with such a decent plan on their own. Smiling to himself at the thought, he exited the shower, dried off, and walked into his bedroom.

Thoughts of their aptitude always turned into thoughts of their father, Leif realized as he tossed the towel in the hamper and dressed in a pair of loose sweatpants and a T-shirt. Garren had adopted them in childhood, after they'd all been orphaned. Leif, Jiro, Tripp, and Delta—all their parents had been abducted and murdered by a powerful coven of witches.

Leif's dear old friend vengeance seared hot in his gut as he imagined, probably for the thousandth time, his parents being sacrificed in some gruesome, brutal way during a dark magic ritual, leaving him utterly alone in this world. With no remaining family to speak of, Leif remembered feeling empty as he was unceremoniously dumped into the foster care system alongside his adopted siblings. The emptiness had been so complete it'd felt like his insides were painstakingly carved out, scoop by scoop, with a dull spoon, leaving behind a hollow shell.

Leif cleared his throat as he dropped to sit on the edge of his bed, attempting to banish the echo of the void that had once made a home in his chest. Sighing, he placed his elbows on his knees and let his head fall into his hands. He massaged his temples as he forced his thoughts in a different direction.

As Leif's head raised from his hands, he recalled what had come next. Garren had heard of the coven's horrific ritual sacrifice, and the children's resulting misfortune, from one of his fellow witch hunters. The tension in Leif's jaw eased with the knowledge that a crew of skilled witch hunters had succeeded in exacting their revenge. The night after the sacrifice—after their parents' murder—witch hunters had annihilated the lot of them.

Even in his exhausted state, Leif's heart beat a faster rhythm as a small dose of adrenaline flooded his veins. At least the snakes who'd killed his parents no longer drew breath. What little peace Leif had found over the years was thanks to that fact.

And now Leif was determined to follow in his adoptive father's footsteps. He was confident he could do it. Garren had said he wanted them to be able to protect themselves in case they ever crossed paths with another coven, so he'd trained them from a young age. But Garren had never forced anything upon them. Witch hunting was a path each of them had chosen for themselves, and even though this was going to be their first official hunt, Leif knew they were ready despite their inexperience, all thanks to Garren's diligent training.

With a sigh, Leif let his head fall back on his shoulders. Light from a passing car crept into his bedroom through thin slits in the blinds, streaking across the popcorn ceiling like a meteor. He remembered, even all these years later, why he'd chosen this path for himself—for revenge, of course, but also due to his fierce desire to make his father proud. To prove to Garren that he'd made the right choice in adopting Leif. Kicking ass at witch hunting was the only way Leif knew, without a doubt, would appropriately demonstrate to Garren just how grateful Leif was for this family—for this life.

Leif flung himself down on the bed, letting the exhaustion take over. His eyes closed, and lazy, half-formed thoughts bounced haphazardly around his mind. The last thought he had before unconsciousness took him was of Octavia's eyes, dark as the depths of space.

Leif was a young boy again, running through a lush forest in summertime, his breath coming in heavy pants. His friends trailed behind him, their shrill laughter interrupting the soft sounds of the forest. He lifted his face up toward the sun, the golden light warming his skin. He was completely and utterly happy.

In the blink of an eye, the warmth of the sun turned icy and the light faded to darkness. The forest became barren, leaves and brush withering to nothing. The giggles morphed into screams. His happiness curdled into fear.

Dizzyingly psychedelic swirls of color suddenly disoriented him. A wild kind of panic tore through his chest as he slammed his eyes shut and pressed the heels of his palms hard against them. Slowly, the flashing light on the other side of his eyelids receded, and the darkness returned, pure and uninterrupted.

Trembling, he removed his hands and opened his eyes. The woods in front of him were bathed in ivory moonlight, every surface covered in fluffy, untouched snow.

A movement in the corner of his vision drew his attention. A woman emerged from behind a large oak tree, her long hair glistening like a pearl in the dim light. Her kind blue eyes were misty, and tears stained her cheeks. She dropped to her knees in front of him; he was so young that they were face-to-face.

Leif raised a small hand to wipe a tear from her cheek. She grabbed his wet hand and kissed the center of his palm. His skin tingled where her lips touched.

She returned her gaze to his and placed his open palm to her chest, right above her heart. Beneath his hand beat a rhythmic cadence, strong and true. The woman raised her free hand to caress his cheek, and a small, sad smile tugged at her lips.

Tears welled in Leif's eyes when the woman's heartbeat began to slow. His eyes frantically searched the woman's. There was no fear in them, only sadness and longing. As the erratic beats faded beneath his fingers, the woman grew cold, her skin paled, and her lips turned blue. She was dying.

Leif's mother was dying.

Her hand drifted from his cheek to the center of his chest; her fingers closed against something at the base of his neck and pulled.

With her last breath, his mother pressed her forehead to his and whispered words he couldn't understand. Her voice was too soft, too breathy to make out. But the words ignited something in him, like the thrum of an idling engine.

The heart beneath his hand stopped beating.

And then she was gone.

Her body went limp, falling onto the cold snow. Her cloudy eyes, dark as a thunderstorm, looked straight through him, into a place beyond. Her hand lay open, a small white gold cross pendant and chain resting in her palm.

Sorrow seized the breath from his lungs.

He was all alone. Again.

Leif shot up in bed, chest heaving as he gasped for air. A tear fell down his cheek as his hand instinctively reached for the small white gold cross pendant on his chest. It was still there, where it'd been since Garren had gifted it to him years before.

The recurring dream had haunted him for as long as he could remember. But even after so much time, Leif had no idea what it meant. That necklace was one of his most prized possessions, so why would his mother yank it from his neck? He knew the dream was a figment of his imagination. He hadn't been there when his parents were murdered, so this version of her death was just a dramatic reenactment that his subconscious tortured him with.

Leif rose from the bed and rubbed his hands briskly over his arms, then went to the bathroom. A tingling sensation always lingered on his skin after the dream. He splashed cold water on his face and raised his gaze to the reflection in the mirror. Pale blue-gray eyes stared back at him, and light stubble peppered his jaw and cheeks.

He dragged his hands through his hair and shook his head, tossing away thoughts of the dream he knew so well, before he reached for his razor. He had to look presentable if his plan was going to go off without a hitch. As his concentration returned to his role in their plan, his stomach flipped nervously—in apprehension or excitement, he couldn't say. A muscle in Leif's jaw flexed at the sensation. Either was a sign of weakness.

He wasn't going to fail Garren like he'd failed his mother.

I'll bring down this coven or die trying.

CHAPTER 10
OCTAVIA

O ctavia had delayed texting Michael back all day, unsure of how to reply. A small part of her did want to see him again—okay, *more* than a small part—but she had other priorities at the moment. Dating simply wasn't one of them.

But she'd zoned out at the dining table next to Quintin and left the text message up on her phone screen for all the world to read.

"Is Michael the guy from this morning?" Quintin asked, pointing at her phone, his voice unusually clipped and harsh.

Octavia startled in her seat, clearing her throat before she said, "Yeah, it is." She flipped her phone over, placing a protective palm on it.

"Are you going to respond?"

"I honestly don't know," Octavia said, shrugging. "He seems like a nice guy, but I have other stuff on my plate right now."

"Bullshit," Sage chimed in as they rose from the table, sauntering off into the kitchen.

June followed close behind, sitting on the living room floor next to her cauldron. "He has a bright aura, Tavi. You should say yes. You might end up having a great time." She smiled warmly as she secured her hair into a ponytail.

"I agree completely," said Sage. "Getting to know more people outside of the coven might be good for you. Don't you agree, Quin?" Sage eyed him pointedly.

"Uh ... yeah," Quintin murmured, refocusing his attention on his plate of spaghetti. "I mean, I think making new friends is a good idea and all, but I also respect your decision not to date anyone you don't want to."

"Great," Octavia snapped. "The next time I want your opinions, I'll be sure to ask." Octavia pushed her plate away, leaving a good portion of her meal untouched.

June rose from her spot on the floor and came to stand behind Octavia, gently wrapping her arms around Octavia's shoulders. "We don't mean to pry. We just care about you and want to see you happy." She inhaled a quick breath. "You just haven't seemed happy lately, and we don't know how to help."

June pressed her cheek to Octavia's and squeezed her tight before letting go. Like taking a sledgehammer to glass, the tenderness of June's embrace shattered Octavia's indignance. Octavia's throat strained against the emotions building there. Around June, she was an open book, no matter how hard she tried not to be. She wanted to hate June's ability to see through her mask, but Octavia found she couldn't. As scary as it was to be truly seen, it was a little wonderful too.

Octavia turned in her chair and reached for June's hand. "I know you all mean well. I'm sorry for snapping." Her gaze drifted to the others, and she sighed reluctantly at their hopeful faces. "I just—I don't even know what we'd talk about. All I think about nowadays are hexes and jiu-jitsu. Watching paint dry would probably be more exciting than talking to me."

Octavia dropped June's hand and let her forehead fall to the table, a groan of frustration escaping her mouth. She knew the others were exchanging looks without even having to lift her head. They knew she was right. Michael was a lost cause.

Then the idea hit her like a slap in the face. She lifted her head from the table and looked around at her friends, who were all staring at her in return. Octavia knew they wouldn't approve, so she'd have to tell yet another little white lie.

"Well, now that I think about it, he does like history."

"What kind of history?" Quintin asked, curiosity glinting through his narrowed gaze.

"I'm not completely sure, but I know he's interested in local history. I could probably talk about history long enough to sustain a first date; if not, I might need to find a different subject to get my masters in." Octavia laughed dryly.

"Whatever gets you to say yes, Tavi," said Sage.

June shot Sage a warning glance, her lips pressed tight and irises armed with daggers. Sage's mouth snapped shut.

June turned to Octavia. "That sounds great! You should see some historical sites around the city or visit a museum."

Or visit a library in Salem.

The idea was perfect. Octavia could kill two birds with one stone. She could continue her research on how to break hexes while going on a date with Michael and—at least temporarily—getting her roommates off her back.

And who knows? Like June said, it might even be fun.

The others waited up, eager for a play-by-play of Octavia's text conversation with Michael. She left out the Salem part when she relayed their texts. By the time they had called it a night, June and Sage were practically bursting with excitement for her.

Quintin, however, had been unusually quiet all evening, despondent even. Octavia had asked him if he was all right, to which he'd responded he was fine, just tired. But having known Quintin all her life, she could tell there was something he wasn't saying. Even so, she respected his privacy enough not to pry further.

They were chatting over their coffees in the living room the next morning—or rather, Octavia observed while Sage and June gabbed and Quintin rifled through cabinets in the kitchen. She couldn't help the envy that poured, hot and sticky like tar, into her stomach as Sage lit the Bunsen burner beneath June's caldron with a snap of their fingers. Like blowing at the muzzle of a smoking gun, Sage raised their flaming index finger to their mouth and extinguished the flame with a puff of breath.

"Water too, please?" June asked, eyes still puffy from sleep.

Sage smirked, flicking the hand that had been on fire at the wrist in a series of circular movements. They trapped the water molecules that formed in midair in a ball between their hands. Sage rose from the couch and brought the floating ball of water to June's caldron. Water splashed over the edges as Sage dropped their spell and gravity regained control. June pushed her grimoire out of the splash zone just in the nick of time.

"Sorry." Sage grimaced, retaking their seat on the couch. "I conjured a bit too much."

"Here." A kitchen towel flew out of a portal that materialized next to them.

June caught it with ease, chuckling. "Thanks!" she called to Quintin; he was filling up a portable thermos with coffee in the kitchen.

Octavia felt Quintin's eyes on her as she watched Sage and June. They laughed as they cleaned up the mess. Her skin crawled uncomfortably. She hadn't been schooling her expression. Her envy was probably written all over her face.

She was pushing away from the dining table when a strong hand grabbed the back of her chair, holding her firmly in place. The next moment, Octavia was yanked from the seat, and then she was falling. Falling in a space between spaces—a place she could never have entered on her own. She was falling through a portal teeming with brilliant, pale blue light, so bright it reminded her of aquamarine gemstones. The veil separating *in here* from *out there* was almost see-through, but not quite.

Then Octavia hit Quintin's chest with a *smack*. Vibrant technicolor swirls spattered her vision, fading with every blink. Quintin's hands on her shoulders steadied her, but her head continued to spin as she oriented herself. They were standing in Quintin's bedroom. She looked to the left, vision still blotchy, toward the wall lined with bookshelves, and then to the right toward his immaculately made bed. She smiled at the sight of his violin in the corner by the nightstand. But her happiness wilted when she realized how long it had been since she'd asked him to play. Months, perhaps? Maybe even a year. Octavia flashed herself a mental middle finger.

I'm the worst.

A cheerful, lilting sound filled the room. Quintin was laughing, Octavia realized. His smile was wide and bright as she returned her gaze to his. "What are you laughing at?"

"You, obviously. Every time I take you portal jumping it's like you forget how to stand on your own two feet." He laughed again, deeply, tears welling in the corners of his eyes.

Octavia slapped at him playfully, shrugging his hands off her shoulders. "It's not my fault. The space between the portals is disorienting as hell! Up is down—right is left. If you didn't use them all the time, you'd feel the same. You're lucky I have an iron stomach, otherwise I'd be puking on your fancy sneakers right now."

Quintin's laughter faded as his arms fell to his sides, his smile with it. His eyebrows pulled together uncertainly. "Listen, I—" Octavia opened her mouth to cut him off, but Quintin raised a hand to silence her. "I know the way June and Sage are with each other hurts you."

A choked noise escaped Octavia's lips, but no words formed. It's not like he was wrong, so the sharp sting lancing through her heart shouldn't have been a surprise. But Octavia knew better than most just how much the truth could hurt.

Quintin plowed on, "So, why don't you just join in with them? They'd love it. You'd love it. I just—" Quintin's mouth fell into a frown as he studied Octavia's face. Sighing, he turned away and walked to the window. "I just don't understand, and it's frustrating."

Octavia didn't know what to say. He was right. He didn't understand, and she didn't think there was a way to adequately explain it to him.

Desperate, she decided to go with the first analogy that came to mind. "It's like trying to be friends with the most talented musicians in the world," she said softly.

Quintin turned at the waist, his full lips parted in a hopeful little O.

Octavia gestured to Quintin's violin with a lazy hand. She had no idea if the analogy would even work. "Imagine learning to play the violin at the same time as all of your best friends, and growing up, that's all you did with them—play your instruments together, write songs, put on performances. And then, out of the blue, your friends start getting better—playing more difficult pieces, getting all the praise and attention—and you fall behind, into the background. Your friends are still there, and you're still surrounded by music—you still love it more than air or water or food—but . . . you're no good at it. So, you sit back and watch your friends grow, and develop, and win competitions, and you—" Octavia's breath caught in her throat. She collected herself with the briefest of nods before continuing. "But you're standing still, falling further and further behind. So, you get jealous and grow resentful because you're human, and we . . . well, we fuck everything up. And before you know it, you wake up years later surrounded by the most talented musicians in the world, and you hate . . ."

"Hate what?" The pity in Quintin's eyes made Octavia queasy.

"*Everything.* Me. You. Them." Octavia pointed to Quintin's closed bedroom door, toward Sage and June, the volume of her voice raising with every word. "Hexes. Guns. Witch hunters. Magic. Everything! I *hate* everything!"

Quintin flinched—a single moment's hesitation—before he bounded for her. When he wrapped her in his arms, she realized she was shaking.

"I get it." Quintin sighed against her hair. She relaxed as the cinnamon scent of him enveloped her. "I mean—of course I don't, but now I can imagine better. I'm—"

"Don't." Octavia's voice was a whisper. "Don't be sorry." She raised her arms to hug Quintin back, dropping her forehead against his chest and breathing deeply.

One day, I'll break the hex separating me from my magic. I'll get it back and work harder than ever to catch up to them. It'll be worth it— putting magic above everything else. Above family, above friendship, above the possibility of a relationship. It has to be worth it.

June's melodic voice drifted into Quintin's room from the hallway, pulling Octavia from her thoughts. "Tavi, it's already after ten. You should start getting ready. You said he's picking you up at eleven, right?"

Octavia pushed herself out of Quintin's arms. "Oh crap, yeah."

Quintin nodded, and she smiled sheepishly. She'd never opened up that much to him before. She didn't know what to say, so she walked to the door in silence. Halfway through the door frame, she turned back to him. "Thanks for caring enough to ask the hard questions—questions I don't want to answer."

Quintin smiled, but his lips were pressed tightly together, and the warmth didn't reach his eyes, almost as if he didn't believe her. "You're welcome."

Octavia padded barefoot down the hallway to her bedroom. Standing in front of her closet, she assessed her options as she shook off the weight of her emotions with a quick shimmy of her shoulders. The last thing she needed was to bring her emotional baggage on this date. As she poked around her closet, she was surprised she'd never realized just how much black clothing she owned.

Like grandmother, like granddaughter, I suppose.

After pulling out a few different options, she settled on a pair of black jeans, leather booties, and a soft, form-fitting turtleneck. She didn't want to get too warm in the stuffy library later. Fully dressed, she sat at the desk in her room and applied a light layer of makeup. Her grandmother had taught her how to put makeup on when she was a teenager, but she'd never been very good at it. Her classic look consisted of plain black winged eyeliner with a colored lip. Today she painted on a vibrant red.

She tossed her hair over her shoulder and studied it in the mirror. The long chestnut strands fell limp and straight to her lower back. She briefly considered curling it, but then thought better of it. Today wasn't about impressing Michael; it was about finally finding out how to break the damn hex.

She shook her head as thoughts of the hex threatened to awaken the voice again. She felt a familiar fog seeping into her brain as she grabbed a stack of notebooks and stuffed them into an empty tote bag. Those notebooks contained years' worth of research notes, and she wasn't about to leave them behind.

Non est umbra sine lumine, the voice said, more softly than usual.

Grimacing against the noise and her inability to keep it at bay, Octavia took one last look in the mirror before exiting her room. On the way to the living room, her cell phone rang.

"Hello?" Octavia answered, still trying to shake off the voice echoing in her mind.

"Don't worry, I'm not super early." It was Michael. "I was just wondering what your favorite road trip snacks are." His voice was cheery, and she couldn't help but chuckle.

"Flaming Hot Cheetos or bust."

"Roger that. Chocolate preference?"

"Hmm, that's a hard one. Let's go with Reese's."

"Thank God. That's what I was hoping you would say." His deep laugh heated her cheeks. "See you in twenty?"

"Yep. Looking forward to it."

I really am, she realized as she hung up the phone, her mind thankfully silent again. *Maybe I don't have my priorities straight after all.*

CHAPTER 11
LEIF

The leather jacket cloaked over Leif's shoulders did little to protect him from the fierce wind. Leaning against Garren's black BMW, he stuffed his hands farther into his jean pockets, trying and failing to protect them from the chill. Garren probably would've been pissed if he found out that Leif took the BMW out, but this wasn't a joy ride; it was business.

The sound of a door opening reclaimed his attention, and Octavia stepped out of her apartment building and into the wind. While he was dressed in a cream-colored sweater and blue jeans, she wore all black. Her dark hair fell over her shoulders in a sleek waterfall, and a sudden flashback of his fingers tangled in those strands clouded his vision. Willing the memory away, he smiled and waved. She returned the gesture with a tight smile.

"You ready to nerd out all day?" she asked, tucking a wind-swept tuft of hair behind her ear. Leif noticed the glint of multiple ear piercings.

"Definitely." Leif opened the passenger door for her.

"Thanks," she murmured as she hopped in, tossing her heavy tote bag on the floor.

Leif jogged around to the driver's side and climbed in. Garren rarely drove the BMW, given his fondness for the vehicle, so it still had that new car smell even though it was a couple of years old.

"Nice ride. Do you have to pay a small fortune to park it?" Octavia asked, twisting in her seat to check out the interior of the car.

"It's actually my dad's. So no, luckily, it doesn't cost me a thing." Leif chuckled, putting the car in drive.

Salem should only be a forty-five-minute drive this time of day. Plenty of time to gather intel.

"I don't want you to think I'm not grateful for the invitation," Leif began, "because I am. But I'm curious about something. Why didn't you ask any of your roommates to join you instead?" He chanced a look at her through the corner of his eye.

She was hesitating, obviously debating whether or not to tell him the truth. "Well, to be honest, they wouldn't really approve of me going in the first place," she finally relented after a long pause.

"Is it too nosy of me to ask why?"

Octavia gave him a wily smirk that was all the answer he needed, but she humored him with an answer anyway. "I'm researching something specific at the moment, and my friends think it's become a bit of an obsession. But they're wrong. It's not," she said matter-of-factly.

His curiosity surged, and he struggled to keep it at bay. "Well, I'm happy to be of assistance."

"No way. I won't bore you with my research. I want you to use the opportunity to research whatever you're interested in." A small smile tugged at the corners of her cherry red lips.

"If you insist," Leif acquiesced.

A few minutes passed in comfortable silence as Octavia gazed out the window, watching the cramped Cambridge streets pass by. Eventually, she turned her gaze to Leif, and he focused all his attention on the road in front of him. He could feel her eyes on his skin, like a cool breeze, drifting from his face down to his chest.

"I didn't notice the cross last time. Do you always wear it?" she asked, eyeing the pendant around his neck.

Leif coughed as he resisted the urge to reach for the cross. "Uh, yeah. It was a gift from my dad. I always have it on." He chanced another sidelong glance in her direction. "I guess we were a little too busy to get caught up in the details." One corner of his mouth curled up into an exaggerated simper.

"I can't deny that," Octavia replied with a chuckle, returning her attention to the world passing by the window. "What about your mom?" she asked.

"She died when I was young. So did my biological father."

"I'm sorry." Octavia turned back to face him. Her mouth was downturned in a small frown, her soft gaze focused and unblinking. Her sympathy seemed genuine.

"It was a long time ago," Leif dismissed the subject.

"Doesn't make it any easier," Octavia countered, a knowing look in her eyes.

"What about your parents?"

"Also dead."

Leif's gaze snapped to hers, disbelief crashing over him. He took a moment to compose himself. "So, you know, then."

Octavia sighed deeply. "Yeah, I know."

Another minute passed in silence. Leif was nervous to push the subject further, but his curiosity won out, and he went on. "I was placed into foster care after my parents died. Luckily, my foster dad adopted me and a few other foster kids. So I got to grow up with a father and siblings."

Octavia smiled. "I'm glad to hear it."

Damn . . . that smile's beautiful.

She continued, speaking blithely, but a flicker of darkness passed over her face. "I was raised by my grandmother. She's given me everything."

"Yet you can't help hoping—praying even—for a different life. A different path," Leif ventured, treading lightly.

Octavia's eyes widened, quickly finding his own.

"Yes, exactly," she whispered. "Well, minus the praying part." She laughed softly. "No offense."

"No offense taken. I wear this cross because of my father, not because of my faith."

Octavia nodded in response, and silence enveloped them once more. Leif reached his arm behind the passenger seat and pulled a grocery bag full of refreshments forward, setting it on his lap. He gently tossed a bag of Cheetos at Octavia and handed over some napkins and a bottle of water before retrieving some for himself. The grocery bag *thumped* against the floorboard as Leif returned it to the back. Using his teeth to open the snack bag one-handed, he popped a corn puff into his mouth and chewed, glad to see Octavia following suit.

Octavia cleaned off her fingers with a napkin before reaching for the car's touchscreen interface and clicking on CarPlay. The last song Leif had been listening to pulsed through the air around them, a happy, upbeat indie rock song.

"Why am I not surprised?" Octavia laughed.

"What do you mean?" Leif retorted as he cleaned the cheese dust off his own hand. He cocked an eyebrow at her mischievous grin.

"Bright, happy song for a bright, happy guy," Octavia said, her nose wrinkling playfully.

Of course she's being sarcastic. That couldn't be further from the truth.

"You still have a lot to learn about me. I might not be as bright and happy as I appear," Leif joked back, but his voice was too tight, too raw, as the words tumbled out.

Damn it. I didn't mean to say it like that. Why am I being so candid with her? *This isn't necessary to get the job done.*

She was eyeing him carefully again.

"I—" Leif shook his head, hoping his ears weren't turning the color of the stoplight he was braking for.

In Leif's peripheral vision, Octavia cocked her head. "You what?"

"Nothing, never mind."

"Do I have cheese dust on my face or something?" she asked as she wiped at her face with a fresh napkin.

"No, no—it's not that." Leif smiled. She was so easy to talk to, and he was getting far too comfortable. "It's just . . . I noticed those polaroid photos in your room, and I . . . I just wanted to say they were great."

Octavia let out a loose, wry chuckle. "Oh, those? Thanks, but they were just for fun. I'm not a real photographer or anything."

Leif's gaze flicked back to Octavia. "That's what photography's all about. That's the only thing that makes it 'real.'"

"What is?"

Leif grinned. "Fun."

Octavia chuckled. "I take it you're a photographer, then?"

Leif's hand flexed around the steering wheel. "Yeah. My dad is too. We love it."

"That's so cool." She paused. "Can I see your work sometime?"

Leif hesitated, but only for a moment. "Well, since I've seen yours, it's only fair, right?" Leif unlocked his phone and tossed it over to her. "The album labeled 'Photography' has my most recent stuff. You can pick the next song too."

The pair was silent for a minute, the sound of the music pumping through the speakers mixing with the steady hum of tires against asphalt.

Leif tensed when Octavia murmured a quiet, "Wow."

"That bad?" He cringed.

"No, you idiot. They're *amazing*. Especially this one of the coastal tree lines you inverted, where the reflection of the trees on the ocean is right-side up. It looks more like a painting than a photograph. I can't stop staring at it."

This time there was no question whether Leif's ears turned red. "I—uh, thanks."

"Now there's solid proof. You're the only photographer in this car. I have more fun looking at your photos than I do taking them."

The way she was looking at him, with that spirited expression on her face, Leif suddenly wished he hadn't left his Nikon at home. He suppressed a smile of his own. "Let's hear that song, DJ."

The song she played was a rough, angsty ballad. The melancholy melody made the hairs on the back of Leif's arms rise. Octavia's mood visibly shifted as she stared out the window again.

A realization dawned on Leif as he watched her mouth the lyrics silently out of the corner of his eye. Her hands were fisted in her lap, the skin on her knuckles white as bone. She wasn't frowning, but somehow, her bottom lip hung heavier than it did before. The skin between her eyebrows was permanently creased, like she'd spent too many years pinching them together. That's when it clicked. This hauntingly beautiful, mysterious woman was *sad*—almost incredibly so. Beneath the charm, wit, and humor, there was a lifetime's worth of sorrow. Another wave of goosebumps rose on his arms, but this time for an entirely different reason.

He recognized her suffering. It was the same as his. But instead of hiding behind a mask of evasion, false confidence, and anger, she embraced her pain and let herself truly feel it. Leif couldn't fathom the amount of strength that took. It'd always been so much easier for him to hide.

There was no denying it now. This woman wholly and utterly intimidated him.

Leif took Octavia's hand into his. Her head whipped in his

direction, eyes wide. The look of shock on her face as her red lips fell open echoed his own surprise. He hadn't made a conscious decision to hold her hand. It was as if his hand had acted of its own accord, drawn to her like the tides to the moon. Leif returned his gaze to the road, eyebrows furrowed.

After a few moments of pulse-quickening silence, her hand lightly squeezed his in response. Leif knew then that she understood. They were the same. The sadness that tormented her also tormented him.

And for the first time in what felt like an eternity, Leif felt seen.

CHAPTER 12
OCTAVIA

Watching the quaint streets of Salem slip by the window, Octavia expected to feel . . . well, after her grandmother's warning, she wasn't quite sure what she'd feel, but she'd expected to feel something. However, driving through her birthplace, she felt nothing. Just numb.

She navigated Michael to the Archives Library, a nondescript brick building near the center of town. They parked in a metered spot and disembarked. Octavia grabbed her tote bag from the floor mat, and Michael tossed a backpack he retrieved from the back seat over his shoulder.

They walked together, shoulder to shoulder, the backs of their hands occasionally brushing. His slightest touch sent her stomach into somersaults. Why was he so incredibly distracting? She was going to have to practice some serious self-control if she was going to get any work done.

They climbed the front steps of the building and entered through a pair of large wooden doors. A sprightly woman staffing the reception desk turned to them as they entered. "Good afternoon! How may I help you?"

"Hi, yes," Octavia replied, forcing as much sweetness into her voice as possible. "We have a meeting with Patricia Barlowe at noon."

"Oh, you mean Charlotte Harold?" she asked Octavia, her

heavily penciled eyebrows squeezing together in confusion. "If you're here to talk about special collections, that's probably with Charlotte, Patricia's supervisor."

The rhythm of Octavia's pulse ticked up, but just by a fraction. Definitely not enough to wipe the smile off her face. "Of course, her," she said, not wasting a moment.

"Just give me one moment. I'll call Patricia and see if Charlotte's ready for you." The woman picked up the telephone and dialed. She spoke softly to the person on the other end of the line, then hung up. "Right this way, please."

The receptionist stood and motioned for them to follow her down the hall to their left. Various artworks decorated the walls, all depicting local historical events. A shiver slithered down Octavia's spine as she passed a painting illustrating a courtroom full of angry Puritans, their fists and crosses raised accusingly toward a young woman.

The Salem witch trials.

Jaw clenched tight, Octavia scowled at the painting. That poor woman in the painting was an innocent scapegoat, wrongfully targeted due to the rampant fear and mass hysteria of the day. Whether she was a witch or not hadn't even mattered. Witchcraft had never been a gift from a deity or a force of evil, but rather a gift from nature—a magical testament to the connection humans have with all things.

Michael pressed his hand gently against the small of Octavia's back, urging her on, his face unreadable. They continued down the hall, toward a small office. A short woman with curly, graying hair waited for them just outside the doorframe. Octavia assumed she was her grandmother's friend, Patricia.

"Thank you, Sylvia. I'll take them from here," the woman exclaimed, nodding.

"Of course," said Sylvia as she waved goodbye.

"You must be Octavia, Jocasta's granddaughter. It's lovely to meet you. I'm Patricia." She reached out her hand.

"Hi," Octavia replied, shaking it. "Thank you so much for seeing us. My friend, Michael, and I are both getting our degrees in history, so we're grateful for the opportunity."

"Oh, honey, it's my pleasure. I owe Jocasta a favor or two anyway," Patricia said as she winked at them. "Charlotte is out at lunch, so we have time, but I want to make sure I get you both squared away in the library before she gets back."

Patricia turned to their right, and Octavia and Michael followed her down the next hallway and down a small set of stairs. They eventually came to two large black doors. A placard on the wall read SALEM ARCHIVES LIBRARY.

Patricia held her employee badge up to an electronic keypad, and an internal lock clicked. She pulled the doors open wide and shepherded them quickly inside.

The library was smaller than Octavia had anticipated, approximately the size of a university lecture hall. Rows of bookshelves reached from the hardwood floor to the crown-molded ceiling. Tables and chairs were scattered throughout the room, some cramped between bookcases, others arranged in a line down the center of the room. Dim gray light spilled in through tall tinted windows, and swirls of dust motes danced happily in the muted sunlight.

Michael let out a low whistle, seeming impressed.

"You should've seen this place before I got here. It was an absolute disaster. Historians and professors have been using this library for years, but could any of them be bothered to clean up after themselves? Of course not!" Patricia exclaimed. "I've done a fair amount of cleaning, but I'm sorry to say there's still plenty of dust. I hope you don't have allergies." Her nose wrinkled in disgust as she sniffed the stale air around them.

"We'll be fine. Thanks," Octavia replied, smiling politely at her concern. "My grandma told me you found some particularly interesting documents while you were doing inventory."

"Ah, yes, I did. Our inventory list hadn't been updated in years, so while I was cleaning and organizing, I updated it. I came across several items that have never been included in the inventory before. Very peculiar, if you ask me. No one is ever allowed in without authorized access. Well, except for you two, that is," she said with a small giggle, sounding very pleased with herself. Patricia obviously wasn't as straight and narrow as she appeared.

She gestured for them to follow her to the back of the library. A long row of wooden cabinets lined the wall, just tall enough to fit beneath the windows. Patricia bent down and took a small silver key from her pocket. She unlocked one cabinet's padlock, pulled out an armful of books and stray documents, then carried them over to the nearest table.

"This is it," Patricia said as she set them down with a soft *thump*. "This is everything previously left off the inventory. I haven't added them yet. I wanted you to get what you need from them first."

"Thank you, Patricia. This is extremely helpful," Octavia replied, fingertips brushing over the documents.

"Two of them are in Latin, and another is incredibly old and fragile, so take care."

"Yes ma'am." Octavia nodded. "And we'll make sure to clean up after ourselves."

"Do you mind if I ask what you two are studying?" Patricia asked, eyeing them curiously.

"Um, my personal area of interest is American folklore, and Michael's is . . ." Octavia paused, suddenly realizing she didn't know.

"Still under deliberation," Michael finished her sentence.

"Well, you've come to the right place. Hopefully, the information in this library will help both of you." Patricia smiled, and the crow's feet framing her eyes deepened. "Now, no one should bother you in here this afternoon, but if anyone does, just call me, and I'll come shoo them away. I'm here until five this evening, so you can stay until then."

"Thanks again, Patricia," Octavia reiterated.

"Yeah, we're grateful," Michael agreed, setting his backpack on a chair.

Patricia batted her hand at them as if she could knock their thanks out of the air. Walking back toward the doors, she called over her shoulder, "You two have fun!"

The doors closed behind her with a *thud*, and the stuffy air in the library grew suddenly dense with expectation. Octavia pivoted to the table, eyeing the small pile of old books and texts. *Please let one of these finally hold the answer.*

Michael was watching her intently, his blue eyes reading her expression. "These books are important to you," he guessed.

Octavia would have to work on her poker face.

"Yes. There's a very specific piece of information that I've been searching for, but it has, uh, evaded me. I hope I can finally find what I'm looking for here . . . today." Octavia swallowed hard, the gravity of her expectations suddenly weighing her down, threatening to crush her.

"Well then, I won't stand in your way." A timid smile brushed Michael's lips as he turned away and began browsing the shelves.

Octavia sat and watched him as he went, his hands clasped loosely behind his back as he studied the shelves. He seemed at ease here, surrounded by books and knowledge. An academic through and through.

A pang of guilt sliced through Octavia's chest. He deserved better than what she was doing to him now. Using him as a means to an end—an evasion tactic. He seemed like a genuine person. In fact, she knew he was. She'd sensed as much in the throes of their intimacy. He hadn't hidden anything from her then, like so many had. Instead, he'd chosen to expose himself to her. And deep down, she was able to recognize how much she liked what she had seen and what she continued to see.

If she was a different person—or, how had Michael put it? With a different life, on a different path—perhaps she could've sparked something real with him. Her heart clenched, a dull throbbing ache, because she knew she didn't have room for him in there. She was who she was, and her resentful, lonely path had been set in stone the night she lost her parents and her magic.

Michael pulled several volumes down from the shelves, then turned to walk back to the table. Octavia yanked open the nearest book, cheeks burning when she realized she'd been staring. She grabbed a notebook and pen from her tote bag.

Michael pulled the chair opposite her out from the table. She glanced at the titles of the volumes he'd retrieved; all appeared to be related to registries, censuses, and even genealogies of the people who'd originally colonized this area. Octavia smiled internally. He was at least getting *something* out of this—even if it wasn't her.

Her teeth ground painfully together as she returned her attention to the book in front of her and began flipping the pages. This one would likely be useless. It was old, its spine sewn together by hand, and it contained handwritten minutes from previous coven meetings. The dates ranged from 1752 to 1812. While the book might've been historically interesting, all coven spells and counter spells were kept in grimoires, not jotted down in meeting notes for just anyone to read.

A few family names caught her eye as she flipped through the remaining pages: several Wardwells, a Foster, a Faulkner, and a Bishop—all ancestors of her coven. Some family lines had been lost several generations ago, and others much more recently. She skimmed an index finger over the name Gregory Martin.

He was one of her ancestors.

Suddenly, tears swam in her eyes, blurring the page and startling her.

"Find something worthwhile?" Michael asked with his pen poised over a notebook.

Quickly wiping away the tears, Octavia laughed it off. "No, not at all. Must be the dust getting to me. This volume is filthy," she said as she gently pushed the book away.

Michael's brow was wrinkled with worry, but he remained silent, inclining his head before returning to his own work.

Octavia pulled a pile of documents toward her; they were held together by a thin, measly strip of aged leather. She untied the sheaf and sifted through the pages. Most were old maps of neighborhoods in the area. Again, the maps were interesting but not at all helpful for her purposes.

Octavia tossed one map in Michael's direction, which landed lightly on the open book at his side. "Check this out." She smirked. "As I promised, you'll learn a bit about the Salem witch trials today."

"Great!" A bright smile broke across his face as he inspected the map. "Now, what exactly am I looking at here?"

Octavia rose from her seat and circled the table to stand next to him, the scent of pine filling her nose. "This is a map of Salem back in the early seventeen hundreds. For centuries, it was widely believed that the nineteen innocent people who were executed during the 1692 Salem witch trials were hanged at the summit of Gallows Hill. Right here." Octavia pointed at a spot on the western side of the map. "However, the exact site of the executions was not memorialized . . . understandably so."

Michael tensed next to her. She couldn't blame him. The unlawful death of nineteen innocent people was truly horrific.

Octavia continued, "But then, in 1921, a local historian named Sidney Perley claimed he'd pinpointed the real location of the executions at the base of a hill on land called Proctor's Ledge. The City of Salem purchased part of that land in 1936. The townsfolk deemed it 'Witch Memorial Land.'" Octavia paused to point at a second location on the map, though it was unmarked due to the year this map had been drawn. "They still didn't build a memorial—not until later. In 2010, a team of researchers came together and reconsidered all the historical evidence. Eventually, they concluded that Sidney Perley had been right. So, in January of 2016, the real location of the executions was formally confirmed to be Proctor's Ledge—and *then* they memorialized it. Some of the evidence he used to confirm this location were handwritten accounts from the neighbors, who witnessed the hangings through the windows of their very own homes!"

Heat flushed through Octavia's body as her finger circled Proctor's Ledge once more. Her hand clenched into a fist.

"You're angry," Michael noted, his face once again unreadable.

"Well, yeah. Of course," she scoffed. "It's a shameful part of Salem's history."

"Did you grow up here?" Michael asked, rotating in his chair to face her.

"No, I didn't. I grew up in Vermont, but I was born here, and my ancestors lived here for generations before me. Salem is a part of me."

Michael nodded, considering her response. A strange, confused look flashed across his face, so quick she almost wondered if she'd imagined it.

"Do you believe in them?" he asked after a moment.

"Believe in what?" she asked as she circled back to her chair.

"Witches, magic, fairytales, and folklore?" His azure gaze met her own.

"Of course I do," Octavia confided. "The world would be extremely boring if I didn't."

"Do you know any witches? You know, personally?" Michael's gaze was so piercing a suspicious chill ran down her spine. Suddenly, she felt too exposed, too *seen*.

"I'm sure we could go to any restaurant or store in the area and meet modern-day witches," Octavia replied, evading the question. Determined, she held her own under his scrutinizing gaze, refusing to break eye contact. The tension in the air became almost palpable.

Just what is he playing at?

"Of course." His responding smile was dazzling, and, she now guessed, also deceiving.

Octavia swallowed against a bitter, metallic taste at the back of her throat as disappointment churned into nausea. *This man I'm staring at now isn't the same Michael from the other night, or the car ride here, or even from a few minutes ago. What changed? Was that all an act, or is this the act? He seemed so genuine, I—*

It didn't matter anymore. Her guard was up now.

Her gaze cut from Michael's; her resolve solidified. She reached across the table and returned the map to its rightful place in the stack. As she twisted the buttery strip of leather between her fingers, securing the stack once more, a warm hand covered her own.

Michael gently grabbed her chin and guided her face upward, so that her brown eyes stared into his blue. His head cocked to the side, asking for her permission before he continued on. For a moment, her brain stuttered, unable to comprehend how they'd gotten here, how they'd transitioned from narrowed, wary gazes to eager, parted lips in mere seconds. She couldn't conjure up an explanation. But in spite of her sudden suspicion, she wanted his lips on hers. Plain and simple. She'd been daydreaming about it since he last kissed her on the stairs of her apartment building. He had a magnetism she just couldn't resist, so she tilted her head in return, freely giving the permission he sought so earnestly.

The kiss was reminiscent of the sweet, fleeting moments before dawn, when cool nighttime air warmed under the first rays of sunlight. She thawed under his touch and couldn't help but wonder if she'd misread the situation.

Did I mistake his harsh gaze as calculating instead of simply assessing? Or am I kidding myself—searching for excuses to explain away my idiocy?

Shocked and flustered, she pulled back from his tender grasp, cutting the kiss off early.

"I'm sorry the history of the trials causes you so much pain, Tavi," Michael murmured softly.

"I—uh, thank you," Octavia stammered. Half-formed thoughts buzzed around her mind like nervous bees, making her dizzy.

Michael returned to his side of the table, grabbed a book, and returned it to its spot on a shelf. Continuing his search, he disappeared between the rows of bookshelves.

Flabbergasted, Octavia stared, open-mouthed, after him. Perhaps she *had* read him incorrectly. Perhaps his tension and confusion had just been him trying to figure her out—a tall order, since she could barely figure herself out. But something tugged at the edges of her mind; something felt off.

Michael wasn't her priority, she forcibly reminded herself.

While her lips still tingled from the kiss, she reluctantly pinned a bright yellow sticky note to the forefront of her mind that read: *Reminder! Have at least some semblance of skepticism. Don't be an idiot, no matter how blue his eyes are.*

CHAPTER 13
OCTAVIA

The next couple of hours passed in comfortable silence. Octavia finished skimming through the remainder of the books Patricia had pulled for her. The two remaining books, the ones in Latin, were the most promising of the lot. They resembled grimoires the most. But while Octavia had come to learn some elementary Latin through her witchcraft education, she was by no means fluent. Jocasta, however, could easily translate the entirety of the texts with a flick of her wrist during a full moon. Octavia hoped Patricia would agree to let her sneak them out of the library for a little while.

So, disappointingly, Octavia hadn't been able to find a way to fix her little hex problem right then and there. But she'd waited so long, what was another couple of days?

Since Jocasta had scoured the rest of the library decades prior, Octavia didn't feel compelled to search much further than the books and documents in front of her. Instead, she helped Michael with his research. He ended up having no real goal in mind, which made it much easier for Octavia to be of assistance.

In the early afternoon, Patricia popped in to see if they were hungry, then returned twenty minutes later with a couple of chicken salad sandwiches from a deli down the street. Michael and Octavia abandoned their work as they ate, making small talk and sharing stories. Octavia was extremely careful to keep all talk of magic and witches out of the conversation.

Michael's demeanor had gone back to normal, and Octavia was surprisingly delighted to see how talkative he'd become. She learned that he had several adopted siblings, and while he claimed that each was annoying in their own unique way, it was clear how much he cherished them.

One of his brothers was apparently extremely athletic and could've gone to the Olympics for gymnastics if he'd wanted to. Another was quite techy, and he'd proved as much by hacking into their high school's computer system and successfully stealing the answers to their AP calculus final.

But Michael described his sister as being very moody and controlling, which Octavia felt was understandable, given the fact that this woman had grown up with three brothers. Octavia figured Quintin must feel similarly sometimes, having grown up around so much feminine energy.

Some of the stories Michael recounted were so delightfully embarrassing, she actually belly-laughed listening to them. Even though she knew his family was far from a "normal" nuclear family, it sounded whole and happy.

They didn't realize time was passing until two hours had gone by, and the remnants of their sandwiches had grown stale on the table. The sky outside the windows was growing dark; dusk was well on its way. Michael threw away the uneaten food, and Octavia returned the unlisted documents to the cabinet beneath the windows. She retrieved her phone from her back pocket, checking the time while she rose to stand.

"We only have one more hour until we have to get out of here. Want to see what else we can find?" she asked.

"Sure," Michael responded, flipping through the notes he'd made in his notebook. "Try focusing on records, pedigrees, or registries from more recent years. I want to see if I can connect some of these older family names with families that may still live here."

"Right." Octavia set to exploring the rows of shelves. She stared in wonder at the books. Over two hundred years of local history were housed between these four walls. Magic was deeply ingrained in the very fabric of this land and its people, and her chest swelled with pride seeing how clearly that was represented with these books.

Out of the corner of her eye, a gold foil title caught her attention on one of the top shelves. The title on the seam matched that of the first book she'd skimmed through earlier today, only the dates ranged from 1990 to 2003. She rolled onto the balls of her feet and pushed against one of the lower shelves as she stretched toward the book. Grunting, she jumped, trying to get a grip on the tome.

A chuckle came from behind her as Michael's hand pressed against her hip. He reached over her head, retrieving the book with ease, and handed it to her.

"Thanks," Octavia murmured, slightly out of breath.

"Of course," Michael replied, his voice a purr in her ear. She could feel the warmth of his breath against the side of her cheek, causing her skin to catch fire.

She opened the book, noticing that Michael's hand hadn't left her hip. She felt his other arm wrap around her abdomen, pulling her in close. His sweater was plushy against her back. She glanced sidelong at him, finding him reading over her shoulder.

Smiling to herself, she returned her eyes to the book, which was quite the accomplishment considering the demanding ache that was unfurling several inches south of the arm he had wrapped around her waist. He rested his chin on her shoulder, and she felt his head move rhythmically as his eyes traced the words along the page.

Several pages in, it became apparent that this was another book full of coven meeting minutes, except the meeting location had changed in this volume. Instead of Salem, they'd moved to a small town in Vermont. The notes were also written in secretarial shorthand and thus very difficult to understand. Octavia could only clearly make out the names of the attendants. Quickly she saw names she recognized, the first of which was Thaddeus Green, Quintin's grandfather. He must've been the coven registrar for several years, because his signature was at the bottom of each of the minutes from 1990 to 1998. Then the signatures changed to that of a woman named Gwyn Hutchins. The name rang a bell, but Octavia couldn't recall why. She'd been so young when the coven was still intact, it was unrealistic for her to expect to remember each of their names.

They were nearing the end of the text when Michael's fingers swept the long strands of Octavia's hair away from her neck, exposing the sensitive patch of skin behind her ear. Her heart galloped in anticipation before she felt the brush of his lips there, and her breath hitched in her chest.

Lost in the sensation, Octavia let go of the remaining pages, letting them fall against the front cover. Briefly, she noticed the backside of the last page had only been half filled out with no signature from the registrar. Then her eyes rolled into the back of her head, reacting to the graze of Michael's teeth against her earlobe.

Michael's quick intake of breath made her open her eyes.

Every muscle in his body had gone tense, and a slight tremor now coursed through his body. Looking at him once more over her shoulder, she saw him staring—no, glaring—down at the page Octavia held out in front of them. His face was usually pale, but now it was completely drained of color, a sickly pallor remaining.

She saw it then. The deadly intensity that danced in his eyes.

Following his gaze, she studied the final page.

Realization dawned on her, dropping like an iron anvil in her stomach. The date. The date on the page was December 30, 2003.

The night of the attack. Her eyes, quickly darting across the rest of the page, found her own name, written clear as day within the list of meeting attendees.

Seeing her name there might be a reason for him to question her, but it didn't explain Michael's tense reaction. A lame explanation formed on her lips as Octavia turned toward the statue behind her.

Faster than she would've thought possible, he untangled himself from her and ripped the book from her grasp. He flipped back through the pages, tearing them in his fervor. The look on his face was terrifying, almost deranged.

Octavia took several steps back from him as fear froze her throat, its icy hand gripping at her windpipe, effectively cutting off airflow. "Michael, what is it? What's happening?" she asked in a shaky, choked voice. She still couldn't breathe.

"Leif. Jiro. Tripp. Delta. They're all here," Michael whispered, more to himself than to her. "Gwyn. Fitzgerald. Why are their names in here? I don't remember. Why can't I remember?"

His whole body was visibly shaking now as fitful tremors wracked his limbs, causing his teeth to chatter.

"Michael, what don't you remember?" Octavia asked, cautiously stepping toward him. His frightening behavior had her stomach dropping worse than any roller coaster, but she couldn't walk away without figuring out what was wrong.

Emotions warred on Michael's face—confusion, sorrow, loss, helplessness—until finally, one won out over the others: fear. The wild look on his face set all the fine hairs on Octavia's body on edge. The large blue eyes that just moments ago had been so warm and loving were now grim and wounded.

"Was none of it true?" he whispered, the erratic, broken pitch of his voice freezing the blood in Octavia's veins. "Is it all a lie?"

CHAPTER 14
LEIF

The air in the library was suddenly too thin. Leif couldn't catch his breath. Stars danced in his peripheral vision, threatening to drag him into unconsciousness. Legs numb, he stumbled, catching himself against the bookcase.

Within the blink of an eye, Octavia was next to him, helping steady him on his feet. She was speaking to him, but the roar of the blood pulsing through his ears was deafening. She was asking him a question, perhaps. He didn't care. He also didn't care about the fear etched in her face.

She should be afraid of me right now. I'm afraid.

Leif forced his lungs to take in air. Forced his mind to work. The book he and Octavia had been looking at was a compilation of notes from years of coven meetings. That much was obvious. The last page, and all the pages through early 1997, had his name included in the list of attendees. His birth name—the name he was given before he was adopted.

Covens never let outsiders in, especially not during sacred events. There was no other explanation for why his name would be on those pages. Or Jiro's name, or Tripp's, or Delta's.

But not Garren's. Leif's father's name was conspicuously absent.

Had Garren *lied*? To all of them? For their entire lives? They'd been taught to hate witchcraft since they were young children. So then why—

Had Leif just discovered he was the very thing he'd been told to despise?

No. No fucking way.

Heart hammering, Leif ripped his arm from Octavia's grasp. He bent down to retrieve the book from where it'd fallen, his sweaty palm slick against the dark green cover. He stormed out of the aisle and threw the book into his backpack before a strong tug on his arm wheeled him around on the spot.

"Tell me what's going on. Right now," Octavia demanded. The fear in her face had been replaced with steely determination. He couldn't respond. The words caught in his throat. "Why do you think you've been lied to?" she huffed, her impatience growing by the second.

"Don't worry about it. I gotta go," Leif bit out through clenched teeth, wrenching himself from her grasp once more. He threw on his jacket, picked up his pack, and fled.

As he jogged down the darkening hallways, his heart continued to gallop furiously. With every step, surmounting rage poisoned his blood. The tenuous hold he had over his emotions threatened to shatter. He couldn't be here when he lost control. His pace quickened as he willed his legs faster.

Leif threw himself through the heavy main doors and out into the cold as the final strand of his control frayed and broke. He cursed into the night as a harrowed sense of loss consumed him—loss of his identity, loss of his purpose. Hot tears scalded his cheeks and red flooded his vision as his shaking hands clamped into fists. He couldn't see, couldn't breathe. There was only anguish.

Leif's muscles twitched under his skin, desperate for an outlet. He had to get out of here. He had to leave. Storming toward the car, his strength faded quickly as he fought against the treacherous current of his emotions. By the time Octavia's insistent hand landed on his shoulder, the current had won, and he was numb. He barely registered her presence.

"Michael!" Her voice was distant, barely audible beneath the red waves. Time moved too slowly. Leif's mind couldn't make sense of the scene around him.

He whirled when she yanked his arm. The slant of Octavia's inner eyebrows rose in disbelief. "What the hell is going on? Talk to me!"

Leif could hardly process her words. At his silence, the corners of her lips—red faded to pink—turned down, mimicking the outer slopes of her brows. He couldn't deal with her. He couldn't do anything but float, benumbed.

Leif tried to pull away, but Octavia was done playing nice—her sudden grimace told him as much. Her booted foot wrapped around the back of his ankle, and she jerked his leg out from under him.

As he fell, time leapt forward. Leif blinked and his back was on the asphalt. She had tossed his bag and guided his fall with the arm she still gripped, so the impact hadn't hurt, just startled him—enough to banish the paralyzing tide. Like rapidly assembling puzzle pieces, the scene clicked together before him, and Leif could breathe again ... if just for a moment.

Octavia crouched over him, her forearm crushing his windpipe and a knee digging into his thigh. Her dark eyes were livid, and judgment ebbed off her in tangible waves, scraping against his skin. Leif squirmed beneath her, attempting to toss her off, but his struggle only crushed his windpipe further.

How in the hell is she this strong? For the second time in minutes, stars spotted his vision.

When he was on the precipice of losing consciousness, Octavia lessened the pressure on his throat. Reflexively, he gulped down the brisk air as the world slowly came back into focus around him.

"I'm not letting you go until you tell me what the fuck is going on," Octavia barked.

Leif only spent a moment weighing his options before he went slack beneath her in defeat. His simmering blood chilled instantly, turning to ice. He was exhausted.

"Okay then," Octavia murmured, lifting herself. She extended a hand out to him. Reluctantly, he took it.

She guided him to a brick wall behind them, leaning him against it for support. She backed up and positioned herself in front of him, blocking his escape. She had good instincts, he had to give her that.

Octavia grabbed Leif's backpack off the ground next to her and pulled out the book that had ignited all of this. "Now, tell me. Who do you think lied to you, and why does this book have anything to do with it?"

Fresh tears welled in his eyes as the reminder of his nightmarish discovery scathed his heart. He turned his head, refusing to look in her direction as the tears fell. Taking in his surroundings, Leif realized she'd dragged him into a small alley. Dusk was giving way to night, and as if on cue, a streetlamp at the end of the alley flickered on.

"My father, Garren," Leif grunted, throat choked with emotion.

"What did he lie to you about?" Octavia asked, eyeing him cautiously.

"I don't know. Maybe everything," Leif huffed quietly, his gaze falling to the dirty ground. "He might've lied about *everything*."

"Right, 'cause that's not vague at all," Octavia murmured. "So, how did this book help you figure that out? This is obviously what triggered you." Octavia gestured to the book between them with her free hand.

Leif's teeth ground together. "My name. I saw my name."

Octavia whipped the book open, carefully scanning the back pages, but Leif knew she wasn't going to find what she was looking for.

"I don't see anyone named Michael listed in here," Octavia said, raising her gaze to meet his. Whatever she saw in his face helped her solve it. Her wide, bewildered eyes narrowed with suspicion. "Your name isn't Michael, is it?"

"No," Leif replied simply, holding her scrutinizing gaze. Betrayal morphed her delicate face into something unfamiliar, cold, and hard as stone.

"What. Is. Your. Name?" she demanded, biting out each word.

"I go by Leif Jones now, but I was born Leif . . . Hutchins." More traitorous tears blurred the alley.

"Hutchins?" Octavia echoed, assessing the book again. Leif noted the recognition in her face each time she saw his name, along with the other Hutchins listed in that book. "Were Gwyn and" — she consulted the page again— "Fitzgerald your birth parents?"

"Yeah. I mean, they must be. But how did their names even end up in that book? How did mine, or my siblings'? I just—my parents were small business owners. They owned a bookstore! They weren't—they couldn't've been . . . this is fucking crazy!" Leif angrily wiped the tears from his cheeks with the back of his hand. Air hitched in his chest as anxiety constricted his diaphragm, keeping him from drawing in a full breath. Returning his gaze to Octavia, he saw fresh tears staining her face as well, surprising him.

"I found you," she whispered hoarsely. "Finally."

The book fell to the ground as Octavia enveloped Leif in a tight embrace. The scent of honey and citrus threatened to soothe his frayed nerves. "We thought we lost you, that you were dead all this time. But you're here. You're alive!" She trembled against him.

Without a moment's hesitation, Leif broke the embrace, thrusting Octavia away from him. She stumbled over her own feet and fell to the ground. Confusion and disbelief twisted her damp face into a pained expression.

"Get away from me," Leif spat. "I am *not* one of them."

"One of them?" Octavia croaked.

"A witch," Leif snarled, the old hatred instantly flaring from somewhere deep in his heart.

Octavia stared at him; he could feel the irrepressible loathing in his expression. "I don't understand," she said at last.

"Of course, you wouldn't. I'm very good at my job, after all," he replied, a warped laugh passing his lips.

"Good at your job," she echoed quietly. "What is your job, Mich—Leif?"

"Do you really need me to say it? Or have you figured it out by now?" Her eyes darted across his face, her mind trying and failing to put the pieces together. "I'm a witch hunter, Octavia. I was raised to be a weapon against witchcraft. That's what I mean when I say I'm not one of *them*."

Octavia's face turned ashen as a fresh stream of tears spilled from her eyes. She was speechless. All she did was stare at him. The fear and hatred in her eyes grabbed at him like the hands of a reanimated corpse. He flinched.

"I know you live with them and grew up among them, but I still cannot fathom your loyalty to them. They are evil, vile, *unnatural* creatures." Leif shook his head, trying to make sense of it all.

"You mean 'we,'" Octavia whispered as she rose to stand in front of him, the book clenched in her hand.

"What?"

"You mean 'we' . . . me, and *you*. We are evil, vile, unnatural creatures. This book is proof of that. My name's in it too." Octavia held the book between them.

Leif scoffed, unwilling to acknowledge the truth. "You are *not* what they are. You're normal. There's not even an ounce of magic on you." His thoughts drifted to the dagger at his calf. It hadn't heated in her presence—but then again, it hadn't heated in reaction to him either. Perhaps the magic imbued in the dagger was faulty, if this book was to be believed.

Despite the mascara-stained tears streaming down her face, Octavia laughed, the melody eerie and disturbing. "Looks like you're not *that* good at your job. I'm one of the last living members of my coven, the only remaining descendants of the original Salem witches." Her chin rose pridefully. "But despite the fact that the witch trials were ruled unlawful long ago, our coven has remained the target of creatures far more evil and vile than ourselves—the witch hunters you so readily associate yourself with." White teeth flashed behind her grimace. "Slowly, over the course of two hundred years, we were picked off, one by one, until our coven was *mass murdered* by a cult of witch hunters eighteen years ago. I was hexed that night, and I haven't been able to access my magic since. That's what I've been researching: how to break the hex and get my magic back. So, you see, Leif, I am still *very much* a witch," Octavia explained, a lethal gleam in her eyes. "And what I lack in magic power at the moment, I more than make up for in strength and speed."

Octavia assumed a fighting stance in front of him, her feet wide and fists raised to the level of her eyes—transforming into a goddamn warrior.

Leif gawked at her, disbelief exploding through his mind. She *was* one of them.

His godforsaken dagger had been hoodwinked by a magical loophole. Which meant there could've been another loophole, one that concealed him and his siblings from the dagger's magic as well.

His right hand twitched, itching to reach for the useless slab of metal secured to his calf, but he restrained himself. Was he really going to fight a magicless witch in an alley in the middle of witch country? For all he knew, she could signal others for help and overpower him in a heartbeat. No, that wasn't the smart move.

"What happened to the other three?" Octavia asked, all pretense tossed out the window. "Jiro, Tripp, and Delta. What happened to them?"

Oh shit. They're about to go on a fucking killing spree.

Leif grabbed his phone from his back pocket, causing Octavia to flinch, and checked the time. 4:50 p.m. They were already clearing the apartment building, but at least they wouldn't be entering the loft anytime soon. There was still time.

But time to do what? *Should I call them off? Let them continue? What's the right thing to do here?*

Logic and reason warred against emotion and instinct in his mind. He could deny it to Octavia all he wanted, but the evidence was overwhelming. If this book was accurate—if it wasn't fabricated like he desperately wanted to believe—it was proof Leif had been born into a coven of witches, which meant his parents must've been witches as well. Regardless of the fact that he didn't have any memories of magic from his early youth, he could've still had magic and not known it, especially if he'd never been taught how to wield it. Or perhaps he'd been hexed too, just like Octavia.

If Leif was a witch, that meant that Jiro, Tripp, and Delta were as well. Their names, and what he assumed were their birth parents' names, were in that book too. How would they take the news? Would they even believe it? If they did, how would they feel? Would they be as conflicted as him, or would they feel differently? More importantly, how would they feel if Leif didn't tell them until after they killed their alleged covenmates?

No, he couldn't break the news that way. Not after the fact. He had to call off the strike. It was the only way.

A pounding headache bloomed under his left temple, distracting him from his conflicting thoughts. Squinting his eyes at his phone screen, he found his message chain with Jiro and sent him a text.

SOS, abort the mission. New intel and our cover's been blown. Return to headquarters and STAY THERE until I get back.

The moment after he pressed "send," his hand exploded in pain, and his phone went flying down the alley, landing hard on the pavement. Octavia ran after it.

Leif held his throbbing hand to his chest. "What the fuck?" he yelled before jogging to catch up with her.

Octavia was already reading the text through the newly cracked screen when he caught up to her. Once she was finished, she let the phone drop heavily to the ground, still facing away from him. Leif watched as her breathing quickened, her chest heaving. Her fists clenched at her sides, and he could've sworn he heard her teeth grind together. Silently, she raised a booted foot and stomped on his phone, destroying it with a resounding *crunch*.

"Are you serious?" Leif yelled at her back. "I was doing you a favor calling the rest of them off!"

"You were planning to attack my coven tonight," she said in a hauntingly calm voice. "But not me, because you thought I wasn't a witch." She released a steady breath. "You were going to keep me from going home tonight, before all of this."

"Yes," Leif breathed, tensing at her ominous calm.

"Were you planning on seducing me?" As she shifted her gaze, her profile was tossed into shadow.

Nausea washed over him at the subtext of her question. They were mortal enemies, born to war until the end of time, and they'd slept together. They'd each successfully betrayed their people, their way of life, and their own hearts.

His silence must've been answer enough. Without warning, Octavia dipped low, throwing her leg out wide and kicking Leif's legs out from under him. Caught off guard, he fell hard. His head cracked against the ground, then bounced once. Pain seared at the point of impact, compounding upon his preexisting headache. His eyes watered profusely.

Octavia circled him, watching as he lay there writhing in pain. Leif couldn't stand the smug look on her face, so he reached for his dagger, the only weapon he needed.

But she caught on quickly—too quickly. Pain flared anew as she stepped on his already injured right hand. Leif howled as the bones in his hand threatened to snap beneath her weight. She followed the path his hand would've taken, wrenched up his pant leg, and unsheathed the hidden dagger from its holster. She studied the dagger, taking note of the engravings on the handle. A sour taste flooded Leif's mouth. He could do nothing as he watched her scrutinize one of his most prized possessions.

"'*Damnatio ad bestias,*'" she read, twirling the dagger in her hand. "'Condemnation to the beasts,' I believe. I'm assuming witches are the beasts in question." She sneered at him. It wasn't a question.

Leif bared his teeth in response, wincing as the throbbing in his head beat a steady, disorienting rhythm.

"I thought you said you weren't religious," she said, rubbing a thumb over the cross etched in the metal at the tip of the hilt.

"I'm not," Leif bit out through his teeth. "I don't hunt witches because of blind religious beliefs; I hunt witches for . . . revenge."

"Revenge?"

His voice was tight, strained. "All my life, I was told that my parents were murdered by witches." Octavia tensed above him. "Offered up as sacrifices for a ritual. Something involving dark magic. That's what we were told."

"That's a lie," Octavia snarled.

"Yeah, I'm beginning to suspect that," Leif relented, rubbing his throbbing temple with his free hand.

Octavia's boot rose, releasing Leif's injured hand. Backing a few paces away, she kept his dagger in her grasp. Leif sat up slowly and assessed his hand, grimacing from the pain. At least he could still move it. Thankfully, nothing seemed broken, just severely bruised.

"Your parents died that night, just like mine did," Octavia murmured. Again, not a question. It took Leif a moment to register her words. "I remember now," she went on softly. "Your mother, I mean. I remember her."

Leif's gaze snapped to Octavia's. Her dark eyes were somber.

"She was beautiful," she told him. "Blond hair like yours. My grandma told me she was supposed to be the next matriarch of the coven, so she must've been extremely powerful."

Images of Leif's mother invaded his thoughts. Her hair glowing in the moonlight; her hand caressing his cheek; his necklace in her cold, dead hand.

Are my dreams about her . . . real?

"I remember her the night of the attack," Octavia shared. "Your mother was brave, fearless. She stood up to the leader of the witch hunters and refused to give in. She was willing to sacrifice everything, including herself, to keep us safe."

Leif rubbed the heel of his good palm against his breastbone, a new ache blossoming there as her words painted an illustration of a night he couldn't remember. A knot formed in his throat, accompanied by a sob that threatened to break loose. Leif swallowed hard, willing the emotions into a box he could shove away. But they were too big, too demanding. There was nothing to do but feel them.

Octavia continued, "I don't know how you disappeared that night, but we never stopped looking for the four of you. Especially the moms—Jiro's and Delta's. Since they're normans and not a part of the coven, they weren't there during the attack. They survived . . . if you can even call living with that kind of heartbreak surviving."

Leif gaped at her, the aching muscles in his jaw falling slack as disbelief consumed him all at once. A torrential downpour. Dry one second and soaked the next.

There's no way. She's lying. If their mothers were alive, they would've . . . what? Found us? How? We were . . . kidnapped? Or were we saved? Stolen? Liberated? Who's even the enemy here? I just can't believe this. Any of it.

His eyelids blinked rapidly, like the rolling shutter of a camera, as his thoughts came and went faster than he could register them. "Wait," Leif managed, mind still reeling. "Did you call their moms Norman?"

"Oh, yeah," she answered with a dip of her chin. "It's short for 'normal humans.' Everyone in the coven happens to have a normal, non-magical parent except you and me. Lucky us." The last part was meant to be sarcasm, but there was no humor in that alley. She continued when she saw his expression grow grim. "Jiro's mother stayed for years, searching for him, but eventually she moved back to Japan to be with family. Too heartbroken to stay. Delta's mother still lives in Vermont, where all of you are listed as missing persons." Octavia leaned against the wall beside her and let out a deep sigh. "I guess the only reasonable explanation is a witch hunter survived that night and kidnapped you. You all were there before I passed out and gone when I came to."

Leif didn't know how to respond to that. He couldn't believe Garren was the villain in his story, nor any other witch hunter, for that matter. He just couldn't. But if witches weren't the villains he'd always assumed they were, then who was? Someone had to be. Right?

A moment of awkward silence passed between them.

"Your fa—" She stopped; apparently, she couldn't even say the word. "Garren, he manipulated you, Leif. He made you believe what he wanted you to believe." Octavia's eyes were fierce, but sincere. "He took our family from us," she finished through clenched teeth.

"I—" Leif couldn't say it yet, but he understood what he had to do next. He needed the truth. More than anything right now, he needed the goddamn truth. Whatever he discovered, good or bad, he wasn't going to let it break him. "I'll figure out what happened."

"Good. You should."

She pushed herself off the wall and sauntered over to where Leif sat. Exhausted and in a considerable amount of pain, Leif kept his head down, refusing to acknowledge any more of her judgment.

"Goodbye, Leif," Octavia whispered, gently dropping his dagger in his lap.

Still processing slowly from the pain, Leif didn't look up quickly enough. By the time he did, Octavia was gone, the book along with her.

He rose gingerly, the cold air a soothing balm against his injuries. He gathered his now filthy backpack from the front of the alley and slowly made his way back to the car. Looking up at the sky, he contemplated the complexity of this new reality. His whole life had changed tonight. A rug had been yanked out from under him without warning. And now he was falling.

With every passing moment, everything he'd been taught to believe felt more and more like a lie.

CHAPTER 15
OCTAVIA

Weighed down by several pounds of notebooks and two technically stolen Latin texts, Octavia ran through the streets of Salem. She passed cafes, restaurants, and gift shops—all perfectly suitable places to seek shelter from the cold—but instead, she ran. She ran away from the library, away from Michael—*Leif*—but most of all, she ran away from her mistakes and the overwhelming guilt that came with them. She felt she would have given anything now for just a sliver of the numbness she'd resented earlier.

Octavia couldn't believe she'd put what little remained of her family in mortal danger. Leif never would've known her roommates were witches if Octavia hadn't been so horny and self-destructive. But even deeper than that, she should've known the moment she'd met him something was off. In fact, she *had* known. She'd consciously registered the eerie familiarity she felt when she met him. In hindsight, the reason was crystal clear. That feeling hadn't been an ordinary sensation of déjà vu. It'd been different, the recognition of a bond—the ancient bond that flowed through both of their veins. They were witches. They were the same. And she should've known. Magic or no magic.

The freezing breeze breathed down the back of her neck and stung her damp cheeks as she neared the edge of town. Out this way, the streets grew dark, and the tourists were few and far between. She slowed as she came upon an old cemetery. Driven by something beyond her control, Octavia stopped at the threshold and threw open the old iron gate. As if on autopilot, she wove her way through rows upon rows of old headstones, their epitaphs illegible in the darkness.

Her right shoulder ached painfully beneath the weight of her bag. She desperately wanted to fall to the ground right where she stood and sulk in a well-earned pit of despair, but she couldn't force her muscles to cooperate. Something was pulling her—a force akin to gravity. It tugged at her, lazy and assured, almost as if it knew its will would be obeyed. Despite her misgivings, she was compelled beyond logic and reason, so she followed the feeling toward the dark center of the cemetery.

Behind a large, sweet-smelling evergreen, Octavia saw a woman standing alone before a headstone. With what little moonlight broke through the clouds, she could see the woman had a tall, lithe figure with long black braids that fell down her back in a textured waterfall. Smoke plumed from her mouth in torpid tendrils.

As the magnetic feeling continued to pull at her, Octavia considered approaching the woman, but quickly thought better of it, turning to leave before she disturbed her. Octavia winced when she realized how creepy it would've been to approach a random stranger in an old cemetery at night like this—and the mysterious pull only made it creepier.

"I can feel your distress from here," a strong, smooth voice echoed across the deserted graveyard. "I think you might need this more than I do." The woman hadn't moved except to smoke from a joint.

"I'm sorry, I didn't mean to disturb you," Octavia replied hesitantly from the shadows of the evergreen.

"Bad vibes seek company. I was already disturbed, as are you." The woman brought the joint back to her lips and pulled a drag.

Drawn forward by the numbing haze she knew the weed

would provide, Octavia left the shelter of darkness and approached the stranger. They stood in silence for a moment, gazing at the headstone. It was small, old, and cracked right down the middle. Darkened by shadows, it was impossible to read.

Octavia took the joint from the woman's extended hand and inhaled a long drag. The smoke that swirled in her lungs was fresh and flowery, good quality. "Are you here to mourn? Have you lost someone?" she asked. As she spoke, she exhaled ghostlike plumes of smoke.

"In a way, yes," the woman provided vaguely.

"Who did you lose?"

"Myself," she responded simply, taking the joint back.

Octavia could relate to that. But she'd stopped mourning the loss of herself a long time ago. Now she was angry, resentful, and jealous. She wished she could go back to simply being sad.

"Are you here for the same reason?" the woman asked on an exhale.

"No," Octavia replied, suppressing a shiver. "No, I guess I'm mourning a person I've found, in a sense."

"Ah, I see." The stranger chuckled, passing back the joint. "That might be worse."

Octavia inhaled deeply and said as she coughed, "You know, I think it might be." Her mind buzzed contentedly. "I thought finding him—or *them*, rather—would make my family stronger, but instead it put them in grave danger."

"The Fates have their twisted ways of surprising us," the woman murmured, shifting her face toward Octavia to get a better look at her. Octavia returned the woman's gaze, twin sets of brown eyes reading each other in the darkness.

"I'm fucking sick and tired of surprises," Octavia muttered, taking another drag before passing it back.

The woman made a gruff noise in agreement before taking a

final puff, finishing off the joint. "The world is a chaotic place filled with complex, messy creatures. We shouldn't let our mistakes and failures keep us from our destinies. Mother Nature knows who we are. We're her children, after all. She's already made adjustments for our shortcomings." A hint of a smile settled on the woman's lips. "The only barrier keeping you from your destiny is yourself. Your rage, resentment, and self-loathing will be your downfall. It'll feed on you until there's nothing left but a shell of a person." She released a clipped chuckle. "From what I can sense, you're already dangerously close to becoming that."

Octavia bristled, but before she could act, the woman continued, placing the joint's roach on top of the fractured headstone as if in offering. "Find a way to accept this and move forward. You need this newfound family, and they need you. You don't have the luxury of failure in what comes next."

The woman spun on her heel without another word, her long braids billowing behind her. Stunned, Octavia stared at the woman's back as she walked away, her hazy mind unable to fully comprehend what had just transpired.

Annoyed and completely exhausted, Octavia dropped her bag as she sat down in the damp grass. She leaned against the headstone and gazed up at the cloudy sky.

Who the hell even is that woman? How could she act like she knows my life after a ten-minute conversation? Seriously, can tonight get any worse?

Still spinning from the weed and the strange interaction, Octavia pulled out her phone and ordered an Uber. She needed to get to her grandmother's house and tell Jocasta everything that had happened with Leif. She didn't know how the rest of the coven would take it, but they needed to know. She couldn't keep this to herself.

After hesitating for a moment, Octavia read through the *many* responses she'd received to the vague text she'd sent to her roommates while fleeing from the alley, asking them to cast a protection enchantment on the loft tonight. They were definitely freaked out, wondering why she was asking them to do such a thing, but this wasn't the kind of news she could share over text. She'd wait to elaborate until she could tell them everything in person.

The app said her ride was fifteen minutes away, so she had plenty of time to sulk in that pit of despair she'd been daydreaming about earlier. She closed her eyes and immediately winced as several thoughts clamored for the spotlight. That woman might've been a total loon, but something in Octavia's gut knew she'd had a point. She'd been angry and selfish for so long. She was tired. But was she really ready to be done?

Was it even that easy? Could she simply choose to stop being the person the anger and resentment had molded her into after all these years? Maybe she could. If she stopped trying to fix what she so ardently thought was broken. Maybe if she let go of the Octavia she used to be, the happy little girl with parents and magic, and accepted the Octavia she was now, orphaned and magicless but also strong and resilient.

She'd found a way to cope, a way to get herself through the worst of it, but maybe that wasn't serving her anymore. Instead, perhaps it was draining her of everything she was, of everything she could be. Maybe the only way for her to move forward was for her to break her ties to the past.

Octavia dragged the tote bag toward her, pulling out the two large books she'd stolen from the library. Their leather covers shined dully in the moonlight. She flipped through them, her heart racing faster with the passing of each page. She could return them to the library, leave them unread, and walk away from this fear that had haunted her so viciously—the fear that, no matter how hard she worked or how far she searched, she'd never be able to break her hex.

And maybe now, it wouldn't matter as much if she never did. It wasn't likely; Octavia knew that, especially after witnessing Leif's reaction tonight, but a part of her still wondered . . . still hoped.

A coven as small as theirs was easy pickings for the witch hunters. The whole reason Octavia had been pushing her combat training so hard was to be able to, in her own small way, help protect the coven if the hunters ever came hunting again. But she knew those skills were next to nothing compared to having magic. If she really wanted to help protect her family, she needed her magic back, desperately.

But now, she'd found them. The missing members of their coven. If they still had access to their magic—if they'd been somehow repressing it this whole time—then they could do what she couldn't. *They* could help protect the coven. *They* could help put their family back together again.

But Octavia—*she* could do nothing of the sort. She was just a burden, a hinderance—for all intents and purposes, an ordinary woman with knowledge she shouldn't have, regardless of what she'd just spewed to Leif about being "still *very much* a witch." Even as she'd said it, she'd known it was a lie.

If the hunters do ever decide to rejoin the coven, maybe I should . . . walk away.

That would be best for everyone, wouldn't it? I wouldn't be dragging them down anymore. I wouldn't have to hate myself for something I don't have—something completely out of my control.

I could just . . . be.

Fresh tears pricked her eyes as she considered this hypothetical alternative. On the ground next to her, her phone buzzed, notifying her that her ride had arrived at the cemetery gates. She shoved the books back into her bag and made her way through the cemetery to the street, where a car was idling. She slid into the backseat and took a deep, grounding breath.

"To Brookline?" the driver asked, eyeing Octavia curiously in the rearview mirror. She supposed they weren't used to picking people up from cemeteries in the middle of the night.

"Yes, please."

A single tear fell down her raw cheek as she clutched her overflowing tote bag to her chest. She couldn't give up hope. Not yet.

The ride back to her grandmother's house was exhausting. In spite of the high, Octavia was standing at the precipice of a panic attack, and she felt like she was trying to hold back a tsunami. Every muscle in her body braced against the weight of it. But she had to hold it together, at least until she was back in her grandmother's arms—the only place she trusted herself to lose control.

By the time the car rolled up to the beautiful brick home, Octavia's head was pounding and her limbs were trembling. She dragged herself up the front steps, moving slowly and gingerly, as if she'd been physically injured. She unlocked the front door, stepped inside, and closed it silently behind her. When the lock slid safely back into place, the tsunami reached its apex.

She slid to the floor. Her body became instantly wracked with sobs, her chest heaving uncontrollably. The air she hauled into her lungs felt like it went nowhere. Her heart sprinted so fast she worried it might falter or stop altogether. Cold sweat dripped down the base of her spine as her eyes frantically searched the room for help, for safety, for redemption. Her vision blurred, and she saw nothing. The only thing she could see, hear, smell, and feel was fear.

She was drowning in it. Suffocating in a room full of air.

Octavia barely noticed the soft texture of fur brush against her cheek. She hardly registered the worried, far-off cries of her grandmother. The sensation of Thad's strong grip felt miles away.

And then she felt nothing, suspended in the peaceful tranquility of anonymity.

CHAPTER 16
LEIF

"**S**hit," Leif cursed loudly. He put the car in park behind their house, then slammed the palm of his uninjured hand against the steering wheel. "How the hell am I going to tell them?"

He looked over at his broken phone lying on the passenger seat. He guessed he wasn't going to be Googling "how to break very, very bad news to your family" anytime soon. Leif's fingers shook as he curled them around the steering wheel. He'd have to figure out how to do this on his own.

But he barely had a hold on his own emotions at the moment. How was he going to be able to keep them in check long enough to attend to his siblings? The numbness tried resurfacing during his drive back from Salem, but his exhaustion, combined with the pain of his wounds, had kept them at bay. Thankfully, that had given him the mental capacity to appreciate the gravity of what he had to do. He had to share what he'd discovered with his siblings . . . and potentially blow up their entire world view.

His throat constricted as he suppressed a gag. But he couldn't suppress the next one. With lightning speed, Leif flung himself out of the car and stumbled toward a small patch of grass next to the parking lot. He dry-heaved as he fell on his hands and knees, wincing at the shooting pain in his wrist. Gulping down air, he waited for the next wave of nausea, but it never came.

I probably have a concussion from when Octavia laid me out. Great.

Leif sat back on his heels, wiping at his sweaty brow with the back of his hand. After a few moments spent breathing in the cold night air, he felt steadier. He stood and returned to the car. Grabbing his phone and backpack, he dusted the pack off before swinging it over his shoulder. He tossed the destroyed phone in the trash bin next to the back door before entering.

His chest tightened as he closed the back door behind him. The first thing Leif noticed was the silence. No music. No television. No voices. Nothing.

This isn't good.

Leif took slow, measured steps as he walked down the main-floor hallway before bending over the stairwell banister to look toward the upper floors. He sighed as he dropped his backpack and began climbing. On the second-floor landing, Jiro's apartment door was thrown open wide. Even from this distance, Leif could see the monitors in his living room displaying the schematics for their plan. Leif's stomach flipped guiltily.

On the third floor, Delta's apartment door was closed, darkness seeping out through the cracks. Leif's pulse quickened as he continued up the staircase.

Tripp's door was left hanging ajar a few inches on the fourth floor, and the apartment lights shone brightly through the gaps. He rubbed his uninjured hand against the back of his pounding skull as he readied himself. One deep breath later, and he was pushing the door open.

Three pairs of eyes, each narrowed in unparalleled fury, swung to Leif. His gut turned to stone, anchoring him to the spot. His siblings had *never* looked at him like that before.

They'll understand. I just have to explain everything, and they'll understand . . . won't they?

Delta broke the silence first as she stood. "So, you get your kicks with some girl you slept with *once* during a drunken one-night stand, and what?" The volume of her voice rose with every word. "Fall to your knees and blow our fucking cover the second you get the opportunity? You ruined everything!" She was yelling now. Her chest heaved with barely suppressed rage.

Jiro sat on the leather couch, looking out Tripp's living room window. He wasn't even glancing Leif's way anymore. Tripp was leaning against the wall, his face tilted toward the floor as he side-eyed Leif. It took every ounce of resolve Leif had not to look away from them in shame. The tips of his ears burned regardless.

"You've got it all wrong, D," said Leif, in a voice far less convincing than he wanted it to sound. "I've got a good explanation for calling off the hit tonight."

Jiro's face finally turned to Leif. Delta opened her mouth again as if to keep yelling, but Leif raised a hand to silence her—his injured hand, which was quickly swelling and bruising.

Tripp was next to him in a second. "Leif, what the hell happened? This looks broken."

Leif flinched against a flash of pain as Tripp gently grabbed his hand, rotating it and turning it over to assess the damage. "It's nothing—well, I mean, it's not. Obviously, it hurts like a bitch, but I don't think it's broken. And it's not important right now. What I have to tell you is."

That got their attention.

"Talk," Delta demanded as she folded her arms over her chest.

As Tripp released his hand, Leif said, "Let's all sit."

Jiro rotated in his seat to face the group, and Tripp took the empty seat next to him on the couch. Delta—ever the stubborn one—remained standing. Leif took a seat on the love seat opposite them.

The anxious beat of his heart hitched up a notch as he cleared his throat. He still had no clue what to say. He gently rubbed his sweaty palms together as he weighed his options—trying to decide where to start.

"You look like you're about to puke. What is it?" Delta uncrossed her arms, eyebrows pinching in concern—a rare emotion to see from her.

"We learned something important at the Archives Library in Salem." He tried to keep his voice steady, but he couldn't. It cracked like fragile glass.

"Learned what?" Jiro asked, his hard gaze softening a fraction. "Something about the coven?" He lifted a leg onto the couch, wrapping an arm around his knee.

"Yes and no."

"Leif, just spit it out," Tripp urged, loose, shoulder-length curls falling into his face as he leaned forward to place his elbows on his knees. He clenched his hands tight together.

"Octavia and I learned something about *our* past." Leif gestured among the four of them with a swivel of his index finger.

In rapid succession, Jiro asked, "What do you mean? How could you possibly find information about us at a library in Salem? Do they keep a running catalog of active witch hunters or something?"

"There's no way," Delta cut in. "We're not even initiated into the organization. This was our first hunt."

Leif shook his head. "It has nothing to do with us being raised as witch hunters." He paused, dropping his gaze to the floor. "It has to do with what we were *born* as." His voice broke on the penultimate word.

Deafening silence pushed against Leif's eardrums. When he raised his face, his siblings' mouths hung slack.

Here it comes. The bomb. I can't delay it any longer.

For what felt like the hundredth time tonight, Leif swallowed hard as emotion knotted his throat. "I found convincing evidence that we were born witches, into the very coven we were going to eliminate tonight."

A choked, gargled sound came flying from Jiro's mouth.

"Excuse me?" Delta asked. She even had the gall to chuckle a little.

"That's impossible," Tripp whispered, his eyes wide in disbelief. But as Leif stared at Tripp, those wide eyes misted over. He could see the truth in Leif's hard expression. Leif wasn't lying. "Oh my—"

"Octavia seemed pretty convinced, but I—I'll find out the truth. I promise. I won't let this go unanswered." Leif had never been more determined about anything in his entire life. He knew what he wanted the truth to be. The book forged. Octavia mistaken. Garren as honest and true as he'd always been. But what if . . . what if he found the opposite? How could he accept that? How could any of them accept that?

Leif's chest ached as he watched a single tear fall from Tripp's eye. After a moment, Leif had to look away. Seeing his brother in pain hurt too much. Leif fought against tears of his own as his gaze swung to the others. Jiro had blanched, his entire body now trembling. Delta still stood, eyebrows raised so high they almost touched her hair line. He couldn't stand the silence. He had to fill it.

"Apparently, when we were young, a crew of witch hunters attacked the Salem coven. That's when they . . ." Leif swallowed hard, the motion as painful as the throbbing in his hand. "They took us. Then Garren adopted us and raised us as witch hunters—as weapons to be wielded—" He couldn't verbalize the end to that statement, was surprised he could even think it with all the doubt in his heart. *Against our own kind.* He wouldn't admit it was true, not until he got his hands on every scrap of evidence, the proof he desperately needed.

Delta took several determined steps toward him. "Tell us everything."

So he did. He told them about the library, about the grimoires and maps and registrar texts, about the book with all their names, about his confrontation with Octavia in the alley, about her hex, about what she'd shared of the attack on the coven all those years ago—about the potential lie they'd been living.

"Let's see this book, then," Delta said, throwing an expectant hand out toward him.

Leif sighed, shoulders dropping to lean against the back of the couch. "Octavia took it . . . after she kicked my ass."

She huffed a frustrated breath, tucking her short hair behind her ears. "Well, then, let's go get it back. I'm not believing any of this bullshit until I see the proof for myself."

"Do we really need it, D?" Tripp asked in a hoarse voice, the whites of his eyes bloodshot. "Leif wouldn't lie to us about something like this."

"And Garren would?" she asked incredulously, the volume of her voice so high it made Jiro flinch. His gaze hadn't moved from the floor in over twenty minutes. Tripp placed a comforting hand over Jiro's knee.

Leif stood. "I get it, D. I do. I don't want to believe it either. I'm still not even sure I do. I need more proof. But regardless, it makes me want to . . . break down, rage, barf—you take your pick." He took a deep breath. "I just couldn't let us go through with the hit if this is real. We need . . . time to—to figure this all out."

Tripp nodded as he wiped at his eye. Delta finally sat, dropping to the couch on Jiro's other side, the expression on her face cold and distant. Jiro looked toward the door. Without a word, Jiro rose off the couch and left, somewhat wobbly on his feet. Leif took a step, intending to follow him.

"Leave him," Tripp instructed. "He needs some space."

"But he hasn't said a word since I started explaining everything," Leif argued.

"You know Jiro. He'll talk when he's ready. He's just . . . processing, in his own way."

Leif rubbed a hand against his pounding head again as he looked toward the door. Silence enveloped the room. The only sound puncturing the stillness was the steady *tick, tick, tick* of the clock on the wall.

Until Delta laughed, deep and throaty. Leif and Tripp stared at her in disbelief. If ever there was a time to be laughing, this was *not* it. But she kept laughing. For a whole minute, and then two. Then she was crying, doubling over in pain from laughing so hard.

"D?" Tripp raised an uncertain hand toward her.

She batted it away. "Dad's a genius," Delta choked out between bouts of laughter. "Quite possibly the greatest con artist of our time, if this is true. I mean, the man hates witches more than anything, and yet, somehow, he was able to raise four of them as his own? You'd have to be crazy!"

Leif couldn't disagree with her logic, but her behavior made him question every word that tumbled out of her mouth.

"God, that's hilarious," she said as she finally calmed down, wiping her eyes with her sleeve. Suddenly, she stood. "We'll talk more about this tomorrow. I'm going to bed."

"What?" Leif asked as she walked to the door. "You're just going to bed?"

She turned back to face him. "What else am I supposed to do?"

"I don't know, but not this—not laugh, and sigh, and go to bed like it's any other day!" Something feverish and nauseating was brewing in Leif's core, the sensation quickly gaining momentum. Anger. Hot, blistering anger. He was angry. No—he was *enraged*. "Aren't you angry? Aren't you furious?" Leif looked to Tripp, his eyes cutting across the room. "Aren't you?"

"I don't know how I feel," Tripp admitted.

"And I still don't believe any of this," Delta said with an obnoxious flourish of her hand as she gestured toward Leif. "The wanna-be witch could've fabricated the evidence, for all you know."

Anger took control. The words gushed from his mouth before he could even register them. "She didn't," Leif said through clenched teeth. "She was over the moon when she first realized I was Leif and not Michael, before I told her we were witch hunters. She wasn't acting. That was real."

Why am I getting so mad? Why I am I defending her like this? She's not the same person she was earlier today, at least not to me. So I can't feel the same way now as I did then. I won't.

"Whatever. I'll believe it when I see it. Until then, I'm not going to waste my time worrying about it." Then she turned and left the apartment, leaving Leif and Tripp in stunned silence.

"This is insane," Leif whispered as he turned back to Tripp. "It doesn't feel real."

Tripp released a wet, broken laugh. "Maybe we'll wake up tomorrow and realize this has all been a sick dream."

Leif climbed into bed several minutes later, after crushing his brother in a hug and wishing him goodnight. He prayed Tripp was right. Maybe this *was* all a dream. Maybe they'd wake up in the morning and their family wouldn't be their enemy, and their enemy wouldn't be their family. All would be right with the world again, and they'd be able to continue as they always had—living in blissful ignorance.

But even as Leif failed to succumb to sleep, deep in his soul, he knew he'd wake up in a world turned upside down.

Chaos was his home now.

CHAPTER 17
OCTAVIA

Non est umbra sine lumine.

The all-too-familiar words echoed in Octavia's mind as the scent of burning sage filled her nostrils, stirring her senses and dragging her mind from its place of rest. Octavia's eyes flashed open, and she heaved forward, almost falling out of bed from the momentum.

Catching herself with her hands, she surveyed her surroundings. Weak morning sunlight illuminated the room. She was in her grandmother's house, she realized gratefully. Her room was the same as it'd always been: purple bedding, purple curtains, purple wallpaper. Octavia covered her eyes to shield herself from the oppressive color scheme. She'd grown to hate the color over the years, so much that she couldn't believe there'd been a time when she'd loved it.

Nevertheless, the room instilled a sense of comfort, and Octavia found she could breathe easier, perhaps more easily than she had breathed in months. She rose from the bed, painfully aware of how sore she was. On the bedside table sat a glass of water, which she took and drank greedily.

Sufficiently hydrated, Octavia wandered down the hall to the bathroom to relieve herself and shower. The warm water and steam brought the memories from the night before flooding back, but she felt far more in control—no doubt due to a little magical interference from her grandmother. Normally, that would've bothered Octavia, but today she was glad.

Once she'd gotten dressed and combed her hair, she hurried downstairs. Octavia expected her grandmother would be a nervous wreck. The buttery, sweet aroma of pancakes filled the foyer. Walking through the dining room, she heard Jocasta's and Thaddeus's soft, muffled voices coming from the kitchen. Octavia braced herself for the onslaught of questions she knew was only moments away.

She stood in the doorway to the kitchen. Jocasta was flipping pancakes, and Thaddeus was sitting at the table reading a newspaper. A bark came from the backyard, and Octavia looked out the window just in time to see Luna lunge for a bird sitting on a low tree branch. The scene before her was beautiful, peaceful even, and she was about to ruin it. Octavia bit her trembling lower lip as she second-guessed her next move, but she knew what she had to do, and it made her sick to her stomach.

"Good morning," Octavia said as she entered the kitchen, not bothering to hide the dismay in her tone.

Jocasta wheeled around at the sound of her voice, the deep worry lines around her eyes and mouth relaxing a fraction. "Darling! Are you all right? How'd you sleep?" Abandoning the pancakes on the griddle, she wrapped Octavia into a warm embrace.

"I'm fine, Grandma. Thanks to you, probably."

Jocasta chuckled softly in confirmation. "It was absolutely necessary. I've never seen you in such a state before. You had me worried half to death."

"I'm sorry. To both of you." Octavia pulled out of the embrace. "I didn't mean to worry you. It's just . . ." She didn't know where to begin. "A lot of stuff happened last night. Stuff you need to know about."

"Yes, of course," said Jocasta. "Well, sit down and make yourself comfortable. I'll make you a plate, and you can eat while you tell us everything."

Thaddeus moved his newspaper to make room for her at the table. Jocasta flitted around the kitchen like a hummingbird, making her a plate, pouring her tea, and calling Luna inside, before finally settling herself down at the table beside them.

Jocasta and Thaddeus waited patiently while Octavia took a few bites of her breakfast. The fluffy pancakes melted on her tongue. With some food in her stomach, Octavia finally felt steady enough to tell the story.

"I found him, Grandma," Octavia started, eyes remaining on her half-eaten breakfast.

Jocasta's head tilted to the side. "Found who, dear?"

"Leif. Leif Hutchins."

Octavia's shoulders slumped as Jocasta and Thaddeus tensed, both their postures going ramrod straight. The growing pressure in the room had Octavia wilting farther into her seat. It was too heavy—the weight of this knowledge. She released a shallow, anxious breath. Regardless, she had to carry it.

"How?" Thaddeus asked, his unblinking gaze flat.

"By accident," Octavia admitted. "I met him at a pub in Cambridge last week."

"Then why have you waited until now to tell us?" Jocasta asked, then pressed her lips into a thin, severe line.

"Because he told me his name was Michael," Octavia explained. "I didn't know who he really was until last night when we went to Salem."

Jocasta's eyes widened in alarm. "You took this man with you to the library?"

"Yes." Octavia winced. "The others were harping on me about never getting to know anyone new, and I wanted to get them off my back, so I decided to bring him with me. You know, kill two birds with one stone? Pretend to be dating and doing research, all in one fell swoop."

"I see," was all Jocasta provided in response.

"How'd you come to the conclusion that this boy was Leif?" Thaddeus asked.

"We were looking at old texts full of coven meeting minutes when he saw his own name, his birth name, listed as an attendee. Then he freaked out."

"Why would he freak out?" Jocasta took a tiny sip of tea. "Even if he didn't *know* he was a witch, he should've suspected as much by now given his magical manifestations."

"I don't think he's consciously registered any of his magical abilities yet."

"That would be extremely improbable, unless his magic is being suppressed somehow."

"I honestly have no idea. Our conversation didn't get that far." Octavia picked mindlessly at her split ends. "Do you think they were hexed too?"

"It's impossible to say without evaluating them in person," Thaddeus said.

"I still don't understand why he had such a negative reaction," Jocasta said as the corners of her mouth turned downward. "You'd think most people would be thrilled to discover they have magic."

Octavia's gaze reached Jocasta's, and she silently implored her grandmother to brace herself for the bomb she was about to drop next. "Because he was taught to hate witches."

Jocasta lifted her chin defensively. "Why would—"

Octavia cut her off. "He was raised by a witch hunter, Grandma."

Jocasta's face drained of color, but she didn't say anything.

"A witch hunter named Garren kidnapped him the night of the attack. He kidnapped all of them: Leif, Jiro, Tripp, and Delta.

They've probably been brainwashed, poisoned against witchcraft, against their family . . ." Octavia faltered for a moment, then went on. "Garren told them their parents were murdered by a coven of witches during some horrible, evil ritual. They were lied to and brutally manipulated."

Octavia felt hazy, the intangible wisps of pain those words caused floating at the edge of her consciousness. The emotions clawed desperately against her grandmother's charm, the only thing keeping them at bay, but they couldn't break it. Gratefully, as the wisps dissipated, Octavia felt nothing but the pleasant numbness of the charm.

"That's why he went by a different name when you first met him," muttered Thaddeus.

"Yes," Octavia said. "But he didn't know I was a witch until I told him last night. I don't know how he can sense magic, but he can. He thought I was a norman because he couldn't sense my magic."

"I see," Jocasta repeated, her forehead wrinkling.

Octavia couldn't bring herself to tell them about the attack the witch hunters had planned to take down the coven. The guilt was still too much for her to face.

"He lost it last night, Grandma," Octavia said softly, surprising herself with the pity lacing her voice. "Finding out he's the very thing he's been taught to hate, to despise with every fiber of his being, for all of these years. It almost broke him. I watched it happen."

Jocasta and Thaddeus met each other's gazes, and not for the first time, Octavia felt sure they were having a silent conversation with their eyes—the kind only the best of friends can make any sense of.

"There's only one thing left to do, then," Jocasta said aloud.

"Yes." Thaddeus nodded. "Let's go put our family back together."

Octavia glanced between them. "What?"

"It won't be easy, but it's necessary. They're a part of us. We won't abandon our family." Thaddeus stood and turned to Octavia.

"Will you help us, dear?" Jocasta asked gently, placing a warm hand over her granddaughter's.

Octavia had no doubt in her mind that Leif would refuse to hear them out. After what she'd seen last night, she wouldn't be surprised if he threw his dagger at her face the moment she stepped on his turf. But the epiphany she'd had last night in the cemetery stopped her from scoffing in her grandmother's face. If they could somehow convince the hunters to rejoin the coven, the coven would be safer, happier, more whole. And maybe then, she could finally move on from this crippling sense of . . . insufficiency. She could finally be guilt-free because her family would be adequately protected. Sure, it was a long shot, but it was worth an attempt.

"Yes. I'll try," Octavia replied.

Feeble hope bloomed behind her grandmother's fading charm.

CHAPTER 18
LEIF

L eif was so angry he almost couldn't breathe. Thoughts of betrayal seared his internal organs, threatening to set him ablaze from the inside out. His jaw ached from the constant tension, and a dull throbbing had taken up permanent residence behind his left eye. Sleep was impossible. Food tasted like ash in his mouth. The only solace from his misery were the fantasies he conjured up about all the brutal, creative ways he was going to exact his revenge—*if* all this was actually true, if he actually was a stolen witch, viciously raised as the archnemesis.

He'd given the others the night to themselves to process the news however they needed. But now it was time to start laying down a plan for Garren's return, a plan to extract the truth. They had a little less than a month before he was expected to return from the hunt, and Leif wasn't willing to waste a second of that time. Garren was strong enough that it would take nothing short of a small miracle to . . . to what, exactly? These were the gaps he needed to fill.

Leif rolled over in bed. His bare room was covered in the thick shadows of early morning, their long arms reaching for him, inviting him to join them in the dark.

I wish I could, Leif admitted, but he knew he had to get up and start moving.

He tossed the covers away and climbed to his feet. Venturing to the bathroom, he freshened up, all the while running through what he was going to say to the others in his head. After dressing in the receding dark, Leif walked to the kitchen. He got the coffee maker going and popped some toast in the toaster. While he waited, he walked out of his apartment into the hallway and called up the stairwell, "Hey! Breakfast and meeting in five!"

Several curses drifted down from the third floor—Delta. Leif rolled his eyes. The world could be ending, and she'd still be as predictable as ever. It was eerie how much control she had over herself.

Leif turned to re-enter his apartment when a knock sounded from the front door of the building. Every muscle in his body tensed, and a cold sweat broke out across his brow. Never in the fifteen years they'd lived in that house had there ever been a knock at the door.

Leif heard three doors slam open from the floors above him. Looking up, he saw his siblings staring back down at him. Each face was tense and cautious. Leif raised his uninjured index finger to his lips.

Several minutes passed before a second knock echoed from the door. He took a step backward toward his apartment, intending to grab his dagger, when a voice called from the other side of the door.

"Leif? Um, it's me," the voice said slowly, cautiously. "Octavia. Octavia Martin. I—I'm here to talk to you, and the others. Just talk. I promise."

Leif looked up, his eyebrows raised in question. The others swapped several uneasy looks among themselves before they seemed to reach a conclusion. Looking back down at Leif, Jiro nodded, mouth parted, Tripp bit his lower lip, and Delta scowled. Their collective decision was clear to Leif: *Let her in—at her own risk.*

The others scrambled back into their apartments. A minute later, fully dressed, they silently descended the stairs and convened with Leif at the bottom of the stairwell.

Octavia's muffled voice drifted through the door again. "Come on, Leif. Just give me a few minutes to explain why I'm here."

He motioned for them to wait in his apartment. Once they were in place, he walked to the front door, squaring his shoulders and wiping his face clean of emotion. His hand hovered above the handle. He hadn't expected to ever see her again. Scenes from their confrontation in the alley swam in his mind's eye: her make-up-stained tears, her bared teeth, her boot crushing his hand, which was terribly bruised and still ached. She was a force to be reckoned with, there was no doubt about that, but this time he had backup. Comforted, he took a deep breath and opened the door.

On the small, brick porch stood Octavia and two strangers, an older man and woman. The woman was likely Octavia's grand-mother, Leif realized quickly. The resemblance was uncanny. They had the same dark brown hair and piercing eyes. Octavia was taller than the woman, and yet despite her small size, her steely bravado intimidated him.

The man next to them, in stark contrast to the woman, was tall and appeared friendly—docile even—with his soft smile and kind eyes. However, if he was with these two, the man must also be a witch, so Leif maintained a healthy level of skepticism.

The woman spoke first. "Hello. My name is Jocasta Wildes, and I've come to welcome you back into our coven—your coven."

Leif's jaw dropped, despite his attempts to remain unfazed. "Pardon?" was all he could manage.

"Please, Leif," Octavia implored, her gaze as captivating as ever. "Let us in and listen to what we have to say. Give us a chance."

Delta, Tripp, and Jiro gave me the green light to let Octavia in— not three of them. But what will these witches do if I don't let them in? They caught us off guard in our own home . . . and they have magic at their disposal. We probably wouldn't stand a chance against them. So what's the best move here? Play nice or slam this door in their faces?

They waited in silence for his answer, seemingly unaware of the heated dispute taking place within his mind. Sighing, Leif pulled the door open farther and stepped aside, waving them in.

His siblings' razor-sharp glares and flaring nostrils told Leif they were not at all happy he'd invited two additional witches into their home. His decision to let them in was difficult to explain, even to himself, but strangely, despite all of the lies from both sides, Leif trusted Octavia enough to give her this one chance.

Leif offered the witches chairs at his dining room table, while he huddled with the others on his old, dingy couch. The arrangement provided just enough space between them to help make everyone slightly more comfortable, which was good because whatever conversation was about to transpire would likely be a difficult one.

Octavia studied the others. She was probably assessing their strength, figuring out if she could take them on, if it came to that. But just like Octavia, Leif's siblings were capable of taking care of themselves.

Clenching his hands into fists, Leif's gaze shifted to the witch named Jocasta.

She cleared her throat, demanding their attention. "I'd like to introduce myself. My name is Jocasta Wildes, and I'm the current matriarch of the Salem coven. This is Thaddeus Green" —she gestured to the man— "and this is my granddaughter, Octavia. Thank you for welcoming us into your home." She paused, making eye contact with each of them. She held Leif's gaze a fraction of a second longer than the others before she continued.

"We would like to formally welcome you back into the coven."

Jocasta held up her hand when she noticed Leif and his siblings had tensed. "Octavia has already explained the situation. I understand how this request must sound to you. However, I want to address the elephant in the room and see if there's a way we can come to an understanding." Jocasta spoke clearly and slowly, obviously choosing her words with care.

A dense silence filled the room, which Delta interrupted with a guttural scoff as she rose from the couch. Leif's heart rate quickened as he watched her walk the short distance to the door. From her stiff posture, he could've sworn she was going to leave, but instead, she pulled a one-eighty, leaned her back against the door, and crossed her feet at the ankles, barricading the only exit. She jerked her chin in their direction, which Jocasta took as an invitation to continue.

"The night we were all separated was . . . tragic. Every one of us sitting in this room lost someone important the night of the attack. Our coven was ripped apart at the seams. The only members of our coven who survived are Thaddeus, myself, and you children." Jocasta cleared her throat again. "Sorry, you *adults*. I forget how much time has passed."

Octavia reached out for her grandmother's hand, which Jocasta took. While Jocasta's face remained calm and somber, Octavia's was contorted with sorrow. Leif figured the conversation was painful for them in a different way from how it was painful for him. The tension in his body ebbed slightly at the sight of their pain. It made them seem more . . . human than he'd been expecting—than what he'd been *taught* to expect. He glanced sidelong at the others, but their faces were hard as stone, completely unreadable.

"What happened that night?" Tripp asked, his eyes still red and puffy. "Leif already gave us the highlights, but I'd like to hear it from you." His brown eyes flicked to Leif momentarily before he continued. "We still don't know what to believe."

"Completely understandable—Tripp, if I'm not mistaken?" Jocasta asked.

Tripp nodded.

"This question is exactly why I brought Octavia with us this morning. You see, coven elders don't usually attend meetings unless they have a specific reason to. It's tradition to leave the governing of the coven to younger generations. Instead, we act as advisors when we're needed. I personally wasn't in attendance that night, and neither was Thaddeus. So the only person here who can share the events of that evening with you is Octavia." Jocasta turned to her granddaughter.

Leif shifted uncomfortably in his seat as Octavia took a deep breath to steady herself. All the eyes in the room turned to her, but she looked resolutely unfazed—prepared even. She must've known beforehand that this would be her role in the conversation.

She talked for several minutes straight; no one interrupted her. They clung to her every word, the sinking feeling in Leif's stomach worsening with every minute she talked. Octavia's description of the attack was exhaustive, not a single moment left to the imagination. The events of that night played back like a movie in his mind's eye—a tragic, horrific movie. Leif had no memory of the night she recollected—not the house, nor the fight, nor the destruction left in its wake—and yet, as he listened, he felt the icy wind on his skin, smelled the noxious smoke in the air, saw the bloodied bodies littering the floor. This night must haunt her, Leif realized. Replaying over and over again on a never-ending loop. His heart ached for her. Listening to this story once was enough of a nightmare. For Octavia to have relived it so many times she was able to recall the memory with this excruciating level of detail . . . it was unfathomable to him.

By the time she was done, nearly everyone was crying, including Octavia. Leif's and Delta's were the only dry eyes left. His rage wouldn't let him cry anymore, but he expected the tears would come for him again eventually. He wondered if Delta felt the same, if perhaps she was also angry, angrier than she was letting on, or whether she still didn't believe a word they spoke.

"Thank you . . . for telling us," Tripp choked out through the hand covering his mouth.

Octavia only nodded in response, finally uncurling her hand from her grandmother's grip to wipe the tears from her cheeks.

"What about our parents?" Jiro piped up, his eyes glistening.

"Ah, yes," said Jocasta softly. "After you disappeared, the four of you were listed as missing persons. The remaining coven members stayed in Vermont for almost a year after the attack, hoping to eventually find you all. But we were so afraid of another attack, Thaddeus and I eventually made the decision to relocate to Boston. Returning to Salem was too much of a risk. Witch hunters visit all the time. That's why the coven moved to Vermont in the first place twenty-five years ago.

"I am very sorry to say that your magical parents perished in the attack. We buried them in Salem. I'm happy to take you to visit them any time, to mourn and pay your respects." Jocasta's shoulders pulled back, her posture straightening. "Your non-magical parents, however, are very much alive, and completely unaware that magic exists." She dipped her chin slowly as eyebrows rose simultaneously around the room.

"Yes, I know," said Jocasta. "Witches having romantic relationships with non-magical partners is not unusual. There are simply not enough witches left. We've always encouraged relationships with normal humans—normans, as we call them—but we've always had the rule that a witch must never disclose the practice of witchcraft to anyone outside of the coven. That little caveat has been strictly enforced for centuries."

"Why?" Jiro asked.

"Witch hunters," Thaddeus murmured simply. Jiro's jaw snapped audibly shut. "Witches have been picked off by witch hunters over the centuries," Thaddeus went on. "So covens tend to grow smaller and smaller with each new generation. Our magical prowess gives us only a very slight upper hand. I guess you could classify us as an endangered species," he joked darkly. "As far as Jocasta and I are aware, we're the last coven in the northeast."

Leif considered this new information. It made sense. In fact, it would even explain why Garren had been traveling so much the past couple of years. There were simply no more witches to hunt in this area apart from them. Reluctantly, Leif remembered he was now supposedly a part of "them."

The thought brought a new slew of questions. Why had they even been kidnapped in the first place? It would've been far easier to just kill them and be done with it. Whoever had taken them had to have had an ulterior motive. Leif considered raising these questions to the group, but he suspected their answers would just be speculation. The only way to get a real answer was to ask Garren himself.

"I still talk to your mother, Jiro," said Jocasta. "She stayed in Vermont for several years after your disappearance before she moved back to Japan to be closer to family. She'll be ecstatic to hear from you after all this time."

A small, relieved smile broke on Jiro's lips.

"Delta, your mother still lives in Vermont," Jocasta continued. "Unfortunately, she and I have lost touch, but I believe I can get you in contact with her."

A flash of an emotion that Leif couldn't name flickered across Delta's face. One moment it was there, and the next it was gone, replaced by Delta's eternal mask of indignance.

"Tripp—" Jocasta started, but he jumped in to interrupt her.

"My mother told me when I was young that my father abandoned us while she was pregnant with me," Tripp bit out through clenched teeth. "She was the only real parent I ever had."

Jocasta nodded before turning to Leif.

"I already know too. You don't have to bother," Leif grunted. "My mother and father were both witches, and they died that night trying to protect us."

Tripp placed a hand on Leif's shoulder. He had the immediate urge to shrug it off, but suppressed it. It wasn't easy for Leif to accept help from others, especially not when the person offering it was giving him a look dangerously close to pity. But Tripp was in a similar situation. They were both alone. So, for once, he accepted the support.

"There's a fatal flaw in your little story," Delta said, her tone menacing as she pushed off from the door, ignoring the obvious emotional tension in the room. "If all of this is the truth, then why the hell don't we have magic?" She walked back to the couch and leaned her elbows against the backrest.

"That's a very good question," Thaddeus responded. "I'm not sure we have the answer just yet."

"The only explanation that makes sense is that your magic is being suppressed by something," Jocasta reasoned. "It could be a hex, like what happened to Octavia, or it could be some kind of magical object, something you always have with you."

"It's their necklaces," Octavia stated matter-of-factly.

Four hands immediately reached for matching white gold crosses.

"But how—?" Jocasta started.

"Leif told me he hasn't taken his off since Garren gave it to him. I noticed when we first walked in; they all wear matching ones. They're supposed to be a symbol of his love. It's a flawless manipulation tactic, really. Of course, they'd never take them off if they were steeped in sentimental value," Octavia explained plainly, as if it were the most obvious thing in the world—which, to Leif, it now very much felt like it was.

Delta cursed under her breath as she unclasped the necklace around her neck.

She's probably just pissed she didn't figure that out on her own, Leif thought darkly. Ridding herself of the necklace might not be a big deal to Delta—after all, she'd just ripped it off with zero hesitation—but Leif knew for him, Jiro, and Tripp, removing their necklaces would be like removing their identities, like shedding a layer of skin they'd grown immensely comfortable in. The thought of taking off his necklace was foreign and a bit scary. *But what if this provides the proof we're looking for? What if we take the necklaces off and something actually happens? Would we be able to turn a blind eye and deny it then?*

No, Leif didn't think they would.

Not to mention, this could be what gave them an edge when it came time to exact their revenge. Magic could give them the element of surprise, which Garren had taught them was so crucial when opposing an enemy who outmatched them. If they communicated with Garren as usual and acted like nothing was wrong, they'd have time to hone their new abilities, and maybe, if they were lucky, be able to use them effectively if it came down to a confrontation.

Slowly, Leif unclasped the necklace and let it drop to the floor in front of him. For several long moments, nothing changed. Jiro removed his necklace next, then Tripp. They all looked between each other, waiting for something to change, or for something to feel different. Almost a full minute passed in stony silence.

"Obviously you were wrong." Delta sneered at Octavia as she pushed off the backrest of the couch and returned to her seat. "I guess *someone's* not as smart as she seems."

Delta studied her nails intently, as if the simple act of sharing air with everyone in this room was decidedly beneath her. Octavia glared back, dark pupils dilated.

Leif hoped Delta would just leave it alone. She'd made her point. The witches were wrong. Leif and his siblings didn't harbor any magical abilities. Removing the necklaces had proven that. And he was wildly, completely, utterly thrilled. It was taking everything in him to keep his elation locked in his chest. He wanted to whoop and holler and cry with relief because it was real after all—Garren, his siblings, his entire life. It wasn't a lie. It was real. And he wanted nothing more than to celebrate that fact with his siblings after ushering their guests out the door as quickly as humanly possible.

But of course, he'd overestimated Delta. He cringed as she continued, her voice full of judgment and contempt, "I wonder what else you could be wrong about? Oh yes, perhaps this entire pathetic fucking sob story you just bored us all with for the last hour." She glowered, her eyes narrowing to dark, dangerous slits as they slid from her nails to Octavia. In a heartbeat, Delta was on her feet, index finger pointing toward the door. "Get out. Get out of our house, right now! Before I make you regret it!"

Leif was about to intervene—when suddenly Delta shifted, changing before his very eyes. Her short black hair lightened, taking on a reddish hue; her fingernails lengthened until they resembled claws; and her black pupils elongated, the top and bottom coming to a deadly point. She no longer looked like the Delta they knew. Instead, she resembled a vicious, feral fox, moments away from killing its prey.

CHAPTER 19
LEIF

The truth stared him in the face, and it was terrifying.

We were wrong. I was wrong, Leif thought. Magic was the only explanation for what Leif was seeing. Delta had altered her appearance, though she didn't seem aware of it at the moment. He had to tell her. He had to say something. He had to . . .

Leif blinked, and the world bled red. Fury unlike anything he'd ever experienced charred his fracturing heart; flames licking every deep, dark corner of his soul. And in the span of a few galloping heartbeats, he died. Not the flesh he inhabited; that sorry sack of cells continued on as well as it could under the current emotional circumstances. No, he felt the difference in his meaning deep within the marrow of his bones. Instead, *he* died—the person inside. Everything that had made him *him* dissolved to ash, scorched under the righteous flames of truth.

He wasn't a witch hunter. He wasn't saved. He wasn't lovingly adopted. He wasn't any of the things he'd been moments ago.

He was something else entirely.

I'm a motherfucking witch.

When Tripp and Jiro saw Leif gaping, they leaned forward to look at Delta too, their sudden movement wrenching Leif back into the moment. Another blink, and the red faded to shades of gray, the world suddenly as empty as his heart.

After a beat, Jiro and Tripp quickly scooted as far as they could to the right side of the couch. The fox woman eyed them warily, clearly confused.

Jocasta and Thaddeus were absolutely beaming, their smiles spread from ear to ear. Obviously, they knew something Leif didn't, because nothing about this revelation seemed even remotely pleasant or amusing.

"A specialist in glamours, it would seem," Thaddeus boomed, his deep voice laced with amusement.

"Ah, yes," Jocasta agreed, "what a marvelous facet of magic! One of my personal favorites. Sadly, I'm not particularly skilled myself."

"What're you people talking about?" Delta asked, the sharp tips of her elongated canines flashing dangerously.

"Do you have a mirror, my dear?" Jocasta asked her granddaughter.

"Um, maybe in my bag somewhere," Octavia replied, quickly rummaging around in her tote bag. She found a small compact and placed it into her grandmother's waiting hand.

Jocasta stood and walked over to the vulpine version of Delta. She handed the compact over and waited. Delta opened the small mirror and peered at herself. The look of pure shock on her face was like nothing Leif had ever seen from her.

Delta's knees trembled slightly before they gave out, and she fell to sit on the couch again. Leif wanted to reach out, to console her, but—how? How could he make this better for her? How could anyone? He didn't have the answer. He had nothing. He *was* nothing, completely hollow. The anguished expression on Delta's face told Leif she was too.

"As I said, your change in appearance indicates that your area of magical specialty is probably glamours. Beginners can usually change their hair or eye color, their height and body, while more skilled witches can change into specific people, animals, and sometimes even objects. It's a niche facet of magic."

"How do I make myself go back to normal?" Delta asked, concern softening her tone.

Something in Leif's chest twisted at her voice's change, breaking him from his stupor. He hadn't heard Delta sound this vulnerable since they were children. He scooted toward her, close enough that their shoulders brushed—a silent reminder she wasn't alone.

"Emotions can enhance the intensity of your magic, so the key is to rein your emotions back in. Put your hands on your knees. Close your eyes and breathe in time with my voice. Imagine yourself looking into a mirror; now, imagine the reflection looking back at you is your normal appearance. Drain your mind of all thought and emotion as best as you can. Ready?" Delta nodded as she closed her eyes. "All right, I'll count down from ten. You focus. Ten, nine, eight . . ."

Within moments, Delta began shifting back to normal. Slowly, her auburn hair darkened back to black, her nails rounded and retracted, and her teeth widened, losing their conical shape. By the time Jocasta reached the count of one, Delta was herself again.

She checked her reflection in the compact, her hands shaking. Ostensibly pleased with her reflection, she returned the compact to Jocasta and said in a fragile timbre, "Thanks."

"You might feel a bit tired for the next few hours. This is brand-new to all of you. Magic has been repressed inside you for so long, it may drain your energy more quickly until we can train you up a bit." Jocasta walked back to her seat and sat down.

"You're going to train us?" asked Tripp, his usually golden complexion blanching.

"Of course. We want to welcome you back into the coven. You'll be full members, able to study and practice witchcraft to your heart's content."

If there was ever a wrong thing to say, that was it. The momentary shock and novelty of Delta's transformation vanished like a strong wind whisking away a cloud of smoke. Suddenly, it became clear to the others: Delta had performed witchcraft. In front of their very eyes, they'd witnessed irrefutable proof of their abilities and their new identities. Leif fell back against the couch cushions as Tripp wrung his hands and Jiro gnawed at his already bleeding cuticles.

Next to Leif, Delta gagged. Quickly, she rose from the couch and sprinted for the kitchen sink. She barely made it before she vomited.

"Oh, dear," Jocasta proclaimed, rising in her seat, but she was stopped by both Octavia and Thaddeus. Octavia shook her head gently in response to her grandmother's questioning glance.

Leif had to admit he was both surprised and impressed that Octavia seemed to be sympathizing with them, especially given the fact she knew exactly what they would've done to her covenmates last night if everything had gone according to plan. And it didn't appear as if she'd told Jocasta or Thaddeus about their plot either, which was particularly confusing. Why was she protecting them?

Leif waited until Delta was done gargling water before he spoke. "We've been taught to despise witchcraft; told witches are a lethal enemy, ready to strike us down at their earliest convenience. Until now, we believed witches murdered our parents. And now we learn we're witches ourselves? This isn't something we can transition into easily . . . if at all." Leif ran a clammy hand through his hair.

"I understand," Jocasta said as Delta returned to her seat on the couch. Her dark skin had taken on a sickly pallor and was glistening with sweat.

"We don't want to force anything on you," said Thaddeus softly. "You've already experienced enough of that to last a lifetime. We're simply extending an invitation. It's yours to take or refuse. Our only request is if you decline our invitation, do not speak of this to anyone, magical or otherwise. We also hope you'll avoid, uh, *hunting* us in the future."

The four of them shared a silent, contemplative moment, each of their gazes tense and uneasy. Eventually, they nodded in unison. The room was enveloped once more in silence.

After what felt like several minutes, Octavia spoke. "I can only imagine what you must be feeling right now. I can barely understand how I'm feeling at the moment." She paused to breathe. "I was hexed the night of the attack, and my connection to my magic was severed. I'm magicless, orphaned, and fucking pissed off. Sorry for swearing," she murmured quickly to her grandmother. "If you're pissed too, then join us. Maybe there's something we can do about it."

A small, warm light sparked to life in Leif's chest, causing his heart to beat faster. She felt the same as he did. Well, maybe not exactly the same, but similar. She was angry, and more importantly, she was motivated to do something about it. And here she was, asking for their help, just as he'd considered asking for theirs, somewhere deep within the recesses of his mind, in a place he hadn't been willing to explore. Now, he didn't have to.

Together. That could change everything.

A plan began forming in his head, before he'd even had time to register that he'd already silently agreed to Octavia's plea.

A gasp from Tripp pulled Leif from his thoughts. He was staring at Leif, wide-eyed. A glimmer of light reflected off the thin sheen of oil that had accumulated on Tripp's forehead, but Leif couldn't see the source. Confused, he turned to the others, each of whom was looking at him with a similar expression of surprise.

"How fitting," Jocasta whispered. "Light magic, just like your mother."

Leif looked down at the palms of his hands. The air evaporated from his lungs, sending his heart into overdrive. His palms were quite literally glowing, emitting dim waves of ethereal golden light. The air around his body warmed a few degrees, and he felt sweat prick on the back of his neck. For a moment, he felt afraid, but as he stared at the light a while longer, the fear was chased away by a surreal sense of peace—of rightness. He swallowed against the emotional whiplash.

"Your hair," Octavia exclaimed, a matching look of awe on her face.

"That's not glowing too, is it?" Leif asked, for some reason feeling embarrassed, pulling long strands of hair from his bangs down in front of his eyes. They didn't appear to be glowing, but they *had* changed. His hair was no longer the dull, ashen color he'd become so accustomed to. Now it was platinum blond, almost white as snow.

Pushing his hair back into place, he gazed at the others on the couch, trying to gauge their response to Octavia's statement. Thankfully, their resolute, wrathful expressions each said the same thing: *we're with you.*

"We're livid," Leif said frankly, "and we want justice. Garren and the hunters have to answer for what they've done." Leif took a few deep breaths like Jocasta had instructed Delta to do, imagining his normal self while forcing the glow and warmth around him to slowly recede. Though the light from his palms quickly faded, leaving a chill in its wake, the hair framing his vision remained blanched; it appeared the change in hair color was permanent. *At least the glowing isn't,* he thought gratefully.

"A natural," Thaddeus noted in an impressed whisper.

"We can help with that," Octavia chimed in. Excitement glinted in her eyes.

Jocasta's head whipped in the direction of her granddaughter, her gaping mouth evidence of her dismay.

"It's the least we can do, Grandma," Octavia said. "They need this to move on."

Jocasta hesitated, her lips pressing into a firm line.

"This witch hunter, Garren, may end up being of use to us, Jo," said Thaddeus. "He was obviously the one who kidnapped them the night of the attack. If he was there, then he probably witnessed Octavia being hexed. If we could glean even a sliver of information from him, this could be the breakthrough we've been searching for. He could be the key to getting Octavia's magic back."

Jocasta released a shaky breath. "You're right," she agreed, glancing over her shoulder at a stony-faced Octavia.

Something was off about Octavia's response. The way she was averting her gaze, refusing to meet her grandmother's eye, made it clear to Leif that she hadn't considered this before. He would've imagined she'd be thrilled at the possibility of getting her magic back at Garren's expense. But that wasn't what he saw in her face. She didn't look happy or even hopeful at the moment.

Jocasta noticed it too and furrowed her perfectly manicured brows.

"So, we have a deal, then?" Leif asked. "We'll rejoin the coven if you help us question Garren."

"Fine," said Jocasta, "as long as we're able to glean the information we need about Octavia's hex too."

Leif turned to the others. They nodded in silent agreement.

"Deal," he said. "We'll make sure Garren's questioning is mutually beneficial." Leif stood and chanced a quick glance at Octavia as he crossed the room. Her face remained stoic, the excitement from moments ago leached away.

Jocasta stood to meet him and shook his hand firmly. "Welcome back, my dears. It's been far too long."

Thaddeus stood next to her. "Let's meet tomorrow morning

to start your training. We'll start slowly, and we'll introduce you to the other three then as well."

"Sounds good," Leif agreed, shaking Thaddeus's hand.

"I'll text you the address," Octavia murmured as she stood.

"Thank you for your hospitality," Jocasta said. "We look forward to seeing you tomorrow." She waved at the others, who were still sitting on the couch looking even more uncomfortable than they had when their guests had first walked in.

Leif guided them to the front door and held it open for them, and Jocasta and Thaddeus filed out. At the threshold, Octavia paused briefly before she reached into her bag. When her hand resurfaced, it gripped a leather-bound book. The book that had started it all.

"I already showed it to Grandma and Thad. Neither of them has any use for it. I thought you might want to show it to the others. Hearing it and seeing it are two different things, as you've realized."

"Um, thank you," Leif replied dumbly as he took the book.

Octavia walked onto the front porch as Jocasta and Thaddeus climbed into a small car parked at the curb.

"Octavia!" Leif heard himself shout.

She turned to face him, a tight mask of indifference upon her face. He realized he wished she was smirking at him—that smug little half-smile that had his heart pounding so fast the night they met. A night they'd never repeat—a mistake they'd never make again. Leif hated the way his stomached knotted with regret. Nothing like a one-night stand gone wrong to make their disagreeable circumstances even more uncomfortable.

"Why are you helping us?" Leif asked. "It doesn't make any sense. Last night you were ready to murder me with my own dagger, and now you're standing up for us. Why?"

Octavia stared at him thoughtfully. "Whether I like it or not, you're a part of this coven now. We look out for our own," she replied simply, then turned her back to him. As she walked to the car, she called over her shoulder, "And I trust that you know by now: if you ever raise a finger to my family again, I *will* murder you with your own dagger. That's a promise." She climbed into the car and didn't give him a second glance as they drove away.

Leif returned to the apartment and slumped down onto the couch next to Jiro. Tripp was now pacing nervously near the dining table as Delta brushed her teeth in the hallway.

"What the hell have we gotten ourselves into?" Jiro asked no one in particular.

"They're a means to an end," Leif replied. "They're the advantage we need if we're going to have any hope of challenging Garren. From there, it's up to each of us how we move forward." He paused to sigh and lean his head back against the couch. "I don't know about you, but if Garren confirms everything the coven's told us, I don't think I can move on until he's six feet underground."

The silence that followed was the only answer he needed.

CHAPTER 20
OCTAVIA

"Where the hell have you been?" Sage demanded.

Octavia pulled her keys out of the lock with a sigh and shut the door behind her. "Can I at least sit down before the interrogation starts?"

Sage ripped Octavia's coat and bag from her and tossed them unceremoniously onto the floor before dragging her to the couch. The worn, lumpy cushions welcomed her gladly.

The meeting at the hunters' house had only taken a couple of hours, but to Octavia it'd felt like days. Her body and mind were spent, both in desperate need of sleep. But Octavia understood that her roommates' need for an explanation was more important at the moment.

"Okay, you're sitting. Now spill," Sage commanded, their hands on their hips. Their posture was in direct contrast with their cottagecore aesthetic for the day; they were dressed in oversized overalls and a chunky wool sweater. They couldn't have looked less intimidating if they'd tried.

June wasn't sitting on the floor hovering over her cauldron like usual; instead she was sitting on the opposite end of the couch with a novel at her side, her attention now resolutely on Octavia. As always, her eyes were brimming with concern, but her lips were pursed in uncharacteristic disapproval. Octavia flinched internally, realizing that she must be the source of June's disappointment. Octavia hated disappointing any of them, but especially June. And, unfortunately, she'd done it a lot lately.

"Didn't Grandma call you and let you know I was with her?" Octavia asked hopefully.

"Granddad called," Quintin said as he entered the room. "He let us know where you were, but he didn't give us details. What happened?"

Octavia sighed heavily, her sore muscles protesting at the effort. "You should sit down."

"Now I'm worried," June said, her voice brittle as she shifted uncomfortably.

Quintin took a heavy seat in the armchair adjacent to the couch. Sage remained standing, their face darkening with anticipation.

"Where to start?" Octavia murmured. "Michael wasn't what he appeared to be," she began. "In fact, his name isn't even Michael. He used an alias."

"Why would he do that?" Quintin asked in a guttural voice, his posture straightening as if a steel rod had just been jammed into his spine.

"Because he didn't want us to know who and what he really was."

"Who is he, then?" June inquired around a thumbnail she'd started gnawing.

"A witch hunter," Octavia replied tremulously. She hated every quivering note.

Quintin's fists clenched so tight Octavia heard his knuckles crack, and June covered her mouth to suppress a gasp. A heavy silence stretched out among them.

Then Sage burst into laughter. "That's fucking hilarious, Tavi! Good one," they boomed, doubling over in a fit of chuckles.

Octavia stared at them dumbly, unable to find even a scrap of humor in this new sick, twisted reality.

Sage's laughter quickly faded, turning into shallow breaths. "Holy shit. But . . . how?"

"He ran into Quintin downtown last week and sensed his magic." Quintin tensed further in the armchair. How that was even physically possible Octavia had no idea, as he'd already been coiled so tight. "He followed him to Tucker's that day but lost him, so he came back the next night hoping to find him there again. Instead, he found me."

"So he knew you were a witch too?" June asked from behind her hand.

"No, he couldn't sense my magic. It was seemingly a normal one-night stand for both of us."

Quintin's teeth ground together audibly.

"Until the following morning, when he met all of you," Octavia finished, suffocating as waves of guilt crashed over her anew.

June must have seen the emotion on Octavia's face because she reached over to clasp her hand tightly. "There's no way you could've known, Tavi."

"I'm still confused over here. How did you even find this out? I doubt he told you willingly," Sage asked, eyeing her curiously.

Octavia laughed darkly. "Now *that's* an interesting story. We were at the Salem Archives Library doing research on our date," she explained, ignoring their judgy looks at her confession that she'd misled them. "We came across one of our coven's old texts. That's when he saw his name . . . his birth name."

"Why would he find—?" Quintin started, but then he trailed off.

"No," Sage denied, shaking their head vigorously.

"Tavi . . . what's his name?" June whispered through her fingers.

"Michael is Leif. Leif Hutchins. He's one of us."

They all spoke at once, talking over each other.

"Shut up!" Sage cried.

"That's impossible," Quintin muttered.

"How?" June asked simply.

Octavia rubbed her neck; a throbbing tension headache was forming at the base of her skull. "They were kidnapped by a witch hunter the night of the attack, all four of them. Then the sick fucker suppressed their magic and brainwashed them, teaching them how to hunt down their own coven."

Octavia's mouth suddenly tasted of pennies as a violent swell of nausea consumed her. Now she understood why Delta had lost her breakfast earlier. Thinking about it from their perspective was almost unbearable. She closed her eyes and leaned her head back against the couch, willing the nausea to subside.

"That's some twisted, maniacal bullshit," Sage murmured, slowly lowering to the floor in a squat, their elbows on their knees, fists to their forehead.

June nodded fervently in agreement, finally dropping the shaky hand from her mouth.

"I had to tell Grandma and Thad, so I stayed at their house last night," Octavia continued, purposely leaving out the details of the witch hunters' murderous plot, as well as her embarrassing emotional breakdown. She didn't want to give them any more reason to harbor negative feelings toward the others.

"So, what happened next?" Quintin inquired.

"Grandma, Thad, and I went to visit them this morning. We got them to agree to reconnect with their magic and join the coven. You'll meet them tomorrow morning when they start their training." Octavia rubbed her aching neck again.

"Training?" June asked quietly.

"Well, they didn't necessarily phrase it this way, but we're going to help them get revenge on the hunter who kidnapped them.

They're furious, rightly so. They want answers and they want them straight from the horse's mouth, not ours." She paused. "But I saw their faces. Squeezing the truth out of the bastard won't be enough. They won't be able to move on until they get justice."

"Hold on," Sage cut in hotly, popping up to stand. "How in the hell can we even trust them?"

"Sage!" June scolded. "They're family!"

"Sage is right," said Quintin. "They've been identifying with the enemy for almost two decades. How can they switch sides so easily? Especially if they'd been so sufficiently manipulated that they forgot they were ever witches."

June's mouth snapped closed.

"They were a wreck this morning. All of them. Delta actually puked after she realized she'd subconsciously cast a glamour spell on herself. The reaction was so visceral . . ." Octavia pressed her fingertips against her eyelids, willing away the mental image. "But Quin is right: we can't let our guard down around them. At least not yet. Maybe someday," she amended when she noted the look of distress on June's face—the eternal optimist. Octavia squeezed her hand, still intertwined with her own.

"This is seriously fucked up. I mean, how long have we dreamed about finding them?" Sage asked, their lower lip trembling slightly. "This isn't how it was supposed to happen."

"You're right," Octavia agreed. "It's not."

Silence permeated the room for a few minutes as each of them processed the news.

"So, tomorrow?" Quintin asked, breaking the silence.

"Yeah," Octavia confirmed, "we'll meet them tomorrow morning at Grandma and Thad's house."

Sage ran a tan, freckled hand back and forth over their hair, a nervous tic they'd developed since cutting it short. "What if they betray us? What if we let them in, share all our secrets, teach them how to use their magic, and then one of them double-crosses us in the end?" Sage pondered. Octavia felt sure they were addressing the questions that had been silently reverberating through all of their minds, questions no one else was willing to ask out loud.

"Then I'll kill them," Octavia said simply.

Sage's eyes widened disbelievingly behind their glasses. Quintin gaped, his mouth hanging open soundlessly. June fell into a coughing fit, as if she'd choked on her own saliva at the mere mention of such violence.

"Don't get me wrong," Octavia went on. "I want to help them. In fact, I'll do everything in my power to help make sure they fit in with our coven, because we simply aren't whole without them. But if they cross us, I won't be merciful. Leif knows that. He knows it's not an empty threat."

Now that she'd made her point clear, Octavia found she could hardly keep her eyes open. Slowly, they fluttered closed despite her valiant efforts.

"Tavi, you need to sleep. You're a right hot mess," Sage said. Their rough words didn't offend Octavia. She knew there was genuine concern beneath them.

"Yes," June agreed, "we can continue this conversation in the morning over breakfast."

Octavia nodded drowsily, her eyes still closed. She was so warm and content on the couch, she couldn't imagine gathering the strength to move to her bed. The last thing she felt before sleep took her were Quintin's strong arms holding her tight against his chest as he picked her up off the couch and carried her away.

This feels familiar, Octavia thought, recalling momentarily how Thaddeus had carried her to bed the night before. How similar they were, grandfather and grandson. The thought left the ghost of a smile on her lips as she gratefully succumbed to sleep.

CHAPTER 21
OCTAVIA

O ctavia woke early the next morning and found the others already awake as well. They were all anxious about seeing their childhood friends, who were now complete strangers—and their mortal enemies.

They planned over a breakfast of scrambled eggs and buttered toast, which they only pretended to eat, pushing the food around their plates aimlessly. They'd decided to approach the witch hunters as openly and welcomingly as they could. It'd only serve to benefit them if they gained the witch hunters' trust before they gave over their own.

June would lead the charge, of course. There was simply no other choice. Octavia, Sage, and Quintin were about as warm and cuddly as a pack of hungry mountain lions. But, regardless of their natural demeanors, they'd promised June they'd put their best foot forward.

At eight o'clock, they trekked out into the damp cold to catch the red line. Each of their hoods was raised against the frigid drizzle except for Octavia's. She lifted her face to the sky, letting the icy numbness settle in. Droplets of near-freezing water clung to her eyelashes, threatening to wash away the little makeup she'd put on. But she didn't care. All she cared about was getting through the day unscathed.

They rode into Boston in near silence before transferring to the green line. On the ride out to Brookline, Octavia did her best to describe Leif, Jiro, Tripp, and Delta. She warned them that Delta was likely to be unpleasant, whereas Tripp seemed to be the most in touch with his emotions. Jiro had been the quietest during their meeting, but something told her he was likely the most perceptive.

Leif, however, remained a complete mystery to her. She didn't know who he was or what his goals were anymore—but then again, she guessed she never really had in the first place. He'd always been a stranger. It'd been made clear enough that night in Salem. Leif had felt terribly betrayed, and yesterday he expressed a fierce desire for revenge, but somehow, Octavia knew deep down there was more to him than that. She thought she'd felt it before—his true nature. Before she'd learned who he was. Before *he'd* learned who he was.

Could he even be the same person he was before he learned his true identity? Hell, she knew *she* wasn't. This had certainly changed her. Hadn't it? If she was being completely honest with herself, she believed the sudden change in her also had something to do with what the woman from the cemetery had said and her warning about Octavia's current mental state ending in her ruin. Nevertheless, the Octavia meeting with him today was not the same Octavia who'd fled that dank alley in Salem—no longer were her own selfish desires her main priority. She'd convinced herself everything she'd done up until that point was for the coven, but she'd been telling herself pretty, fallacious lies. Every move she made up until that night was motivated by her own selfishness. No more. She owed it to herself and the coven to be better than that.

When they reached their stop, they piled out onto the street and beelined through the brownstone-lined neighborhood toward her grandmother's house. Eventually, they rounded on the house, finding the car belonging to the witch-hunting bastard, Garren, parked out front on the street.

Octavia halted at the familiar threshold, turning to nod at the others, mutely confirming their plan. They adorned their matching masks of solemnity and entered the house without knocking. They deposited their coats, scarves, and boots in the foyer as nearby voices drifted their way.

The four witches ventured into the massive sitting room. It was an old, dusty room that their family rarely used. In fact, Octavia could only remember sitting in there a handful of times over the last decade. The rectangular room was decorated in shades of neutral cream and vibrant ochre. The vintage Victorian furniture contrasted strikingly with the Greco-Roman décor of white marble bust sculptures displayed on fluted pedestals and quirky olive branch wallpaper. Nothing in the space matched, and yet somehow, it worked. Whether or not Jocasta's magic had played a hand in that would always remain a mystery.

Jocasta and Thaddeus were seated on a loveseat with a tray of tea and cookies spread out on the coffee table in front of them. The four supposed ex-witch hunters sat spread out amongst the remaining couches and accent chairs, leaving the others no option but to disperse among them for seats. A smug smirk spread across Delta's face when she saw Octavia's unease.

Her poker face must really have been dreadful. She suppressed the urge to roll her eyes and headed for the seat next to Delta on a cream-colored Phyfe sofa. Two could very well play at this game.

Delta released a huff as Octavia made herself comfortable, crossing her legs beneath her. Quintin waved before taking the seat next to Tripp, which was as far across the room from the others as he could get while still being able to engage in conversation. Sage and June sat on either side of Jiro on the final couch, each muttering little "hello"s, while Leif half-stood, perched against the arm of an obnoxiously bright accent chair.

"Wonderful," Jocasta started, setting her teacup down gingerly on the coffee table. "Now that you're all here and comfortable, let's go around the room and introduce ourselves." She gestured to Leif on her left.

"Um, okay. I'm Leif Hutchins," he murmured quickly, crossing his arms and turning his face from the others in discomfort, causing a tuft of his newly lightened hair to fall into his eyes.

"Leif's parents were Gwyn and Fitz Hutchins," Jocasta explained to the others with a small, proud smile. "It would seem he shares his mother's affinity for light magic."

Leif tilted his head in recognition, obviously unwilling to speak further.

Disregarding the group's rigid posture and wary sidelong glances, Jocasta motioned for the next in line to continue.

June smiled brightly. "Hello! My name is June Foster, and I use she/her pronouns, and it's really great to see you all, after all this time." She drifted off, enthusiastic, but still uncertain as she studied the newcomers' less than friendly expressions. She started fidgeting with the ends of her long, thick braid before she noticed Jocasta's expectant glance. "Oh, right! And I specialize in potions."

Jiro was next in the circle. "I'm Jiro Jon—" He paused as his ears turned red. "Jiro Bishop, he/him, and I guess I'm not sure what my magic type is yet."

"We refer to them as 'specialties,'" Jocasta corrected kindly. "Most witches can perform basic spells and enchantments, but we tend to show remarkable skill within one specific facet of magic. Many choose to hone their skills within their specialty, as opposed to spreading their efforts thin across each of the different facets. But ultimately, it's up to the individual how they want to conduct their practice."

Jiro nodded, rapidly tapping the heel of his sneaker against the shag carpet.

Sage dipped their chin as the room looked to them. "I'm Sage

Wardwell, and I use they/them pronouns. My specialty is elemental magic."

"What does that mean?" Delta chimed in with a look of hesitant curiosity.

"It means I can manipulate the elements," Sage explained in a bored tone.

"Which elements?" Tripp asked, leaning forward to place his elbows on his knees.

"All of them. But I'm training to make my manipulation more precise, like manipulating specific minerals in metals, electric currents through the air, or the water in blood," Sage finished with a triumphant smirk on their face.

Based on the newcomers' bulging eyes, Octavia felt certain they were impressed with Sage's abilities, and maybe even a little intimidated, which explained Sage's smugness. They'd clearly accomplished their goal: *intimidate the outsiders.*

Which was exactly what they had agreed *not* to do back at the loft.

"Show us," Delta demanded, looking much less confident than she had when they'd arrived.

"There will be plenty of time for that later," Jocasta cut in, forcing all the eyes in the room to return to her, which dispelled some of the tension that had formed thanks to Sage's thinly veiled boasting. Jocasta turned in her seat to look expectantly at Octavia.

Great.

"I'm Octavia Martin, and I use she/her pronouns," she said, quickly raising a hand in a gesture of welcome. She returned her hand to her lap and waited. The attention of everyone in the room remained fixed on her, waiting for her to continue. The muscles between her shoulder blades strained against painful knots as she squared her shoulders and held her head high. "You already know I don't have my magic anymore."

Leif met her gaze for a moment, his bright eyes shining with an unreadable emotion, before she broke the connection, looking down at her hands in her lap.

"And you have no idea who hexed you, or why?" Jiro asked softly.

"No."

"What was your specialty before you were hexed?" Tripp asked next.

"I don't know," Octavia replied honestly. "Witches don't usually start showing proficiency for a specialty until they're older. In fact, most can't even use their magic effectively until they're like ten. I lost my magic when I was six."

"That's why we're interested in questioning this Garren fellow," Jocasta added. "He had to have seen or been in cahoots with whoever hexed Octavia that night if he was able to whisk you away before the police arrived."

Octavia's fists clenched at her grandmother's words. *What difference would that even make? Who cares who cast the spell if we aren't able to break it?* She *had* to move on from this. If she didn't, it was going to ruin her. If she kept searching for something that might never be found, she'd end up always refusing to love any version of herself that was magicless. It was toxic. Nevertheless, vibrant, traitorous hope bloomed in her heart. She didn't let it take root.

"That shouldn't be our main priority. Our main priority should be justice." Octavia's voice sounded stronger and more level than she felt. Without looking up, she knew the jaws around her had gone slack, falling open in surprise. Their laser-focused gazes made her skin crawl.

"Well, isn't that *generous* of you?" Delta drawled as she reached forward and plucked a bite-sized cookie from the tray before popping it in her mouth. She looked back at Octavia. A mischievous smile tugged at the corners of her lips as she chewed.

Distrust, and something dangerously close to hate, sparked a blaze in Octavia's chest at Delta's taunting words. Even though she did her best to keep her face neutral this time, something must've given her away, because Delta's close-lipped smile deepened as she swallowed her treat.

Tucking silky raven strands behind her ear while glancing around the room, she said, "Delta Faulkner, she/her, and my specialty is something called glamours." She grinned openly then, flashing two rows of brilliant, perfectly straight white teeth.

Tripp was quick to jump in, perhaps wanting to yank the attention away from Delta before she had the chance to do something nefarious with it. "I'm Tripp Bradbury, and I use he/him pronouns. I'm not sure what my specialty is yet either," he announced, raising a polished hand to tousle a handful of unruly brown curls held back by a thin headband. He wore a white V-neck T-shirt under a thick navy cardigan. Octavia noticed a large tattoo peeking out above the neckline of his shirt that seemed to extend from one shoulder to the other. Upon subtle inspection, she realized the tattoo consisted of several intertwining snakes just beneath his collarbone. The intricacy and level of detail was remarkable. She could almost make out each individual scale, even from across the room.

"Each of your specialties will make themselves known in due time, I have no doubt," Jocasta chirped enthusiastically, turning to Quintin.

"Quintin Howe, he/him, and portal magic," Quintin mumbled quickly, all too eager to be out of the spotlight.

"No way!" Jiro exclaimed excitedly, scooting to the edge of his seat.

Quintin nodded once in response.

"So, you can basically teleport?"

"I guess so, yeah. But it's extremely difficult magic, even for me. The farthest apart I can comfortably conjure portals is like three or four yards."

"Damn, really? So, you couldn't send me to Paris, for example?" Jiro asked. The joke did little to hide his disappointment.

"Nope. A portal from one side of Boston to the other would take me an entire day to conjure and zap every ounce of energy I have," Quintin explained.

Jiro nodded, leaning back on the couch again.

"Well then, Thaddeus, I think it's your turn," Jocasta prodded.

"Ah, yes. My name is Thaddeus Green. I'm Quintin's grandfather, and I also go by he/him pronouns. I specialize in green magic, which means my magic helps plants grow. You'll soon discover I spend most of my free time in the greenhouse." He gestured to the backyard behind him with a thumb, soil permanently packed into the nail bed. He'd probably been out there gardening for hours before this meeting.

Octavia smiled fondly at him, which he returned in earnest.

"And that leaves me. Jocasta Wildes. I use she/her pronouns, and my specialty is lunar magic. This means I can practice many different facets of magic proficiently, but the strength and power of each of my spells is determined by the current phase of the moon." She picked up her tea from the table and took a sip. "As you all know, I'm the matriarch of the Salem coven, so it's my responsibility to make sure you're all properly educated and protected. Now that we've been reunited, I'll uphold that responsibility with my life, if I have to. Our coven has always been more than an organization of witches. It's a family. I hope that will continue moving forward."

Apart from June's fervent nodding, the room faded into eerie stillness. For the first time that morning, Jocasta seemed to notice the tension, her gaze bouncing between many lowered brows and pursed lips.

"Well, we can at least try," she barked. "Understood?"

The stillness shattered as several heads nodded around the room in agreement, to which Delta clicked her tongue rebelliously but said nothing.

"Very good. Now, we have scheduled some time for you to re-acquaint yourselves before the beginners' lesson with Thaddeus at ten o'clock. The rest of you can do your independent studies per usual. Just stay on the property, please." Jocasta straightened her sweater dress as she stood.

Octavia picked at a ball of lint on her leggings, anxious to get this little meet and greet over with so she could spend her independent study time pouring over the Latin texts she'd taken from the Salem Archives Library. She itched to get back to the routine she'd grown so accustomed to, the need for normalcy almost strangling her.

"Quintin, can you show me your portal magic?" Jiro asked as Jocasta and Thaddeus left.

"Uh, sure," Quintin replied as he surveyed the room. "Go stand at the other end of the room, and take this with you," he instructed, handing Jiro an empty teacup.

The knots in Octavia's stomach pulled tight as Jiro crossed the room. This was either going to be the best icebreaker or the worst.

Jiro walked obediently to the other side of the room and wait-ed. Quintin hovered his hands in front of his chest and closed his eyes. His brows furrowed in concentration as the rest of the group kept their eyes on him. Octavia sensed the newcomers' anticipa-tion mounting with each passing second. She tried to put herself in their shoes, to imagine a world where magic was brand new again, but it was impossible. Magic was her whole world—always had been—so she really couldn't imagine a life in which she wasn't sur-rounded by it. But she figured someday that would become her reality. Her covenmates, with their magic intact, would always be welcome here, but she was different. Eventually, she'd have to leave, banished to the world of normans. She wouldn't just be imagining it.

With shaky hands, she reached for one of the full teacups on the table, her mouth suddenly bone-dry. She'd only managed a sip before a small, silvery oval of light appeared before Quintin, and Octavia knew it was ripping through atoms upon atoms, creating a tear in space.

After only a fraction of a second, an identical shimmering oval formed in front of Jiro. He gasped and jolted backward.

"Don't worry, it won't hurt you." Quintin chuckled. "Now, pass the teacup through."

"What?" Jiro asked, mouth slack.

"Just do it already," Delta commanded from her spot on the sofa.

Hesitantly, Jiro put the hand holding the teacup through the iridescent portal. Instantly, his hand and the teacup popped out of the other portal. Quintin grinned at the look on Jiro's face as he retrieved the cup. After Jiro had removed his hand from the portal, the rip in space zipped closed.

Leaning forward, Jiro waved a hand through the air where the portal had been. "That's insane," he whispered.

"Welcome to the coven," Quintin replied. He was certainly warming up quicker than Octavia had expected, or else he'd become a convincing actor overnight. "Just wait till you see what Sage can do."

Sage opened their mouth to join the conversation when a wicked laugh came from the corner of the room. Delta had risen from the sofa and sauntered over to a small writing desk, where she now stood flipping through a stack of what appeared to be hand-written letters.

Octavia's stomach dropped.

"Why would we ever be excited to see such blatant acts of devilry?" Delta asked as the muscles in her jaw feathered fiercely beneath her flawless skin.

Guess I have my answer: showing off your magic to a crew of ex-witch hunters is indeed the worst icebreaker ever.

"Excuse me?" Sage asked, their eyes suddenly glistening with rage.

It wasn't until then that Octavia noticed the small alterations in their body language. Leif was determinedly staring out a tall window with his arms crossed. Tripp's head had fallen into his hands, his chest rising and falling in time with carefully measured breaths. Jiro's gaze was cold and flat as he analyzed the hand that had crossed through the portal. They were clearly repulsed.

They shouldn't have started off with portal magic, which Octavia had to admit was visually shocking, even though Jiro had asked. He'd seemed excited enough, but their years of psychological conditioning were the real issue here.

Octavia stood from the couch and walked over to Sage, placing a calming hand on their forearm. "Sorry. We should've guessed our magic would make you all uncomfortable. We won't do it again. Not until you feel ... more comfortable with the current circumstances. But that being said, you need to learn that our magic doesn't come from the devil—or any other evil entity, for that matter—so please don't refer to it like that from now on," Octavia demanded, desperate to defuse the rising tension.

Delta rolled her eyes, tossing the stack of papers on the desk. "I'll do what I want, Octavia," she sneered, saying the name like it left a bad taste in her mouth. "Always have, always will."

"D," Leif cautioned in a low voice, still facing the window.

"You can go to hell, Leif," Delta spat. "There's no way I'm going along with this ridiculous farce. I refuse to play nice with these *necromancers.*"

Sage tensed under Octavia's hand. "Okay, bitch, you wanna go?"

June raced between them, holding out her arms as they lunged for each other. "Stop it! We're all the same. Why are we fighting?" she asked in a desperate tone.

"Because we're not the same, not really," Leif remarked from across the room. All eyes snapped to him as he turned around, finally facing them again. "Our lives couldn't have been more different. Sure, we're from the same community. We were all born with magic." He paused to clear his throat, as if just saying the words was physically painful. "But we are *not* witches, not like you are. We don't remember the night of the attack. Hell, we barely remember our own parents. All we know is what we've been taught since we were taken. You are our enemy. It's as simple as that."

He paused, gazing at the others around the room until his ice-blue eyes finally fell on Octavia.

"We are not the same," he said again. This time, Octavia knew he was speaking directly to her.

CHAPTER 22
LEIF

H e didn't know exactly why he was saying it, nor why he was speaking directly to her, but—

Leif cut himself off, internally laughing at his arrogance—more in a self-deprecating way than in good humor though.

Who was he kidding? That was a lie. Of course he knew why he was saying this to her. Because on the drive to Salem, back when Octavia was just a woman who'd made some dangerous friends, and Leif was—well, Michael (admittedly not the best memory to put on a pedestal, but still), he'd thought the exact opposite. He'd thought they were the same, especially in their sadness. Now he knew how disturbingly wrong he'd been. She couldn't begin to fathom the depths of Leif's sadness, his horror, his rage. But Leif supposed he couldn't fathom hers either. So, no, they weren't the same. No use pretending that they were.

But even though he knew all of this, knew that his logic was as sound and true as the heart beating in his chest, the pull remained. Like gravity, but less generalized. More direct. More specific. Tugging him toward *her*. Which is why he needed to wedge more space between them, as what space he'd already developed seemed to dissolve with every passing glance.

In the midst of all this confusion and pain, they couldn't be friends. He was sure none of them could. So they sure as hell couldn't be anything more. He needed to sever whatever it was that held Octavia and himself in each other's orbit. He wasn't sure the best way to go about doing it, but he figured this was a decent place to start.

Based on Thaddeus's warm smiles and Jocasta's welcoming cups of tea, he could easily guess what the coven was hoping to get out of this arrangement. A big, happy family. But that's not what Leif was in this for. Leif was obtaining a weapon, and without this weapon he wouldn't stand a chance in hell of pinning Garren down long enough to get what he wanted out of him.

A means to an end, Leif had said to Jiro, and he'd meant it. After Garren spilled his guts and confessed the truth, Leif would exact whatever revenge was due and be on his way. Perhaps he'd re-clasp the magic-suppressing cross around his neck. Perhaps he'd simply try his best to forget his sorry excuse for a life. Sure, it wasn't the most pleasant future to strive for, but it was his, and no one would take it away from him. Not this time.

Octavia nodded, snagging his attention and surprising him all at once. Was she agreeing to his statement as it was, or was she acknowledging the double meaning? He couldn't be sure.

"You're right," said June, still standing between the aggressors. "I'm sorry. But that doesn't give any of us the right to treat each other with contempt. We were all friends once, even if some of us can't remember, so let's please try to be civil, at the very least."

"I agree," Leif stated, his gaze whirling to Delta accusingly.

Delta raised her hands in reluctant submission and sauntered out of the sitting room through an arched doorway.

"We need some ground rules, then," said Quintin.

"Good idea," Octavia seconded, turning her gaze from the empty doorway to Quintin. "First, we'll keep our magic to a minimum in your presence, until you're more comfortable."

"To be safe, let's keep chatter of the good old days to a minimum too," Tripp chimed in, lifting his head to face them. "It's triggering to be reminded of all of the things we should remember but can't."

"Perfectly reasonable," Octavia affirmed, glancing at the others to see if they agreed. She was met with three nods of approval.

"And lastly, we'll all try our best to be civil," June concluded.

"Deal," Leif decreed, solidifying their strange pact.

"What about Delta?" Sage asked, their eyes boring fiery holes into the wall of the room Delta had disappeared into.

"I'll talk to her," Jiro assured them, "but I can't promise she'll stop being so bitchy. That's just how she is."

"I think we can all adjust our expectations where Delta is concerned," Octavia replied, turning to face Sage again.

"Yeah, all right," Sage huffed.

"It's time for your lesson." Thaddeus appeared in the doorway, beckoning toward Leif, Jiro, and Tripp. "Please, will you follow me?"

The trio followed Thaddeus into the next room, leaving the rest behind in awkward silence. After that debacle, Leif was grateful for the change in scenery.

By the look of it, this room was the coven's library. A large, embellished Bonaparte fireplace, alight with a roaring fire, stood at the center of a wall comprised of floor-to-ceiling, cherry wood bookshelves. The thousands of books adorning the shelves came in every shape, size, and color imaginable. Most were tattered and worn, a likely side effect of decades of use.

Normally, Leif would've beamed at the sight of such an obviously beloved collection, but this wasn't a normal collection of books. This was a collection of grimoires. He clenched his jaw tightly to stave off the nausea.

In the middle of the library, a massive ornate rug covered the glossy hardwood flooring. Five wooden upholstered chairs were arranged in a circle at the rug's center, likely dragged in from the dining room. Delta was already seated, surveying her surroundings.

Jiro quickly took the seat to her right and leaned over to whisper something in her ear. Whatever he said was not to her liking, if her pursed lips were any indication. She wholly ignored Leif and Tripp as they took the seats to her left.

The group's mutual discomfort was rough and abrasive, sawing painfully against Leif's already frayed nerves. As they sat in silence, waiting for Thaddeus to begin the lesson, their nervous tics were on full display. Tripp picked at his chipped nail polish while Jiro's heel bounced up and down. Leif wiped cold sweat from his brow with the sleeve of his sweater. Slowly, he forced his breaths into an even, steady rhythm. Delta might've looked as cool as a cucumber to anyone else, but Leif hadn't missed her occasional deep, anxious breaths.

Trying to distract himself from his own anxiety, Leif looked down to admire the elaborate pattern on the rug. There were several deep indents in the fabric. They must've removed whatever furniture was usually here and replaced them with these chairs.

Why wouldn't they just leave the space as it was?

Thaddeus finally took the remaining seat in the circle and crossed his legs. The crackling fire at his back tossed his face into shadow, despite the natural light seeping in through the large windows on the adjacent wall.

"Moving the furniture was no problem at all," Thaddeus said, correctly guessing the question etched in the lines of Leif's face. "Jocasta and I might look our age, but you seem to have forgotten we have magic at our disposal. We only had to lift a finger." Thaddeus paused, smiling to himself. "We used to have a classroom in the basement when the others were younger, but once they moved on to their independent studies, we converted the space into a potions workroom for June, so we'll make do with the library for now."

Leif nodded a wordless thanks, but it did little to relay his gratitude, since Delta chose to scoff at the same exact time.

Thaddeus graciously ignored her and pressed on. "Now, you've made it clear that your goal is to get answers regarding your kidnapping. In order for me to help you, I need to know what your tentative plan is and your timeline."

"Garren probably won't be home until the end of the month," Jiro explained. "He's on a hunt in the pacific northwest."

The corners of Thaddeus's mouth tugged downward at the mention of an active witch hunt, but he recovered quickly. "That gives us about three weeks, which is a very tight timeline. How often will you be available to train?"

Leif looked around at the others before replying, "Daily."

"Good, and your plan?"

"Basically nonexistent at the moment. We know magic will give us the element of surprise, but since we're starting from ground zero, I'm not sure how much of an advantage it will actually give us beyond that."

"I understand," Thaddeus murmured, now thinking aloud. "Maybe we should take lessons from you as well." Thaddeus chuckled slightly at their pinched expressions. "Well, you're all trained witch hunters. You know their advantages and weaknesses, their typical fighting tactics. Being privy to that information also gives you an advantage. And if we're going to be truly helpful to you during the confrontation, we should know about witch hunters as well."

"You're planning to confront Garren with us?" Tripp asked, his eyes narrowed, skeptical.

"Of course. The entire coven will," Thaddeus confirmed, patiently folding his hands in his lap.

Tripp rubbed his forehead, disbelief chiseling grooves beneath his hand. "Why would you put yourselves in harm's way like that? Why not just train us and leave us to fight our own battles?"

Thaddeus tapped his foot in the air as he explained, "That's not the way of our coven. We never stand alone. But we also have our own desires. We hope to obtain new information that could help break Octavia's hex."

Tripp swallowed thickly and leaned against the back of his chair, apparently at a loss for words.

"Now, once we get into training a bit, we can work together to come up with a strategy. There's no need to put the cart before the horse." Thaddeus rose from his chair to grab a book from one of the shelves on the wall behind him. "Let's begin, shall we?"

Their first lesson consisted of the basics. They learned about grimoires; apparently, most of the Salem coven's grimoires were kept within this very room. The rest resided under the protection of the Salem Archives Library, which is why Jocasta had stayed connected to the employees there. After reviewing several grimoires from the library's bookshelves himself, Leif determined that witches were meticulous in their record-keeping and note-taking. The sheer level of detail contained within the pages of those spell books was astounding.

Thaddeus also briefly recounted the history of magic. The practice of witchcraft had been documented across almost every continent and culture since humans had invented written language. Thousands of witches over the ages had dedicated their lives to investigating the source of magic. No single source had ever been identified, so it became widely believed that magic derived from nature itself, in all its various forms. Magic was a product of the powerful connections that bound all things together—like an intricate spiderweb, perpetually weaving and bridging. Witches simply had to learn how to manipulate these connections, how to intertwine their will with nature's.

Ever since Thaddeus had stepped foot into Leif's life, it'd been apparent he was a man of few words. However, it was turning out that Thaddeus had plenty to say when it came to magic, and a smile often blessed his face as he lectured. Not only was he clearly a passionate educator, but he was also exceptionally talented at it. Despite himself, Leif often found his interest piqued. The corners of his mouth had made several sneaky attempts at ticking upward, but he refused to acknowledge them—for that would require admitting just how much of his previous beliefs had been fallacy. Regardless of his intellectual curiosity, he wasn't going to let his hatred of magic be one of them.

Lastly, Thaddeus spent a fair amount of time explaining the sensation of magic. He described it as a vibration or a hum, small waves of energy that witches could feel in their bodies and the environments around them. According to Thaddeus, connecting with these waves of energy—with magic—could take a lot of practice, which was why many witches didn't harness their full magical abilities until their forties or fifties. Apparently, very few witches were born with innate magical talent, and thus, the most powerful witches were typically the most dedicated.

That realization might've bothered Leif, given their time constraints, if he hadn't been so convinced they didn't need outrageously powerful magic to face Garren. They just needed the element of surprise to stay one step ahead of him.

"What about incantations?" Jiro had asked near the end of their lesson. "Don't you need them to cast spells?"

"The answer to that question isn't a simple yes or no," Thaddeus explained. "Years ago, witches used spoken incantations to channel their magic when casting. Nowadays, however, witches have identified several alternate methods. For some, simply thinking the incantation is sufficient, while others use physical movement to coax their magic in the right direction. But regardless of how a witch chooses to practice their craft, the benefit of limiting spoken incantations is obvious: it provides yet another layer of protection against witch hunters."

Jiro's jaw snapped shut; clearly, he hadn't expected the question would bring them back to the topic of witch hunters.

"Without incantations, witches could hide their identities better—that is, until the witch hunters learned to produce magical items that could sense magic."

Leif thought back to his dagger, which he'd left in its sheath on his bedside table. His calf still felt naked without it, but ever since he'd taken off his necklace, it'd been too hot to touch.

"Out of curiosity," Thaddeus started cautiously, "did Garren ever tell you how those nifty little items can sense magic?"

Leif felt a sharp pang behind his sternum as he sensed yet another unveiling of truth—truth they desperately desired, but never asked for.

"He told us they were forged from a special metal," Delta answered in a frosty tone, "but I'm assuming that was just a bunch of bullshit too."

"Ah, I see. Yes, I guess that was another area in which he chose to mislead you. In truth, those magic items were originally spelled by a witch."

Leif scoffed internally. *Of course, how Shakespearean. It's diabolical—using magic against magical people. It's also hypocritical as hell. But considering the raging shit-show that has been the last forty-eight hours, it tracks.*

"But ho—why?" Jiro stuttered.

"Eventually, the witch hunters became much cleverer than we originally gave them credit for. They captured and forced witches to create magic items for them—a difficult task for our brethren to have achieved, as the spells required are quite advanced. It was brilliant, really, finding a way to use our own magic against us." Thaddeus sighed deeply and rubbed his temple.

A large black Labrador retriever trotted into the room, coming up behind Thaddeus before barking loudly, easily pulling him from his thoughts. "Ah, yes. Thank you for the reminder, Luna," he said as he briefly shook his head. He gave the dog a gentle pat.

"Is she a familiar?" Tripp asked, eyeing the dog distrustfully.

"Yes, Luna is Jocasta's familiar. She was just coming to remind me that lunch will be ready soon. I want to give you a proper tour of the house before we eat."

"Will we be getting familiars too?" Jiro asked, locking gazes with the dog.

Leif suppressed the urge to roll his eyes. *Why does Jiro even care? Does he honestly think having a demon dog is cool?*

"It's always a possibility, but typically only the most powerful witches bond with familiars. You'll have to train hard and hone your craft if you want to catch the attention of a familiar one day." Thaddeus rose from his seat, gesturing for the others to do the same.

"Wicked," Jiro said under his breath.

Guess that answers my question.

"Now, the main floor of the house makes a circle, with the staircase at its center. This hallway leads to the kitchen," Thaddeus began explaining as they walked into the kitchen where Jocasta was hard at work preparing lunch. Leif noticed a spatula hovering in midair above a frying pan, patiently waiting to flip over a sizzling panini. A few moments later, it moved on its own, slipping beneath the browning bread and tossing the sandwich onto its other side.

Jocasta smiled at them over a pitcher of freshly squeezed lemonade as they passed. Leif shook his head in frustration as the citrusy scent reminded him instantly of Octavia. Hazy memories—of skin, lips, and eyes he wished he could forget—flashed before his mind's eye, sending an incredibly awkward pang of guilt darting through his gut. Reflexively, his stomach clenched against the sensation, which was made instantly worse by the sight of a smiling Jocasta holding out a glass for him to take. Her eyebrow ticked up almost infinitesimally as he shook his head, denying the offer. *Too familiar.* The pang deepened, digging back toward his spine. He couldn't look away fast enough.

Forcing his tense muscles to relax felt like trying to move a mountain. Impossible.

Through the next door was the dining room. The mahogany table was massive, large enough to comfortably seat twelve people. A dazzling chandelier hung above its center. At the end of the long rectangular dining room, they found themselves back in the entryway before descending the large central staircase.

In the basement, they passed a small potions room where June was working diligently, humming along to music playing from a small, wireless speaker. But an enormous wood-paneled room took up the majority of the lower level. When they entered, they found the space almost completely void of furniture.

Quintin, who'd shed his sweater in favor of a plain white undershirt, was manipulating a shimmering portal to their left, the exposed skin of his arms glistening with sweat. It appeared as if he was trying to stretch the portal large enough for several people to pass through. Leif chuckled to himself as Quintin nervously eyed the portal's shuddering edges.

"Think you could help me out here, Sage?" Quintin grunted through gritted teeth.

"You wish," Sage laughed from the corner of the room, where they sat at a table with multiple transparent glass containers laid upon it. They were separating water from what looked to be a variety of substances. In contrast to Quintin, who looked as if he was mere moments away from bursting a blood vessel in his brain, Sage hadn't broken a sweat and went through the motions of their practice with ease. The speed at which they could separate the different components from the water mixtures was thoroughly impressive. Leif had a hunch that if there was ever a witch with a natural knack for magic, it was Sage.

Thaddeus cleared his throat as the others filed into the room behind Leif, finally drawing the attention of the witches. Quintin's portal quickly receded while the previously separated liquids within Sage's glass containers mixed together again.

"Sorry for interrupting," Thaddeus said to Quintin and Sage before turning his attention back to the group. "This is the training room. We keep it pretty empty so you have space to practice."

When they ascended the central staircase, they found the top two floors of the house consisted of many bedrooms and bathrooms, as well as an office. On the top floor, they came across Octavia, spread out on the floor of an oppressively purple bedroom amongst a sea of open grimoires. Her forehead crinkled as she rapidly flipped through the Latin dictionary in her hand. Dark eyes flicked up from the page when they entered.

"Any luck?" Thaddeus ventured to ask.

"Of course not," she huffed, blowing at several stray strands of hair.

"Perhaps it's time for a break?" he suggested with even more caution. Octavia had obviously done a marvelous job of training her family to walk on eggshells around her. Leif sneered at her blatant hubris.

Octavia took a deep breath before she looked up at him, declining with a soft shake of her head. It wasn't her remarkably poor attempt at a pleasant facial expression that caught Leif's attention; it was her eyes. For the first time since they'd met, her eyes were dull, shallow, and—he realized with a pang—hopeless.

Hot, stifling anger prickled his skin, causing the fine hairs on his neck to stand on end. *Why am I feeling so . . . frustrated?* Thoroughly jarred, Leif did his best to shove the emotion away as Thaddeus closed the bedroom door behind them.

They trooped back downstairs to the dining room, where they nibbled on sinfully delicious tomato, mozzarella, and pesto paninis, trying their best to avoid unnecessary conversation. Delta was the only successful one, not uttering a single word the entire meal, even though Jocasta had asked her not one, not two, but several direct questions. Delta simply stared at the poor woman with a sharp, icy gaze. Eventually—and quite reluctantly—Jocasta got the hint and let Delta be.

Jiro, on the other hand, was rapidly warming up to the witches, chatting happily with Quintin, June, and Thaddeus throughout the meal. Somehow, he was having a much easier time compartmentalizing than Leif was. Leif had no idea how Jiro could be so impressionable. They couldn't even trust the man who'd raised them, so how could he sit there making small talk and laughing with these strangers like it was nothing? Perhaps Jiro's ability to trust hadn't been completely annihilated by Garren's betrayal, but Leif's had.

The rest of their afternoon was spent in the library, practicing connecting to their magic. As Tripp pointed out, the exercise was essentially meditation.

At first, Leif struggled magnificently at sitting still and quieting his mind. His thoughts kept floating back to that defeated look in Octavia's eyes. It'd been so disturbingly out of character. The Octavia he knew was determined, vicious, and *never* accepted defeat. What happened since that night in Salem? He figured he may never find out. After all, he wasn't supposed to care anymore. Octavia was a witch—was his enemy, his target, up until a day ago—and he was . . . no, he couldn't think about that right now either. He had to focus.

But at the moment, focus was almost painful. No, not *almost* painful. It *was* painful.

In an attempt to pull his thoughts away from Octavia and the predicament he and his siblings were currently in, he took mental stock of his body. And what he found . . . hurt. His muscles ached from the weight of the truth, his chest constricted with loss, his stomach twisted in fear. He was carrying his emotions around physically, and shit if that didn't make them even more real. So, he breathed through the pain and visited each affected area, giving the emotions space to be felt, to move, to vacate. It wasn't a cure-all. He still felt like crap, but the stillness, the breathing, it helped.

After an hour or so of fidgeting and sighing, Leif's breath eventually found a steady rhythm and his body stilled, no longer seeped in discomfort.

There! He inhaled sharply when he finally felt the pulse of his magic humming through his body at a constant frequency. A dull roaring like the ocean filled his ears, almost drowning out the sound of his own thoughts.

I recognize this sensation. But from where? It feels like . . . like the thrum of an idling engine.

Sweat coated his body as an unfamiliar heat flared beneath his skin. Alarmed, Leif tried shifting in his seat, but an invisible weight pinned him to the chair. He couldn't move an inch—couldn't speak, couldn't breathe. The weight of his magic was overwhelming.

He tried to call out, but instead of words filling his mouth, a smoky, metallic taste did, as if he'd licked sunbathed copper. Inconceivably, the taste soothed him, evoking memories of long summer days spent adventuring the city with his siblings. He relaxed, giving into the pressure instead of fighting it.

He touched his magic cautiously with his mind, then was briefly overcome by a peculiar prodding sensation before the frequency spiked in recognition. It was as if his magic had assessed Leif's intentions before giving him permission to continue, like being rapidly frisked by airport security, only way more invasive.

Once the connection was made and his entire body hummed comfortably with the bond, he imagined himself floating on an ocean surface, moving with the waves, letting the current push him wherever it pleased. When Leif finally opened his eyes, his hands were glowing intensely, and the air around him was as warm as a summer's day.

Shit. This is . . . amazing.

"Well done!" Jocasta cooed.

And, just like that, the balloon of excitement in Leif's chest burst with a *pop*. Her approval only made Leif nauseous, the panini sitting like a ball of lead in his stomach. He imagined returning to land and rising from the waves—severing the connection with his magic, letting the light fade and the warmth ebb away. He didn't want to admit that his body felt strangely hollow now without the thrum of the engine. The first few seconds of acclimating to his magic had been terrifying, but the last few had been exhilarating. He hated that he was already looking forward to trying it again.

During the remainder of their session, Delta successfully changed the color of her hair from black to a coppery auburn, but she refused to try anything more than that. Leif guessed the shock of seeing an unfamiliar reflection in the mirror was likely lingering from the day before.

Jiro and Tripp both felt that they also successfully connected with their magic; however, they did nothing notable during the exercise. Thaddeus reassured them that was quite normal, especially since they weren't using their magic to cast any specific spells, and he reiterated that it might take some time before they could determine their magical specialties.

But they didn't have the luxury of time. Leif's nerves wavered under the weight of that knowledge.

Tomorrow they'd be starting basic spell craft and enchantments, so Jocasta and Thaddeus encouraged them to get a good night's rest. But Leif knew resting was the last thing he was going to do.

CHAPTER 23
LEIF

L eif spent the night brooding, pacing back and forth in his bedroom, trying desperately to gain control of the whirlwind of emotions he was trying not to feel.

He'd never been any good at dealing with his emotions. He usually repressed them or projected them onto unsuspecting passersby, so he hadn't gained the emotional intelligence necessary to safely and properly "feel" his emotions. He knew that much about himself. Regardless, these emotions were too big, too overwhelming. If he retreated back to his typical coping mechanisms now, the emotional storm would probably kill him.

Leif fell backward on his bed, releasing a frustrated breath as he stared at the ceiling. He hadn't even really started processing yet, and already he wanted to do something, anything, to avoid feeling these feelings. He wanted to envelope himself in static noise, drowning out everything but the feeling of his beating heart. Instead, he took a deep breath.

No more avoiding.

Using the meditation techniques he'd learned earlier that day, Leif cleared his mind of everything except how his current situation made him feel. Immediately, anger blazed like a raging inferno. Leif's chest constricted, his lungs so tight he felt dizzy. Then the tips of his fingers tingled as if he'd just taken a drag from a cigarette. He wanted to stop. He wanted to run. But he forced himself to lie still, to continue breathing, no matter how hard it was or how much pain he felt. Because . . . because that was the truth of it, wasn't it? His anger was a mask for the pain.

His father—the man he loved and idolized above all others—had deceived him. For the majority of his life, Leif had thought Garren loved him, but deception wasn't love. Had he ever been loved? Had he ever deserved to be?

Hurt. Sadness. Fear. That's what I really feel . . . and it fucking blows.

Leif shoved a fistful of hair from his face and closed his eyes, blocking out the dim lamp light and cocooning himself in temporary darkness. He'd never been afraid of the dark, even as a child. He'd always found it to be a safe harbor, a place of peace and tranquility. In the darkness, away from judging eyes, he could be himself. Not a witch. Not a witch hunter. Just Leif.

Leif relaxed, carried by the tide of his depressed thoughts until he came across one that made his entire body tense: *What if . . . what if the truth was under our noses this entire time?*

When he opened his eyes again, he had an idea. Bounding up the stairs two at a time, Leif passed the other apartments until he reached the top floor. He didn't have a key to unlock the door, so he'd either have to pick the lock or barrel the door down. Picking it would probably be easiest.

Just as he was about to head back downstairs to retrieve a pin and credit card, a hand reached out in front of him, holding a lock picking kit. Leif looked up at Jiro's somber face and smiled sadly.

"It's time," Jiro said. "We need to figure out how this all really went down. I can't keep feeling like this."

"Me either," Leif agreed. He took the kit from Jiro and dropped to his knees in front of the locked door.

"Me three," Tripp called from the top of the stairs behind them. His eyes were red and puffy again, and Leif's heart squeezed painfully at the sight. Tripp was far more in tune with his emotions than the rest of them. He felt everything deeply, and Leif wanted nothing more than to protect him from the pain he must've been drowning in. He wanted to protect them all.

Jiro clasped Tripp on the shoulder as he joined them. With his brothers at his back, Leif returned to the lock and kit before him.

"Where did you get this?" Leif asked as he grabbed two of the metal instruments and began maneuvering them in the keyhole.

"Amazon Prime," Jiro replied with a shrug.

Leif laughed deeply as he fiddled with the lock. After several minutes spent in silence, the lock clicked open. Leif zipped up the kit and handed it back to Jiro.

"All right, let's split up. Call out if you find anything odd or incriminating," Leif instructed as he stood up again. He reached for the door handle when a venomous voice reached his ears.

"Were you really going to do this without me?" Delta asked from behind them. Leif turned to find her at the top of the stairs with a hand still on the banister, looking far more docile than she sounded in a red robe and slippers, her short hair in a tiny pony-tail at the nape of her neck.

"We knew you'd hear us and come stalking," Tripp replied, waving a hand dismissively. "You always do."

Delta rolled her eyes but said no more, getting in line behind them as Leif opened the door and entered Garren's apartment. None of them had been in this apartment in over five years. This was Garren's private space. As children, they'd only been invited in when they were sick or upset, but when they'd reached adult-hood, those invites had stopped altogether.

The apartment was almost as bare as Leif's, not a single dec-oration in sight apart from the far wall, which was plastered from floor to ceiling with maps, photos, and handwritten notes. To an outsider, it might've looked like Garren made a hobby of solving cold cases, but they knew better. That wall was the product of decades of hard work hunting witches. Leif's mouth grew dry at the sight of it.

Only a couch, lamp, and television furnished the living room. Tripp walked to the couch and began searching, pulling the cushions off and looking in the crevices. Jiro joined him. After they deemed the couch cleared, Jiro eyed the cushions again, pulling out a small pocketknife. Tripp smirked as he tossed the nearest one Jiro's way. He caught it and used the pocketknife to tear the cushion fabric, then began fisting the stuffing out onto the floor. Tripp was toppling over the couch to scan the bottom as Delta began inspecting the coat closet across from the door.

Leif took it upon himself to check the flat-screen TV mounted to the wall. The back was bare, and Garren wasn't tech savvy enough to be able to hide something of value inside and then put it back together.

They moved into the dining room and kitchen, ransacking to their heart's content. Delta had the brilliant idea of breaking Garren's dinnerware against the TV in the living room. So, they took turns, chucking plates, cups, and mugs against the wall, watching each of them fracture and break with immense satisfaction. It was only after the damage was done that Leif felt the heavy hands of guilt fall upon his shoulders. His back twinged under their weight, rib cage threatening to cave in. But then he remembered why they were here, what they were looking for, and the remembering straightened his spine, brought air back into his lungs. He could do this. He *needed* to do this.

After clearing the kitchen, they moved to the bedroom and adjoining bathroom.

It only took Tripp five minutes to clear the bathroom. "The most damning piece of evidence in there is an unopened bottle of Viagra," he said. "Why in the hell would you go through the trouble of getting a prescription and then not use it?"

The others had been tearing the mattress apart. They knelt among a pile of stuffing next to the gutted mattress, their brows slick with sweat. Delta released a breathless laugh as she stood.

"Toss this back on the bed frame," Leif instructed, "and keep checking the rest of the room. If we don't find anything here, we're shit out of luck." He turned to search the dresser, emptying the drawers of clothes and removing them to inspect for false bottoms. Nothing. Completely clean.

Tripp inspected the bookcase, flipping through each individual book, checking for hidden compartments. Delta rummaged through the closet, diligently turning out the pockets of every item of clothing. Jiro checked the desktop computer's hard drive, deeming it clean as a whistle.

"The bastard knew how to keep a secret," Jiro breathed, blowing a tuft of hair out of his eyes.

"There's got to be something in here," Delta exclaimed, turning in a circle, looking for places they could've missed.

But Leif knew Garren was meticulous. They should've expected this. He was adept at remaining invisible until he chose not to be, always waiting for the perfect moment to strike. The chance of them beating him at his own game was frustratingly slim. Leif cursed under his breath as he scanned the room again, looking for any stone they might've left unturned, no matter how small.

"We checked everywhere, D," Tripp said. "Garren's been doing this shit longer than us. He's just better." Sighing heavily, Tripp leaned against the now-empty dresser.

The dresser slid under his weight, revealing a sliver of a hole in the wall behind it.

"Tripp, stand back up," Leif commanded, walking over to the wall.

Tripp moved out of the way, and they all gathered around Leif. He ran his fingers over the hole in the drywall and pushed the dresser further away, exposing the small cavity.

The hole was only big enough for a single hand to reach through. Delta, being the smallest, volunteered and reached deep into the hole. When she pulled her arm back out, she was holding a plump, sealed envelope that had a single flash drive taped to the outside.

Delta ripped the flash drive off and handed it to Jiro, who whirled back to the computer. While he pulled the files up, Delta broke the seal and removed the documents from the envelope. Tripp and Leif watched over her shoulder as she laid them out on the desk next to Jiro and assessed them, eyes roving over the pages.

"They're our foster and adoption papers," Delta finally concluded. She held them up to the lamp light, searching for hidden messages. "They're clean," she murmured. "They have the official stamp seal of the state of Massachusetts, so they have to be legit, right?" Her gaze bounced around the group.

"Maybe he didn't lie to us about everything," Tripp said with a shrug. But Leif knew there was no preserving Garren's dignity, even if he had followed the law in this regard.

"Oh, he lied all right," Jiro whispered in a hollow voice, his eyes glued to the computer screen. "He lied about everything."

Leif could've sworn his heart skipped a beat, but not from surprise—from met expectations.

"What do you mean?" Tripp asked. His palms smacked the desk as he crowded in, looking over Jiro's shoulder.

"This flash drive contains everything. All of the evidence we need. All the information from the police report from the night of the attack. Our missing persons reports." Jiro paused, and the others shared grave glances. "There are even incriminating messages between Garren and the chief of police insinuating that Garren bribed him to share this information. He kept the missing person search isolated to Vermont." Tripp's fingernails clawed against the desk as Delta gnawed on her lower lip. "There are also messages here between Garren and some hacker, who, by the looks of it, was able to create perfect replicas of formal Massachusetts adoption papers. He paid a pretty fucking penny for those," Jiro exclaimed, then gave a low whistle. "One hundred thousand dollars."

Leif scoffed. *This is more like it. Exactly what I expect from him. He's good at this, far too good.* His abs tensed against the coiling in his gut.

"Why the fuck did we grow up in this shit hole if Garren had a hundred thousand dollars to spare?" Delta whined.

"Guess he spent his life's savings to keep us hidden and compliant," Jiro murmured, still toggling through files on the computer.

Leif watched as Jiro opened the last folder of files on the flash drive. It looked like it was full of surveillance pictures. Jiro clicked through them slowly. Most featured people Leif didn't recognize, but as the photos got noticeably older, the resolution far below today's standards, he started getting flashes of recognition from the people in the photos. A short, red-haired woman smiling, hand in hand with a tall brunet man. A beautiful Black woman with short curly hair, cradling a toddler against her hip. A young couple, both with dark hair and even darker eyes, sitting at a cafe patio, grinning from ear to ear at an infant in a stroller.

Those had to be June, Quintin, and Octavia's parents. Leif's eyes stung and his heartbeat galloped, making him dizzy, as he stared at the photos. He reached out to the corner of the desk for support.

Delta looked at him with wide eyes. "What? What is it?"

"It's their parents," Leif choked out. "Garren found them. He's the reason they're dead."

Delta's mouth fell open as she returned her gaze to the screen. The next photo pictured her mother and father getting into a car. Leif watched his sister's features twist in rage, then regret, then longing, until tears as thick and heavy as rain drops fell from her eyes.

Next was a photograph of Tripp's mom shopping. The computer monitor shook slightly as Tripp trembled, his hands still on the desk. After a moment, Leif could hear Tripp's teeth chattering too but had no idea how to help him.

Then came a photo of Jiro's parents doing laundry at a laundromat. As if suspended in time, Jiro froze. His eyes didn't wander the image, nor did he blink. Leif was concerned he'd stopped breathing until Jiro suddenly hunched over, catching his head in his palms. Only then did his brother let a sob pass his lips.

Silently, Leif leaned over Jiro to tap the keyboard, moving on to the next image.

It was a photo of Leif's mother, sitting alone on a park bench. The photo was hazy and slightly pixelated, as if a printed photo had been scanned into a digital file. She was incredibly young, not a day over eighteen.

Leif's teeth ground together against a dreadful sense of foreboding. Jiro noticed him tense and lifted his face from his hands. Jiro's gaze was red and swollen but surprisingly soft as he waited.

"Keep going," Leif ordered quietly.

Jiro obeyed, toggling through the next ten or fifteen photos. Every single one of them pictured Leif's mother. Grocery shopping, getting gas, reading a book at a bus stop, out on a date with his father, coming out of a church in her wedding dress.

This was evidence. Evidence that Garren had stalked the coven for years. Perhaps an entire decade or more. But the photos of his mother hadn't been taken by a man formulating a plan to destroy. Garren had taken those for his own sick, twisted pleasure.

Leif's limbs began to shake then too, his heart beating so fast it felt like it'd stopped pumping oxygen to his brain. *If only I'd done this years ago. If only I'd known where to look. If only I'd had the courage to question Garren's authority earlier. If only, if only, if only . . .*

His vision blurred as Jiro exited out of the files and removed and pocketed the flash drive, then turned to face him.

"We'll make the sick bastard pay. I promise," Jiro bit out in a voice more ferocious than Leif had ever heard from him. His expression was warped by hatred, but his ferocity was grounding, bringing Leif back into himself.

Tripp's hand gripped Leif's shoulder in silent agreement. Delta's red-rimmed eyes glowed with vengeance. Together, they would bring the enemy down.

The true enemy.

CHAPTER 24
LEIF

"I still can't believe I let you talk me into this, hunter," Sage scoffed as they shrugged out of their coat. They hung it on a hook on the back of the door as they closed it behind them.

"My logic's solid," Leif reminded them. "We both know Jocasta and Thaddeus would've been pissed if we'd woken them up this late at night."

Sage grumbled, "I'd have gotten an earful, that's for sure." They shrugged. "That's the price we pay for their genius, I guess. No midnight office hours."

Leif didn't know what he'd expected Sage's room to look like, but it somehow wasn't this. Their perpetually sarcastic attitude somehow drastically contradicted the sea of thriving houseplants before him.

Sage must've read the surprise on Leif's face. "What? I like plants." They smiled. "And they like me back. Just look at this baddie monstera." They pointed to a flourishing, leafy plant in the corner.

Leif dipped his chin before clearing his throat. "So, um—I wanted to get your advice on something." His hands dug deeper into the pockets of his coat.

Sage pulled out an oak wood chair from a matching desk. They plopped down on it backward, legs straddling the backrest. "Yeah, so you said back at the house. What's this about?" Their squinted hazel eyes sparkled with mischief. "Octavia?"

Leif scoffed. "No."

Sage's forehead wrinkled disbelievingly. "Wanna try that again?"

Scowling, he said, "Octavia and I aren't a thing anymore. That ended the second all of *this* started."

Sage nodded dramatically. "Uh-huh, uh-huh. 'Cause it's just that easy to flip the switch off. No sweat." They smirked, shifting forward to lean their elbows on the backrest.

"Yeah, it is." Leif's temper was rising precariously. He took a deep breath, trying to lock it down.

"But you can't hate Tavi. No matter how hard you try." Sage laughed. "Poor thing."

Leif shot them a withering glare.

"What?" Mockingly, Sage held their hands up in the air, palms facing forward, as if Leif's glare was a firearm. "I'm only an innocent bystander . . . an innocent bystander that had to listen to the two of you screw all night." Their expression was wicked: a twisted, curling smirk complimented by a nauseatingly knowing gaze. "Sorry. The walls are thin—but it sounded like it won't be easy to forget."

Leif choked on air, his face flaming in an instant. He averted his gaze, coughing profusely into the crook of his elbow. It took him a moment to catch his breath.

Fuck. They were able to throw me off guard so easily. Now I'm pissed.

Leif whirled on Sage, only to find their face as angry as his. "So, what is it you want from me, then?" Their pale lips pressed into a thin line, and fire burned behind their eyes.

Damn, they know how to be intimidating when they want to be.

Leif swallowed his pride. If Sage could turn on a dime, so could he. "You're more powerful than the others. Somehow, your magic comes easier. I want you to teach me how."

A flicker of surprise dashed their scowl away, but only for a moment. "I can't."

Leif bristled, his stomach dropping. "Why not?"

Sage averted their gaze, looking toward the bedroom window and the night beyond. "I don't know why I'm stronger than the others."

"Come on. There has to be a trick to it."

They clenched their jaw, a muscle pulling tight in their cheek. "Damn, you're arrogant." They sighed. "There's not, okay? And even if there was, why the hell would I teach it to you?" Sage returned their gaze to Leif's, a gaze meant to sear.

"Because, right now, I want justice more than I want air in my lungs." Leif's hands fisted at his sides. "And I can tell you want it too."

Leif took a bold step forward. Sage tracked it, their tense hazel eyes dipping to measure the distance between them. "You're strong and capable," he continued. "And you don't let *anyone* fuck with the people you love. Whatever it takes. You'd do it . . . for them—for justice." The muscle in Sage's cheek flexed. "You're different from the others in more ways than one." Leif paused. "Desire for vengeance runs through my veins too. But to have it, I need *power*. As much as I can get."

Leif stared, unblinking, as Sage swallowed.

Checkmate.

Sage huffed before muttering something under their breath. To Leif it sounded suspiciously like, "Guess I get what she sees."

They stood, their face inches from Leif's. "I can only teach you what's worked for me."

The weight in Leif's chest lightened. Sage frowned at the smile he couldn't keep tied down. "You're too used to getting what you want, you know that?"

Leif laughed and nodded as he backed away a few paces. "So, what works for you?"

They crossed their arms over their chest. "My magic works in a few different ways. I can conjure the elements or transmute them depending on the spells I use. Do you have any idea how yours works yet?"

Leif considered this for a moment. "Transmutation, I think. I feel the light in my body, or in the air around me, and then I just reach out and . . . turn it on."

"Good. That gives us a starting point."

Leif worked with Sage for an hour.

Their magic was deeply rooted in movement, so they taught him various gestures and hand signs that might help strengthen and focus his casting. Sage was a good mentor—patient, straightforward, concise. They saw every mistake as an opportunity for improvement. Leif had never been instructed like that before. He was so used to viewing his errors as failures. Their approach to coaching made him feel comfortable, safe.

Once Sage let their guard down, they were ridiculously easy to be around.

"Okay, now try it with a spell from the grimoire," Sage said, dropping to sit on the edge of their bed.

Leif studied the open page of the grimoire lying on Sage's desk. He'd borrowed it from the house's library.

Following the notes carefully, he straightened, adjusting his posture. He placed his hands before the center of his chest, held out an arm's length away. He connected his arms at the wrists, palms of his hands facing forward.

Leif closed his eyes. A deep breath. The low thrum of the engine. The current flowing in his veins. Floating along with it. Ears ringing, shoulders heavy. Smoke and metal on his tongue.

Okay, ready.

He twisted his wrists, hands pinwheeling, as he thought, as loud and hard as he could, *IGNIS!*

Leif opened his eyes.

Light exploded from his palms, shining with the intensity of a football stadium spotlight. Heat quickly followed, pulsing off him in waves, raising the temperature in the room considerably. Several beads of sweat dripped down his back.

Sage had covered their eyes with their forearm. "I think you got it," they chuckled.

Leif closed his eyes again, mentally stepping out of the current, as he lowered his arms. Bright flashes of color winked behind his eyelids like fireworks. He'd have to be careful in the future, otherwise he might accidentally blind someone—like himself.

"Just keep practicing with the addition of small hand movements like that and you'll get better in no time," Sage said as they stood from the bed.

Leif released a relieved breath. "Thanks, Sage. Really." He grabbed his coat from the back of the door. He'd been forced to take it off when they'd started practicing. The heat his magic generated had him sweating like a pig.

"It's whatever." They shrugged. "It's not like you'll get stronger than me anyway, so there really wasn't much of a risk either way."

Leif laughed. It was surprising, given how Sage first came off, but they were *funny*. Like really funny. He was honestly shocked how much he enjoyed their company.

"Why are you looking at me like that?" Sage asked, raking a hand over their pink buzzcut. "No, no, no—uh-uh. We're not besties, lover boy. Save that face for your hunter buddies."

Leif's smile fell from his face like a stone in a lake—heavily.

"This was a one-time thing, okay?" they continued. "If you need more help, go to Jo or Thad."

All sense of camaraderie evaporated, like early morning fog under a sweltering summer sun. Leif's eyes narrowed as he resisted the urge to rub the center of his chest, right where their harsh words were meant to wound.

"Roger that?" As they cocked their head, their wire-rimmed glasses reflected the golden lamp light with a flash.

He sneered. "Loud and clear."

As Leif closed Sage's bedroom door behind him, he heard them mutter again, only this time he swore he heard, "At least he's smart. Another point to blondie." A pause. "Octavia's in deep shit."

Leif's smile returned with a vengeance as the door clicked shut.

Leif walked down the coven's apartment hallway. He told himself he would keep his gaze to the floor—that he wouldn't let it catch his eye. But it did.

Her bedroom door hung slightly ajar, the soft notes of a somber song wafting out into the hall.

Keep walking, Leif commanded his feet. But he stopped. Walked to the door. Rapped it softly with the back of his knuckles. *What the hell are you doing? Turn around and leave!*

"Come in," she called, her voice low and rough from fatigue.

Every nerve in his body sparked to life, as if electrified.

Walk away. Right now.

But his blood called out to her, pulling him through the door like metal to a magnet.

Octavia was lying on her bed in an oversized band tee and pajama shorts. Her long hair was wrapped in a messy knot at the crown of her head. One ankle rested on the opposite knee, the gap between her legs a perfect triangle. Through the space he watched her expression change as she looked from her phone to him. Leif paused just inside the door, leaning a shoulder against the door frame.

Her relaxed brow furrowed, and her sleepy eyes narrowed. He wasn't a welcome visitor.

Good. This is good.

She sat up straight, discarding her phone on the comforter. "What are you doing here?" she asked, her tone turning icy.

He used the sharp pang in his chest to fuel the fire in his stomach. "Here to get some advice from Sage. Nothing to do with you."

Her dark eyes narrowed further. "Then why the hell are you in *my* room?"

Leif looked around, scanning the space. The only other time he'd seen it, it'd been cloaked in darkness. He cocked his head to the side, thinking he liked it better that way.

These four walls—this room where we . . . no, not right now. Don't even go there. All that matters is that it haunts me. Endlessly. That's why I'm here. For closure.

He settled on, "I have something to say."

"What?" Octavia scoffed, rising from the bed, her eyes never leaving his. "You didn't say enough yesterday morning?"

So she did catch that. Also good.

"Just want to make sure we're on the same page."

Octavia stalked a few steps closer. "Nope, I think we're good. Your message was crystal clear. 'You are our enemy' is pretty hard to misinterpret."

Leif's jaw clenched. "I know it's harsh, but it's the truth. We can't just stop being hunters overnight."

She smirked. "Right. Of course. That explains why you're here snooping around for extra magic lessons—because acclimating has been *so* very hard for you."

Leif released a shallow breath. "You don't know what you're talking about."

"Fine. I don't." She took another step and then another. "But neither do you."

She was less than a foot away, and the citrus smell of her was overwhelming. Leif breathed her in deeply. A wave of dizziness crashed over him, making him grateful he was supported by the wall.

"Regardless." Leif jerked his chin toward the bed. "You have to forget what happened between us."

Octavia smiled. It was the opposite of nice. Her gaze flicked to the bed before rounding back to him. "You really want me to forget?"

Leif could only nod. His whole body warmed, every nerve ending tingling. She was too much—and at the same time, just enough. Perfectly enough.

The devilish smile fell from her lips. "Fine." Her gaze sharpened—from daggers to scalpels. "You forget it too."

Leif's pulse roared in his ears, too fast, too loud. "Done."

"Then we're finished here." She whirled around, walking back to her bed. Leif hated himself for tracking her every movement. Forcibly tearing his eyes away, he turned to leave.

"Leif." He stopped, glancing back at Octavia over his shoulder. Blue eyes met brown. "You are not my enemy."

The words sliced him like a knife—cutting deeply, savagely. Leif opened his mouth to slash back, but she cut him off.

"Prove me wrong."

Leif thought about those three words the entire commute home: *prove me wrong.*

I can't.

Chapter 25
OCTAVIA

Non est umbra sine lumine.

Eyes squeezed shut, Octavia loosed a shuddering breath as she fisted the roots of her hair in her hands. With a foot, she shoved away the books lying open around her before falling back against the plush carpet. Staring at the excessively purple walls of her childhood bedroom, she fought to keep her irritation at bay.

If only Grandma was as concerned with helping me translate these books as she is with getting the newbies to fall in love with magic, who knows? I could be casting spells and kicking ass right now.

Octavia winced as the voice sounded again, the hex reverberating against the inside of her skull, making her more than a little woozy.

Between the brain fog and the endless, echoing voice of her curse—which had only been getting louder and louder—Octavia had been plagued by horribly selfish thoughts. But if she was being honest, most of her thoughts were far worse than the one that just clawed its way to the surface. The thoughts tended to oscillate between baneful resentment and unbridled rage, fueled by the injustice she felt when she saw how quickly her newest covenmates were developing their magic.

Day by day, everyone around her grew stronger, more adept, and more confident. Overnight, Leif and Delta had completely transformed. They began devouring their studies and threw themselves into their training. They were gaining skill at a pace so remarkable it could only be explained by sheer determination. No one could doubt they were pushing their limits.

Octavia, on the other hand, felt like an anchor drifting to the ocean floor, slowly becoming more isolated, more distant, and more maddeningly aimless. Her research, as always, was getting her nowhere, and she wasn't helping the others in any tangible way. What was the point? What was her purpose here?

She still had no idea.

And so, with the dumpster fire raging in her head, Octavia had never been less productive in her life. Apart from her training sessions with Dante, she spent the rest of her time trying to decode the Latin grimoires she'd stolen, spending far too much time in this room. Her grandmother had tried to translate them with magic several times, but there was some kind of protection spell in place, safeguarding the information within. So, ever the determined soldier, Octavia dove in headfirst with a Latin dictionary and Google Translate in hand.

From what she'd gathered so far, the grimoires contained conjuring spells. Many of the spells required multiple witches, some requiring so much magical power that even their coven of ten wouldn't have been sufficient. Octavia often stopped to marvel at how large covens must've been at one point in time for spells like this to have been created.

She could only suffer the madness of translating for so long, though, and often found herself helping Tripp and her grandmother cook. It turned out that Tripp had a real passion for cooking, much to Jocasta's delight. For dinner one night, he'd made pasta from scratch, so soft and decadent it melted in your mouth. It might've been the best meal Octavia had ever had.

Occasionally, she also assisted Thaddeus in the greenhouse. He'd been working on growing a few rare, temperamental plants for one of June's newest concoctions, but he'd been having some difficulty. Octavia quickly realized she was more of a hindrance than help. She wondered if his struggles were due to the plants themselves or the level of distraction in the house. Like clockwork, just about every half hour, someone would come barging into the greenhouse to ask Thaddeus a question.

Octavia was already unbearably restless only halfway through the week, so she decided on a whim to attend one of her graduate program lectures on campus. Somehow Octavia was stunned at how far she'd fallen behind despite all the classes she'd missed recently. At the end of the lecture, her professor called her to the front of the class to interrogate her after all the other students had departed. Did her showing up today mean she was recommitting herself to her studies? Could they count on her to be a reliable student? Had she made any progress toward her thesis?

When Octavia walked out of the lecture hall, she decided she wasn't coming back. She made straight for the Graduate Program Office and withdrew herself from the program. In the grand scheme of things, a graduate degree just wasn't important to her. Nothing really was. Not anymore.

By the time Saturday rolled around, Octavia needed a drink. It was only eleven in the morning, but she desperately needed a release. Fuming from her fruitless efforts translating, she stomped down the stairs to the kitchen. *This isn't worth it anymore. I'm not doing anything useful. Leif and the others are acclimating better than I ever could have imagined. They don't need me here.* Octavia's breath, hot and suffocating, caught in her throat. *I'm not needed anymore.*

Jocasta was lecturing the newcomers down the hall in the library, so she wouldn't catch Octavia snooping around quietly. She searched the dark corners of cabinets, the top shelf of the pantry, and even the hall closet, which was full of cleaning supplies. Nothing.

"Someone's jonesing," a low voice said from behind the closet door.

Octavia jumped, leaning to look around the door with her hand to her chest, her startled heart pounding beneath it. Leif was standing there with a mischievous tilt to his lips. *Asshole scared me on purpose.*

"What are you doing here?" she asked Leif, scowling as she closed the door.

"Bathroom," he answered, pointing at the door a few feet down the hall, as if it was painfully obvious.

Octavia rolled her eyes irritably, refusing to be embarrassed.

"It's a little early to be looking for a drink, don't you think?" he asked as he took a few steps closer, not wanting to be overheard by the group in the library.

"Who says that's what I was looking for?" she asked, crossing her arms over her chest.

"That look in your eyes," he replied simply, insinuating, once again, that the answer was obvious.

"As if," she scoffed at him.

"You okay?" he asked, his eyes scanning hers closely—too closely.

His concern surprised her, but she wouldn't let him see it. "Why do you care?" she retorted, turning to reenter the kitchen.

"Just morbid curiosity."

"Figures." She heard the bathroom door close behind her as she continued into the kitchen. *He really is the worst,* she thought. But then a second, quieter voice chimed from somewhere deep in the recesses of her mind, *Except for the fact that he's not. Not even a tiny bit. And you hate him for it.*

Octavia shook her head sharply to dispel the unwanted thoughts.

Having come to the conclusion that her grandmother must

be upholding the infuriating witchy tradition of keeping a sober household—magic and booze often didn't mix well, after all—she fell into a chair at the kitchen table, a large sigh passing over her lips.

Out of the corner of her downcast eye, she saw Quintin walk in from the dining room. "Penny for your thoughts?" he asked in a way that let her know he was smiling before she even saw it.

She raised her head, a pathetic, half-baked smile plastered on her lips. "Ha! You don't want to pay for anything going on up here. Trust me."

"Duly noted." He took the seat across from her, nodding as he folded his hands in his lap. "But I'm doing it anyway."

The tension in Octavia's chest loosened slightly, the same way it always did when she was around Quintin. Sometimes, being around him was like being wrapped in a warm, weighted blanket, grounding and comforting.

"I'm useless," she murmured, wincing as the words brought her shame to life.

"That's bullshit," Quintin replied dismissively.

"Is it, though? Sure, I can fight. I'm agile, strong even, but how's that going to help anyone during a confrontation with a man just as skilled in combat whose favorite weapon is a gun?" Quintin's lips pressed into a hard line as he considered her. "At this point, I'll just be a hindrance if I went with you to confront Garren," she concluded, feeling pathetic.

"You just need a little magic, Tavi. That's all."

Octavia leaned back in her chair and laughed, a deep, belly laugh that led to a humiliatingly loud snort.

Quintin's eyes grew as wide as saucers before he collapsed into a fit of throaty chuckles. Octavia did her best to shush them both before her grandmother came bounding in with a heavy book to smack them with.

"I'm serious, though," Quintin continued when they finally caught their breath. "I've come up with an . . . experiment of sorts."

"What do you mean?" A single eyebrow arched up in challenge.

"Well, since you've had no luck finding a solution to your hex problem in those grimoires from Salem, I had to start thinking outside the box." His dark brown eyes flashed mischievously.

"How do you—"

"It's obvious, Tavi. You've been moping around here like a depressed zombie for a week."

Ouch, that kind of hurt. Quintin was nothing if not honest.

"Listen, we only have two more weeks until we meet up with Garren, and our research efforts have gotten us nowhere for years, so we can't really expect to get lucky now," he pressed on.

"That's *why*—"

"Why you were giving up? Yeah, I figured," he interrupted again. If he wasn't going to let her finish a sentence, then she wasn't going to explain the other reasons she'd considered giving up her research.

"So, instead, I spent some time researching magic items, and . . . I think I may have found a temporary loophole."

Her heart stuttered. "Explain."

"What if we could store magic within an object, so a third party—in this case, you—could use it to fight? Kind of like what witch hunters have done with magic-sensing items in the past, but different."

Octavia nodded vigorously, gesturing for him to continue with a circular hand motion.

"So the magic-sensing items hunters use work like a light switch, right? Once the spell alters the item's properties, the spell remains active, maintained by a very low level of magic, until the enchantment's removed, no outside influence involved. Well, a spell like that isn't going to work for the kind of item I'm hypothesizing. We'd need to be able to interact with the magic—and I'm talking about a lot of magic here—stored inside for it to really be useful in combat. Luckily, I came across a spell in one of our coven's old grimoires that would allow a magic item to work more like a battery, to be charged, used, and recharged with as much magic as needed." His face was aglow with excitement.

Octavia tried to reason with her speeding heart. This would just be a Band-Aid to her problem, not a solution. *Calm down.*

She leaned forward in her seat, setting her elbows on the table, cupped fists under her chin. "All right, I'm with you, but here's the thing: How would I be able to dispel the magic from the item when I needed it? Without magic, I wouldn't be able to control it even if I did have an object like that."

"You're right, but that doesn't mean that one of us" —he waved a finger toward the rest of the house— "couldn't control it for you. It'd take teamwork, but I think we can do it."

"Holy shit," Octavia murmured. Her chest flared with the first real hope she'd had in weeks. She wanted to be impressed with Quintin, but she wasn't. Quintin was a genius. Coming up with a brilliant scheme like this was nothing for him.

"What type of spell is it?" she asked, desperately hoping the type of spell required would match up with Garren's return *and* the lunar calendar. If anyone could make this happen, it was her grandmother, but only if the moon cycle lined up properly.

"A sealing spell," Quintin said, rubbing his brow absentmindedly.

"Great, then we just need to talk to Grandma—"

"No need," Sage's voice interrupted a moment before they slid into the kitchen, their fuzzy purple socks gliding easily over the smooth vinyl, just like that famous scene from *Risky Business*.

"Were you—"

"Out there eavesdropping on your entire conversation? Yup!" Sage said as they came to a stop, their stance wide.

Quintin doesn't like the taste of his own medicine, does he? See how he likes being interrupted.

Ignoring the irritated look on Quintin's face, Octavia asked, "Why no need?"

"Because the one with the pretty hair discovered he specializes in containment magic yesterday," Sage explained, jumping up to sit on the kitchen counter.

Quintin rolled his eyes. "For goodness' sake, just use Tripp's name, Sage."

"Sealing is a faction of containment magic, right?" Octavia asked Quintin. He tilted his head in affirmation. "That's great! I mean, I'm sure Grandma could've gotten the job done, but now with Tripp . . ." Octavia trailed off as she watched Quintin's eyes squint, forming little crow's feet at the corners. "What?"

Quintin shook his head. "It's a big spell, really advanced stuff."

Sage bounced their heels against the wooden cabinets. "He's the athlete, though, right? Maybe he'll relish the challenge."

Quintin tapped his chin, his gaze drifting out the kitchen window.

Sage pulled him from his thoughts as they said, "Regardless of the difficulty, we know what the real tricky part will be."

They all nodded at each other.

"Getting him to agree to help us," Octavia said.

"Exactly."

They sat ruminating in silence; Octavia had no idea how to achieve their goal. What if he denied them outright? What if they couldn't get this plan to work and she really was . . . left behind? The thought made goosebumps rise on her arms.

Sage's face broke into a wide smile as they hopped off the counter. "Thank goodness we have June."

"That's an amazing idea!" June exclaimed over her lunch plate. "Of course I'll help you talk to Tripp about it, but I can't imagine he'd say no."

Quintin, Sage, and Octavia shared quick glances of uncertainty before Octavia responded, "Great! Thank you."

"When do you want to talk to him?" June asked before popping a plump red grape into her mouth.

Sage waited until June started chewing before they grabbed a fistful of her grapes off her plate for themself. Sage was notorious for stealing other people's food. It annoyed everyone to no end. Well, everyone except June, who simply offered them the remaining half of her turkey sandwich as well.

"They're supposed to be giving us the inside scoop on witch hunters later this afternoon," Quintin suggested after taking a sip of his tea. "We could ask him after that."

"Sounds good," June said, happily watching Sage devour the rest of her sandwich.

"So, what've you been working on all week?" Octavia asked June.

"Well, I've been brainstorming ways I can be helpful, and I came up with an idea," June explained slowly, color blooming in her cheeks. "Basically, I'm trying to create substances that can be used during a fight instead of fists or weapons."

"Sounds cool! What type of substances?" Sage asked through a mouthful of bread, meat, and cheese.

"I think a powder would work best, something with enough density to travel a decent distance when thrown."

"What would these substances do?" Quintin asked over his mug.

"I hope I can come up with a few different ones. Incapacitation by robbing the assailant of their senses? A poison powder? Maybe something explosive with a delayed reaction time, like a grenade? I don't have all the details worked out yet."

"That's insanely cool, June," Octavia said, smiling.

"Seriously!" Sage agreed. "This sounds like it could give us a huge advantage if it came down to a fight. Robbing an enemy of their senses, even temporarily, could give us the perfect opening for an attack."

June's cheeks flushed scarlet. She'd never been any good at taking a compliment.

"What could give us an opening?" Tripp asked as he strutted into the dining room and grabbed an apple from a fruit bowl at the other end of the table.

"I—I'm working on creating some magic powders that could be useful in a fight, should it come to that with Garren," June replied, nervously averting her eyes as Tripp studied her.

"Sounds promising. Good thinking outside the box. Garren will only be anticipating straightforward magical attacks." Tripp took a large bite from his apple, then wiped away a trickle of juice with his sleeve.

June's blush deepened, her face now almost as red as the apple in his hand.

"Of—Of course. Happy to help."

Octavia suppressed a giggle as she met Sage's gaze. *Looks like someone has a crush.*

"Actually, Tripp," Quintin said, "if you have a sec, would you mind joining us? We have a quick question for you."

Tripp was rarely without the other ex-hunters. Perhaps Quintin was right in wanting to ask him now, while he was free from the influence of Leif, Jiro, and Delta.

Tripp shrugged half-heartedly and sat down, his mouth still full of partially chewed apple.

"What's up?" he asked after he swallowed, positioning the apple in front of his mouth for another bite.

"I'm afraid I won't be of any help when it comes time to confront Garren," Octavia explained, meeting his gaze. His warm brown eyes were soft, and he gave her his full attention. "So Quin came up with an ingenious plan to help make me more useful." Octavia gestured for Quintin to take over with an open hand.

Tripp took another bite from his apple, turning his attention to Quintin as he chewed.

"I think it's possible to seal some of our magic into an item," Quintin explained, "similar to what witches did for the witch hunters to create your magic-sensing objects. Then, during the fight, Octavia can use the object with the help of another witch, who would cast a spell to dispel the magic stored in it, giving her an advantage."

Tripp considered the proposition thoughtfully as he swallowed. "Wouldn't it be counterproductive to split our attention during a fight just to boost your ego?" he asked brusquely.

Four jaws dropped in unison.

"Excuse me?" Sage asked.

"Well, as you said, one of us would have to help her use the magic stored in this item," Tripp said simply, like he was solving an arithmetic problem, "so whether or not she has it, her presence will put us at a disadvantage. I think it'd be more tactical to keep the attention of the witch assigned to help her solely on the enemy."

"But we need Tavi there," June piped up, her voice louder and more assertive than usual. "None of us can fight as well as her. We'd be stupid not to take advantage of her physical prowess."

"Physical prowess . . ." Tripp echoed, the sound resembling the purr of a contented cat. He discarded his half-eaten apple on the table. "That's high praise."

"Because it's true."

"Just ask Leif," Octavia said.

He considered June for a moment before asking, "So, why are you talking about this with me? Why not just do what you want and leave me out of it?"

"Because the type of magic we need to create the item happens to be within your newfound specialty," Sage enlightened him.

Tripp's perfect, cupid's bow lips twitched. "Do you know if I'll even be able to do magic at the level you need by the deadline?"

"We don't," Octavia answered, "but you're the best chance we've got. My grandma's ability to perform sealing spells is tied to a specific phase of the moon. If the timeline doesn't line up, her magic might not be powerful enough to do it."

The weight of his silence was substantial. It took an impressive amount of self-discipline for Octavia not to start begging. She really needed a fucking win.

"I have one condition," Tripp said at last.

"Yes?" Octavia asked as June and Sage low-fived under the table. She didn't let it show on her face, but she was already celebrating with them. She knew she'd agree to whatever Tripp's condition was.

"I won't be the one to help you control it. I refuse to be distracted when the time comes. There's too much at stake."

"Deal," Octavia agreed quickly, reaching her hand across the table to shake on it.

Tripp simply looked at her extended hand and chuckled. "No need for formalities. I said I'd help, and I will. I'm true to my word."

As quickly as he'd come, he stood, grabbed his half-eaten apple, and walked from the room.

"Well, that was interesting," Quintin murmured. "I underestimated how well he could play the game."

"Thanks for standing up for me, June," said Octavia.

"Of course. I just can't believe he insinuated we'd be better off without you. That was a completely incompetent thing for him to say."

The love and respect glinting in those forest green eyes brought tears to Octavia's own. She leaned over and embraced her life-long friend, affectionately kissing her cheek.

"J, you were picturing him naked earlier, weren't you?" Sage asked, gleefully ruining the moment.

"Wait, what?" June asked, ripping herself from Octavia's arms.

They broke out into a fit of laughter again, lifting Octavia's spirits higher than they'd been since the night she'd met Leif. Her friends—her family—were always there when she needed them.

CHAPTER 26
OCTAVIA

A knock at the door interrupted the slew of colorful curses erupting from Octavia's mouth. "Yeah?" she called.

The door to the guest room cracked open an inch. One inquisitive, dark brown eye peered through. "Is it safe to enter?"

Octavia dropped the grimoire she'd been attempting to translate, letting it fall to the floor. "Jiro? Is that you?"

What does he want?

The eye narrowed. "Will you keep cursing if it is? 'Cause if so, the answer's no."

The ghost of a smile curled her lips. "What's up?"

Jiro pushed the door open, standing in the doorway.

"Does Grandma need help with something?"

Jiro crossed his feet at the ankles, standing at an awkward angle. "Nah, nothing like that."

Octavia stood, crossing her arms over her chest. "Then what's it like?"

Jiro cleared his throat. "I, uh, wanted to chat."

Octavia's lips fell open with a soft *pop*. "Chat? With me?"

He flashed an uneasy smile. "Yup."

"What about?" Octavia cocked her head as she shifted her weight on her feet.

"Well—and please don't take this the wrong way or anything—but we're the only two left in the group without our magic, so I—I don't know. I thought we could . . . ugh, this sounded way less lame in my head." Jiro raked his hands through shiny raven hair as he struggled. "Want to start like a support group or something?"

Octavia balked. "A *support group?*"

Jiro grimaced. "Shit, no. Sorry." He turned on the spot, taking a step back out into the hall. But before taking a second step, he whirled around again. "No. No. Never mind. I'm not sorry." He rattled his head. "Yes. A support group." A quick sigh. "'Cause being left out of shit sucks."

His gaze captured hers, and her stomach flipped like she'd missed a step going down the staircase. She didn't know what to say.

"I know we don't know each other very well. Or at all, really. But I thought it might make it suck a little less. To have someone to talk to about it who gets it. You know?" His eyes gleamed hopefully.

His hope burned the back of her throat like scotch. She hated scotch.

"No. I don't know. Your magic will kick in any day now. Mine—" Her eyes drifted to the pile of books on the floor. "Mine might never come back."

Jiro frowned down at the books as well, a heavy beat of silence passing between them. The air in the room shifted as Jiro closed the door before leaning against it, his gaze still downcast. "Can I tell you something I haven't been brave enough to say out loud?"

Octavia tilted her head the other way, one eyebrow perked in interest.

"I don't want my magic to surface." He gulped. "Ever."

"I don't think that's much of a secret," Octavia said, the softness in her voice surprising her.

Jiro chuckled, returning his gaze to hers. "Nah, I guess not. Given our history. But it's the reason why that I'm—" His angular jaw tensed. "My siblings wouldn't understand."

Hesitant lines framed the outer corners of Octavia's eyes. "And you want to tell me this reason?" He nodded, crossing his feet at the ankles again. "Why?"

His brows furrowed and relaxed, quick, like a reflex. "Because you've got your heart and mind set on something important to you, something personal, and yet you let the needs of the people you love come first. So you might get where I'm coming from, better than anyone else could."

Octavia studied him. His thick-lashed eyes were sincere, the soft curves of his lips relaxed. His shoulders tensed a bit under her scrutiny, but she could tell he was being candid. "What if your perception of me is all wrong?" She cocked her hip, leaning on it. "Where'd you even get that impression of me in the first place?"

He smiled softly. "When we were reintroduced, you said breaking your hex shouldn't be our main priority—that getting justice should." His eyes hardened. "You don't know us. And up until a few days ago, we were your enemy. I mean, we literally had a plan in motion to eliminate—"

Octavia interrupted him, her throat tight against the guilt. "Your point?"

He pushed off the door, standing straight. "My point is, despite your feelings about us, despite your own goals, you knew us joining the fold was the safest option for the coven. Leif, Tripp, and Delta can provide them the extra protection that you and I—" He paused. "We can't right now."

She lifted her chin, denying it the chance to quiver.

"You chose them—continue to choose them—over everything. Even if that choice breaks your own heart." At that moment, his face was like a mirror, reflecting her pain with his.

"What's your story, then?" she asked, strolling to sit on the corner of the bed. She motioned with an open palm for Jiro to join her.

He stepped over the puddle of books on the floor and sat, leaning back on his arms for support. His head lolled back on his shoulders as he released a heavy breath. "I have a boyfriend." Octavia sat up straighter, sensing an important shift in his tone. "Unlike the coven, witch hunters aren't required to keep their profession hidden from their partners. But I have." Another heavy breath. "Because I was ashamed. I've always been ashamed."

"Of being a witch hunter?" Octavia asked quietly.

"Yeah." Jiro's head turned in Octavia's direction. Their gazes locked. "My siblings don't know that." Octavia could only nod. "I'm not . . . *like* them, in a lot of ways, but especially in this. I'm not a killer. Murder is wrong, no matter which way you slice it."

Octavia watched his gaze darken, pupils dilated, as if his worst fear had materialized before him.

"Witch hunters kill people." His haunted expression crumpled. "Thank God witches don't." A choked sound left him. "I've never been so happy to be wrong about something, but I still don't want—"

"You don't want this—hunting, magic, the coven." When he looked at her, Octavia gave him a small, watery smile. "You want *him.*"

He slumped down onto the bed. "Yes. I want Ryan."

The weight of this secret must've been slowly crushing him. But can we ever really be free of them? Our secrets?

"Ryan knows I hate my job, but he thinks it's some boring techie office job. Basically, I'm the worst boyfriend in the world. I've been lying to him nonstop for a year, and now, if I want to keep him, I have to lie to him even more." Jiro laughed humorlessly, raising his torso off the bed. He pushed his sleeves up to his elbows and then placed his elbows on his knees, displaying colorful tattoo sleeves Octavia had never seen before.

She blinked rapidly, her eyes devouring the intricate designs.

"Holy shit, Jiro. Those tattoos are gorgeous." She leaned toward him, unable to look away.

Jiro smiled as he twisted his forearms around, giving her a better view of the entire design. "Thanks. I designed them myself, but Ryan's the tattoo artist. He did them for me. That's how we met, actually. Tripp and I wandered into his shop, and the rest was history." His smile was that of a man in love.

Octavia leaned back. "Well, if you designed those yourself, it looks like you're a tattoo artist too."

He laughed again, this time lighter. "You sound like Ryan."

"Well then, Ryan must be something else since I have it on good authority that I'm *amazing*."

Jiro's eyes startled wide. Octavia laughed, the tension in her shoulders dissipating with every word passed between them.

Am I actually enjoying myself? This is good, right?

But Jiro's smile faded, eyes glossing over. "But I'm not an artist. I'm a witch hunter." His amused breath was hollow. "Nah—I'm a witch. A witch who'll have to lie to the love of his life forever." He rubbed a hand against the illustrations on his forearm. "I'm tired of lying to him, even if he's oblivious to it. I love him too much to keep . . . disrespecting him like this."

Octavia's eyes burned. She reached a hand toward him but stopped halfway. Jiro watched it as it dropped to the bedspread. His gaze lifted to hers.

"I get it now."

Jiro's Adam's apple bobbed.

"You've got your heart set on Ryan, but you're willing to break your own heart if it means Ryan's safe—loved the way he deserves to be . . . because you can't walk away." Octavia's heart sputtered in her chest. "You can't walk away and be with Ryan the way you wish you could because of your family."

Color bloomed in Jiro's cheeks.

"Magic or no magic, you chose your people—Ryan and your siblings—over yourself."

Jiro nodded, eyes snapping to his wringing hands.

He's brave, honest, and warm . . . shit, I like him, don't I? Well, okay then.

Octavia released a breathy laugh. "A support group."

His head continued to bob. "A support group."

Octavia slid off the bed suddenly, reclaiming Jiro's gaze. "We have to make it official then."

Jiro's mouth perked up in a half smile. "What?"

"Our group!"

"How?"

She just grinned as her eyes dropped to his tattoos.

"What? No way. I just draw. I don't even know how to use a tattoo gun."

Octavia shrugged. "So learn."

"Are you serious?"

Her smile widened. "*Dead* serious."

CHAPTER 27
OCTAVIA

After learning about witch hunter tactics, Octavia figured she'd have no problem holding her own against a witch hunter in a fistfight.

The coven was assembled in the library, seated in a circle of chairs pulled from the dining room. The ex-hunters were teaching the others everything they knew about witch hunters and how to beat them at their own game.

"We were all trained in hand-to-hand combat," Leif explained, "and taught to wield an array of weapons from a young age, but fighting isn't our main thing."

"He's right," Tripp agreed. "Our greatest strength is stealth."

"Hunters take reconnaissance seriously," Jiro added. "It might as well be their eleventh Commandment."

June chuckled quietly.

"That's why an ambush is the only realistic way to approach this," Delta chimed in. "The element of surprise is essential."

"So we should lure him to a space we can control?" asked Quintin.

"Exactly. Going after him on his turf would put us at a disadvantage," Leif agreed.

"But even the element of surprise might not be enough," said Tripp. "He'll have the knowledge and the skill to evade us, so we have to be strategized to a T."

"Luck favors the prepared," Thaddeus muttered under his breath.

"You all know this is only one man we're talking about here, right?" Sage interjected. "It's not like we're going up against a whole crew of these assholes."

"Garren has single-handedly taken down over fifty witches during his time with the organization," Leif warned in a low tone. "He's not a person you want to underestimate."

Sage *tsk*ed as they draped an arm over the back rest of their chair. "We're the ones who shouldn't be underestimated." There was fire in their eyes.

"That kind of arrogance will get us injured if we're lucky." Delta made a slicing motion against her neck, her long fingernail grazing her skin. Behind it, a long, deep laceration cut the skin of her neck in half, thick droplets of blood beading on the flayed skin before it gushed from her like a waterfall. "And dead if we're not."

She really is getting better at her glamours, Octavia thought, *even though it's only seemed to add to her dramatics.*

Delta blinked and the illusion faded, the smooth skin of her neck once again whole and unblemished.

"Magic still beats anything this guy could throw at us," Sage said, eyes narrowed.

"You're right," Leif replied with a slow nod, "but only if we cover all our bases. That's what we're trying to do here."

Sage huffed, averting their gaze.

"So we get him isolated in a location of our choosing," said June, "and then what? Fire at him all at once so he can't evade us?"

"That's a joke, right?" Delta laughed.

June pursed her lips at the snide remark. "Nothing about this is funny."

Delta's smirk fell from her face as if June had slapped her.

"That's a good idea, June," said Jiro, "but no. The best tactic is to first use our magic to try to restrain him, and then attack if we have to."

"Remember, our goal is for this to end peacefully," said Jocasta. "Once he's restrained, we can interrogate him and hopefully convince him to yield."

Heads bobbed in agreement around the room.

"But what about weapons?" Octavia asked. "Is it really the smartest idea to give him time to fire a weapon instead of going straight for the KO?"

"It doesn't matter which tactic we choose to go with," Leif said darkly. "If we can't disarm him, we're screwed."

It appeared that Octavia's only disadvantage was that she'd never trained with actual weapons. She considered asking Jiro or Tripp to teach her the basics, but they were so focused on honing their witchcraft, she didn't want to be a distraction.

The next day, she watched a few hours of YouTube videos on how to use knives for self-defense in one of the spare bedrooms on the second floor of the house. It was the only room with a twin bed, so it gave her the floor space she needed to practice the techniques in the videos. She practiced drill after drill for an hour or more. Her sports bra and leggings clung to her uncomfortably damp skin as she smoothed her hair up into a sweaty ponytail.

She took a deep breath and practiced a quick combo move with her arms, adjusting her wrist as instructed in the video, forcing the flimsy steak knife in her hand into a new angle. Frustrated, she huffed a heavy breath.

This is going to be impossible without a real weapon. I need to get used to the weight and feel of it if I'm ever going to get the hang of this.

But I can't just go around ordering a weapon on Grandma's Amazon Prime account.

Octavia set the knife down on the dresser and paused the video on her laptop to take a swig from her water bottle. As she drank gratefully, a low chuckle came from the doorway behind her. She gasped, choking on the water as it flew down the wrong pipe, threatening to douse her lungs. She doubled over, coughing uncontrollably, forcing the water back out.

"Shit, sorry." Leif walked toward her, hands extended, brow wrinkled. "I didn't mean to scare you like that."

He placed a gentle hand on her upper back. Octavia took several ragged breaths that burned her lungs, causing her eyes to water. She angrily wiped the tears away, frustrated that Leif was seeing her like this: so painfully human.

After her breaths evened out and the heat in her throat dulled, Octavia stood up straight, shaking off Leif's hand as she stepped a few paces away. She hadn't forgotten their recent interactions.

We're not the same.

You have to forget what happened between us.

He didn't want anything to do with her, and she was all too willing to oblige.

So, why is he here now, what is he angling for?

"Sorry," he said again, his hand dropping to his side.

"What are you doing up here?" Octavia asked, her voice gravelly.

"I—uh, heard you . . . from down the hall," Leif replied awkwardly, shoving his hands into his pockets. "Just curious what you were doing."

"Why?" Octavia turned from him to snap her laptop closed on the bed.

"Because you don't usually do this here," Leif murmured vaguely.

"You're going to have to be more specific than that," she snapped, picking up her sweatshirt from the bed and pulling it over her head.

"You usually work out at the gym, but today you're training here, upstairs, in a dusty bedroom at the end of a hall I've never seen anyone use, instead of the designated training room," Leif clarified, sounding from inside her sweatshirt as if he'd moved across the room.

Octavia yanked the fabric down, her ponytail catching against the neck of the sweater, preventing her head from popping through. She cursed, readjusting the fabric so she could get the damn thing on.

When her head was finally free, Leif's eyes were glinting with amusement and his lips twitched, fighting against a smile. "It's interesting."

Octavia scowled at him as she blew stray hair from her now-messy ponytail out of her face. "What's so interesting about it? Everyone's practicing more important things in the training room right now, so I'm staying out of the way. It's decidedly *not* interesting."

The soft pitter patter of rainfall on the window cut through the silence.

Leif squinted, his expression slightly suspicious, but also slightly—well, she didn't know what exactly, but it made her feel strange. Almost heady. "You're wrong. It *is* interesting. You changed up your entire routine today, not just this. You haven't worked on translating the grimoires either; this is the first day I've seen you without them. I want to know why."

"Have you been watching me or something?" Octavia scoffed. She tried her best to appear nonchalant, but her lungs constricted at the thought of him watching her without her knowledge. What had he seen? It couldn't have been good considering how pissed off she'd been lately. Had his opinion of her changed at all? *Why do I care if it has?*

"Yeah, I have," he said levelly.

Octavia's stomach flipped. She'd hadn't expected such blatant honesty.

"Why?" she asked. The question was hard as stone.

"Because no matter what, you keep moving forward," Leif answered quietly. "This past week has been hard, and I've needed . . . Watching you gave me . . ." He shook his head despondently. "Well, let's just say it's been motivational."

Octavia stared at Leif as his eyes dropped to the floor. Were the tips of his ears more pink than usual? Was he *blushing?*

"So, fess up," Leif went on, his chin raising defensively. "Why are you up here training with cutlery instead of translating the grimoires?"

Octavia hesitated, debating whether or not to lie. "I returned them to the library," she responded honestly. "Earlier this morning, actually."

Leif shifted on his feet. "So, they didn't have any helpful information in them after all?"

Octavia shrugged as she watched him scrutinize the steak knife she'd been practicing with. "I don't think so, but I can't be sure. I didn't end up translating all of it."

His eyes snapped back to hers. "Why not? You went through all the trouble to start. Why wouldn't you at least finish?" He leaned back, perching against the windowsill behind him, the soft winter light shimmering against his hair. She hated how beautiful he was. How much he resembled a living, breathing work of art, standing there with that infuriatingly genuine look of concern on his face. Without her consent, her eyes devoured him, the sharp angle of his cheekbones and how they so perfectly contradicted the soft fullness of his lips. His eyes were warmer in this light, more aquamarine than frosty diamond.

"You're doing it again," Leif murmured, bringing her back into the moment, never breaking eye contact.

"Doing what?" she demanded, refusing to look away first.

"Staring. Reading me. Trying to figure me out, maybe," Leif speculated. "Feel free to continue, but I'm not leaving without an answer to my question."

Heat flooded Octavia's face, the tips of her ears now blazing hot. "Because I finally figured it out. My obsession was killing me . . . and could've killed what's left of my family." She couldn't quite put the bite into the words that she wanted to.

Leif crossed his arms over his chest. "How do you figure?"

"Damn it, for so many reasons," Octavia exclaimed. "If I wasn't so obsessed with getting my magic back, I wouldn't have been so resentful and jealous. I wouldn't have felt the need to self-destruct." Her throat constricted with every word. "Hell, I probably wouldn't have been at that bar on a Wednesday night, wouldn't have run into you, wouldn't have brought you home and put my family at risk. They wouldn't have felt like they needed to pressure me into going on a date with you." She pointed a shaking finger at Leif. "There never would've been an opportunity for you to plot, or *scheme*, or whatever it was you all did when you decided it was a good idea to kill my *only* reasons for living!" By the end of her rant, she was out of breath from yelling. But not at Leif, she realized—at herself.

He pushed himself off the windowsill and stepped toward her.

"Don't," she choked, her throat tight. She looked away from him, wiping the corner of her eye before a tear could fall and betray her emotions.

Leif stopped and waited a moment before he said, "That wouldn't have changed anything. I still would've run into Quintin downtown that day and followed him back to Tucker's. I'd have pursued him—for months, if that's what it took. I wouldn't have given up. Because I didn't know who I was then. I had no idea. I was living a *fucking* lie. Every day. Until you—" Leif's voice was rough, his breath ragged in his throat.

Octavia's gaze snapped up, searching his face for the lie. The falsehood. The audacity. Because it had to be there, somewhere.

"Your desire to get your magic back is what makes you *you*, and that person saved me. She saved all of us. She helped show us who the *real* enemy is."

The real enemy? Did he—did he listen when I said that?

You are not my enemy.

Or did something else go down that changed his mind?

His angry gaze bore into her own. "Stop punishing yourself for that." He was serious, deathly so. Octavia felt her limbs begin to quiver, even though she was the furthest thing from cold.

He was giving her an out, offering her the acknowledgment and acceptance she'd been famished for her entire life. Every instinct told her to reject him, to mentally spit on what he'd said. Label him a liar. Dismiss his very existence. But instead, she forced herself to listen.

"There has to be a way to get your magic back," Leif continued, his face pleading.

Her stomach fluttered uncomfortably. Tripp must not have told him about their conversation from the other day. *Why would Tripp keep that from him?*

His gaze consumed her. Suddenly, her sweatshirt was too tight, too warm, the air in the room too thin. She shook her head, but the sensations remained. "Why do you want to help me? Just last week you made it perfectly clear you didn't want anything to do with me. What changed?"

"Seeing you so defeated and aimless . . ." Leif began. "I don't know. I can't really explain it, but it pisses me off watching you give up. You're too tenacious for that." He chuckled as her eyes widened in surprise. "I know it sounds weird, but I felt the same way after learning the truth about us. Everything I'd worked so hard for was suddenly worthless, and I was aimless too. I guess what I'm trying to say is: I get it."

A beat of silence passed between them.

"What I couldn't find the words to tell you earlier is that, in a completely unintentional, roundabout way, you've helped me get through it—the stagnancy, the uncertainty, the depression." Color spread from his ears to his cheeks. "So let me repay the favor."

Octavia's legs tried to liquify beneath her, but she locked her knees, steeling them against the blush in Leif's face. "I don't know what to say," she murmured, averting her eyes. She'd never seen him this vulnerable before. Wait, that wasn't true. She'd seen him like this one other time, in a dark bedroom.

"You don't have to say anything," Leif said, peeling Octavia away from the memory. "Just accept my help."

"Fine," Octavia relented, meeting his piercing gaze once more. A shiver ran down her spine. "But we don't have a lot of time before Garren gets back, so that takes priority."

"Fair," Leif agreed, lifting his hands in surrender, "but that means I'll also have to help you with whatever it was you were doing when I walked in here."

The heat in her face blazed anew. "My trainer doesn't let me train with real weapons, so I've never actually learned how to do it," she admitted as she crossed her arms defensively. "I figured if I'm going to be of any use at all, I should learn."

"Smart," Leif said, stepping a pace closer. "Let me help train you then. We have plenty of weapons at our place. I'll bring a few tomorrow, see what you like best. We can train in the evenings after our magic lessons."

"Are you sure? It's going to take time away from your practice."

"No, it won't. Plus, I haven't practiced hand-to-hand combat in a while, so it'll be good for me too."

"All right. If you insist."

"I do."

His smile was brighter than the sun, and it took every ounce of self-control she had to keep her stomach from somersaulting. They might be agreeing to work toward a common goal, but they weren't friends. He'd made that clear enough, despite his sudden kindness now.

Her face cooled as his smile faded.

Leif headed for the door. Before he exited, he turned to look over his shoulder at her once more. "In the meantime, you should use a chef's knife instead of that flimsy thing. It still won't be the right weight, but it's closer to the real thing than what you've got."

"I—uh, all right. Thanks," she replied to his back.

"No problem. See you tomorrow," he called, lifting his arm in a lazy, half-wave.

Octavia exhaled a heavy breath as she listened to him gallop down the stairs.

CHAPTER 28
LEIF

It was five o'clock in the afternoon, and Leif was already exhausted, both mentally and physically. With Jocasta's help, he'd created a training regimen that pushed his limits without overwhelming him. He knew he couldn't relent until Garren was dealt with, and this allowed him to achieve more within a shorter period of time, but the grind came at a steep price. His muscles ached so much it even hurt to lie down, and his head pounded like a never-ending war drum. He'd spent the last twenty-four hours convincing himself that he wasn't in fact getting sick, he was just magically drained.

But Leif couldn't stop now. He couldn't afford to rest. He had to get stronger, as fast as his body would let him.

Jocasta had explained to him that light magic was exceptionally rare. Very few witches had ever specialized in it. His mother had been one of them. And now, so was he.

His magic was drawn to the unique vibrations of light waves like a magnet to steel, enabling him to alter them. Essentially, he could create and manipulate visible light.

The different applications for his magic were what inspired Leif most.

"Of course, light magic would come in handy in a dark corridor," Jocasta had said, "but the applications of light magic go much further than that. For example, manipulating light also means you can manipulate sight." Her eyes had twinkled with the memory she shared next. "Your mother was very good at using her light magic to create illusions. She could conceal things without hiding them, just by manipulating the light around them. Eventually, she could even create mirages, causing people to see things that weren't actually there."

Leif had developed a new appreciation for Delta's specialty after ruminating on the potential benefits of being able to control what another person sees. *After all, isn't seeing believing?*

But Leif was admittedly most excited about one particular application of light magic that had been mastered by only a single witch in history: honing light into a laser.

Laser magic. Like fucking *Star Wars*.

"The first and only witch to be able to create lasers from light magic was a Scottish witch named Phelix Douchter," Jocasta told him. "Due to the immense power of his magic, he went into hiding in the Scottish Highlands shortly after his discovery. Witches and witch hunters alike searched for him for over a hundred years to no avail. And his grimoires have never been recovered," Jocasta explained with a sigh. "What a shame. I'm sure he was one interesting man."

But even without Phelix's grimoires to learn from, Leif was determined to become the second witch in history to wield that magic.

Leif sat down heavily onto a dining room chair and his spine smarted like it was barely able to hold the weight of his body.

Delta and Tripp sat at the table across from him, eating their dinner. "You look like shit," Delta said, the corners of her mouth curving downward.

"Right back 'atcha," Leif responded moodily.

"Fuck you. I look flawless," Delta said, tossing a long lock of strawberry blonde hair over her shoulder. He had to admit she'd gotten much better with her glamours. The blonde almost looked natural.

Leif's stomach churned with nausea as he assessed the dinner laid out on the table, but he swallowed the sensation. He had to eat something. His nose guided his hands toward the aroma of spiced meat and tomatoes. Chili.

He ladled two large scoops into a bowl and topped it off with a sprinkle of shredded cheese and a cornbread muffin. This was one of Tripp's favorite meals to cook, easy to make but fun to experiment with, so it'd become one of Leif's too. The perfect comfort food.

"Let me know if the chili is too spicy," Tripp said from his seat next to Delta. "Jocasta and I might've gone a bit overboard with the spices."

Leif blew a billow of steam from his spoonful of chili. When it had cooled, he placed the spoon in his mouth and relished in the savory, spicy flavor. It was spicier than most might like their chili, but Leif didn't mind. With every bite he took, he felt the knots in his shoulders loosen, his mental fog dissipate, and his strength return.

"What's in this chili exactly?" Leif asked through a mouthful.

"Magic," Tripp said, his eyebrows dancing mischievously.

It was astounding how quickly they'd acclimated to this new world of magic. Thankfully, the mere mention of it no longer sent Leif's body into a death spiral of anxiety, which made what they had to do much easier.

Within minutes, Leif was stuffed. He also felt almost completely recovered from the side effects of his overuse of magic. Satisfied, he pushed the empty bowl away.

"Where's Jiro?" he asked.

"Watching another K-drama with the others upstairs. They ate earlier," Tripp explained between bites.

"He's getting far too comfortable here," Delta pronounced, dropping her fork atop the remainder of her salad. "Watching him with them now, you'd never know he spent almost two decades of his life learning how to kill them."

"Leave him alone," said Leif. "We don't get to judge him for adapting better than the rest of us."

She simply scowled in response, poking a cherry tomato around her plate with a knife.

"At least he's found something to bond with them over," Tripp mused, pushing away his empty plate as well. "He's already gotten close with them all. Even Octavia. I saw them at breakfast this morning, laughing over Jiro's sketchbook. They seemed tight."

"Yeah, well, Jiro's always been a pushover like that. I don't think I've ever seen him hold his ground on anything," Delta said, dropping the knife on her plate with a clatter.

"Does it always have to be us versus them?" Tripp asked. "It's getting exhausting."

"I agree," Leif breathed, grateful that someone besides himself had finally worked up the courage to say it.

Delta bristled.

"Look," said Tripp firmly. "All I'm saying is that they've shown us no ill will. They're actively helping us get stronger, knowing damn well we could easily turn around and use that power against them. Plus, they've promised to help us get revenge on Garren. I'm just having trouble seeing what's so bad about them anymore."

Delta opened her mouth to retort, but no words came out. Her lips flapped open and closed a couple of more times before she eventually gave up, slumping back in her chair dejectedly.

"They asked for my help the other day," Tripp continued after a moment of silence. "With something only I can do."

"What was it? What do they want from you?" Delta asked, sitting up straight. She was like a moth to a flame, looking for any reason, no matter how small, to keep on hating them.

"To create something they can store magic in. They want to find a way for Octavia to be able to temporarily use magic, since she's basically useless without it."

"Creative," Leif murmured.

Why didn't she tell me about that when we talked yesterday afternoon? She probably still doesn't trust me. I haven't exactly done anything to earn it back. I've only pushed her away.

Or maybe, Leif speculated, Octavia was worried Tripp wouldn't be strong enough to do it. They'd only been practicing witchcraft for a couple of weeks, after all. Jocasta assured them they'd catch up in due time, but there was certainly a chance he wouldn't be able to do the magic they needed.

"And they can't create this item without you?" Delta asked, pivoting in her chair to face Tripp.

"That's how they made it sound," Tripp said.

"Have you agreed?" Delta asked.

Tripp locked eyes with Leif before he responded. "Yes."

"Did you negotiate?" she went on. "Make any demands?"

"No, Delta. I didn't."

"And why the hell not? Are you stupid?"

"No, I'm not," Tripp replied, his voice low and laced with venom. "I've simply decided to trust them—a decision you're obviously too emotionally stunted to understand."

Delta's face went blank, wiped clean of all traces of emotion. Without another word, she rose from the table and left the room. Several moments later, they heard a door slam from somewhere within the depths of the house.

"You can't beat fire with fire, you know," Leif said, shaking his head.

"You sound like a damn fortune cookie." Tripp exhaled heavily. "But yes, I know. That wasn't my finest moment."

"She really has a way of getting under your skin and provoking the worst in you, doesn't she?"

"That's the understatement of the year."

Leif chuckled softly, enjoying the moment. He had a full stomach and was relaxing in a comfortable chair, chatting with good company. Tripp must've been thinking the same, because they fell into comfortable silence.

The reprieve was fleeting, lasting only a minute before the silence was broken by the sound of someone bounding down the stairs. Leif and Tripp turned their faces to the doorway.

Octavia swept into the room, her cheeks rosy, long hair loose, and a dazzling smile upon her face. Leif realized with surprise that this might be the first time he'd seen her smile genuinely.

She halted mid-step when she noticed Leif and Tripp watching her.

"Am I interrupting something?" she asked uncertainly.

"Not at all," Tripp assured her with a smile of his own. "It was just impossible to continue our conversation over the sound of your large feet clamoring down the stairs."

"Ha-ha, very funny," Octavia said flatly, walking to their end of the table. "You almost ready?" she asked Leif when she reached them.

"Ready for what?" Tripp asked.

"I'm helping her with weapons training," Leif explained simply.

"Ah, I see," Tripp replied, trying and failing to suppress a shit-eating grin.

Leif kicked him under the table in warning. Tripp only laughed, bending over to rub his shin.

"Speaking of," Leif said to Octavia, "Tripp informed me you two have struck a deal as well." Leif smirked as he watched the obnoxious grin dissolve from Tripp's face.

"Uh, yeah," Octavia began, appearing to catch on to the faint undertones of pettiness within the exchange as her eyes narrowed suspiciously. "Tripp agreed to try and help us make a magic item."

"I heard. Very creative. Who came up with the idea?"

"Quintin."

"Not surprising. He's smarter than he lets on."

"Really?" Octavia asked. "Because to me it seems like all he ever talks about are his clever schemes."

Tripp chuckled. "He does think highly of himself, doesn't he?"

"Did he decide what item you should spell?" Leif asked.

"Nope, not yet," Octavia replied, shaking her head. The long strands of her hair danced just below her ribs.

"Well, it's obvious, isn't it?" Tripp asked as he tapped his index finger against the glossy wooden tabletop.

"What is?" Leif and Octavia asked in unison.

"We should spell whichever weapon Octavia fights with best," Tripp replied.

Leif grinned. "Tripp, you're a genius."

"I don't think so." Tripp stood. "You're all just really dense."

Leif balled up his cloth napkin and threw it at Tripp, who caught it easily in midair and returned it to the table.

"Good luck, you two," said Tripp. "Let me know once you've chosen the weapon you want me to hocus pocus."

"Tripp, wait," Octavia called after him.

Tripp paused in the doorway and turned to face her.

"Thank you. Honestly."

The simple words took almost zero effort on her part, but it meant everything to Tripp. Leif could see the appreciation in the slant of his outer brows, the disbelief in his wrinkled forehead, before he smiled, wide and bright. Octavia had acknowledged him and appreciated him. She was obviously glad to have him in her corner. Leif understood perfectly now why Tripp had been so willing to say yes and offer his help.

It really doesn't have to be us versus them.

CHAPTER 29
LEIF

In the training room, Octavia swung a large rubber training knife in a wide arc from right to left, slicing through the air.

"You need to adjust your stance if you're going to hold it like that," Leif instructed.

"Adjust my stance *how*, exactly?" she asked in an irritated tone.

Apparently, he wasn't half the teacher Sage was.

Leif sighed, shaking his head at himself. "Sorry. Center your hips toward your target," he explained, demonstrating as he squared his frame toward Octavia.

"All right." She adjusted accordingly and swung again. Her stance looked better, allowing for more power and accuracy. "Okay, I think I got it," Octavia said, tossing her plaited hair over a shoulder. "Let's spar again."

"Just remember, your blade will find its target as long as you square yourself toward it."

"Got it," she replied, adjusting her stance again.

Leif got into position in front of her, his frame squared, arms raised to chest level. Even though he was used to fighting with weapons, he'd also chosen to use a rubber training knife, which mimicked the weight of a knife without the sharpness.

Leif held back, waiting for Octavia to attack first. She didn't hesitate. She twisted, using agile footwork to distract him, before she sliced her knife at his chest, aiming for his most vulnerable spots: the neck and heart. The distraction tactic was clever, but not enough to fool Leif.

He ducked, avoiding the blow easily. As he popped up on the other side of her, he swiped his rubber blade against her forearm. Octavia gasped in surprise, offering him an additional momentary opening, which he took advantage of by swiping against her upper arm too.

She stumbled out of his reach and cursed. Octavia looked down at her arm, her eyes wide. "What the hell was that?"

Leif chuckled, tossing his rubber knife up into the air, then caught it by the hilt with ease. "Sorry, felt like showing off a little."

Octavia scowled at him. She chewed the inside of her cheek, pursing her lips as if she wanted to ask him a question, but was resisting for some reason.

"I can't read minds," he said. "You're going to have to actually ask me if you have a question."

"Ugh, sorry. I just—I don't understand why you chose to attack my arm when my vital organs were exposed," she explained, rubbing the inflamed skin where his rubber blade had met her forearm. He winced against a twinge of guilt. She was in pain. The swipe must have given her a friction burn.

"Several reasons," Leif began, twirling the fake knife between his fingers. "An enemy always expects their opponent to go for the obvious kill, so when you go for the limbs, they're surprised. It also puts more distance between you and their weapon. Injuring or disarming your opponent can be just as effective as killing them. If I'd actually sliced the muscles and tendons in your forearm, you'd have dropped your hold on the knife. Then, if I'd really gotten your triceps, you wouldn't have been able to extend your elbow for a second attack."

Her lips parted slightly. "Oh, that makes sense."

Leif forced his gaze away from her mouth. "Despite what you

may think about me, I don't relish the thought of taking a life," he murmured, twirling the prop again, giving him something else to look at.

"I have a hard time believing that. Just a few weeks ago you seemed all too eager," she bit out critically. The ice in it made his stomach clench.

"You're right. And I'd have agreed with you back then. I honestly thought I *would* have relished it." Leif sighed deeply, finally ready to share the thoughts that had been haunting him since he'd discovered the truth. "But I would've been wrong. What I actually would've relished was Garren's approval. Killing someone in cold blood would've eaten me alive. I'm sure of it."

Octavia was staring at him when he met her gaze once more. Her brows were pinched in confusion. "But I thought you and Garren had a good relationship . . . you know, before."

"I thought we did too. But again, I was wrong. I was wrong about so many things . . ." His gaze drifted over Octavia's shoulder, going far and away, back to days without sadness or resentment. He shook his head, returning to the present. "Come on, let's switch weapons and go again."

They switched out their rubber knives for rubber daggers.

"Now, the fighting style to use when wielding a dagger is drastically different from the style you used with the knife," Leif began as they got into position across from each other.

"Why? They're the same weight and size."

"Because a knife's made for cutting and slicing, whereas a dagger's meant for stabbing. See the difference in the edges?" he asked, gesturing toward the symmetry of the prop dagger in her hand. She nodded. "Knives can be extremely useful for disarming, but daggers are useful for stabbing and killing, so there are fewer fighting techniques that make sense to use with them. Dagger fighting usually involves attacking your opponent from behind and stabbing them under the ribs and up into the kidney or between the fourth and fifth ribs and into the heart. Attacking from the front with a dagger often leaves you vulnerable."

"Got it."

"You need to grip the dagger differently based on which angle and direction you're attacking your opponent from."

"Just like with knives."

"Exactly. Do you want to go through some basic moves first or just jump in?" But he anticipated her response, choosing not to wait for it. "Never mind, stupid question. Let's jump in," he said.

At the sight of her smile, his mouth flicked up into a smirk before he could stop himself. She caught it and cocked an eyebrow. Leif shook his head and forced his lips back down. *She's like a bad habit I can't seem to shake—that I don't know if I want to shake anymore.*

They took their stances, feet wide, hips centered, fists and daggers raised. Since they were facing each other, Leif held the dagger like an ice pick, blade facing downward, hoping to find an opening from the front despite the instruction he'd just given Octavia.

Octavia held her dagger backward, the blade resting against her forearm. It wasn't the smartest grip to start off with, but Leif decided to wait and see how it played out before correcting her.

"Go," Leif instructed. Then he charged toward her, his dagger arcing toward her chest.

She immediately assumed a defensive stance, making an X with her arms and blocking his attack. His forearm caught against hers, between the crooks of her wrists. With one great heave, she shoved him away.

Leif jumped back, choosing to change tactics. He twisted his wrist to change his grip, the blade of the dagger now facing upward. He didn't hesitate, bounding forward once more to attack, his dagger held out before him.

In the blink of an eye, Octavia's weaponless arm shot out to meet his, their wrists slamming together. Her daggered hand remained tucked at her side, the hilt still facing him. Then her wrist pushed against his, throwing his arm wide. She guided Leif's arm up and around, twisting it painfully behind his back. He kept his grip on his dagger, but just barely.

Without skipping a beat, Octavia's right hand jutted out. She pressed the blade of the dagger against his back, where his kidney was. She released a soft, throaty laugh in his ear, sending an unwelcome but not at all unpleasant shiver down his back, before she released him.

"I think I like this one better," she mused, flipping the dagger over in her hand. "Less flailing around."

Leif chuckled as he watched her. "Don't get cocky. It's probably just beginner's luck."

"Want to test that theory?" she challenged.

"Absolutely."

They spent the next half hour sparring, and Leif quickly discovered it hadn't been beginner's luck. Octavia won every single match. Her ability to expose an opponent's vulnerabilities was truly impressive. At the end of their final spar, she flung Leif face-first onto the hardwood floor and jammed her elbow against his ribs where she would've plunged the dagger, right into his heart.

Now she's the one showing off.

Since Leif had fought against her before and seen her skill level, he should've anticipated a dagger would've suited her fighting style. "We shouldn't have even wasted our time with the knives," he said as he stood and brushed the invisible dirt off his clothes.

"No, it's good for me to know. Just in case," she replied as she returned the prop weapons to the case Leif had brought them in.

"You're really good. I think you might end up being good

enough to train me," Leif half-joked before taking a drink from his water bottle.

"Thanks," Octavia murmured, locking the case before leaning against it.

Leif joined her, perching against the table at her side. Her neck was exposed, covered by a light sheen of perspiration that reflected the dim light in the dark, wood-paneled room. Instinctually, he raised a hand to wipe away a drop of sweat that threatened to fall from behind her ear. The feel of her damp skin against his was familiar, achingly so.

Her breath hitched at his touch, but she didn't flinch from it. Instead, she met his gaze, her somber eyes the color of freshly tilled earth. He let his fingers linger a moment before he returned his hand to his side.

She asked quietly, "What were you wrong about?"

Leif winced. He'd almost forgotten he said that earlier. "It's a bit of a long list."

"I've got time."

Leif sighed deeply, considering where to start. "Well, after our first day here, we went home and ransacked Garren's apartment, looking for evidence that everything he'd told us had been a lie."

Distracted by the memory, his gaze drifted toward a desk lamp in the corner of the room. He let his magic call out to the light emanating from it. The bulb flickered slightly as his magic formed a connection. His heart rate spiked, fresh sweat slicking his palms.

"We found what we were looking for. Proof we were never officially adopted. Proof Garren paid off the local county sheriff in Vermont to limit their missing persons search. Proof he discovered the existence and location of our coven years prior to the attack." Hatred burned through his core like a red-hot fire poker had impaled him. Leif hesitated, unsure of how to continue. His jaw clenched against the words his gut told him to say, but his brain told him to hide.

But he was tired of hiding. Garren had taught him how to do it too well. Plus, this attraction he felt toward Octavia—there were only two ways to deal with it: fight it or accept it; fear it or master it.

He glanced sidelong at Octavia. She was watching him intently, dark eyes sharp, full lips soft. The angry heat in his core cooled; raging blue flames simmered into molten lava.

His heart threatened to falter as he braced against the weight of his choice.

I choose the latter.

"I believed it when I saw my name in that book from the library, but something in me still hoped it was wrong. A part of me still wanted to believe in Garren. But seeing the proof for myself, hidden inside a wall in his bedroom, in the house I've lived in for most of my life—there's just no denying that."

"I'm sorry," Octavia whispered before pressing her lips together firmly.

"What for?"

She blinked, long lashes grazing her cheeks. "For everything." Pain and sympathy twisted the tight set of her mouth.

The light from the lamp intensified, emitting a high-pitched hum. Leif ignored it, his attention locked on Octavia.

"He stalked my mom for years before the attack," Leif shared through clenched teeth. "I found the photos he took of her. Mostly surveillance photos, as if he'd been tracking her movements. But some of them were different. More intimate, and old, probably from when she was seventeen or eighteen."

Octavia's hands tensed, causing her nails to scrape harshly against the durable plastic case behind her. Her gaze fell to the floor. "That's sick."

"Yeah," he agreed, chin dropping, eyes following hers to the hardwood floor, covered in years' worth of scrapes and scuffs. Evidence of the coven's tenacity. Their fight for survival.

It still shocked him how very wrong he'd been. About everything. About every*one*.

Voice tight, she asked, "Are you going to kill him?"

The light bulb in the lamp popped under the pressure of Leif's surprise, tossing half of the room into shadows. They both startled, arms brushing. Octavia quickly shifted, returning space between them. The skin on Leif's arm tingled in her wake.

Octavia continued briskly, "I just mean we've been talking about getting justice—revenge, whatever you want to call it—on Garren for a while now, but nobody's clarified what that's actually going to look like. Will we kill him? Try to send him to prison? Use magic to punish him some other way?" Octavia's face was shrouded in shadows now, but she hadn't moved her gaze from the floor.

"I don't know," Leif answered honestly.

"If it came down to it, and you were forced to make the choice, do you think you could do it?"

"Kill him?"

She nodded.

Leif considered it. Immediately, the thought of Garren being dead was gratifying, but the feeling didn't last long. His mind flooded with memories of Garren teaching him how to drive, congratulating him on good report cards, recounting his escapades with his fellow witch hunters. The onslaught of memories made Leif sick to his stomach. "No, I honestly don't think I could."

"Even after everything?" she asked, voice low.

"Yes, even after everything," he admitted. Guilt—or perhaps shame—stirred in his chest.

Octavia nodded again before she raised her gaze to his. "Then

I'll do it for you. If it comes to that." Her expression was stony, ruthless. There wasn't a shred of hesitation there.

Leif's mouth went dry. "Why would you offer to do that for me? For us?"

Her eyes glimmered with protective intent, primal and deadly. "Because that's what we do in this coven. We protect each other. We compensate for each other's weaknesses. It's how we survive."

Leif had heard a similar version of that excuse before, when he'd questioned Octavia the day she'd come with Jo and Thad to convince them to rejoin the coven, but there was something different about the delivery this time. The words fell flat. A flutter unsettled Leif's stomach when he realized what that meant. *She's lying. There's another reason she's feeling protective. One she's not willing to admit.*

Leif reached out, taking Octavia's hand, her skin soft against his. Touching her was like being struck by a million tiny bolts of lightning—hot, paralyzing, and all-consuming. His breath caught in his throat.

Startled, she began to pull away, but he squeezed back gently, silently urging her to stay. He wasn't ready to let her go.

She paused, wide eyes searching Leif's expression.

Shock waves skittered across his nerves, heating his face, as she laced her fingers between his own. They stood in silence for a while, their beating hearts the only sound between them.

"Thank you," he breathed, barely more than a whisper, into the half-dark room.

Her "you're welcome" was a quick pulse of her hand before she let him go. His hand immediately went cold, contracting like thunder after a lightning strike.

She grabbed the case from behind her and turned to leave. "We can leave this under the bed in my old room upstairs," Octavia said. "Grandma wouldn't approve if she found it down here."

"All right," Leif agreed, rubbing his tingling hands together as he pushed off the table to follow her.

They made their way upstairs to the main floor and paused in the foyer, Octavia weighed down awkwardly by the case.

"Same time tomorrow?" she asked.

"Sure thing," Leif responded, smiling weakly, his mind still hazy with the lingering feel of her.

Octavia set her jaw. "It's going to be okay. No matter the outcome, we're going to beat him. He won't get away with what he did."

The confidence in her words was meant to be inspiring, but she'd never met Garren. The outcome of their efforts couldn't be predetermined, not with an enemy as powerful as him.

CHAPTER 30
OCTAVIA

The first snow of the season had fallen the night before, and the day was exceptionally cold. The only comfortable place in the whole house was near the fireplace in the library, so the room was packed, all eight of them attempting to relax after a full day of studying and practicing. Eventually it had dawned on Octavia: this was the first time they'd all been in the same room together outside of their lessons or meals since they'd been reintroduced almost two weeks before.

Quintin and Tripp were whispering at a desk in the corner, leaning over an old grimoire, studying the spell they needed to imbue Octavia's weapon with magic. Tripp was going to have to practice the spell every day if he was going to learn it in time to perform it to help Octavia, and Quintin was devoted to making sure that happened.

Sage and June were sprawled out on the rug, chatting incessantly, their woolen socks mere inches from the fire. Every ten or so minutes, Sage pushed up onto their elbows to stoke the fire with their magic. Jiro was lying beside them, joyfully playing a game on his Nintendo Switch, only occasionally jumping into their conversation.

Delta was seated in an armchair in the opposite corner of the room, reading a novel. It turned out Delta was an avid reader and extremely dedicated to keeping up with Reese Witherspoon's monthly book club. Delta hadn't spoken a word since she'd entered the room, but the mere fact that she was sharing space with them was progress.

Which left Octavia and Leif, who were currently sitting on opposite ends of a loveseat—yet somehow still close enough their shoulders occasionally bumped as they each pursued their own distractions. Every brush sent a jolt through Octavia, but despite the constant intrusion of his closeness, she wasn't in any hurry to find a roomier seating arrangement.

Leif was cleaning the glass of a very fancy, expensive-looking camera lens with a microfiber cloth while Octavia was re-reading one of her father's old grimoires, a self-soothing habit she'd developed sometime in her childhood. She'd all but memorized the text by now, but there was something therapeutic about studying his handwriting. His pen had always leaked ink at the end of a sentence, and he'd alternated between writing his Ys with loopy and straight tails. But her favorite parts were the small notes he'd made in the margins. The notes appeared to have only ever been for him, even though he'd known the book would eventually be shared with the entire coven.

Her favorite notes were the non-magical ones: *Buy diapers for O* and *Anniversary on the 7th, don't forget a present this time!*

Her father had been scatterbrained, but she'd grown to adore that about him. The flaws made him more real, more relatable. There wasn't much Octavia wouldn't have given to be able to hear her mother scold her father for forgetting her birthday or failing to pick up milk on the way home.

While memories from the night of the attack stood out in Octavia's mind like fireworks against a black sky, her earlier memories of her father had become frustratingly hazy, like trying to see through fogged glass. But the few memories she had of her mother were slightly more tangible. She remembered her mother brushing her hair, singing her lullabies in bed, cooking her breakfast in the morning. Simple, monotonous moments. Moments that happened every day.

She held them close to her heart regardless.

Out of the corner of her eye, she caught Leif watching her run her fingers over the loops and curves of her father's words. He'd taken a break from cleaning, camera assembled and pointed at her. He smiled as he peered through the viewfinder. A soft *click* sounded from the camera as Leif pressed the shutter button.

"What was that for?" she asked him in a playful tone.

Leif gazed down at the image on the display screen. His smile deepened. "Nothing. It's just nice to see you smile. You don't do it often, so I wanted to document it."

Octavia hadn't realized she'd been smiling. "This grimoire was my dad's. I like to read it sometimes when I'm feeling . . ." How was she feeling? She was a bit sad, but mostly she was hopeful, possibly even content. A month beforehand, Octavia would never have believed she might someday feel content, but sitting here in front of the fire with the people she cared for most, she felt that contentment was closer than ever.

"I get it," Leif said softly, placing the camera back on the side table. Octavia was grateful he didn't make her try to put the feeling into words. "Thaddeus showed me where my parents' grimoires are." He pointed to a spot high up on the bookshelf to their left. "But I don't think I'm ready to read them yet. It feels like opening Pandora's box. I don't know why."

"That makes sense," Octavia said. "Once you face those emotions, it's impossible to shove them back down."

"Exactly."

"We're here for you whenever you decide to read them." The words were barely even out of her mouth before a wave of heat flooded her face and neck. *"We"! I said "we," not "me"! So why am I blushing like I just said something suggestive?*

Quick as a flash, Leif had the camera in his hand again, snapping several more photos. Octavia's instinct was to blush further and throw her hand in front of her face, but that look in his eyes—the playfulness glinting in them—stopped her. Instead, she posed, sticking the tip of her tongue out before flashing him the middle finger. His deep laugh vibrated right through her, fine hairs rising in its wake.

"Will you two please stop your incessant flirting?" Delta called at them over the top of her book. "It's making me nauseous."

Octavia's stomach clenched, her spirited expression falling from her face.

Delta smirked to herself for a moment, then flicked her eyes up and around the room. Everyone's gazes were now focused on her.

"Fuck me," she murmured as she closed her book.

"Did you end up calling her?" Leif asked before she could decide to leave.

Delta's eyebrow perked up. "Calling who?"

"Your mom. I saw you enter her number into your phone after Jocasta tracked it down for you."

Octavia's chest tightened with anxiety, wondering how Delta would react. Jocasta had spent the better part of last week tracking down Delta's mother's phone number.

"And why would I do that?" she asked impatiently, scowling at him from under a thick layer of obsidian lashes.

"To reconnect, of course," June replied from the floor, as if it was the most obvious thing on the planet.

"And what if Garren kills us after he discovers we've turned on him? Wouldn't it be rather cruel to reconnect a mother with her long-lost daughter only to go and die on her a week later?" The bite in Delta's words was scathing. She'd considered this scenario thoroughly, although Octavia doubted she'd ever admit it.

"I—I suppose so," June relented, color blooming in her face, "but to be honest, I hadn't considered the possibility of us dying."

"Of course you wouldn't have," Delta scoffed. "You don't know Garren."

"That's the reason I haven't called my mom either," Jiro chimed in, setting his Switch down on the rug next to him. "Well, that and the fact I'm terrified she'd hop on a plane from Japan."

"Why would that be terrifying?" Sage asked, the fire beside them growing dimmer as their attention drifted.

"Because we're strangers now. I'm not the same person I would've been if Garren had never taken me. I—" Jiro pulled at the fibers of the rug nervously. "I'm afraid who I am now will be a disappointment."

Delta shifted uncomfortably in her chair at his words. Octavia suspected she shared Jiro's fear.

"But you're amazing, Jiro," June said with a small smile. "I know sometimes it's hard to see these things within yourself, but trust me when I say I know she'll love you just as much, regardless of who you've become."

Jiro swallowed hard, his Adam's apple bobbing. He seemed at a loss for words. June reached out a hand across the rug toward him. For a moment, it lay there, palm up, waiting to be accepted. Jiro considered it briefly before taking it, smiling gratefully at her. Octavia's heart warmed for Jiro. She relished knowing the others were opening up to him as much as she was.

"Well, I'm pretty sure there's not a single one of us in this room without raging parent issues," Tripp proclaimed. "Hell, my dad abandoned me and my mom while she was pregnant with me, so my daddy issues pre-date the attack *and* Garren." He gave a dark chuckle, leaning away from the desk.

"You too?" Quintin asked next to him. "My parents got divorced when I was three, and then my dad hauled ass to California. He used to come visit every year on Christmas or my birthday, but eventually he stopped. I don't think I've talked to him in four or five years, actually."

"Well shit, who would've thought?" Tripp replied, seeming to reevaluate Quintin with a considerate gaze.

"Isn't it severely fucked up that the one thing we can all bond over is our parental trauma?" Sage asked, sitting up. June followed suit.

"Yeah," several of them replied in unison, followed by barks of hollow laughter.

Octavia's gaze dropped back to the grimoire on her lap as silence draped over the room. A sudden jarring feeling of rightness fell over her, causing goosebumps to wash over her skin. This was the way it was always meant to be, the eight of them together. They'd been deprived of this, of each other, for far too long. Never again.

All at once, four phones buzzed around her.

Leif pulled out his phone first. "Fuck," he murmured.

Octavia closed the grimoire, abandoning it on the armrest. "What?" she asked, the rhythm of her pulse picking up tempo.

Jiro and Tripp whipped out their own phones, then read their screens carefully and quietly.

"It's Garren," Jiro said to the room.

"What did he say?" Quintin asked, forehead creased anxiously.

"'Finishing up in Seattle,'" Tripp read aloud. "'Booked a flight back the evening of the thirtieth. I'm excited to see you all.'"

Octavia inhaled a deep breath, suddenly feeling dizzy. That was so soon.

"Shit," Sage breathed, "that's it then? That's the deadline?"

"Sounds like it," Delta replied monotonously, her phone untouched on the armrest next to her.

Octavia stared at her incredulously. *How is she being so nonchalant?*

"That's only ten days from now," Tripp whispered, the hand holding his phone trembling slightly.

"We have enough time," Quintin said, his voice strong and steady. The fist in Octavia's chest unclenched a bit, giving her more freedom to breathe.

"Well, if it's not enough time, then we die. Problem solved," Delta mused, nuzzling into the armchair as she cracked her book back open.

"That's morbid as hell, D," Jiro said, scowling at her.

"How should we answer him?" Leif asked.

"Just like normal," Sage instructed. "We can't have him expecting anything."

Leif typed on his phone briefly, and Octavia knew he'd hit "send" when three phones buzzed. Leif read aloud, "'We're excited to see you too. Let us know if your flight gets delayed. See you soon.'"

Tripp nodded. Jiro swallowed hard again, falling back down to his spot on the floor. Delta continued ignoring her phone, seemingly engrossed in her book. As they relaxed, Octavia loosed a tense breath.

Quintin met Tripp's gaze. "Guess it's time to get back to work."

Tripp dipped his chin, tossing his phone on the desk and returning his attention to the grimoire.

Sage, June, and Jiro gathered their belongings from the floor and exited the room. Delta remained in her chair, reading happily, as if the world hadn't just shifted beneath them. The room was suddenly so still, and yet the world seemed to be swimming in

Octavia's vision. It felt real; this was really happening, and now they had a definite timeline.

Octavia leapt up off the couch, but a sudden warmth around her arm—Leif's hand, she realized when she looked back—stopped her.

"Where are you going?" he asked, brows furrowed.

Octavia swallowed against the dryness in her mouth. "Downstairs to run drills."

Leif frowned. "But you've already trained for like four hours today."

Octavia shrugged his hand off. "And?"

"And you need to rest. You won't be of any help to us burnt out."

Octavia sighed. "Fine. But I have to do something. I can't just sit here helplessly." She motioned to the loveseat with a palm.

"Help me with my training. With my magic, I mean." His silver-flecked eyes were pleading.

Octavia looked down at her father's grimoire, considering Leif's request. Her father had written some interesting theories that might be applicable to Leif's light magic.

"Yeah, all right," she finally relented, picking up the grimoire from the arm rest and leading the way out of the room.

The stronger Leif got, the better off they'd be. At least that's what she told herself, in spite of her racing heart. How she felt about him, how her body responded to his, had absolutely nothing to do with it.

CHAPTER 31
OCTAVIA

O ctavia gripped the couch for balance, squeezing her eyelids shut against the glaring light. Vivid purple and pink swirls danced across her vision. When the colors finally faded, they were replaced by a sea of flashing stars as she opened her eyes. She really needed to be using sunglasses for this.

It took several long moments for her vision to adjust to the dim lighting in the sitting room. Eventually she located Leif on his hands and knees in front of her. He was dripping with sweat. His black T-shirt clung to his soaked skin, and strands of platinum blond hair were plastered against his forehead and neck. He sucked in short, labored breaths, and his arms and legs shook viciously. He was getting more powerful by the day, but right now he was completely tapped out. He'd pushed himself too far again. Octavia cursed at the sight of him.

She walked toward him as his arms failed. She caught his shoulders just in time, a fraction of a second before his face hit the ground. Grunting, she rolled him over onto his back, placing his head in her lap.

"Come on, you have to drink this," Octavia pleaded softly as she patted his cheek and pulled a potion vial from her pocket. His eyes rolled, and a miserable moan escaped his lips. "That's right. Okay, now drink. It'll help."

She lifted the glass vial to his chapped lips. Using her other hand, she pulled his chin down, opening his jaw. The clear liquid dripped into his mouth as she tipped the vial. Watching his throat bob, she released the breath she'd been holding. He'd feel better in moments. Octavia had been given the very same potion only a few weeks ago. She'd asked June to make a revitalizing potion after she'd started helping Leif practice magic and seen how hard he was pushing himself.

But the potion was only a temporary fix. Leif would still feel unbelievably sore, sick to his stomach, and generally like a big, fat pile of shit when they were done. But that was his choice. He didn't have to push himself so hard. Octavia had reminded him of that fact several times until it had started to visibly irritate him, so she'd stopped, and instead started forcing magical steroids down his throat.

Leif's eyes fluttered open.

"You have to slow down," Octavia scolded as she brushed the drenched hair off his brow. "This is getting dangerous. You've only been practicing magic for two weeks."

Leif nodded and rolled up to a seated position, clutching his head in his hands.

"Dumbass," Octavia murmured while rising to retrieve his water bottle. He accepted it gratefully, drinking deeply when she brought it to him. "Why are you so damn insistent that you have to be the strongest?"

He shrugged. "That's funny coming from you."

The flicker of a rage-fueled fire sparked in her chest, but she smothered it. She took a deep, calming breath before saying, "There are nine others in this coven. Lean on us rather than kill yourself trying to do the impossible."

"I can do it," he croaked, throwing her a harsh sidelong glance.

"Yeah, you *can* do it, but at what cost? Do you think you'll be helpful to anyone when you're passed out on the floor like this?"

He tilted his head side to side, stretching his neck and rolling his shoulders.

Octavia dropped to the floor across from him, wielding the only supposed power she had against this infuriatingly stubborn man. She stared—and stared—until he twitched uncomfortably under her gaze like an ant under a magnifying glass. She had no idea why this tactic worked so well with Leif, but it did. It broke down his walls, letting her in. To see the man behind the mask.

"My power has no real offensive applications," he admitted gruffly, "but it would if I was able to hone the light into a laser."

"That's bullshit and you know it," Octavia said brusquely. "How is temporarily blinding your opponent not offensive? My vision still hasn't completely recovered, and I had my eyes closed."

Leif simply drank from his water bottle in silence.

"Plus, you're an amazing fighter. You're absolutely lethal . . . with magic lasers or without." Her voice broke on the last word.

Just like her, he felt inadequate without powerful magic. In spite of everything he'd been able to teach her about fighting, in spite of his brilliantly tactical mind, in spite of his physical strength, he still couldn't see the value he brought to the coven. *How can he not see his versatility?*

Rage flared again, trailed by envy. Both burning hot and fast behind her sternum.

Octavia stood up, meaning to storm out of the room, but found herself held back by Leif's hand. His expression was twisted in regret, the corners of his mouth pulling into a deep frown. It didn't suit him.

"I'm sorry. I was being an asshole. Please stay."

"I—Why should I?" she asked exasperatedly. "You're tapped out, and I wasn't even helping."

"Yes. Yes, you were," he breathed, scooting back to lean against the wall.

"How?"

"I'm stronger when you're near."

She scowled. "Wicked pick-up line."

Leif chuckled. "I'm telling you, it's true."

Octavia observed him for a moment. His eyes flicked between hers. From his soft expression, he didn't appear to be lying. "It might seem like I'm helping your magic, but that's technically impossible. Witches can syphon each other's magic, but the necessary spells are extremely complex. Not to mention, I have no magic to syphon even if you tried."

"I can't explain it, Tavi. But it's true."

This was the first time he'd called her by that nickname since Salem. Their date in the library felt like it was ages ago. Their last moment of blissful ignorance together. She wished she could go back to the moments when he'd looked at her like there was something in her worth looking at. When he made her feel like she just might belong—like she might just be enough without magic.

But I'm not enough. I know that. So I'll go. Right after we face Garren.

It hurts, living in a world I no longer belong.

"Plus, you're good company." He winked at her, cracking a hundred-watt smile.

Leif had been the only one to quiet these thoughts of hers, but whether those thoughts were loud or quiet, the pain was still there. Her feelings for him—feelings she could no longer rationally deny—weren't enough to make her stay.

She flipped him off, unwilling to accept the compliment.

"I shouldn't have implied I was useless without stronger magic," Leif went on hurriedly. "I'm sorry. I can be a prick sometimes."

Octavia looked away, eyes drifting to the carpet. "It's whatever."

"It's not, though." He took a deep breath, leaning his head against the wall. "I'd like to think it's because I'm still trying to figure out who I am, but that's no excuse."

"Seems as good an excuse as any," Octavia said, shrugging as she reclaimed her seat on the floor.

"I lost my sense of purpose that night in Salem." Leif's pupils dilated with the memory, black conquering the blue. "It was like gravity had failed me, and I was falling upward into the vast nothingness of space. Spinning out of control with nothing to grab onto . . . except Garren. Garren and my rage. He could be my purpose, bringing him to justice could be my purpose. But . . . who will I be after that? Will I be flung back out into space? Spinning aimlessly? The thought makes me sick." Leif swallowed hard.

Concern panged through Octavia's chest. *I wish things were different. I wish I could help you find what you're looking for. I wish . . . yeah, I really do, don't I? I wish I could be a part of your purpose.*

"That's a good question. I wish I had an answer for you," Octavia admitted. "But I'm probably the worst person you could ask. I can't even figure out what I'm supposed to be doing."

"Hmm?" he asked, turning his head toward her.

Octavia took a deep breath, steeling her nerves. She'd already come to the decision, so what was the harm in voicing it? Who knows? Maybe he'd even understand and agree with her, giving her the validation she hadn't even realized she'd been craving until right now.

"What's my purpose if I never get my magic back? Am I really going to pretend to be a witch forever? What benefit can a witch without magic even provide her coven?" She paused for a moment, lost in the endless blue of Leif's eyes. "I'll have to walk away at some point."

He tensed at her words, his eyes bouncing back and forth between her own.

"You can't even see it, can you?" Leif said in an awed voice. He leaned forward, the space between them evaporating. "This coven would be nothing without you. Because of you, the coven has doubled in size. I seriously doubt any of us would've agreed to join if you hadn't come with Thaddeus and Jocasta to convince us. You brought proof by giving us the book. You described the horrors of the attack so bravely. We couldn't doubt you after that if we'd tried. Hell, the only reason we're even getting along and working together right now is thanks to you stepping in to lay down the ground rules on day one." His eyebrows lowered in determination. "We'll find a way to get it back. I promised you I would help."

Octavia laughed softly. "Okay. Then I'll help you find your purpose after Garren. I promise."

It was an empty promise, but it had the desired effect. He relaxed. The others were going to have to uphold her promise for her. She wasn't going to be around long enough to keep it herself. *I can't keep playing pretend.*

Octavia watched Leif, a small smile on his lips, as he lifted the hem of his shirt to wipe the sweat from his face. She didn't even bother trying to look away. Because she liked what she saw—beyond just his body. She liked his sharp mind, his devotion, and his hidden tenderness. But more than that, she liked his hot-and-cold mood swings, and even his self-righteousness too. Traits that should annoy her but didn't. Instead, they set her on fire.

But, just maybe, for you . . . I would.

"Hey!" Quintin called from the library. "Leif, Tavi, get in here!"

Octavia stood and held a hand out for Leif. He took it, and she used her weight to help pull him to stand. He was still pale and sweaty, but he was steady on his feet.

They entered the library to find Tripp slumped over the desk, chest heaving, next to a shiny letter opener and an old grimoire. Quintin stood with his hands on his hips at Tripp's side.

"Are you all right?" Octavia asked, running over to him.

He replied between heavy breaths, "Yeah. Fine. Just tired."

"Drink this," she said, pulling a fresh vial from her other pocket and shoving the revitalizing potion into Tripp's palm. He eyed the vial suspiciously. "Trust me, it'll help."

"She's right. I just had some," Leif agreed from Octavia's side, motioning for Tripp to drink with a jerk of his chin.

Tripp lifted his head off the desk and nodded at Leif before draining the bottle.

Within seconds he was blinking rapidly as his shoulders straightened and mouth opened in awe. "Holy shit. Whatever that is, it's amazing!"

"Why were you so exhausted, anyway?" Leif asked as he crossed his arms.

"He did it," Quintin said, a grin the size of Texas on his face.

"I did it," Tripp breathed.

Warmth flooded Octavia's veins. "You're joking."

"Look," Quintin said, gesturing to a silver letter opener on the desk.

It was small, only a quarter of the size of an average dagger, but it resembled the shape. Quintin furrowed his brow in concentration, all of his focus on the letter opener. After a moment, it began to vibrate.

"No way," Leif whispered.

The vibration only lasted thirty seconds.

"I could only get a small amount of magic stored, but I'll keep working on it," Tripp explained. "Hopefully, a week from now I'll have the strength to store enough magic for an entire spell, or hopefully two."

Octavia felt the moisture on her cheeks before she realized she was crying. She yanked Tripp out of his seat by the crook of his elbow and rolled up onto the balls of her feet to wrap him and Quintin in a neck-breaking embrace. They groaned in protest as she kissed each of their foreheads wetly. Leif chuckled happily in the background.

This could change everything. With this loophole . . . maybe I could stay? I could be a part of their world again. Not necessarily in the way I imagined it, but hell! It's better than nothing!

"Thank you so much," she whispered after she finally released them.

"I, uh—sure," Tripp murmured, his cheeks flushing.

"Anything for you, Tavi," Quintin said, the corners of his eyes squinting from the size of his smile.

"I seriously appreciate everything you've done to help me. All of you." Her gaze bounced between the three of them.

"Seriously, isn't one boyfriend enough? Do you really need three?" Delta snarked at Octavia as she sauntered into the room.

"Yeah, so I'm opting out of—whatever this is," Tripp said, gathering the grimoire and letter opener before bounding from the room, sensing Delta's maleficence.

Irritation blazed into ire in Octavia's chest. She guessed now was as good a time as any to get to the bottom of Delta's attitude.

"What's your problem?" Octavia asked.

Delta sneered; a single eyebrow raised in challenge. "Me? Oh, I'm not the one with the problem."

"And what's that supposed to mean?"

"Only that if you keep leading these nice gentlemen on, you're going to do more damage than you're worth." Delta dropped her gaze to the hand she held before her chest, studying her nails as if she didn't have a care in the world.

Octavia bristled. "And exactly how have I been leading anyone on?"

"Darling, can't you see it?" Delta asked. "You're helpless."

Octavia's teeth ground together.

"You can't do a damn thing on your own. Not magic. Not fighting. These poor boys have been carrying your sorry ass with the hope that one day you'll let them back into your pants." Delta laughed. "But perhaps you need them to help you with that as well? Honestly, with how tightly you're wound, I doubt you can even get off on your own."

Octavia's pulse roared in her ears. *Did she really just say that?*

"You're way out of line," Leif warned in a dark tone.

At the same time, Quintin yelled, "Shut your mouth!"

Delta laughed again, the look in her eyes reduced to something savage, hungry. "I wonder . . . Leif? Quinny? Is she even worth it? I can't imagine a girl as pathetic as her would be very good in bed."

Octavia's fingernails bit little half-moons into the skin of her palms.

"Why are you acting like this?" Leif roared. "You're being ridiculous! Stop!"

Quintin stilled, standing frozen as a statue, his expression suddenly fearful.

Delta ignored Leif, her full attention now on Quintin, circling him like a lioness playing with her food. "I see. So you've never actually slept together." Her eyes flicked between Quintin and Octavia. "But not for lack of trying, am I right?" she asked, smirking at Quintin.

Octavia's jaw snapped shut at the insinuation. *The fucking gall!*

Octavia turned to Quintin, eager to watch him defend himself. But he remained silent. Instead, Quintin's ears twitched as the muscles in his cheeks seemed to pull taut. When his eyes fell to the floor, she realized she'd never seen him wear an expression like this before: so purposefully blank. Was her roommate, her best friend since childhood, *embarrassed?*

Octavia whipped her gaze back to Delta. "Of course we haven't slept together, not that it's any of your business. We're friends!"

Delta huffed an amused breath. "Ouch. Friend-zoned." She pushed her lower lip out in a faux dramatic pout, swinging her eyes back to Quintin. "Poor guy. I bet that hurt."

Quintin glared at Delta, avoiding Octavia's gaze like she was Medusa incarnate. Her heart felt like it had been punctured by a serrated knife.

"What are you doing, D?" Leif yelled. "Do you get off on making everyone around you fucking miserable?" The light bulbs in the room flickered in unison, tossing long, angry shadows across the library.

Octavia held up a hand to silence Leif, and he paused uncertainly. She didn't have an ounce of magical power, and yet the air around them crackled with the sparks of her rage.

"Leave. Now," she spat at Delta. "Before I do something I'll regret." Her voice rumbled with a confidence she didn't feel.

"I'd like to see you try," Delta snapped. "But I'm not worried. Not one bit. Want to know why? Because you're *nothing.*"

Then she turned and stalked from the room, leaving heaps of emotional carnage in her wake.

The remaining three stood in silence, staring after her. The tension lingering in the air was almost intolerable, but Octavia worried breaking the silence would be like shattering glass—completely irreversible.

"Quin—" Octavia began quietly, turning to her friend.

"We don't have to do this, Octavia," he murmured, his eyes locked on the door.

Before she could respond, Quintin strode from the room.

Octavia rounded on Leif. "Did you know?" she demanded.

The crease between Leif's brows mirrored the tense set of his mouth. "I suspected, but I didn't know for sure."

"I should've known!" Octavia slammed the heels of her palms against her eyelids. Angry splotches of red and orange colored her vision. Self-hatred seeped through her chest, staining her heart. "Fuck!"

"He's your best friend," Leif began quietly. "And that never changed, so that's what you always saw. You can't blame yourself for that."

Octavia's hands fell to her sides. "Obviously, I can. I didn't know, and now he might never look at me the same." The thought of Quintin avoiding her long-term had her heart racing.

Leif's face softened as he stepped forward, closing the space between them. He placed a warm hand on her shoulder. "He's just embarrassed. He'll get over it."

Octavia was grateful for that small gesture of comfort as tears pricked her eyes. "I do love him," she choked out softly.

He squeezed her shoulder gently before tugging her into an embrace. "I know. You're just not *in* love with him," he murmured, his chin resting at the crown of her head.

"No," she admitted against his T-shirt. She was sure she could feel her heart breaking in half, so strong was the ache.

"It'll be okay," Leif reassured her. "You talk to Quintin, and I'll talk to Delta. We can fix this."

They lingered in the embrace for a moment longer before Octavia pulled back, looking up into his face. The fine lines around Leif's mouth, which were usually smooth and invisible unless he smiled, stood out now, catching her eye. They betrayed the concern his bright, determined eyes were trying to hide.

He's worried about me, she realized as Leif backed away slowly, letting his hands trail down her arms until he was out of reach. He gave her a smile as he walked from the room, leaving her alone.

Maybe I am Medusa. I might not turn anyone to stone, but what good do I do? What do I give the people in my life in return for their love?

Delta's final parting word echoed in her mind, drowning out the kind words Leif had said to her earlier.

Nothing.

CHAPTER 32
OCTAVIA

O ctavia jerked up in bed, her entire body shivering. She wanted nothing more than to go back. Not back to sleep—to the nightmare that had consumed her—but back to the night they'd met. Back to his touch, his smell, his warmth. She *ached* for that night.

His light had always been there, before he'd even known about it, banishing the darkness. She needed it now—this very second—before she fell headfirst into the arctic chasm the dream had conjured.

She rolled over, grabbed her phone, and thumbed the touch screen on instinct. She wasn't thinking about anything beyond the icy feeling that sluiced her veins.

"Hullo?" His voice was gravelly from sleep. A heartbeat passed before she heard the *whoosh* of sheets being tossed in the air. "Shit—it's three in the morning. What's wrong?"

Her teeth were chattering, but her throat had frozen. She didn't even try to open her mouth to speak. She knew she couldn't.

"Octavia!" His pitch rose with every word. "Just tell me where you are. I'm coming. Are you in trouble?" She heard the *bang* of drawers clamoring shut. "Shit, I—" There was a heavy crash, then a groan. "Fuck, that hurt."

The beginnings of a smile cracked the frosty planes of her face. Her next breath came a little easier through her rattling teeth.

"I'm on my way now." The *slam* of a door. The *smack—smack—smack* of heavy footsteps. "I'll be there in ten."

A croak. That's all the sound she could make, but he didn't hear her over the roar of the car engine. Tires skidded against asphalt.

"No." The single syllable almost took her breath away.

"Octavia! Thank God. Talk to me. What's happening?" His voice was bordering on hysterics.

She cleared her throat, her rigid muscles relaxing by the second. "Nothing. I'm fine. I'm sorry. I shouldn't have bothered you." She released a shaky breath. "I don't even know why I called you."

Leif's side of the line was silent.

"Go back home. I don't need anything. I don't need you."

Why do I feel like I'm lying?

"Yeah, all right." His voice was gruff. "See you tomorrow."

Octavia's muscles continued to thaw, sore to the bone, as the icy darkness of the dream she'd already forgotten finally released her. "See you tomorrow."

She hung up, falling back against her pillows.

What the hell was that? The dream? The cold? My instinct to call Leif? For a second, I felt like I really did . . . need him.

Her hand shook as she returned her phone to the nightstand. She was still cold, scared, and confused—but she was also exhausted. Her heavy eyelids drifted closed as she rolled over onto her side, cocooning herself in the blankets as best she could. She was spent. She barely had enough energy to blow a stray strand of hair from her face before she fell back asleep.

A sequence of soft, muffled sounds pierced through the thin veil of Octavia's unconsciousness. A door opening and closing. Footsteps on carpet. Shoes being tossed off. *Who's here?*

She tried to open her eyes to look, to roll over, but she couldn't. She was frozen again. But before the fear had a chance to ravage her heart, she heard a low voice. A voice that made her heart panic for a completely different reason. "Octavia?"

The rush of adrenaline allowed her eyes to flutter open. She registered a fleeting glimpse of a tall figure shedding a coat. The fabric made a soft swishing sound as it hit the ground. *Is that—? No, it can't be. Why is he here?*

Oh, that's right. I called him, didn't I? It felt so long ago.

"Holy shit, you're cold as ice," Leif whispered as he climbed into bed beside her. His jeans rubbed against her bare legs, causing her sluggish pulse to quicken further. Then his arms were around her, strong and safe.

But I changed my mind; I told him not to come.

"You're gonna be okay," he murmured against her forehead. The fresh, familiar scent of pine filled her nose. She leaned into it.

I'm already okay, she thought stubbornly, even though she knew it wasn't true. Despite her current state of exhaustion and distress, she refused to yield.

But then, everything went warm. Her skin, blood, bones—her lips. Eyes snapping open in Leif's fading light, she saw what her lips couldn't feel. His mouth, an inch away, his warm breath emerging in a dissipating cloud, lingering around her lips. He wasn't kissing her. Just breathing. Just gazing at her with this look that brought her back to that first night. The night she yearned for.

Her arms moved on their own, wrapping around him, crushing her to him. Leif held her in return, arms snaked around her, warm hands firm against her waist and shoulder.

"I told you to go back home," she whispered into his sweatshirt, the warmth of his skin radiating through the thick cotton like it wasn't even there.

"I don't take orders from you," he whispered back.

Octavia smiled as her languid breathing returned to normal. But it hitched in her chest as Leif's lips brushed the curve of her ear. He whispered, even quieter than before, "You scared me."

She shivered, but not from cold—from delight.

Leif called on his magic again, misinterpreting her shiver. Heat flared in his palms. The warmth traveled with his hand against her skin, from her hip over her pajama shorts, coasting along her outer thigh down to her knee. She couldn't help but sigh at the sensation.

"Still think you don't need me?" he asked, a smirk in his voice.

"I *don't* need you." But as she said it, she gripped him harder, pulled him in closer.

Leif's breath quickened. "Good." His warm palm moved again, tracing the trail back to her hip. Her skin broke out in goosebumps. "I don't need you either."

Octavia swallowed against the heat building inside her, a heat that had nothing to do with magic and everything to do with Leif.

As if Leif sensed the change in her, his hands stilled. "You need to sleep." His lips retreated from her ear, and she couldn't explain away the wave of disappointment that doused her raging desire— not anymore. There was no denying it. She still wanted him. She always had.

But he doesn't need to know that right now. Not before we deal with Garren.

"Okay," she whispered, nuzzling her head against the crook of his neck.

One thought haunted her as she found sleep again. *With anyone else, I'm ice, but around him, I melt.*

Chapter 33
LEIF

His "talk" with Delta hadn't gone well. She'd used all her typical tactics: deflecting, ignoring, and insulting. So the cause of her outburst remained a complete mystery to Leif. He could try to make her talk all he liked, but the only option he was really left with was to wave the white flag. Delta was a puzzle he was never going to solve.

Octavia didn't seem to have had much luck with Quintin either. He appeared to be doing what he did best: deny and push on as usual. From what Leif had witnessed over the past few weeks, it seemed like that was where Quintin thrived—within a rigid routine. His days were always the same, organized and ritualized. Leif could see how any deviation, no matter how small, might be enough to throw Quintin off-kilter, causing him to hold on to normalcy with a vice grip. Leif might not have been the same, but he could sympathize.

Octavia was harder to convince. She was desperate to repair what she thought was broken, even though Quintin hadn't given any outward indication that anything had changed. Eventually, she heeded Leif's advice and gave him space.

Unfortunately, the strife in the house couldn't have come at a less opportune time. Not only was their meeting with Garren going down in five days, but it was also Christmas—which meant it was *also* Octavia's birthday.

Christmas by itself was an ordeal for the coven, Leif soon learned. The traditionally Christian holiday had been originally inspired by two of the most notable Pagan winter holidays, Germanic Yule and Roman Saturnalia. The histories of Paganism and witchcraft had intertwined so much over the centuries that the winter celebration had been lovingly adopted by the witches as well.

On top of that, Octavia's birthday made the day extra special.

Jocasta and Thaddeus had been preparing for days, cooking nonstop and decorating every inch of the house. Not a single table was without a yule log, and the multiple evergreen trees scattered about the house were beautifully adorned with handmade wooden yule stars. The scents of citrus, star anise, and cinnamon perpetually permeated the air.

It was meant to be a cheery time, but no amount of holiday cheer could dissolve the raw, feral tension that afflicted them all.

The day before, Thaddeus had gathered the eight of them in the library to begin strategizing. They'd brainstormed locations to lure Garren to, eventually deciding on an old warehouse in Southie. Its demolition was ongoing, but due to the recent heavy snowfall, it'd been suspended. The isolated location would give them the privacy necessary to use their magic.

Garren was expected to land at nine in the evening on the thirtieth. Leif's job was to lure him to the abandoned warehouse by ten. The coven would be dispersed across the landscape, cutting off any means of escape.

They would first attempt to reason with him, convince him to confess and surrender. But if that failed, the question remained: What would they do with him? Thaddeus was partial to involving the police. He was a man of honor, after all. Jocasta preferred the idea of reform by teaching him the truth about witches and witchcraft, with the hope that he would walk away from hunting. But Leif knew that was a pipe dream.

The one option no one voiced to the group, even though every mind had considered it, was murder. Of course, Octavia had discussed the possibility with Leif in private, as he assumed the others had amongst themselves, but the thought of declaring it to the group made it feel so . . . premeditated. Like if they got too familiar, too comfortable with the idea, they might decide it was their *only* option. Now that Leif was no longer a hunter, he knew better than to get trapped in that way of thinking again. There was *always* another option.

Jocasta had preached again and again that magic was never to be used to harm, hex, or curse another human being. In doing so, they would perpetuate the infamous stereotype that plagued witches. Leif didn't disagree with her. The logic was sound.

But Leif hadn't always been a witch. At one point, he'd been close to being a regular guy, a norman with a gun and a dagger, taught to be clever, trained to be lethal. Could he become that person again? He wasn't sure he could. And what was worse, he wasn't sure he wanted to.

He still hated Garren for what he'd done to them, but was that hatred worth losing himself? This version of himself he was just starting to get to know?

No.

He'd been deprived of his true identity for too long. He knew it might be selfish, but he was done living life for everyone besides himself. He was choosing himself over his desire for revenge. He'd go along with whatever the others decided, and that was that. There were much more important things to occupy his mind at the moment anyway. Like how bewitching Octavia looked adjusting the star on top of the dining room's decorative evergreen.

She wore all black. A long-sleeved, ribbed sweater dress clung to her every curve, leaving little to the imagination. Her porcelain skin was hidden from view beneath sheer tights, and scuffed Doc

Martens added her signature edge to the ensemble. Her long dark hair was curled in loose ringlets and fell down her back. The curls caught every fragment of light, reflecting in hues of honey and amber, depending on the angle. He longed to run his hands through them.

"Take a picture, perv. It'll last longer," Sage whispered in his ear as they walked past with a stack of plates.

Shit. He hadn't realized he'd been staring. Octavia hadn't noticed, but his cheeks burned regardless.

"What are you two whispering about back there?" Octavia asked as she stepped off the stepstool.

"Oh, nothing," Sage replied in a sarcastic tone, turning back to wink at Leif.

The burn in his cheeks blazed hotter.

"You okay?" Octavia asked Leif, eyeing his face closely.

He coughed. "Uh, yeah. Just a bit warm in here."

"Want to go outside?" Her gaze leveled with his. "I'm a bit warm too."

"Sure."

On their way out, in the foyer, Leif swiped a long, rectangular, gift-wrapped box he'd hidden behind his parka.

They stepped out through the front door of the house and onto the porch, covered in a fresh layer of dusty snowflakes. Their breath clouded before their mouths as they stepped away from the door, stopping between the banister and a porch swing that swayed ever so slightly in the frigid breeze.

"Shit, it's colder than I thought," Octavia chuckled, bracing her arms across her chest.

The knots in Leif's stomach pulled tight. "We can go back in a minute, but before we do, I wanted to give you something." Leif pulled the present out from behind his back.

No going back now.

"What's this for?" she asked, eyes glinting mischievously.

"Your birthday. Christmas. Take your pick."

The corner of her lips curled up playfully. "One gift doesn't count for both, you know."

Leif laughed, his nerves calming a bit. She didn't know it, but she'd made a habit of putting him at ease. It was one of the reasons he couldn't keep playing the role of enemy, one of the reasons playing the role of friend was slowly torturing him. There was only one role left he yearned for. A role he'd play with his entire heart. A role he'd botched before.

Her eyes dropped to the present as she brushed a thumb over the glossy wrapping paper. "I feel bad. I didn't get you anything. The coven doesn't usually give gifts during Yule." Her dark eyes returned to his.

"Jocasta told us. But this present is different," Leif said, grinning. "It's a hand-me-down."

Octavia smirked as she shook the box. The object inside rattled heavily. She tore through the wrapping paper messily, clearly not the type to save it for future use. The paper dropped to the porch, quickly dampening in the snow.

His hands shook nervously in his pockets as she lifted the box top and peered inside. The glint of metal flashed beneath the partially opened lid. Octavia stalled, gaze snapping to Leif, her smirk returning. "A weapon?" She cocked an eyebrow. "Are you flirting with me?"

He beamed. *Absolutely.*

She laughed as she opened the lid completely, the sound light and airy. Her eyes startled wide when she looked in the box. "But this—this is yours."

Leif rolled back onto his heels as he shook his head lightly. "Not anymore."

Octavia pulled his old dagger out of the box, setting the cardboard container on the porch swing. She held it in her hands, studying the engraving on the hilt, just as she had that night in Salem. Leif's whole life had changed that night, in more ways than he'd known at the time.

Like getting to keep Octavia in his life.

Octavia's brows knitted together. "It's cold as ice. Why isn't it heating up around you?"

"I asked Jocasta to remove its enchantment. Now it's just a regular dagger." Leif's lips twitched into a small smile. "That is, until we imbue it with magic for you."

Octavia tore her eyes from the dagger, observing him in that infuriatingly enticing way she did. The plumes of vapor from their breath mingled in the space between them, the only sound the ebb and flow of their breaths.

"I can't accept this," Octavia murmured, pushing the dagger flat against his chest.

Leif placed a hand over hers. "No, it's yours now."

"Why?" Her hand trembled slightly under his.

"Because I believe in you. I want this dagger to be proof of that."

Her eyes creased with concern—or was it fear? "But—"

Leif's rib cage suddenly felt too small for his heart and lungs. "I know you're planning something. I don't know what it is, but I know I don't like it. It feels like you're still thinking of giving up. Of running away from who you're meant to be. From who you are."

She flinched at his words. It was confirmation enough. His hand tightened over hers, still holding the dagger to his chest.

"I want this dagger to give you hope, Tavi. Hope that you'll break the hex someday."

She swallowed thickly, the slightest of quivers crumpling her chin.

He grasped her shoulder with his free hand, pulling her a step closer. "Promise me you won't give up. That you'll keep hoping."

Her eyes searched his frantically, looking for—*what?* Leif had no idea.

"I'm not your problem," she murmured. "So why do you care so much?"

Leif's mouth went dry. He licked his lips.

Octavia's gaze dropped, watching, as her own lips parted.

Leif whispered, "Maybe I want you to be my problem."

Impulse moved Leif's hand to the ends of Octavia's hair, hanging just above her elbows. He rolled the silken strands between his fingers, relishing in their softness. He smiled, if only to himself. *Softer than satin.*

Octavia surprised him, moving her hand out from under his. She discarded the dagger in the box on the swing and rested both palms against his chest, stepping forward to close the distance between them. She was trembling, whether from cold or something else. She was near enough he could count the faded freckles that dusted her nose and cheeks. The honeyed, citrus scent of her filled the air around them.

"We can't be lovers, can't be enemies, can't even be friends . . . What does that leave us with?" she asked breathlessly.

"Who the fuck knows?"

He didn't stop to think about the consequences; he just moved.

His lips met hers with fervent need, a need so deep it frightened him.

She stood on her tiptoes as her hands laced themselves into his hair. Chests pressed firmly together, they eliminated any distance between them. Her tongue swiped urgently against his, and his teeth captured her lower lip in response, pulling gently. A breathless gasp escaped her lips, making him dizzy. He gripped her waist harder, needing *more* of her.

They devoured each other—hands searching, lips bruising.

With each passing heartbeat, the rest of the world faded away. A better witch than he might've been able to bottle up this moment to relive it again and again and again, but Leif was new to the world of magic—new to *her* world—so he'd simply have to live in the moment as long as he could.

Leif was positive he'd never been happier, never more comfortable in his own skin. Being enveloped in Octavia's touch, smell, breath, was like being home—a home he never should've turned away from.

Reluctantly, Leif's hands dropped to his sides as she pulled away, her breath coming in rapid and shallow. His heart pounded haphazardly in his chest, the rush of blood in his ears far too loud. Even in the dark, he could see the flush in her cheeks. "Well, uh— that was . . ."

"Astounding? Brilliant? Earth-shattering?" he offered, joy steadying his sprinting heart.

Her laugh was sweet and melodic. The sound had him aching with desire.

"Yes, something like that," she agreed. She smiled in a way that Leif felt reflected his own—satisfied at last.

Looking into her eyes, watching the way they twinkled as she studied him, Leif felt himself being pulled toward a precipice. A precipice he knew he'd never come back from.

"What does this mean?" she asked under her breath, a hint of fear, or perhaps uncertainty, lacing her tone.

"I think we both know," Leif breathed as he tried to keep the sudden desperation he felt out of his voice. He needed her to choose this on her own; just as he was.

Octavia nodded, bending to retrieve the box and dagger from the swing. She clutched the present to her chest and walked past him.

Leif looked up at the stars, barely visible in the black sky. Before she made it to the door, he said quietly, "I'm still trying to figure everything out. Who I am, what I should be doing . . . but I know one thing for sure."

"What's that?" she asked.

"I know I want you." Leif turned toward Octavia to find her hair and eyes glistening red and green from the Christmas lights bordering the doorframe. "I want us."

A beat of silence passed, Octavia's chest pumping beneath the present pressed against it. Leif froze, feeling as if time itself stood still as he waited for her response.

Finally, she said nervously, "I—I do too."

Leif nodded as his body flooded with heat.

"After . . ." Octavia hesitated. "Maybe after Garren?"

He nodded again. "After."

"Thank you for the present." She smiled softly. "I love it."

Leif's heart clenched. "I'm glad."

In the next breath, he was alone on the porch, trying to quell the emotions bursting forth from his chest. But it was as impossible as trying to stop an avalanche. Eventually, he gave up, letting the emotions swell until, finally—

I think I love her.

CHAPTER 34
LEIF

By the time Leif reentered the house, the dining room was full of food and people for Yule dinner. The table was packed with holiday delicacies, from honey-glazed ham to candied yams to cranberry sauce. There was barely enough room for the plates and silverware. His smile ticked up at the sight.

A bar cart Leif had never seen before rested in the corner of the room. Octavia and June were in front of it, pouring their glasses full to the brim with plum-colored wine. Quintin reached around them and grabbed a full bottle of scotch from the cart, much to Tripp and Jiro's amusement. As he pulled out the cork with his teeth, they held out their empty glasses, which he gladly filled.

Jocasta and Thaddeus sat at the heads of the table and gestured for the others to sit. Leif walked to the bar cart and poured himself an Irish whiskey, neat, as the others took their seats. By the time he rounded on the table, the only seat left was in a corner between Delta and Thaddeus. He sat and returned Thaddeus's welcoming smile with enthusiasm.

"As this is our first holiday gathering as a reunited coven, I was hoping to say a few words," Jocasta called across the table. She smiled wide as all eyes fell on her. "The last three weeks have been . . ." She broke off, emotion rising in her voice. Immediately, Octavia's hand shot to her grandmother's.

Forever the hero. Leif's chest swelled with pride.

Jocasta nodded softly at her granddaughter, took a deep breath, and continued, "These last three weeks have been a dream come true. For myself, for Thaddeus, for the entire coven, including those who watch over us from their place of eternal rest." Her dark eyes glistened with unshed tears. "We are truly, deeply honored to have you with us today during the celebration of Yule and our beloved Octavia's birthday." She took a deep breath. "I know that in the new year, you may not choose to stay with us. You may choose to pursue your own life and interests outside witchcraft. If you choose another path, I hope you walk away with the knowledge of how precious this time has been for us."

Around the table, teary-eyed faces stared at her. Leif felt warm, warmer than he'd felt in years.

"And so, I'd like to make a toast to Leif, Jiro, Tripp, and Delta, for making this the happiest holiday season in recent memory." Jocasta raised her glass of sherry. Glasses clinked around the table, followed by the scraping of silverware against porcelain as food was eagerly heaped onto plates.

Jocasta's eyes swept across the scene in front of her. Her gaze eventually landed on Leif's, and a shiver of familiarity ran down his spine at how she studied him. Having gotten more accustomed to their family's scrutiny, he simply smiled and raised his whiskey glass in response. The slight hitch of a single eyebrow communicated her approval as she returned the gesture, glass raised in a toast.

Leif smiled deeply, drinking in the merriment of the moment. This was what they'd all been waiting for. The moment when they felt like they were finally a part of a family. The witch hunters had played pretend, convincing themselves that they'd had a real family all along. But they were wrong. They were famished for love, for acceptance, for acknowledgment.

This, right here, was it. The real thing. And Jocasta was right. It was precious.

Leif ate and drank like he never had before. Completely uninhibited, he tried a little bit of everything, even the array of steamed vegetables. He went back for seconds during dessert, finishing a whole piece of pie and several freshly baked cookies. The wine and whiskey never stopped flowing, warming his chest and cheeks to their limit.

By the time they began clearing the table, Leif's ribs were cramping from laughing so hard. Even Delta's eyes were watering. Before they could fully recover from their fits of laughter, they were interrupted by an adorably loud snort coming from the other end of the table. Octavia had cracked up at something Jiro said and now held both hands over her face out of sheer embarrassment.

"Jiro, you can't! That's not fair!" she choked out between her hands in deep, shaky breaths.

Underneath the influence of good food, great company, and even better booze, Leif couldn't help himself, he stared. Once again, completely uninhibited. He marveled at her pink cheeks, her wide smile, her tear-brimmed eyes. He drank in the sight of her with the fervor of a dangerously dehydrated man.

"You couldn't be more obvious if you tried, Leif."

"What?" Leif asked, yanked from his thoughts.

"Don't make me repeat myself," Delta said as she sipped from her whiskey glass.

Thaddeus had vacated his seat to help with clearing the dishes. *I should join him.* Leif pushed his chair back to do just that.

Delta scowled. "Sit back down. I was talking to you."

Leif sighed, sitting back down. "Sounded more like you were chastising me, D."

She waved him off with the flick of a wrist. "Potato, po-tah-to."

Irritation sparked in Leif's chest. "You know, that's probably why you aren't anyone's favorite." He flinched at the words as they left his mouth. *Damn it. Why does whiskey always loosen my tongue?*

Delta scoffed at his words, seemingly unfazed. "You really think I care what everyone else thinks about me?" She took another sip from her glass.

"I don't know, D. You're impossible for me to read." Sigh. Drink. Avert gaze.

Her lips pursed as she tapped a ringed finger against her glass. "I didn't used to be, you know."

Leif lifted his brows in question.

"You used to be the only one who got me. When we were younger."

Leif rubbed his forehead. "Was I?" *I don't remember that.*

"I understand why you wouldn't remember. I was your annoying little sister. Why would you pay me more mind than you needed to?" Delta stopped tapping her finger, now gripping the glass firmly instead.

Leif tried to focus on her face, but suddenly, he was finding it quite difficult to do so. "Don't say that. I love you. I don't have to say that for you to know it."

"That was true . . . once."

"It still is true." Another sigh. Another drink.

"Not anymore."

He paused carefully before responding, not wanting to make the situation worse with harsh, drunken words. "How could you possibly know that?"

"Because I have eyes, Leif. I've seen you with her, with the rest of them. You're different now."

"What did you expect? I can't be the same person I used to be. Not after everything that's happened. I had to adapt and change."

"I didn't," she countered, glaring at him.

"Well, that's wonderful, then. Good for you." He was starting to feel uncomfortable. But from the food, drink, or this conversation? *Probably all three.*

Delta rolled her eyes at him.

Leif scoffed. "I honestly don't know what you want me to say to that."

"I want you to understand!" she said, a little too loudly, as she slammed her empty glass on the table.

A few heads swung their way, but Leif waited until they returned their attention to their own conversations before asking, "Understand what?"

She grimaced, biting out the words. "Why this is so hard for me. Why being around these *people* is like listening to nails grinding on a chalkboard twenty-four-seven."

"I'm sorry, but that makes no sense. These people are great."

She scowled and rose from her chair.

"D, stop." He touched her arm, urging her to sit back down. "Help me understand."

Her pinched expression was uncertain. She sat and grabbed Leif's drink, downing it in one gulp.

"My whole life I was alone," she began. Leif opened his mouth to protest, but she waved at him to be quiet. "Just listen. Okay? I was the only girl surrounded by an entire family of boys. The only way to make myself heard was to be the loudest, the toughest, the hardest to swallow. After I figured that out, you three never left me behind, never forgot me, never left me out of the fun. But now . . . now I'm more alone than I've ever been. You three keep leaving me behind, forgetting me . . ." Her voice wavered, and she feigned pushing a strand of hair from her face to wipe at the corner of a teary eye.

Leif's irritation flickered out like a spent candle. "D . . ."

"I'm not the one who changed. You are. And now I'm alone. Again."

"I'm sorry—I didn't know." He reached for her arm again, nudging it reassuringly. "Yeah, you do piss us the hell off sometimes. But we don't want you to change. You're our family, and we want the others to love you as much as we do."

Her eyes narrowed in challenge. "Sure, you say that, but—"

"I'm not just saying it. I mean it." Leif laughed, leaning back in his chair. "A drunk person's words are a sober person's thoughts, right?"

Delta's lips twitched, as if she was holding back a laugh.

"Seriously, life would be terribly, horrifically dull without you. Please, don't ever leave us." Leif raised his hands in mock prayer, putting on his best drunken impression of a puppy dog face.

Delta laughed thickly as she rolled her eyes again.

Leif rapped his knuckles on the table. "But maybe we can work on being just a tad less bitchy."

Another throaty laugh.

"Sound reasonable?"

She finally smiled—a small and reserved smile, but it was *there*. "I guess so."

"Perfect." *Halle-fucking-lujah.*

"Can I admit something else?" Delta asked shyly. "You know, since we're being all drunk and sentimental?"

Leif laughed. "Sure."

Delta clenched her jaw as she hesitated. A heavy breath passed her lips before she finally said, "I considered telling them the truth. Forcing a wedge so big and deep between us that no one could ignore it." She shook her head. "I know I was miserable, but it's terrible I even considered doing it."

Leif's stomach dropped like the floor had evaporated beneath his seat. "What do you mean? What truth?"

"Octavia never told them." Delta nodded toward the other end of the table.

Leif's stomach clenched. "Never told them what?"

"That we were planning on killing them all. That if it wasn't for you and Octavia finding that book in Salem, they all would've died. Instead of reuniting their coven, we would've brought it to its knees, and we would've done it gladly." Her voice slurred slightly as she said the words. She was clearly too drunk to be having this conversation. But the expression on her face was somber, bordering on genuine sadness.

She regretted it too, and the realization sent Leif's spirits soaring.

"What the *actual* fuck?"

It took Leif a moment too long to register the anger in the voice, and then his joy came crashing down into his stomach. He turned in his seat. "Sorry?"

"What the *fuck* did you just say?" Sage bellowed at Delta.

Delta's bulging eyes would've been comical in any other circumstance. She looked like a literal deer in the headlights. "I—uh, I was just telling Leif how I've been having a hard time lately."

"That's not what it fucking sounded like!" A stack of dirty plates dropped from Sage's hands.

No. This can't be happening, Leif thought as the dinnerware fell through the air, slowly, so slowly, until—

Crash! The porcelain fractured into a thousand tiny pieces, scattering upon the hardwood floor. A silence followed, so dense it was as if the barometric pressure in the room had plummeted, sucking out all the oxygen. In the corner of his vision, Leif saw every face turn to their end of the table. His ears rang like a steam engine. He couldn't draw a breath.

Sage's empty hands began to spark, white wisps of smoke dancing in their palms a second before they caught fire. The heat warmed the clammy skin on Leif's face and neck.

"What's going on?" Quintin asked, wasting no time as he dashed behind Sage and restrained them by the elbows.

Dizzily, Leif's head spun as he gulped down a large breath.

"They were planning on murdering us!" Sage snarled, fighting against Quintin's grip. "The night Octavia and Leif went to Salem." Sage jerked their chin toward Delta. "I just heard her admit it!"

"That's impossible, Sage. You must've misheard them," June said in between hiccups from her seat at the table.

"No way! I know what I heard." The flames in Sage's palms flared.

"Watch it, Sage," Quintin growled.

"I can't!" they screamed.

"What in tarnation is going on in here?" Thaddeus yelled as he bounded into the dining room from the kitchen.

"They were going to kill us!" Sage exploded. "This whole time we've been playing house with our would-be *murderers!*"

"Sage, that was before we knew who we were," Leif said in a cautious tone, rising from his seat to face them.

"Don't! Don't you come near me!"

He paused, raising his hands in surrender. *I hate that look in their eye, like I'm a stranger to them again, like I'm the enemy.*

"What's all this about?" Thaddeus demanded.

Leif's eyes met Delta's, which were still thrown wide in fear. He opened his mouth to speak just as Octavia's voice rang out behind him. "It's my fault, Sage. If there's anyone you should blame, it's me."

She was sitting eerily still, facing Tripp and Jiro at the other side of the table. They looked at her with parted mouths. Jocasta edged into the arched doorway beside Thaddeus, watching silently.

"What are you talking about?" Sage spat, their eyes still trained on Leif and Delta.

"I made the decision not to tell you," said Octavia as she rotated in her seat.

"Tell us what, dear?" Jocasta asked.

"Jiro, Tripp, and Delta were planning to attack our apartment the night Leif and I went to Salem. The night we discovered he was actually a witch." Her hands flexed against the wooden back of her chair.

Sage's gaze whipped to Octavia. "You knew?" they asked in a small voice.

Octavia nodded. "I did."

"And you didn't tell us?" Quintin asked, the muscles in his jaw feathering.

Octavia met their glares, regret swimming in her eyes. "I didn't want to give you any more reason to hate them. It was already going to be an uphill battle. Learning they'd planned an attack on us only would've made the situation worse."

The silence in the room pounded against Leif's eardrums.

"I'm sorry," said Delta in a shaky voice. "I—I'm drunk. I didn't think anyone would overhear me."

"Don't you fucking apologize! You will *never* be forgiven!" Sage screamed, straining against Quintin's grasp.

"Sage, cut it out!" Octavia cried, standing abruptly. "I'm tired of your bullshit! They had no idea who we were to them back then. How could you have expected them to do anything different? We were their enemy! We were the villains in their story! Don't you get that?" Her voice was shrill. "Have they even once tried to do anything harmful to us since they learned the truth? Apart from Delta being a royal bitch."

Delta shrugged mildly.

Octavia cautioned her with a glare before returning her attention to Sage. "Are you really going to judge them based on one ill-informed decision they made before you even knew them? And are you going to weigh your judgment of that more heavily than the experiences you've had with them the past three weeks? Because if you are, you're not the person I thought you were, Sage."

Octavia walked around the table toward them. As she approached, Quintin released his grip on Sage, moving back to give them space to talk one on one.

Without saying a word, Octavia took Sage's flaming palms in her own, barely wincing at the pain of being burned.

Shit! Leif lurched forward, heart hammering.

Sage gasped and ripped their hands from hers quickly. Leif stopped a foot away. They quelled the flames and clasped their hands together. But from what Leif could see of the blisters already forming on Octavia's palms, he could tell they'd given her second degree burns, at least.

"What the hell? Why'd you do that?" Sage demanded, a twinge of panic in their voice.

Octavia's burnt hands shook, her eyes locked on Sage. "We all have the power to hurt the people we love. They had the power to hurt us well before they knew about their magic, and they have even more power to do so now. But they haven't, and they won't."

Sage asked, "How do you know that?"

Octavia sighed. "Because they're our family, and I've chosen to trust them."

"Octavia's right," Delta said, her voice still quivering slightly. "We're on the same team now."

A choked sound came from the other end of the table. Leif looked to find June on the verge of tears. Tripp patted her shoulder gently, his eyes downcast. June leaned into Tripp's touch. Jiro met Leif's gaze, the set of his eyes sharp and determined.

"And from now on, we'll all act like it," Leif added, turning to look pointedly at Delta.

She nodded in silent agreement.

Sage's teeth ground together as they scanned the room, united once more. They huffed as their shoulders sagged, the fight going out of them.

Jocasta chimed in, "Well, I think Octavia is right. We can't hold grudges against people for who they used to be. They've shown we can trust who they are now, and that's all that matters. Are we all in agreement?"

She looked around the room from person to person, and everyone nodded in response, except Sage, whose face dipped toward the floor.

"Wonderful," said Jocasta cheerfully. "Now, Thad, dear, would you please pack up the bar cart? I think we've all had enough for one night."

CHAPTER 35
LEIF

The small potions room in the basement smelled of hazelnut and sandalwood. Leif breathed deeply, savoring the woodsy scent. June was hunched over a grimoire next to the large cauldron, tendrils of steam wafting from the center. She chewed her bottom lip, arms crossed, as she read the page.

Leif knocked on the door frame. "How can you make battle prep smell so good?" he asked with a smile.

June's gaze lifted. Her returning smile was warm, framed by petal-pink lips. "Don't flatter me. That's just a candle you're smelling." She gestured to a small candle burning behind her on the workbench with a thumb over her shoulder. Above the candle were shelves upon shelves of potions ingredients, from dried herbs to flowers to powders to liquids. Leif felt dizzy just looking at them all.

"So what's this you're working on?" Leif asked, stepping into the room and walking up to the table. He peered into the pot, finding a simmering pool of onyx liquid. This close, Leif realized the potion was odorless. He looked back to June, his eyebrows raised in interest.

She dipped her head toward the cauldron. "That's the base for one of the powders."

Leif watched the liquid simmer. It seemed to drink in every photon of light that touched it. A chill slithered down Leif's spine.

He took a step back from the concoction. Before June even responded, Leif guessed the answer to his silent question.

"Sensory deprivation," June confirmed. She laughed, the sound hollow, and shook her head slowly. "It's one of the most complex potions I've ever made."

June raised her gaze to Leif's, her bottom lip red and inflamed from chewing it. *She's nervous*, he realized.

"I'm scared I'll mess it up," she murmured as her eyes filled with tears. "If I mess up, if the powder doesn't work, someone could get hurt. I—"

Leif interrupted her. "You won't mess up."

She blinked, tilting her head.

Leif shifted his weight on his feet. "Look. I've learned three important things about this coven since joining. First" —he held up his index finger— "each of you would do just about anything to protect the group. Second" —his middle finger joined the first— "you're all insanely talented. And third" —his ring finger popped up before his hand fell to his side— "even if one of us was to fail at our jobs, we'd have backup."

June's lips twitched.

"You're not alone." Leif stepped back toward her, the table between them. "In this coven, you're never alone."

June looked at Leif with wide green eyes. "She's won you over."

Leif's gaze dropped. He mindlessly flipped through a spare grimoire lying open on the table. "How could she not?" he asked quietly.

June laughed, drawing Leif's eyes again. "The ridiculous part is that she doesn't even know, does she?" Her eyebrows perked up. "The effect she has on everyone around her."

Leif tilted his head in question.

"Tavi thinks she's all doom and gloom, but she's not. She thinks she's useless right now, but she's not. She thinks she doesn't

deserve to be a part of this coven, but she couldn't be more wrong."
June's gaze dipped to the hands she wrung; her fingernails were
bitten to the quick. "Tavi's the only reason we survived the attack.
Did you know that?"

Leif's stomach dropped. He shook his head.

"I don't know how exactly—the memories are definitely fuzzy,
so I don't have the specifics, and she doesn't know either. I've asked
her about it over the years, but she's never seemed to recall what I
do." June swallowed thickly. "I know in my heart that she saved us.
She found me upstairs in the house after they broke in. She helped
me be brave, helped me put one foot in front of the other. We got
captured, and they brought us into the main room with everyone
else. She pushed us all back behind her when the guns started fir-
ing and the magic flared. I think I passed out immediately afterward, but I remember her standing before us with her arms spread
wide . . . like a warrior."

Leif's heart drummed in his chest.

"She's the heart of the coven." June's gaze turned hard. "So don't
make us regret letting you get close to her."

Leif's palms began to sweat. June was small, but that didn't
mean she wasn't intimidating. "Sure," he said, waving a hand toward
the brewing potion. "As long as you stop doubting your mad skills."

Her eyes softened. "Deal."

"What's up?" Leif asked after he entered the dining room
through the foyer.

Jiro, Tripp, and a person Leif didn't recognize sat around the
dining room table with wide smiles pasted on their faces. The
stranger was tall with broad shoulders and a narrow waist. Short

dirty-blond hair framed pale skin and a strong jaw. They were dressed in generic masculine clothes. Since strangers couldn't simply waltz into this house, thanks to the protective enchantments Jo had cast, there was only one explanation, and Leif was impressed. This was easily Delta's best glamour, but he had no idea who she was trying to emulate.

And on top of that, Leif was pretty sure he hadn't seen the three of them simultaneously happy like this since before the "Surprise! You're a witch!" bomb dropped.

"Jiro finally figured out his specialty!" the person who both was and wasn't Delta said in a deep voice.

Leif strode toward them. "What? No way!"

Jiro's ears turned pink. "Yeah. I'm pretty sure."

"Tell him the story," Tripp urged, nudging Jiro with his elbow.

"What story?" Octavia's voice came from behind them.

Leif's heart skipped a beat before kicking up a notch.

"I wanna hear," she said as she walked up beside Leif, her shoulder brushing against his, sending a bolt of electricity through him. His hand instinctively flexed toward hers, but he didn't grab it. Not in front of the others. *Not yet.*

Octavia glanced at Delta. "Hey, nice glamour."

Delta freed a heavy breath, finally releasing the spell. She morphed before their eyes, the oversized clothes now hanging from her smaller frame. She inhaled a deep breath, a light sheen of sweat on her face. "Thanks. I'm getting better at holding it for longer too."

"Who was she trying to look—" Leif began.

He was interrupted when Octavia said, "I'll tell you later." She turned to speak to Jiro. "Tell the story!"

Jiro laughed, looking between the four of them. "All right. So, just an hour or so ago, I was napping in the library."

Delta scoffed. "Lazy piece of—"

Jiro shot her a warning glance. "Hey, this is my story. Shut it." He cleared his throat. "Where was I? Ah, right. So I was napping, when suddenly my magic stirred, waking me from my dream, only . . ." His eyes drifted between them. "I wasn't actually awake. I was still asleep."

Octavia asked, tucking her hair behind her ear, "How can you be both awake and still asleep?"

Jiro snapped his fingers. "That's what I was trying to figure out. And I'm not gonna lie, after about three minutes of not being able to move a muscle, I started freaking out. But then my magic kind of . . . changed rhythm beneath my skin, and I got the urge to . . . float. So, I did." His eyebrows shot high up his forehead.

"What?" Octavia and Leif asked at the same time.

"My soul or whatever *legit* left my body," Jiro said excitedly. "Like one minute, I was in my body, and the next I was looking down at myself, just napping there like a cute little cat."

Delta smothered a chuckle with a hand over her mouth while Tripp clapped Jiro on the back. Jiro's smile couldn't have been bigger. Leif had missed this kind of happiness.

"Astral projection," Octavia murmured, eyes widening.

"What?" Delta asked.

Suddenly, Octavia's hands were on Leif's upper arm, squeezing tight. His body ignited, every cell on fire, until she squealed, loud—right in Leif's ear. He impressed himself when he kept the cringe off his face. *What the heck is going on?*

Octavia cried, "He projected into the astral plane!" She whirled on Jiro, then bounded toward him. "Oh my God, that's so cool!"

Leif just stood there, dazed, arm tingling, ear ringing, heart stuttering. He couldn't take his eyes off her.

"Tell me everything," Octavia said as she leaned over the back of Jiro's chair. He turned in his seat to face her. "How did it feel?"

Jiro grinned. "Shit, it was cool. It felt like being a cloud, floating on a breeze, only the breeze was my magic, pulling me or pushing me wherever I wanted to go, like a magnet."

Octavia's face flushed in excitement. "Then what happened?"

Tripp and Delta leaned in close, hanging on to Jiro's every word.

"Then I floated around the house for a while, and I—"

But Leif stopped listening. His thoughts were loud as he stared at them—acting like a family. A *real* family. This is how it should've been all along. This is what was robbed from them. Screw revenge. This—the *loss* of this—is what they were avenging.

A knot formed, burning the back of his throat.

"Talk about an out-of-body experience, am I right?" Jiro exclaimed, cutting through Leif's trance.

Jiro, Tripp, Delta, and Octavia doubled over in laughter. *Seriously? At that terrible joke?* But Leif knew they weren't laughing because the joke was especially good. They were laughing because they loved Jiro. And Jiro loved them.

Leif's gaze snagged on Octavia again, wide eyed, breathless, and pink cheeked.

She's a bit damaged. A bit chaotic. A beautiful mess. Just like us.
She's far from perfect, and I want her all the more for it.

CHAPTER 36
OCTAVIA

Octavia felt sick to her stomach. If this didn't work, she—well, she didn't want to think about it. So the only other option was to believe it would work. Tripp *would* be able to contain Quintin's magic in the dagger. She *would* be able to help her family during their confrontation with Garren. The other possibility wasn't even an option . . . at least, it wasn't an option she was willing to consider. Her denial was the only thing keeping her nausea at bay.

Quintin and Tripp sat on the rug in the middle of the library, the sporadic *pops* from a hearty fire crackling in the background. Octavia paced next to them as they studied the same grimoire they'd been hunched over for weeks. "Are you sure we don't need anything else?" she asked as she anxiously chewed her thumbnail.

Quintin let out an exasperated breath as he raised his eyes from the book. "Yeah, we're good. We've got the dagger, the spell, and a revitalizing potion from June in case Tripp runs out of gas. We don't need anything else."

Octavia plopped down onto the floor with a *thump*. "I just wish there was something I could do to help."

"You being here is enough," Tripp said, his eyes amber in the firelight, glued to the page. "It'll keep me motivated." He smirked. "No talking once I get started, though, okay?"

Octavia swiped her index finger and thumb across her mouth, gesturing zipping her lips together, but frowned when Tripp kept his focus downward. She rolled her eyes toward Quintin, who laughed under his breath.

"Whatever you two are laughing at me for, I couldn't care less." Finally, Tripp raised his eyes from the grimoire. "'Cause I'm about to save the day."

Octavia swallowed against a fresh wave of nausea as her heart began to jackhammer. She didn't know if she'd be able to watch once they started.

"You ready?" Quintin asked Tripp, shifting on the ground to face him head on.

Tripp removed a hair tie from his wrist and secured his hair in a bun at the nape of his neck. "As ready as I'm ever going to be. All that's left is to do the damn thing." He closed the grimoire and pushed it to the side.

Octavia's hands fisted on her knees, her stinging palms still raw and sore from the burns, as her gaze flicked between the two of them. Quintin nodded, then removed the dagger from its holster and placed it on the ground before Tripp.

Tripp cracked his neck and knuckles in rapid succession. He wiggled his arms as he readied himself. "Let's do this."

Tripp's hands hovered a few inches above the dagger, his fingers splayed out wide.

"Step one: cast the containment spell," Quintin reminded them softly.

"Step two: imbue the dagger with your magic," Tripp continued.

Octavia couldn't resist the temptation. She broke her vow of silence. "Step three: kick some lying, manipulative ass."

Tripp and Quintin grinned at her.

"Exactly," Tripp said as Octavia re-zipped her lips. He turned his gaze to Quintin and nodded once.

"This is a big spell, so it's a marathon, not a sprint. Don't expend all your magic at once. Go slow and steady. You got this," Quintin coached, scooting back to give Tripp some extra space to work.

Tripp closed his eyes, his profile calm and relaxed. He flexed his hands once more before taking a series of deep, even breaths. Octavia mimicked him, breathing in through her nose and out through her mouth. Her sprinting pulse slowed a fraction.

Tripp must have nerves of steel. He looks so calm over there, while I'm seconds away from puking my guts up.

But then the veins in Tripp's hands, arms, and neck ballooned, all the way up to his forehead, giving away his strain. His hands began to tremor over the dagger.

Quintin leaned forward, placing his hands on the floor before his crossed legs. He made sure to whisper, his tone soft and gentle as if he were singing a lullaby. "Breathe, Tripp. Don't forget to breathe."

Tripp's nostrils flared as he breathed in deeply, but his veins still bulged, and his arms still shook.

Octavia captured Quintin's gaze. *Is he okay?* she asked with her face, her eyebrows hitched up high.

Quintin assessed Tripp again, watching the muscles flex in his neck. Air hissed through Tripp's teeth as his mouth cracked open in a fierce grimace. "Fuck," he breathed. Sweat broke out across his face, golden in the firelight.

Octavia didn't consider the consequences of interrupting him; she just moved, crawling toward him.

Quintin's arm whipped out to stop her. He cautioned her with a single shake of his head. Then he spoke to Tripp. "You're burning through your reserves too quickly, Tripp. Use the meditation techniques we talked about. Relax your muscles from the top of your head down to your feet."

Tripp hissed out another breath, his body beginning to shake as if the earth was quaking beneath him.

Quintin raised his voice. "Now. Now, Tripp. Do it now!"

Tripp jerked his chin downward, the tiny movement seeming to cost him as the color in his face deepened considerably.

Octavia covered her mouth with her hands as she watched Tripp breathe, his breaths dragging in too slow, leaking out too fast. "Quin," she whispered, "he's going to pass out."

A muscle in Quintin's jaw flexed. "He'll be fine. He just needs to calm down."

The seconds passed tortuously, sweat dripping and muscles twitching as Tripp fought for stamina. Quintin and Octavia watched him intensely. For a minute, the only sounds in the room were Tripp's ragged breathing and the crackling of the fire. Octavia's lingering nausea was all but forgotten until Tripp began to pale before her eyes, his slick skin taking on a ghostly pallor. "Shit," she hissed.

Quintin moved, removing a small glass vial from his pants pocket. He gripped and opened Tripp's jaw with one hand while he poured in June's potion with the other. Tripp swallowed the potion reflexively as Quintin pushed his mouth closed. Color returned to his cheeks almost instantly, and slowly, his trembling receded.

Quintin smiled as he backed away. "There you go. You got it."

"What's going on?" Octavia asked Quintin.

He grinned at her. "He's almost done."

She looked at Tripp, who seemed significantly more relaxed, his breathing less labored and his muscles steady. "How do you know?"

"The potion helped instead of making him worse."

Octavia startled, staring at Quintin. "The potion could've backfired?"

Quintin shrugged. "If he was really running on fumes, the potion would've given him an extra boost he couldn't have physi-

cally handled." Octavia glared at him, her lips pursing. "Don't worry. I had an antidote, just in case."

Octavia opened her mouth, about to fuss at him, when Tripp's
voice, heavy with fatigue, cut her off. "What did I say about talking
while I'm working?"

Their gazes whirled to Tripp, who was sprawled out on the
floor, propped up by his elbows, head hanging loose over his shoulders. An anxious tumult of rapid-fire questions followed the duo's
momentary shock.

"What happened?"

"Are you okay?"

"Did the spell take hold?"

"Do you think it worked?"

Tripp croaked his answer through chapped lips, "Yeah, I
mean—I'm pretty sure it worked. Felt like it did." He paused to
cough, the sound dry and raspy. "If you two hadn't been busy bick-
ering you mighta you, I dunno, seen something? Or maybe not . . . Gah,
I feel like shit."

Octavia ran to him. He was still covered in sweat, his skin hot to
the touch as she placed a palm on his forehead. "Quintin, water and
a cool compress. Now!"

Quintin stood and strode from the room. "On it."

Tripp groaned as Octavia shifted him back into a seated position. "You better make this worth it. My body feels like a piano fell
on it."

Octavia couldn't stop the laugh that bubbled up from her throat.

Tripp coughed again, his slumped shoulders flexing. "I'm serious. You'd better get that dagger bloody."

She smiled at him. "You got it."

Tripp let down his hair, shaking it loose. "I can't believe I just
did that." He laughed too. "Marathon my ass, that was a fucking
Ironman Triathlon."

Octavia gripped Tripp by his shoulders, shaking him gently. "You're amazing!"

Tripp wiped his mouth with the back of his hand, propping the other elbow on one of his knees. "No, I'm just a perfectionist. Why try at all if you can't do it perfectly the first time, right?"

The smile fell from Octavia's lips. "You've got to be joking."

Tripp's eyes swung to hers. "Nope. That's basically my life motto."

Octavia sat back on her heels. "That's a harsh, and not to mention extremely unrealistic, expectation to hold yourself to."

Tripp squinted. "How so?"

She gaped at him. "What do you mean, 'how so'?"

Tripp shrugged. "I always get things on the first try."

Octavia laughed again as Quintin entered the room with a glass of water and a cool rag.

"What's so funny?" Quintin asked as he handed Tripp the water.

Tripp drank as Octavia answered, "Tripp's apparently never failed at anything, ever, in his entire life."

The guys looked at each other. "Yeah, I can see that being true," Quintin said simply.

Octavia's jaw went slack. "How is that even possible? I fail all the damn time. Like multiple times a day, every day."

Quintin laughed as Tripp cocked the corner of his mouth in a sympathetic half smile.

"That's 'cause you probably just jump right into things," Tripp explained, wiping his face with the damp cloth. "I research and study and obsess over whatever it is I want to do until I'm a hundred percent confident I can do it."

Octavia frowned. "Isn't that exhausting?"

Tripp's expression turned sad. "Like you wouldn't believe."

Quintin nudged Tripp lightly with his leg. "That's anxiety for ya, though." A gesture of comradery.

"Ain't that the truth," Tripp said with a sigh.

Octavia's gut twisted. "I'm sorry I asked you to do this, Tripp. I—I didn't know you felt that way. I didn't mean to stress—"

"Enough of that," Tripp interrupted as he stood, slightly wobbly on his feet. Quintin grabbed his shoulder to steady him. Tripp flashed his thanks with a grin. "You didn't force me into anything, and anyway, it wasn't all about you. This was a challenge I wanted to tackle." Octavia blinked at him. "Plus, now we know I'm a badass. Who knows? Maybe I'll get as good as Sage."

"Don't say that around them," Quintin cautioned with a chuckle.

The group fell quiet as step two of their plan loomed over them like a rain cloud promising spring flowers. Their collective gaze fell to the dagger on the floor.

"Time to test it out," Tripp said, still leaning into Quintin's hand for support.

Octavia bent down to pick up the dagger. It was warm in her hand, but from the fire a few feet away or Tripp's magic, she couldn't say. Silently, she handed it to Quintin.

He released Tripp and closed his eyes, holding the dagger by his palms at chest level.

Nothing happened for several moments—and then a smile slicked across Quintin's face. "Oh hell yeah. We're in business."

Tripp rubbed his hands together. "Charge her up, baby."

An indescribable weight lifted from Octavia's shoulders, the sudden lightness going straight to her head. She felt, in that moment, brand new.

I'll be able to help. Maybe I really can . . . stay.

Chapter 37
Octavia

By the morning of the thirtieth, Octavia had never felt more restless in her life. She fidgeted incessantly, and she wanted nothing more than to crawl out of herself like a snake shedding its skin.

The others must have felt similarly, because no one could sit still for long. After their breakfast of muffins and fruit in the sitting room, which had been left basically untouched, the coven went over their plan again and again as Jiro and June handed out all the equipment they'd need for that night, including June's magic powders.

"Well, my dears, it looks like there's nothing left for us to do but wait," Jocasta announced as she smoothed nonexistent flyaways into the tightly coiled bun at the nape of her neck.

"Have faith," Thaddeus counseled. "He'll listen to reason as long as we approach with logic . . . and control our thirst for revenge."

Octavia noticed Thaddeus dip his head discreetly in Leif's direction. She would've missed Leif's relenting nod if she hadn't been looking for it. Then Jocasta and Thaddeus made their exit, returning their dishes to the kitchen.

Surveying the sitting room after, Octavia felt it was obvious that the rest of the day was going to be absolute hell. Jiro looked slightly green. June had pulled out a strand of her hair and was wrapping it so tightly around her index finger the tip was turning purple. Tripp's nails, which were usually painted, had been stripped of polish and gnawed down to nubs.

The only one of them who looked even slightly calm was Delta. She sat comfortably, legs thrown over one of her chair's arm rests, reading a book.

"How are you so calm?" Octavia asked quietly, leaning toward her across the space between their armchairs.

"Because we have a solid plan," Delta said coolly, but she swallowed hard. "Is your magic dagger all set to go?"

"Yes, thanks to Tripp and Quintin. They performed the enchantment last night," Octavia replied, her heart rate increasing at the memory. Even though she'd thanked them profusely the night before, gratitude blossomed anew.

"Good," Delta said, relaxing further into her chair. "How many spells can you get out of it?"

"Quintin thinks up to three, depending on how big they are."

Delta placed her bookmark in her book and closed it. "Any idea what kind of spells you'll want to use?"

"Offensive spells, if I can get close enough. Though the downside to that strategy is they use up more magic. Defensive spells have the potential to be equally as useful, and luckily, require less magic. So, I guess it'll all depend on how the fight goes."

Delta nodded. "Do you know who will help you wield the magic?"

"Quintin offered last night, so I think I'm going to take him up on it. We always made a good team . . . before."

Delta averted her gaze quickly, but not quick enough for Octavia to miss her pained expression. It wasn't an apology, but it told Octavia that Delta had at least some semblance of human emotions.

"I think we'll be okay," Octavia went on. "He wouldn't have

offered to help if he didn't want to do it. I think that's a good sign."

"Good," Delta breathed.

"Well, shit," Leif said as he came up behind them, leaning his forearms against the back of Delta's chair, "if the two most deadly women I know are conspiring together, we're all in trouble."

"Oh please, you've been in trouble for years," Delta retorted as she lifted her face to him. He smiled back as her face turned serious. "I'm still not sure it'll work."

Octavia chimed in, having seen just the night before how good Delta was getting at her glamours. "It will. I promise."

Delta's eyes met hers. "You can't promise something like that."

Octavia shook her head. "Yes, I can. You know why?" She looked at Leif.

"Why?" Delta asked, her brows knitted.

Leif answered for her. "Because you're the most devious, conniving woman we know. Trust me. If anyone can pull this off, it's you."

Octavia watched Delta's tension melt in the face of his reassuring smile, just as hers always did. His optimism was infectious.

"Stop sucking up. It's not getting you extra brownie points." Delta laughed as she shoved him away. She stood, smoothing down her shirt. "I'll see you later. Time to power up."

"See ya," Octavia and Leif replied in unison, which elicited a cringeworthy eyebrow dance from Delta as she walked away.

"She makes me want to rip my hair out," Octavia exclaimed as she picked at the healing skin on her burnt palms. June had given her a healing potion after Yule dinner, but it was taking some time for the new skin to grow.

"You'll get used to it eventually," Leif said, taking Delta's empty seat. "I'm just glad she's toned down her attitude since Christmas."

"I don't know, I kind of miss it," Octavia joked.

They both laughed half-heartedly, the humor strangely hollow under the circumstances.

"I should go talk to Quin," Octavia said, standing. "He offered to help me wield the dagger's magic. We should come up with a strategy."

"Need help?"

"I'd love to say yes, but this is something I need to do alone."

"I get it," Leif replied with a smile.

Don't melt. Don't melt. Do NOT melt. You have shit to do right now. You can melt all you want tomorrow when this is done.

Octavia looked around the sitting room, but Quintin was no longer there. She ventured into the library, where she found him reading a grimoire at the desk in the corner. He looked up as she approached, one eyebrow cocked.

Octavia stopped a few feet before him, her hands laced together behind her back. "I'd love to take you up on your offer, if it still stands."

"You sure?" he asked as he closed the text.

Octavia nodded. "Definitely."

A pause. Quintin averted his gaze, and Octavia's heart sank.

She said hopefully, "We've always made a great team, Q. I can't see that changing anytime soon."

His smile didn't quite reach his eyes, and her drowning heart throbbed.

He stood from his chair. "All right. Let's get to work, then."

"Thank you." She brushed his arm with her fingertips, just enough to get his attention, but was careful not to linger. "Seriously, without you, I'd be useless tonight. I'll never be able to repay you."

"Uh, yeah," he coughed, eyes dropping to the grimoire on the desk. "Of course. Just kick some ass and we'll be even, okay?"

She laughed softly as the weight on her shoulders lessened slightly. "Yeah, okay."

CHAPTER 38
OCTAVIA

The chill in the air seeped bone deep, causing Octavia's joints to stiffen and ache. Her heart pounded painfully in her chest, the beats alarmingly uneven. She took deep, even breaths, but her attempts to calm herself were futile. There was no quelling the apprehension that writhed in her body.

If any of them get hurt . . . She couldn't even finish the thought. It was too painful. They were finally all together again, and even though it had *not* been easy, it would get easier.

Octavia didn't believe in any one god or deity, but she did believe in the natural connections that brought their magic to life. Magicless or not, she needed to lean on those connections now more than ever.

She dipped her head toward the frozen earth beneath her feet and knelt in the foot-high snow, the knees of her black leggings instantly soaking through. Digging her way to the dirt, she tossed fistfuls of dirty snow to the side. She placed her hands on the earth. Her fingers were numb, but she kept them in place, still as a statue.

Connected to the earth like this, she felt strong. For a fleeting moment, she felt as if she wasn't a liability. Like they were going to make it through tonight and come out stronger for it.

As the numbness spread to her wrists, the ground beneath her hands trembled in time with even footsteps. "Tavi?" Sage called from behind her. "Why are you kneeling in the snow? You're getting wet."

Octavia removed her hands from the earth and stood, wiping

the dirt off her hands absentmindedly as she turned toward Sage.

"What were you—?" Sage took in the dirt on Octavia's pants and hands, their expression growing even more curious.

"Just taking a moment," Octavia murmured.

Sage frowned slightly but stood next to her in silence, assessing the half-demolished building in front of them. Octavia checked her wristwatch.

"Is it almost time?" Sage asked.

"Mhm, we have about twenty minutes." Octavia looked at her soiled hands, silently willing the dirt beneath her fingernails to give her courage. "Is Delta ready?"

Sage dipped their chin. "As ready as she's ever going to be."

"Does she look convincing?" Octavia asked, her voice quivering slightly.

"Yes."

"Good," she said, her head bouncing like a bobble-head. "And Tripp's in place to shield?"

"Yes. We got this, Tavi. Have faith."

"I do."

"Is it time for you to take your place?"

"Just about." Octavia's hands trembled as she reached reassuringly for the dagger sheathed on her right thigh.

"I hope we laugh about all of our unnecessary preparations tomorrow." Sage sounded optimistic—hopeful, even.

"So do I."

Octavia's cell phone chirped. It was time to move into position. Before she could say anything, Sage wrapped her into a tight, chest-crushing embrace. The silence between them spoke louder than words ever could: *Whatever happens, I love you.* As they clung to each other, any discomfort that had lingered from Yule dinner disappeared. It was time to leave the argument in the past, where it belonged.

When they broke apart, Sage walked south, and Octavia north. She entered the warehouse from the only side that remained standing.

"You good?" Quintin asked. She must've really looked like shit for him to have asked.

"Yeah."

"Your earpiece working?"

"Yes. Jiro tested it. It's good to go."

"Good. Just make sure to remember to tell me when and what to cast."

"Got it."

The feel of his hand on her shoulder startled her. She looked toward him to see his handsome face twisted in worry. She was tired of talking, and there was really nothing left to say, so she placed her hand over his and smiled weakly. She was sure he understood well enough.

"Everyone in position," Jiro's voice whispered in Octavia's ear—in all of their ears—through the wireless earpiece. "A car just pulled up outside."

Oh shit, this is really happening.

Octavia felt her heartbeat in her fingertips, and her lungs began leaking oxygen like a popped tire, unable to refill on their own anymore. Stars spotted her peripheral vision as Quintin dragged her behind a large pile of debris.

"Breathe," he mouthed to her. His hand remained at her shoulder, his thumb now moving in steady, comforting circles over her jacket, just above her collarbone.

The act of controlling her breath was tedious and took much more focus than it should have, but slowly it began to work. The stars in her vision receded. Her mind cleared and refocused. *There's no going back now, so let's get the job done.*

She refused to be a hindrance. Not anymore.

"I'm okay," she mouthed in return. Quintin nodded and removed his hand. Its absence chilled her galloping heart more than the frigid air around her.

A car door slammed in the distance. Octavia gritted her teeth as Quintin's hands balled into fists.

Leif entered the building from the north, behind Octavia and Quintin's hiding place. His hands flexed and clenched at his sides. He was dressed in black, and his ash-blond hair looked dull in the moonlight. In the middle of the space, he stopped and pivoted to face the western entrance. From their vantage point, Octavia and Quintin could just glimpse the gaping doorway from around the fallen debris that hid them.

"Now," Jiro whispered through the earpiece.

A tall, slender man with short brown hair and a meticulously trimmed beard entered the building wearing dark blue jeans and a black parka. He walked casually toward Leif. His pale ears had rouged in the cold.

Octavia scoffed to herself. The bastard was handsome.

Garren didn't break stride as he neared Leif. *A good sign.* Ten feet away, he stopped and his face wrinkled in question. "Why did you want to meet here, of all places? What's going on?" Garren's deep voice echoed throughout the room.

"We have a surprise for you," Leif responded, his voice an octave too high.

Garren crossed his arms. "Where are the others, then?"

"They'll be here in a minute." Leif's lips pressed thin.

The muscles in Octavia's face burned. She released a shaky breath, moving her jaw side to side. *So far so good.*

"I don't have time for this," Garren said as he uncrossed his arms, gesturing to himself with open hands. "I'm tired and filthy. Let's go home. You can surprise me there." He turned and walked a few paces toward the entrance before he looked back over his shoulder.

Leif wasn't following.

Garren sighed deeply. "All right. If it's that important. What is it?"

Leif sneered, his lip curling up like a panther ready to pounce. "We know."

Octavia held her breath. *This is it.*

"Know what?" Garren turned to face Leif fully once more. Annoyance pinched the skin between his thick eyebrows.

Leif's teeth flashed dangerously. "Everything."

Garren exhaled, rubbing his brow impatiently. "Could you be more specific?"

"We know you're not actually our adoptive father." Leif's voice shook.

Octavia's eyes snapped to Garren. He straightened but didn't reply. Surprise darted across his features, but he schooled them in an instant, into a perfect mask of indifference as he studied Leif. A chill shot down Octavia's spine.

"Why lie to us?" Leif asked in a low tone. His arms shook with tremors as his mouth twisted into a grimace.

Garren's tone was calm and collected, without a hint of unease. "Because the state of Massachusetts wasn't about to let a single twenty-five-year-old adopt four young orphans all at once. That's not how things are done."

Leif cocked his head. "Are you sure that's the only reason?"

Garren's hands clenched into fists.

"I disabled the transmission in his car," Jiro huffed over the earpiece. "Everyone's in place. The entrance is blocked. Delta, go ahead."

Leif's hands relaxed at his side. Octavia watched in awe as the Leif in front of them transformed. His body shrunk several inches, his thin frame filling out and taking on an hourglass figure. Pale skin and light eyes darkened to a warm brown. Ash-blond hair transitioned to a brown so deep it was almost black, lengthening as it shifted.

Garren recoiled, his eyes bulging as if he were watching his worst nightmare come to life. Perhaps he was.

"Hi, Daddy," Delta cooed.

"Mother*fucker*," Garren whispered.

"Surprise." The smile Delta flashed at him was absolutely feral.

"Of course we know," the real Leif said as he stepped out from behind a pile of rubble and into Octavia's view. As Leif walked to the center of the room, Garren stared at the fierce lightness of Leif's hair, so bright it was glowing in the moonlight. The white strands almost seemed to shimmer—like light reflecting off the ocean—hypnotic and blinding. Garren's face was conflicted, two emotions Octavia couldn't quite place warring against each other.

"How long did you honestly think you could get away with it?" Leif asked.

As if he'd suddenly remembered a vital piece of information, Garren startled, reaching toward a blade hung on his hip. Octavia's body tensed, ready to jump into action.

Garren unsheathed the dagger at his hip and inspected it with a squinted gaze.

"Cold as ice, right?" Tripp sauntered forward from the entrance behind Garren, his hands raised and brow furrowed.

Garren turned toward him, mouth parted in disbelief. "H-how?" he stuttered.

"Just a fancy new trick I learned," Tripp said, dark, twisted amusement coating his voice, thick as honey. "It's called containment magic, and I'm using it to shield our magic from your pesky little radar." Tripp dropped his hands and relaxed his face.

Garren yowled, tossing the dagger aside. He glared at the palm of his now empty hand. It had burned him.

Garren's breaths came in fast and heavy. "How many of you are there?"

"Enough," Jocasta's voice boomed from the east. She strutted confidently toward the enemy, wrapped from head to toe in black winter wear.

"You," Garren spat.

"Yes, *me*." Jocasta smiled wickedly. "Now, tell me, who are you?"

Jocasta's entrance was their cue. Octavia abandoned her hiding place, Quintin close behind her. They walked side by side to the center of the warehouse. In her peripheral vision, Octavia saw the remainder of her coven doing the same. As they'd planned, the ten of them formed a circle around Garren, trapping him in the middle.

Before Garren answered, he swiveled around, taking them all in. A muscle in his jaw feathered at the sight of Sage. *Good. He's smart enough to be afraid of a Wardwell.*

But when he laid eyes on Octavia, he stumbled back as if he'd been slapped. His mouth gaped like a fish's on land, not a single sound escaping it. The fear in his gaze was all-consuming.

What the hell is going on?

"No . . . not you," Garren murmured to himself, as if he was lost in a trance.

"What was that?" Delta asked loudly, successfully snapping him out of it.

Returning his gaze to the group, Garren's dark eyes widened further as he took in the mere feet that separated Octavia from Leif.

Octavia's gaze swung to Leif's, and his expression was pinched in similar confusion.

"No!" Garren yelled, his guttural voice ricocheting off the partially demolished concrete walls around them. "Leif, get away from her! Now!"

"What the hell is going on?" Delta snapped with a fury that surprised even Octavia.

"Leif," Garren tried again, "please, come here. She'll be the death of us all." He stretched his arms out toward Leif but didn't dare take a step closer.

Garren made eye contact with Octavia once more, and what she saw there shattered an old, self-conscious part of herself. This man was terrified of her. He looked at her and honestly feared for his life. It felt . . . it felt *fucking good*. It felt like power. A power she'd been searching for.

Maybe her power wasn't tied to magic after all.

In an instant, the fear and restless anxiety from before melted away. Her blood flowed through her veins to the steady rhythm of her heart. Her skin—suddenly a perfect fit—no longer felt two sizes too small, suffocating her soul.

At last, she felt free.

"No, Garren," Octavia drawled. "I'm only going to be the death of *you*."

CHAPTER 39
LEIF

It was as if his fear fueled her. Her back straightened, her chin raised, and she looked down her nose at him. It was amazing and concerning. Just moments ago, she'd been so anxious and afraid, she'd been trembling.

What changed?

But Leif didn't have time to dwell on the thought. Garren hissed through bared teeth, taking her threat at face value. Leif had never seen Garren in such a state, so uneasy and unbalanced. He didn't understand this fear Garren had of Octavia, but it gave them the advantage they'd been hoping for.

Or so Leif thought. Before he could register, Garren had reached around to his lower back for a weapon concealed beneath his coat. He whipped it from its holster, aimed, and fired. Leif knew with surmounting dread the bullet would find its target, just as it did every time.

Leif's instinct was to charge Garren, but in a fraction of a second, he changed trajectory and threw the full weight of his body toward Octavia. If he was fast enough, he could save her. But the laws of physics simply weren't on his side. There was no way he'd make it in time.

In slow motion, a silvery light ripped open a hole in space just before Octavia's chest, swallowing the speeding bullet whole. Less than a second later, the bullet ricocheted loudly off the concrete walls behind them.

Leif felt a twinge in his shoulder as he thudded to the ground before Octavia's feet. Octavia and Quintin grabbed his arms, hauling him to stand. Even though he'd seen the portal, Leif searched Octavia frantically, gripping her shoulders tightly. "Shit, are you okay?"

"Yeah, fine. Thanks to Quin," Octavia breathed.

Leif looked to Quintin, whose brow was slick with sweat, despite the cold. The talent required to create that portal that quickly ... it was nothing short of phenomenal.

Quintin jerked his chin at Leif. Only then did Leif register the grunts and thuds coming from behind him. *Damn, I should've known better. Never turn your back on an enemy.*

He whirled around to find Garren on his knees, his pistol on the floor several feet away. Jocasta stood before him while thick vines coiled around his hands behind his back. Thaddeus stood behind him, a furious statue. His face was pinched in concentration.

Sage walked slow circles around him, their hands moving in rhythmic motions. Gradually, water began to pool beneath Garren's shins, but it didn't freeze. Sage kept the water liquid, which must've been close to freezing in the ungodly cold.

Jiro, Tripp, and June had moved in closer as well, each of their hands raised and ready. Garren released a threatening growl as he twisted his wrists against the living restraints.

"I was desperately hoping it wouldn't come to this," Jocasta said scornfully, "but it seems you've given us no other choice."

Garren made no attempt to reply except to spit at her feet. His blue lips trembled as they pressed into a thin line.

"Why try to kill my granddaughter, Garren?" She spat his name as if it curdled on her tongue like spoiled milk.

Despite the full body tremors, Garren somehow managed to press his lips tighter together.

Sage and Jocasta locked gazes for a moment before Sage lifted their hands. The water crystalized beneath Garren, encasing his legs in ice. Then they spun on graceful feet, fingers dancing in a careful sequence, some of which Sage had shown Leif during their tutoring session. A small tornado of wind encased Garren, whipping freezing air against his soaking skin, hair, and clothes. The tremors rocked his body now. The blue of his lips began to spread across his cheeks. If this went on much longer, hypothermia would claim him.

Jocasta waved a hand at Sage. Sage's hands fell to their sides and the wind died.

Garren's body shook alarmingly, and his eyelids fluttered as his eyes tried rolling into the back of his head, looking moments away from passing out.

"I will not ask again, hunter," Jocasta threatened.

"I-it's a lo-long story," Garren bit out.

"Then I suggest you speak quickly, before you freeze to death," she whispered, watching him squirm beneath her piercing gaze.

Damn, Jocasta is a badass.

"It—it all started with her . . . twenty-five years ago," Garren said beneath the thick, swirling clouds of his breath, his gaze moving to Leif.

"Her who?" Thaddeus demanded loudly at his back.

"Gwyn," Garren murmured, pain written on every line of his face.

Leif's breath hitched in his lungs as the heat of renewed rage burned in his chest.

"What was your connection with her?" Thaddeus asked.

"I came across her in Salem almost thirty years ago. I-I was a new hunter, straight out of training. I'd been told witches were clever and cautious. That it'd be nearly impossible to find one, even in a city like Salem. But I found her in three hours. She was im-impossible to miss." He paused to take a ragged breath. "The magic coming off her was dense and powerful. I knew I had to end her, for the safety of the entire town, and quickly. So I devised a plan to capture her. But I underestimated her." A dark chuckle left his trembling lips. "She knew what I was right away, and in an instant, she foiled the plan that had taken me a week to prepare. I was completely at her mercy in that dive bar in Salem. She could've destroyed me. But she didn't. She spared me. And then—" His lips quivered as they curved upward. "Then she befriended me. Her mortal enemy. A threat not only to her, but to her entire coven. But she never cared about the risk. She was *fearless.*"

Leif's hands clenched into fists. *Friends?*

"You're a fucking liar," Leif snarled. It took every ounce of self-control he had to keep himself from erasing the few feet that separated them so he could knock the sick bastard out. "You *stalked* her. For years. You were obsessed with her. There's *no way* she was your friend."

Garren's eyebrows sloped as he let out a shaky huff of breath. "I guess you found the pictures, then."

"Yeah, we did." It took every ounce of restraint Leif had to keep from shouting.

"I u-understand how that must have looked. I guess it doesn't paint me in a favorable light."

There was a pause. Leif didn't know what to say. He looked around at his covenmates. Their eyes—all of them angry—were locked on Garren.

"Your mother knew about those photos," Garren said. "Every single one."

Leif tensed, hating how tightly he clung to Garren's every word.

"Photography started off as a part of the job. A means to an end. But somewhere along the way, I fell in love with it." He jerked his chin at Leif. "You know that, of course. I taught you everything I know." Leif swallowed against the bitter taste in his mouth. "The art of capturing a person's essence in a single moment. Your mother was my favorite subject—my muse."

"Why?" Leif choked out. A knot was growing painfully in his throat.

"Because I grew to love her. Hell . . ." Garren chuckled. "I worshiped the very ground she walked on. I was hers—heart, body, and soul."

Only after Leif felt Octavia's warm hand intertwine with his did he realize he was trembling now too. The rage that rampaged freely through his veins was suffocating, threatening to strangle him. He felt himself slipping into that place again, into the red nothingness he'd teetered on the edge of that night in Salem. The place Octavia had pulled him out of.

Leif barely noticed the grimace on Garren's face at the sight of their touch. He swung his gaze to hers, to those beautiful brown eyes. The concern there was deep as an abyss. "You okay?" she asked under her breath, her lips barely moving.

Leif couldn't form the words. *No, I'm not okay. Nothing about this fucked up night—this fucked up life—is okay.*

Whatever it was Octavia saw on his face, she seemed to understand and turned to face the monster. That cold, lethal look was back in her eyes, the look he loved so much. She never let go of his hand.

"But she never loved you back, did she?" Octavia asked in a glacial voice.

Garren's teeth chattered as he bared them at her. "No, *girl*, she didn't. I-I'm man enough to admit it. She only ever had eyes for Fitz . . . the pompous asshole."

Octavia's hand tensed in Leif's. "So, you just watched as the love of your life married another man?" she asked quietly.

"Yes," Garren breathed. "It was that or lose her."

"What does your unrequited love for Gwyn have to do with Octavia?" Thaddeus asked impatiently.

"Everything," Garren said, his voice growing fainter. "Gwyn told me when she got pregnant. We weren't as close then. Not after Fitz. We only met up once a month or so by then, if I was lucky. She was the first of their generation in the coven to get pregnant. She was so excited." He shifted his gaze back to Leif. "She loved you so much—fiercely, with everything she had."

The knot in Leif's throat burned so hot tears pricked his eyes, but he refused to let them fall.

"Then came *all* the pregnancies," Garren continued. "In Gwyn's eyes, it couldn't have been more perfect. Seven pregnancies, seven babies, all due within the same calendar year."

"I don't get it," June said. "What do our mother's pregnancies have to do with anything?"

"Your matriarch knows th-the answer to that question." Garren smirked in Jocasta's direction.

"Seven is a magical number," Jocasta began, her tone cautious. "It was thought if a coven could produce a new generation, comprised of seven witches all born within the same year, they'd be blessed with unparalleled magical abilities. But it's an old hypothesis, based on assumptions and theories. I'm surprised Gwyn even knew about it."

"She did," Garren growled. "In fact, they all did. Do you really think those pregnancies occurred by chance?"

Jocasta's eyes widened, her mask of strength and confidence faltering. It looked to Leif like Jocasta hadn't expected his mother to be capable of carrying out a plan like this behind her back. She'd tapped his mother as the next matriarch, after all. She'd been Jocasta's prized pupil. This must've been especially difficult for her to hear.

"N-no," Garren continued. "Most of them were planned and

achieved thanks to fertility potions. Gwyn and Fitz were the masterminds behind it all. They whispered promises of power and prosperity in their friends' ears, convincing them all one by one. Gwyn wanted to grow the coven more than anything, and obtaining more power would help her achieve that. To my knowledge, the only ones who refused to go along with their scheme were *her* parents." Garren jerked his chin at Octavia. "Alexandra and Sebastian Martin."

"Why?" Octavia asked.

"Apparently, they were against using innocent children to attain more power."

Leif didn't know how to feel. He barely remembered his mother, so learning about her knack for strategic planning made it hard for him to feel anything but proud. He and his mother were similar in that regard; they always had a plan.

But this plan . . .

Leif looked around at the others once more. Their faces were warped in various expressions of confusion and revulsion. This plan obviously wasn't something that should be sparking feelings of familial affinity. He heard Octavia swallow hard next to him. Garren's words were having an effect, sowing seeds of doubt and uncertainty. *This isn't good.*

"Gwyn never held it against them, though. Af-after all, they managed seven pregnancies without them, and Alex was her best friend. She couldn't—or wouldn't—hold her beliefs against her."

As Garren inhaled a jagged breath, Leif's stomach clenched. He knew the story didn't end there. The proof was standing beside him.

"Until she got pregnant too. The eighth. I remember how stressed she was after Alex and Bash told her. All that work and planning . . . for nothing."

Leif's throat burned as if he'd swallowed hot coal. The pain only fueled his hatred. Octavia was not *nothing*.

"That was, until she learned Alex wasn't due until January of the following year."

"But I—" Octavia began.

"Yes, yes," Garren cut her off impatiently. "But you were born premature. Born on Christmas Day, in fact. Gwyn cried for weeks after your birth."

Octavia's hand left Leif's, flying to cover the pained gaping of her lips.

"Your birth ruined everything," Garren whispered through a blue-lipped smirk.

"Shut up!" Leif yelled at him, throwing an arm out in front of Octavia, as if his body alone could shield her from his words.

Garren smiled wickedly at Octavia, causing Leif's chest to tighten. *I'm going to kill him after all.*

"But Gwyn and Fitz were determined," Garren went on. "They planned to try again. Seven years after the first attempt, of course. Her obsession with that infernal number never ceased. And in the meantime, they raised eight very ordinary witches. And for a while, everything was normal again . . . until Fitz found out about me." Leif's pulse pounded in his ears, and he strained to hear every word. "He confronted me. Threatened to kill me if I so much as spoke to Gwyn ever again. Then the coward packed up the coven and moved. I had no idea where she was, when I'd see her again, whether she was all right." His dark eyes flashed like a thunderstorm.

"She was with her husband and child," Octavia snarled. "With her family. Why wouldn't she have been all right?"

"She'd befriended the enemy," Garren breathed. "I had no idea what the coven would do to her for a transgression like that."

"We didn't know," Jocasta murmured, meeting Thaddeus's

hardened gaze. "Fitz never told us. But that explains why he convinced us to purchase the house in Vermont—why he was anxious to move us so quickly."

"I couldn't handle it . . . life without her," Garren whispered, his voice weaker with each breath.

"What did you do?" Jiro asked, his brows raised accusingly.

"I got vengeful," Garren explained, bowing his head warily. "For a year, I drowned in it—the jealousy, hate, and resentment. It—it does something to your soul."

"What did you *do*?" Delta demanded.

"I sold her out!" Garren rasped, his face crumpling.

"You're the reason we were attacked," Jocasta exclaimed quietly, taking two hurried steps away.

"Yes."

"Why?" Tripp asked weakly, his voice cracking.

"I—" Garren swallowed thickly. "She left so easily, and never looked back."

"He wanted revenge," Octavia mused, again looking down her nose at him. "He could handle her rejection as long as he wasn't abandoned. When she left, she crossed a line. A line he drew in the sand of his humanity."

Garren's expression darkened, his shoulders slumping beneath the weight of her words.

"It took me years to find the coven again," Garren said, "and when I did, I didn't hesitate. I rallied all of the hunters in the northeastern region, and then" —he loosed a shaky breath— "we attacked."

"You're a murderer." Leif's voice was as cold and dark as his heart felt.

"I am," Garren agreed as he lifted his head to meet Leif's gaze. "That's what I was raised to be. Gwyn's friendship only delayed the inevitable."

Leif's mind went blank as he stalked toward Garren, stepping around Jocasta. He stopped a foot away and dropped into a predatory squat before his former father. "You were pissed, so you *killed* her."

"That wasn't my intention," Garren replied softly. "I wanted the rest of them to die, but not Gwyn. Never Gwyn."

"You failed," Leif whispered with as much venom as he could muster. He winced as fury deluged his gut like acid, corroding everything it touched.

"I wouldn't have failed," Garren whispered, the sorrow in his eyes churning to hatred as he glared at Octavia once more, "if it hadn't been for her."

"Explain," Leif commanded.

Garren took a moment to study Leif's face before he said, "She's the reason your mother is dead."

Leif heard Octavia's boots scrape along the concrete floor behind him.

"Impossible." Jocasta scoffed. "Octavia was a child. Plus, that night she was—"

"Hexed?" Garren offered.

Jocasta's eyebrows rose sharply. Her original suspicions had been right. He *did* know something about Octavia's hex.

"What do you know about that?" Thaddeus boomed behind Garren.

Garren chuckled darkly, his dusky lips still trembling. "Didn't you ever wonder why? Why she was the only one?"

The coven's silence was deafening. Slowly, their defensive stances began to crumble—hands lowering, legs locked. Their focus was slipping, and Leif wasn't sure what to do about it.

"You have no clue. None of you?" Garren asked incredulously.

"Spit it out," Leif growled.

"Even though we had the element of surprise that night, your coven held their own. We underestimated your magic. We always do. And we would've lost—if it wasn't for her." He glared at Octavia over Leif's shoulder. "Her and her magical *awakening*."

Leif glanced back at Octavia. Her eyes were wide as she shook her head slowly in denial, rejecting the words with every movement. One of her hands moved to grip the base of her neck. His heart ached for her. He wanted to grab her and run, take her somewhere far away from here. But he couldn't. They couldn't abandon the others.

When Leif turned his attention back to Garren, the bastard was smiling.

"Despite what you all must think about us, hunters don't murder children. Yes, we rounded them up that night, but we were going to take them with us and raise them in the natural world by suppressing their magic. We meant to move them before the fighting began, but Gwyn was quick and powerful. She sensed what we planned to do and tried to distract us as quickly as possible." Garren's weak, breathy voice cracked. "It worked."

He swallowed loudly before continuing, "The children huddled in the corner. Some of them watched the whole thing—witnessed their parents die before their eyes. I watched as Alex fell. I'm assuming she watched it too." Garren jerked his chin toward Octavia. Her eyes brimmed with unshed tears. "The emotional turmoil must've released it. Her magic."

"I don't remember what you're describing," Octavia said emphatically. "You're wrong. I blacked out after I saw my mother—"

His next words fell like molasses from his mouth. "You didn't black out, girl." His smile was bestial. "You were consumed by darkness because you *are* darkness." A scoff. "Your magic is death itself. Pure decay and destruction." His every syllable was a knife aimed to kill. "People *died* because of you."

The air evaporated from Leif's lungs. *He's lying. This is just an-*

other one of his lies. Leif's gaze whipped to Octavia. Her face was contorted in a sickening mixture of horror and pain. "You're lying!" she cried.

"I wish I was," Garren said dourly. "If I were, the love of my life would still be alive, and her son would still have his mother."

Leif could almost feel Octavia's emotions take physical form in the room. The air grew dense and heavy, as if a cloud of smog had materialized around them.

"That's impossible," Jocasta repeated, her piercing eyes roving over Octavia from head to toe, as if she could find the truth in her.

"The children and I only survived because we were behind her. She shielded us from the brunt of her magic somehow," Garren explained. "The force of it knocked the younger ones out, but I remained conscious—barely. And so did Gwyn. She tried to shield herself, but it was too strong. She clung to life, desperately, despite the wounds the girl's magic had inflicted. After that surge of power, Gwyn figured it out, and she knew she had to fix it before she . . . let go."

If Garren could have shed a tear, he probably would have. Leif had to give him that much. But hypothermia was setting in, and it looked like it was all he could do to keep talking.

"Gwyn hexed her."

CHAPTER 40
OCTAVIA

The statement rattled through the room. Jocasta shook her head fervently as Thaddeus laid a hand on his chest. June's hand smacked against her mouth, muffling a gasp. Leif stood and turned slowly. When his eyes met Octavia's, all she felt was pain. A pain so deep, so poignant, she wondered if she'd ever recover from it. Just when she'd started to get better, to believe in herself, she was confronted with this. *The truth.*

Octavia's heart felt like it was being torn from her chest.

Garren said to Leif, "With her dying breath, Gwyn asked me to bring you to her."

Octavia tore her gaze from Leif and gritted her teeth. What felt like a gaping hole in her rib cage bled out harder, faster.

Garren's voice was low and soft. "I carried your unconscious body to her and laid you in her arms. So small, but so, so strong." The love Garren had for Leif was undeniable. It was written all over his face. "With the last of her magic, she made you the key to banishing the girl's dark magic." Garren's expression turned grim. "When the spell was done, she asked me—no, *begged* me—to keep you two apart. 'You owe me this,' she said, 'Save my son. Save as many as you can.' So I did. But I could only carry four of you."

Octavia blinked, and the world seemed to tilt slowly, as if gravity was failing her. In slow motion, Leif turned toward her. When their eyes locked, she felt it. The tether, right behind her sternum, pulling taut between them. Her and Leif.

The familiarity. The bond. It'd been the spell this whole time. The spell Leif's mother had cast had woven them together.

Octavia's hand flew to the warmth radiating from her sternum. She could tell he felt it too. Slowly, his hand drifted to the center of his chest, as if he could grasp the tether with his hands. Then, as if the realization cracked a glass brimming with liquid, the emotion on Leif's face drained. He stared at her with a blank expression as he saw something beyond her, beyond this room, beyond this moment in time.

Where'd he go? Octavia thought frantically. Panic seized her, ripping the breath from her throat. *I need him back. I need him here with me. I need him.*

The realization sent her back to the night when she'd called Leif after her nightmare. The night they let themselves slip back into their old skin, the versions of Leif and Octavia that weren't witches or hunters; enemies or covenmates. Just Leif and just Octavia. The night she tried denying with every fiber of her being that she needed him. The thought almost made her laugh, the pressure building in her chest even though this moment—here in this frigid, half-demolished building with the man who was responsible for tearing their coven apart—was the absolute worst time she could be laughing. But she couldn't help it. *Still think you don't need me?* he'd asked. She'd been so stupid. So incredibly stupid, and stubborn, and flat out wrong.

Of course she needed him. And, looking into Leif's vacant blue eyes, this was clearer than ever to her. But then Leif's face suddenly came back to life, the set of his eyes an unusual mixture of pain and—strangely—happiness.

Before Octavia knew what was happening, she was jerked forward a step, matching orbs of light suddenly blooming from the centers of her and Leif's chests. Octavia's eyes dipped to the light. As she beheld it, her face crumpled.

In a moment, her cool, wet cheeks were in Leif's hands, and her gaze was boring into his. "I remember," he whispered to her, and only her. They knew they had an audience, but for a moment, it was as if no one else existed. "I remember your lanky legs, your temper, and those big, beautiful eyes. I remember you, and me, and all of us. Finally."

Octavia choked out a sad, muffled sound. Their chests were still glowing, the warmth of the light chasing away the chill in the air around them.

"You and me. We were *us* before all of this." He gestured toward the light, the tether, the hex. "Back then, I was too young to understand what our friendship would grow into, but I understand now."

The terror and anger and heartbreak of the last ten minutes melted away as Octavia stared into Leif's eyes. She fisted his jacket in her hands, needing him closer. She wished she could stop time, stay here forever. Stay in his—

His words severed her thoughts. "Tavi, I lo—"

But Garren interrupted, shouting weakly from behind Leif. "Don't you *dare* finish that sentence!"

Octavia's heart hammered erratically. She couldn't think. Couldn't move. She could only stare into those eyes. Eyes that made her feel safe and seen and *loved*.

"Son, have you not heard a word I've said?" Garren roared at Leif.

Leif blinked slowly as the spell's light dimmed between them. When he replied, his tone took a sharp turn from the softness he'd been using with Octavia. "Don't ever call me that again. I'm not and have never been your son."

Garren pushed on, his expression deadly even though he was still tied up. "She's the reason the coven is cursed! Her magic could bring down buildings—cities even! You can't be with her!"

Red-hot rage burned fiercely in the hollow of Octavia's chest.

Leif chuckled darkly. "You're full of shit; you know that? Our whole lives, you've been preaching the same crap. 'Magic is bad. Magic is dangerous. We must purge it from our world.' Doesn't it start to get old?"

"This isn't the same—"

Leif cut him off. "Isn't it, though?"

"No." Even with Garren's failing strength, the word boomed throughout the room, and Octavia's breath hitched. "I loved you like a son, Leif. I truly did. It was an honor to raise you, an *honor*." Garren paused to take a deep breath. "I've known for decades I'd eventually have to pay for my sins. Kill me if you want—God knows I deserve it—but please, please, if you take me out, take her out with me."

The silence rang in Octavia's ears. Leif tensed under her touch, but he didn't speak as the muscles in his jaw pulled taut. Every instinct in her body urged her to flee, or attack—to do *something*—but despite herself, she remained still as stone.

Garren leaned forward, practically begging now. "Her dark magic will bring about the end of the natural world. Family, friends, strangers—everyone . . . everyone will die."

Another heartbeat of silence passed. It took every ounce of self-control Octavia had to remain calm.

Garren's eyes were wet and pleading. "Leif, please, it's what your mother would've wanted. She sacrificed her life to ensure Octavia's dark magic never saw the light of day again. What would she say if she saw you now? Spitting on her memory as you cling to the reason she's dead. She would be so *disappointed*."

Octavia took one moment, perhaps only a fraction of a second, to meet Quintin's gaze. Then she jolted forward, pulling her dagger from its sheath.

A silvery, shimmering portal cracked open in front of her. The second portal opened just behind Garren. She ducked down, her speed never letting up as she hurled her body through. The space between portals was blindingly bright—and then it was gone. She barreled out at Garren's back, surprisingly steady on her feet. Before his head could whip around, she grabbed a fistful of Garren's mousy brown hair and yanked hard.

Garren's head jerked back, and he hissed in pain. His eyes reluctantly found hers, and she watched as they widened in a mixture of surprise, pain, and most deliciously, fear. Octavia felt nothing but the thrill of vengeance buzzing through her every nerve. A wicked smile tugged at the corners of her mouth as her dagger found the vulnerable, exposed skin of Garren's neck.

"You don't get to speak to him anymore," Octavia purred in his ear. "You get to speak to me now."

She locked gazes with Quintin and nodded. But Quintin motioned toward Sage with a tilt of his head. Sage's hazel eyes were churning with emotion. Octavia questioned them with a look and was pleasantly surprised to find their eyebrows cocked in a way that said, *Let's make him cry.*

Octavia removed the dagger's blade from Garren's neck, twirled it in her hand, and swung it down in one swift motion. The dagger ripped through denim, skin, and dense quadricep muscle until it hit bone. Octavia felt the resistance vibrate through her entire arm. Garren screamed in pain.

The dagger illuminated in her hand as Sage called to the magic within it. Bright, jagged streaks of electrical discharge exploded from the hilt of the blade, soft and warm as a lover's caress against Octavia's skin. The flickering sparks slid down the blade until they found their target. Garren's jeans disintegrated, and his skin began to bubble. Howling, his back arched as his leg smoked, the scent of burnt flesh quickly filling the air. He convulsed, but Octavia never loosened her grip on his hair.

"Sage," Thaddeus called, "stop!"

Sage's mouth twitched, but they lowered their hands. The flashes of lightning faded, and Garren slumped, limp and exhausted, against Octavia as his fried tissue hissed. His breaths were ragged and irregular.

Octavia shifted beneath his weight and pulled the dagger free. She watched as a stream of crimson blood dripped to the floor, mixing with the puddle of water.

Garren coughed a few times before he spoke, his voice frayed. "You're aiming that weapon at the wrong person."

Sage scoffed, raising their hands into position, ready to strike again.

"Sage," Thaddeus boomed, shaking his head.

Reluctantly, they lowered their hands.

"Tell us how to break the hex," Jocasta commanded. "Now."

"You might as well kill me," Garren replied casually despite the severity of his injury. He pushed off Octavia to lean on his shins once more. "I'm never going to tell you."

Jocasta exhaled, and Octavia could almost feel her grandmother's frustration thinning the air around them. Jocasta hated using magic in this way. Treating any living, breathing thing this way. To her, this was as disgraceful as it got. But she'd do it. For Octavia. Guilt seared through her gut at the thought of her grandmother abandoning her morals on her behalf.

"I'm warning you," Octavia whispered in Garren's ear. "Things are about to get even more unpleasant if you don't cooperate."

Garren chuckled from his pool of bloody water. "Yes, I think they will."

A sharp pang shot through Octavia's wrist as Garren twisted and wrenched his head free from her grip. When her hand reflexively unclenched, a thick, bloody tuft of Garren's hair fell to the ground. She stumbled back a step, almost losing her balance.

Garren took full advantage, grabbing the wrist of her armed hand with a punishing grip. Octavia gasped as he stood, twisting her arm along the way. In one fluid movement, her back slammed against his chest, shoulder aching, as the cool metal of the dagger bit into the skin at her throat. The vines that had previously contained him lay shriveled and charred on the ground.

The fucking lightning.

Octavia whimpered, struggling against his grip despite the pain in her shoulder.

"I'll kill her myself." Garren pressed the blade of the dagger—*her* dagger—further into the skin of her neck. Octavia barely noticed the trickle of warm, sticky blood that slid down her neck and pooled at her collarbone as her mind worked overtime to find a way out.

Fear was already running rampant across the faces of those around her, but they turned absolutely savage at the sight of her blood. June wrenched a handful of midnight blue powder out of a velvet pouch at her hip and held her fist above her elbow, poised to throw. Jiro backed away while Sage conjured a spear of ice from the moisture in the air with several swipes of their wrist. Quintin and Tripp held Leif back as he lurched forward, desperately trying to get to her. The ferocious yell that passed his lips raised goosebumps along her arms.

Garren increased his pressure on the dagger at her throat, and panic seized Octavia's lungs, but then she remembered her promise to herself. She wasn't going to be a liability. Not this time. Not today. She could do this. She *would* do this. Garren was afraid of her, after all.

A baleful laugh escaped her lips. The sound was her, but it was also different—darker. Her but *not* her. A disconcerting heaviness settled in Octavia's stomach.

Garren's grip on the dagger at her neck loosened ever so slightly at the sound. *Perfect.* That was all she needed.

Octavia dipped her chin forward and then rammed her head back with all the force her slim neck could muster.

It was enough.

The *crack* of Garren's nose breaking reverberated through the room. She kicked backward, sending Garren stumbling even farther away. Octavia stalked away from him in a way she hoped looked cool, but inside, her heart was racing. *I can't believe I just did that.* Her chest lightened, and she was grateful she'd found a way to keep her promise.

Octavia turned to find Garren raising a hand to staunch the blood now flowing freely from his face. Satisfaction warmed her chilled skin as the coven released their breaths in unison.

"You're not going to make it easy, are you?" Garren gargled through a mouthful of blood.

"No. I'm going to make it impossible," Octavia bit back as Leif strode up to her. He rested a shaky hand on her shoulder. She leaned into it, her way of saying *I'm okay.*

"Well then," Garren began, shifting his gaze from her to Leif, "if you won't kill her, and I *can't* kill her, then I'll just have to kill the only person with the power to break her hex." His bloody mess of a face turned to Leif, a predator sizing up his prey.

"I'd like to see you try," Octavia hissed.

"Cheeky, aren't you?" Garren said, the flow of blood from his nose finally slowing.

She locked her jaw, refusing to answer.

Garren's arms bent at the elbows, his hands raised in question. "What do you say, Leif? Up for one final spar with your old man?" His crimson-stained lips parted in a foul smile.

Octavia's uninjured hand gripped Leif's shoulder. She wasn't going to let him leave her side.

"You're a persistent little thing," Garren said before he released a long, heavy sigh.

He pounced like a tiger—not toward Octavia and Leif, but straight for his discarded firearm. Octavia's dagger was still clutched in his other hand. He hit the ground, rolling gracefully as he swiped the gun. Still in motion, he took aim and shot directly at Octavia.

She pushed against Leif and propelled herself to the side, narrowly avoiding the bullet's steel bite as she fell. Her palms burned as they chafed against the concrete floor.

Leif's battle cry, a vehement, guttural screech, the sound of shredding vocal cords, rattled her eardrums. Before she could orient herself, Tripp and Quintin were pulling her to her feet.

Leif charged at Garren, knife raised and ready. Octavia's heart stuttered as Garren aimed his pistol at Leif and shot. A scream tore from her mouth.

Diving out of the way, Leif rolled on the floor, popping up mere feet away from Garren. Leif closed the distance, and Garren took aim.

Before he could pull the trigger a third time, Leif kicked the gun and sent it flying out of Garren's hand. Octavia's shoulders sagged with relief.

Now that Garren had lost his firearm, Octavia chanced a glance toward her grandmother. June and Jiro were ushering Jocasta and Thaddeus out of the warehouse. Jocasta was making feeble attempts to resist, but Thaddeus was an unrelenting brick wall. She wasn't getting past him. With one final insistent push from June and Jiro, the four of them were gone.

Octavia released a ragged breath, desperately relieved to know her grandmother was safe, but they weren't in the clear yet.

Delta walked toward the fallen firearm as Leif and Garren

continued to clash; the metal of their blades clinked together loudly. Delta picked the gun up, checked the safety, and twirled it around her index finger. Octavia could only imagine the plans Delta had for that gun.

A grunt of pain tore Octavia's attention away. Her stomach seized.

Leif had been cut. A long slice in his jacket revealed a shallow cut to his upper arm. The muscles in her core relaxed a bit. The wound was painful, Octavia was sure, but not likely to hinder him.

"You've improved," Garren grunted. He was already out of breath, and the blood on his face had begun to dry. The sight of her dagger in his hand set Octavia's teeth on edge.

"I've got a skilled teacher," Leif replied, winking at Octavia. Despite the danger and fear, her heart soared.

If Leif's goal had been to rile Garren up further, he succeeded. Garren wheeled on Leif with renewed vigor. His strikes and evasions were skilled and graceful, despite his age and various injuries. With each clash of fists, flesh, or metal, Octavia's anxiety mounted. Her pulse pounded in her ears. Leif was a skilled fighter, but Garren was disturbingly fast.

Octavia swallowed hard against a wave of nausea as her dagger slid across Leif's cheek, leaving a deep gash in its wake. Leif didn't pause to assess the damage.

He was relentless. A warrior through and through.

Octavia ran over to Sage, her eyes never leaving the dagger in Garren's hand. "Can you electrocute him again?" she asked.

"No, it's tapped out," they said breathlessly. "I'm so sorry; the first spell used too much magic."

Shit.

Somewhere in her mind, buried beneath the layers of crippling anxiety, Octavia felt the tether tug at her. It shifted with each of Leif's calculated movements. She reached out with a mental hand and held onto it for dear life.

Leif would win. *They* would win.

CHAPTER 41
LEIF

The sadistic expression on Garren's face when he noted the fear on Octavia's made Leif want to murder him. He didn't just want to win this fight. He wanted to take something precious away from Garren. Leif grasped for an idea, something he could do to belittle Garren like he'd spent all evening doing to Octavia, but he came up blank. He'd just have to settle for his life. It wasn't enough, but it'd have to do.

During their dance of metal and fists, Leif only caught glimpses of Octavia. Each time, his heart clenched painfully, threatening to stop altogether. The fear plastered on her face was . . . violent. Leif didn't even want to imagine what Octavia would do if he lost, if he fell tonight. So he shoved the thought away and refocused his energy on the battle at hand.

The dagger in Garren's grasp whizzed past Leif's ear, nicking his upper helix. The strike left a sharp pain behind in its wake. Hot, sticky blood pooled in his ear canal. He had to speed up if he was going to have any chance of defeating Garren. How a middle-aged man was still so fast, Leif had no idea.

To counter, Leif spun counterclockwise, ducking under Garren's extended arm. He'd chosen a fighting knife for himself earlier that evening, since he'd given Octavia his favorite dagger. He swiped the knife toward Garren's triceps. If he could just sever the muscle there, he'd gain the advantage.

But Garren had taught him that move. He anticipated Leif's strike and partially evaded the attack. Leif still got a good swipe in, but the cut was far too shallow. They pushed away from each other, like two magnets of the same polarity, and readied themselves to strike again.

Thick droplets of blood dripped from the cut on Garren's arm. The sight brought forth another memory, long since locked away, to the forefront of Leif's mind.

Leif raised his left forearm to block Garren's next strike as the night of the witch hunter attack played back in his mind's eye. *Flames licking up ivory walls. The acrid smell of smoke in the air. His limp body being dragged from the floor. His mother's pale blonde hair stained red. Her lifeless body splayed across the floor amongst a pool of blood so dark it looked black. Being thrown over Garren's shoulder and carried from the burning house. The echoing cries for his parents floating away on the wind.*

The muscles in Leif's arm strained against the force of Garren's blow, Octavia's dagger aimed at his chest. A grunt ripped from Leif's lungs with the effort it took to push him off.

Garren wasted no time, immediately lurching forward to strike again. Leif blinked the memory away as he spun out of the dagger's reach, swinging his arm to slice at Garren's abdomen. *The lying bastard.* "I remember now," Leif said through heavy, panting breaths. "My parents, my childhood, the night of the attack."

Garren grimaced as he readied himself to strike again.

"How did you get us to forget?"

When Garren lunged forward, Leif met the dagger with his own outstretched blade. The sound of metal on metal ricocheted off the walls around them.

Garren jumped back, his breaths coming in fast and short. "Some of your memories were repressed without my intervention. Post-traumatic stress. For the rest I used hypnosis. It wasn't perfect, though." He walked a semicircle around Leif as he spoke, his voice strained and breathless. Leif rotated in synchrony with Garren, never letting him slip out of sight. "Memories slipped through occasionally, and when they did, a specialist helped me . . . *rewrite* them."

Leif couldn't remember ever meeting with a hypnotist before, but he supposed that was to be expected. He raised his knife, assessing the best strategy for his next attack. "You killed our parents, kidnapped us, and fucked with our minds," Leif said as he stepped forward. "You don't deserve a quick death."

Leif struck, and Garren's calf sliced open, exposing flayed muscle. His blade gleamed crimson.

"I don't disagree," Garren grunted through the pain. "I'm ready to pay for my sins when the time comes, but it looks like I'll need to commit one more before I go."

As Garren turned to spit on the floor, Leif's gaze met Octavia's. Her eyes were desperate, pleading, and the message was clear: *finish the fuck up.*

There was only one surefire way to win a fight against an opponent as skilled as Garren, Leif realized. His free hand found the velvet pouch full of June's magic powder in his coat pocket. He grasped as much of the powder as he could hold.

Garren readjusted his grip on the dagger and sprung, only to meet a fistful of dark gray powder in mid-air. He gagged and sputtered as he fell. Delta whooped and hollered behind him.

"What is this?" Garren choked out. His eyes darted around frantically.

Leif kicked the dagger out of Garren's hand as he responded, even though he knew Garren wouldn't be able to hear him. "Just a bit of hocus pocus."

"Finish it!" Octavia called, her voice laced with anxiety.

Leif nodded as he crouched down. Garren was kneeling, his eyes still whirling around aimlessly, unseeing.

"This is for all of us," Leif whispered, taking his time. Garren was unarmed, deprived of his senses, and at Leif's mercy now. It was over.

Leif raised the knife to Garren's neck and held one of his shoulders firmly in place. His muscles flexed as he began to swipe the blade against Garren's throat. But as blood blossomed beneath the steel of his blade, Leif felt—

Pain.

Unlike anything he'd ever experienced before.

It seared and burned, straight through his ribs, and into his . . . *fuck*, into his heart.

"I'm sorry," Garren said in a raspy voice over the thundering of Leif's pulse in his ears.

Leif's heart stuttered around the metal. He drew a sharp breath—almost blacked out. His vision swam. It was excruciating, this pain.

No. He was wrong. The pain of the metal being twisted, then slowly pulled free—sharp edges scraping against his still-beating heart—*that* was excruciating.

Leif gasped for air. Blood filled his lungs and poured from his wound. He didn't even have to look. He knew because he was cold.

He was dying.

Flashes of moments broke through his agony. Like swiping through photos on a camera. Octavia running after Garren. Cries and screams. Explosions of color. Quintin appearing as if from nowhere to cut off his escape. Garren dodging their punches. Sage throwing fire. Garren's coat flaming. Delta aiming Garren's gun. An earsplitting bang.

Then there was only the night sky and cold concrete pressing into his back.

No stars this close to the city, he thought sadly.

June's powder failed. She'll be so upset. It's not her fault.

I made a mistake.

Garren kept his ace hidden in his coat—such a small dagger, such a short blade—so much damage.

What a stupid, stupid mistake.

The cold was spreading. He couldn't feel his arms or legs anymore. His heart missed a beat, and then another. His thoughts drifted to Octavia. Then, as if his thoughts had summoned her, her face hovered over him, framed by the starless sky. Her cheeks were stained with tears, but he couldn't stop the smile that broke out at the sight of her.

He wanted to say her name. One last time.

"Tavi."

The sound was barely a whisper.

CHAPTER 42

OCTAVIA

*T*his isn't happening.

Octavia's quaking hands pressed firmly against the wound in Leif's chest.

Stop the bleeding. Just stop the bleeding.

Hot, thick blood flowed between her fingers.

So much blood.

She'd started crying, and now she couldn't stop. Like a faucet thrust on high, the tears fell and fell and fell. Octavia wanted to puke, to scream, to explode. *If he doesn't make it, if he* . . . She didn't finish the thought.

Because he smiled. That perfect smile that made even her very worst days better; the smile that kept her safe and warm; the smile that gave her space to be fully and unapologetically herself.

And then he whispered her name. "Tavi."

A guttural sob crawled its way out of her throat. "Leif."

His smile brightened at the sound of his name on her lips. Her chest tightened, threatening to stop her heart, crush her lungs, and take her with him.

"Stay with me, Leif. You can't . . . you can't go anywhere, okay? You stay here with me, where you" —another choked sob— "where you belong."

"Okay," he breathed. "I'll stay."

His shoulder tensed beneath her blood-drenched hands, as if he was trying to move his arm.

"No, don't move. Stay still. Please." Her voice broke—along with her heart—into a million fragile pieces.

Leif nodded as she felt his heart skip a beat under her hands. His shallow breathing hitched, and his eyes flashed wide with fear.

"No, no, no, no!" Her own heart stuttered. Every cell in her body went cold, drenched in soul-wrenching fear. "Someone, help! I need help! We—we—" Her breaths were coming too fast, every inhale a convulsive gasp for air that provided no relief.

Leif's pensive cerulean eyes never left her face. They roved over every inch of it, every curve, every angle, every damn flaw. He didn't have to say it for her to know, but he loved whatever he saw there.

He loved her.

His heart was slowing, the soft beats skipping more frequently.

"I love you," she cried. Maybe she whispered it. She wasn't sure. She just knew she needed him to hear it, just once.

"I love you," his ashen lips mouthed. They twitched as he tried to smile again.

She needed to do something. Now. Something. Anything.

She grappled for the tether in her mind, but without Leif's magic to guide her, she couldn't find it. Couldn't feel the connection at all. It was like trying to capture air with a net.

His heart stopped. For one second. One whole second.

A petrified gasp escaped her lips.

"Come here," Leif commanded with a breath.

Octavia bobbed her head shakily as she bent down close, laying her forehead gently against his. He was cold as ice.

He took a deep, shuddering breath, taking the scent of her deep into his lungs. Their tears merged, tracing lines across his pale face.

She didn't know why the words came now. She hadn't been haunted by them for almost two weeks. But they came, with a force so strong and insistent she couldn't ignore them. So, she gave them life instead, speaking them into the small pocket of air they shared.

"Non est umbra sine lumine."

Leif nodded weakly beneath her, as if he understood. His breath rattled in his chest.

She lifted her chin. The brush of their lips was soft as the brush of a butterfly's wing.

"Non est umbra sine lumine." His breath against her cheek was cold.

Submerged in her grief, she barely felt it. The click. The tug. The ... *tether.*

There it was, in her mind's eye, solid and sturdy and real. With mental hands, she grabbed on tight, and pulled and yanked with every ounce of strength and willpower she had left. Until she felt the other end go taut.

There. He was right there.

She wasn't sure if it was instinct, but somehow, she knew what to do. She forced her intention down through the link. *I will save you. You're not leaving; you're not allowed to. I will save you.*

Her soiled hands felt a flash of warmth break through the numbing cold.

Her eyes opened to a blinding white light. She couldn't see anything. Not Leif, not even her own hands mere inches in front of her face, but she could feel *it.*

The healing.

Leif's light magic was *healing* him.

Octavia didn't dare move. Not an inch. Not even a breath.

The blinding light began to recede, growing dimmer and dimmer until Octavia could see its origin. It had come from the tether. From the orb of light at the center of Leif's chest. Blood still caked his skin and clothes, but the wound was gone. She brushed the pads of her fingers along his exposed chest, unable to find a single trace of it.

"Leif," she said, her voice hoarse. "Leif, your chest. It's healed."

She shook him gently at first, and then more insistently. He wasn't moving besides the steady rise and fall of his chest. He must've lost consciousness.

"Leif!"

His eyes fluttered.

Without thinking, her mouth found his, tender and searching. His hands tangled in her hair, pulling her closer. A soft whimper of relief passed between their lips.

"I heard you," Leif murmured against her lips. "You told me you'd save me, that I wasn't allowed to leave." The soft curve of his lips brushed against hers as he smiled. "I was wrong when I said I didn't take orders from you. You can order me around any day, love."

Octavia let her strength shatter then, sobbing in the safety of Leif's arms, soothed by his every heartbeat echoing in her ears.

CHAPTER 43
LEIF

He held on to her like she was a life raft and he was lost at sea. She'd saved him. He didn't know how, but he knew it'd been her. It should've been impossible for her to call to his magic like that, not with the hex still intact, but somehow, she'd done it. She'd saved him.

Because she *loved* him.

The words echoed in his mind as he rubbed soothing strokes along her spine. For an indeterminate amount of time, they simply clung to each other, before her tears began to dry and her breathing regulated.

"Do you want to sit up now?" she asked quietly.

"Yes, please."

She nodded as she moved off his chest. He accepted her extended hand and grunted as she gently pulled him into a seated position. He'd expected pain, soreness, or at least discomfort, but there was nothing. Not a hint of strain or injury in his entire body. Whatever his magic had done, it was impressive as hell.

"Don't you ever scare us like that again," Delta called in a venomous voice from behind him.

"Come on, where's the fun in that?" Leif managed, looking over his shoulder at her.

Delta's cheeks were wet with tears, but she smiled at his retort as she jogged over to them.

"What happened to Garren?" Octavia asked, as if suddenly snapping back to reality. Her head whipped around as she wiped her cheeks with the back of her hand.

Leif looked around to find Quintin, Tripp, Jiro, and Sage jogging toward them as well, from the western entrance.

Quintin answered when he reached them. "The bastard got away."

"What? How?" Leif asked.

"While we were blinded by your light magic, he got past us," Tripp explained as he ran a hand down his weary face. "I have no idea how he could've seen through it enough to get away."

Leif shook his head. "Shit, I'm sorry. I didn't mean to—"

Sage cut him off. "Shut up. No apologies. If you hadn't used that magic, you'd be dead right now."

Leif nodded. "June's powder didn't work on him either, or if it did, it couldn't have lasted more than a few seconds. He must have something . . . some type of magic-repelling device, or maybe he's enchanted with a spell that makes him immune. It doesn't make sense otherwise. Only direct hits from Sage's elemental magic seemed to have any effect on him."

"I noticed that too," Quintin agreed grimly.

"Where are the others?" Octavia asked.

"I told them to wait in the car," Jiro answered. "Your poor grandmother is frozen half to death. June and Thaddeus are with her."

"I bet the crafty bitch is already cooking up a plan," Delta chuckled, rubbing her hands together briskly. "That prick tried to kill you multiple times tonight. She's not going to let him get away with it. Grandma's claws are coming out." Delta's smirk was vulpine.

"What do we do now?" Octavia asked quietly, her hand still shaking slightly under Leif's.

"We go home, I guess. Rest and reconvene," Jiro said with a shrug.

"Try to get your magic back," Quintin added, nodding toward the discarded dagger at Octavia's side.

Octavia picked up the dagger with her free hand, bringing it to her chest. "Sage's spell used up all the imbued magic."

Tripp let out a low whistle. "Damn."

Sage scoffed at the surprise in his tone but smiled despite themself.

"I'm not sure what being 'the key' to Tavi's hex means, but I'm willing to try anything." Leif looked pointedly at Quintin. If anyone could figure out what this new piece of information meant, and how to use it to get Octavia's magic back, it was him.

"I'm in too."

Everyone turned when Delta spoke.

"What?" she asked, her eyebrows reaching for her hairline. "Apparently Octavia has some crazy dark magic. I'm sorry, but I'm not missing out on that."

The group devolved into fits of shaky laughter. This night, this fight, had brought them closer together. There was no questioning it now: they were on the same team. It would be their coven against the world.

June appeared in the entrance. "What are you loons laughing about?" she asked beneath swirls of breath as she jogged over to them.

"Delta thinks Octavia is Lady Death," Jiro explained.

"Uh-huh, sure she is." June rolled her eyes. "Leif, are you okay? I heard everything over the comm link."

"Yeah, yeah. Perfectly fine."

"I'm so sorry. If my powder had worked—"

"Your powder was perfect, June. Garren had the upper hand tonight, that's all."

She dipped her chin in understanding. "Are you ready to leave? It's freezing out here."

"Yeah, let's go."

Octavia helped Leif stand. Her cool skin against his finally started to warm. He tucked her under his arm, and together they walked with the group toward the exit.

After a few steps, Leif felt his magic stirring. It hummed and vibrated, the frequency slightly off. *Too high? No, too low.* Something was different.

"Do you feel that?" Leif asked quietly against Octavia's ear.

"The cold?" Octavia replied, blinking slowly as if she was puzzled.

Whatever this was, she obviously didn't notice. *But she wouldn't, would she? She doesn't have magic.* Leif didn't reply. He simply tucked Octavia in closer, planting a kiss at the crown of her head.

"Tavi, come here!" June called, pulling a vial from her coat pocket. "This will speed up your healing."

Octavia disentangled herself from Leif's embrace. With every inch of space she put between them, the frequency of his magic shifted. Dropping lower. Leif glanced at the others. All their faces were weary and exhausted, but relaxed. Nobody seemed concerned. This must've been some kind of side effect from his light magic. *Or maybe a side effect of getting stabbed*, he thought humorlessly.

But the frequency dropped again, now low enough that it scratched against his nerves like sandpaper. It didn't feel right, didn't feel natural.

Her dark magic will bring about the end of the natural world.

Garren's words echoed in Leif's head a second too late. Her hand left his, the absence of it like a block of ice against already frozen skin, so cold it burned.

She took one step away, and then another before she came to a halt and whipped her head back toward him. The whites of her eyes were stark against the darkness—the blackness—of her irises. She felt it now too.

"Tavi?"

Leif had no idea who had called her name. He was distracted by the pavement lurching beneath his feet.

CHAPTER 44
OCTAVIA

Was the ground shaking, or was she? Octavia couldn't tell. The feeling within her body was almost indescribable. It was as if every atom was waking up. It sent her nerves fraying, her skin tingling, and the hair on the back of her neck standing on end.

Is this—?

No, there's no way.

But even as she tried to shove the thought away, she felt it rising within her, each breath drawing it closer to the surface.

Magic.

The vibrations within her synchronized, calling to the magic within. An unfamiliar force pooled at her core, right beneath her thrashing heart. The force hummed with delight, happy to be set free at last. She leaned into the sensation.

The magic wasted no time as it reached and splayed, snaking down her spine. Her eyes rolled into the back of her head. Ice-cold fingers stroked over every vertebra. Her toes were curling in her boots by the time it reached her feet.

Every cell in her body was *singing*.

When Octavia opened her eyes again, her body was drowning in magic. It was brimming over, spilling into the ground beneath her feet and into the frosty air around her.

And then Octavia took notice of the others. They were scattered around her, kneeling upon the quaking ground. Quintin was screaming her name. Over and over. She could barely hear him over the thrum of magic leaking out of her veins.

She hadn't thought to be afraid. Not until now. She'd been too captivated by the magic. It hadn't felt threatening, at least not toward her. But now, as she registered the fear in the others, terror of her own rose, clogging her throat.

A frozen hand grasped at her neck. It took her a second to realize it was her own. She couldn't swallow, couldn't speak. More screams echoed around her as every pair of eyes tracked her movements.

She moved her hand in front of her face, gaping at the sight before her. Her pale skin was barely visible through thick, heavy swirls of black smoke. Plumes of it billowed from her fingertips, making lazy trails up her wrist and forearm.

She stumbled, taking several steps back. But it followed. Like a faithful beast keeping close to its master. She shook her smoking hand helplessly, trying to dispel the magic. The smoke only clustered, caressing her hand like a lover.

Her back hit a concrete wall, and the hand at her side pushed against it for balance. Her skin burned at the contact. She twisted around to find a blackened handprint seared into the stone. Her head tilted as she watched the handprint crack and crumble. Onyx fissures spread across the surface like disease-riddled veins. In seconds, the entire wall had disintegrated into a fine powder and floated away on the wind.

You were consumed with darkness because you are darkness. Your magic is death itself. Pure decay and destruction.

Garren's words replayed in her mind as she watched the tendrils of ash dance in the wind. Once, and then twice, and then again and again his words echoed in her head, until it was all she could think, all she could feel.

Death. Decay. Destruction.

Garren had been right. She didn't know why she hadn't really believed him when he'd said it. But the proof was here, in the wall that was now a pile of dust because she had *touched* it.

People died *because of you.*

The truth of those words cut sharper and deeper than any blade. Thick, heavy blood oozed from her chest. No, not blood— magic. Waves of smoke, black and opaque as oil, slithered through the air.

The tendrils of her magic reached Jiro first, and she stood frozen with horror as she watched the smoke curl around his neck. He flinched at the contact, and the smoke writhed with pleasure.

Octavia blinked, and the smoke struck. It entered through his agape mouth as smaller wisps broke off to invade his nostrils. Octavia could feel it, the smoke in his throat, swirling toward his lungs.

It wanted to suffocate, to kill.

She quivered, her magic celebrating beneath her skin as every last trace of oxygen evaporated from his lungs. It was the closest thing she'd ever felt to ecstasy. No drug on the planet had ever made her feel like this.

Even as some small part of Octavia's remaining humanity thrashed violently against her magic at the sight of Jiro's lips turning blue, she kept going, ordering her magic to continue its work. Just a few more minutes, and the light would leave his eyes forever. That—death—would be rapturous bliss. She needed to feel it, desperately.

With a flick of her wrist, the smoke spread like a raging wildfire, consuming the rest of the kneeling bodies around her.

Who were they again? Friends? Strangers? She had no idea. All she knew was their deaths would bring about a state of euphoria unlike any other. She couldn't deny herself that. She wouldn't.

The first boy's heart fluttered in his chest. It would only be a minute or so now. A wicked smile tugged at the corner of her lips. The force pooled at her core pulsed impatiently.

"Any moment now," she whispered to it. The sound of her voice was alien, yet intimate. Feminine, yet masculine. Ancient, yet new. It was unlike anything she'd ever heard.

The last threads of Octavia's consciousness clung to her shell of a mind. If Jiro died, she would lose herself entirely, and she knew, without a shadow of a doubt, she could never return once she leapt over that edge.

Her magic had been locked away for a reason—this reason.

Garren had been right. If she couldn't hold on to her consciousness—to her own will—she would bring about the end of the world as they knew it. This dark magic would never be satiated. It would kill and consume until there was nothing and no one left.

I have to stop it. Have to. Have to . . . Have—

What do I have to do?

Who am I?

What am I?

You are mine, an inky voice murmured in her mind, *and I have missed you.*

A gentle wisp of smoke stroked her face, and she shivered with pleasure.

In the distance, a light flickered against her curtain of darkness. The smoke around it recoiled in pain. The light—it hurt her.

The light flared, and her smoke receded further as it sought the safety of darkness. Octavia hissed in its direction. She'd have to stomp it out.

She stalked toward the light. With every step she took, the light intensified and the lovely, frigid air around her warmed to a repulsive degree. The vibration of the magic within her blood hitched. The frequency was too high, too oppressive.

Stomp it out, stomp it out, stomp it—

The light flashed as a glowing hand shot out through the shadows. Octavia whirled, narrowly avoiding contact. She bared her teeth at the glowing person. He was tall and masculine. The hair on his head stood on end, the white strands reflecting facets of light even though he was surrounded by darkness on every side.

"Octavia." The voice was a command. A call to action. But the word meant nothing to her. She hissed and recoiled from the abhorrent light.

"Are you still in there?" the glowing being asked, more softly this time. Something akin to pain laced the sound.

"Esto!" she spat at him.

"Latin?" His shining face etched in worry. "You can't even speak English anymore?"

Her head tilted in confusion.

"Octavia," he repeated, his voice now desperate and afraid.

Good. He should've been afraid. She was going to end him.

The suffocating bodies around them thrashed, their lungs searing and twitching, begging for life. The first would succumb in seconds.

"They're dying," the glowing man said, following her gaze.

Her savage smile was her only response.

"No," he said simply.

"Etiam." *Yes.*

He moved so fast. Before she could counter, her arm throbbed with pain. A long, deep cut along her shoulder now leaked blood and smoke. Her eyes drifted to the wound for only a moment. But it was a moment too long. The light flared, blinding her, sending her tendrils of smoke scattering to the farthest corners of the room.

Desperate gasps for breath echoed all around her. She summoned her smoke and darkness, readying the force within her to strike back when two strong arms wrapped around her. Her magic sputtered as the blinding light invaded everything. Her smoke. Her shadows. Her mind.

"Octavia! Come back to me."

The magic in her veins soured, spoiling instantly. Pain pried her mouth ajar as bliss devolved into torment. Soft, seductive vibrations became electric shocks that slowly, tortuously zapped every ounce of power from her bones. She wanted to thrash and scream and cry, but it was as if her brain had disconnected from her body. Her magic was draining away, and though she pleaded with herself to fight against the pain, to just keep her grip on the magic she'd yearned for so desperately . . . she was no match for the light.

The darkness withdrew further, seeking refuge beneath Octavia's skin as she clawed her way back into herself, her magic continuing to dampen as the frequency rose. Leif's magic followed suit, lowering to meet hers in the middle, until the last of their magic blinked out, together.

The only sounds around them were those of heavy breaths. Octavia could barely hear them. Her ears were ringing in the absence of her magic. She startled as Leif's forehead fell to rest against her shoulder.

"Thank you," Octavia whispered as she collapsed against him.

"I owed you one," he murmured against her hair.

This time, when darkness came for her, she went with it gladly. It was the tranquil darkness of rest and dreams.

CHAPTER 45
LEIF

It had only been ten hours since the coven had returned to the house, but Leif had already tried everything, everything he could think of. None of it had worked.

Octavia had withdrawn back into herself, much like the stranger he'd met in the bar not long ago. And even though it infuriated him, Leif could understand why she was acting like this. Most of Octavia's life had been spent in search for her magic, and now that she'd found it . . . well, he could understand why she might be feeling like all her efforts had been in vain.

Her magic had been unlike anything Leif had ever encountered before—not that he'd had much experience to speak from yet. But still, it had been petrifying. The starving, emotionless void of her magic's darkness was nothing like Octavia herself. It was something wholly different, perhaps a different entity entirely. Octavia *had* to know that. And yet, every attempt he'd made to try and reassure her had been utterly ignored.

He knew she was ignoring him because he hadn't left her side since the incident, at Jocasta's and Thaddeus's recommendation. They didn't know why Leif's magic was able to keep Octavia's in check, but they were working on a hypothesis of sorts, something they could test.

Octavia had made it clear she resented being stripped of her independence, the constant brush of skin against skin, but Leif was trying his best not to take it personally. She had still slept soundly in his arms for a few hours and wiped cream cheese off his lips as he ate breakfast, even though her words had been few and far between. She wasn't rejecting him; she was rejecting herself, and to Leif, that was worse.

He'd tried to tell her how much she meant to the coven—and more importantly, to him—but she'd just shrugged the words off. So he'd tried to show her how much she meant by pressing his warm lips against hers with as much passion and fervor as his heart could summon. She'd kissed him back, but he could tell she'd done it for him, not for herself. The realization had felt like an ice pick to the heart.

He could save her from foes, magical and otherwise, but he wasn't going to be able to save her from herself. That would be up to her. Her battle. Her choice. So, he'd decided to give her space. Not physical space, of course, but mental and emotional space to figure this part out on her own.

Octavia stared out of the window next to the bed they were lounging on in her childhood bedroom. The room was still decorated from floor to ceiling in obnoxious shades of purple, but today he didn't mind. He'd come to realize purple was the perfect color for her: mysterious, powerful, and sometimes dark.

She was twisting her hair between her fingers mindlessly as her eyes roved over the scene beyond the window. Whatever she was considering, it had nothing to do with the sun-washed streets of the Brookline neighborhood beyond.

Leif moved his hand that had been gently stroking her neck above a bulky cable-knit sweater to rest on her exposed knee. "Are you hungry yet?" he ventured, looking up at the shadows staining her profile.

"Hmm . . ." she considered. "No, I don't think so." Her face remained pensive as she continued staring out the window.

"You haven't eaten a solid meal since the day before yesterday," he said carefully. "Please. Let's ask Jocasta to bring an early lunch up."

"All right."

He was pretty sure she'd ignore anything her grandmother set in front of her, like she had with breakfast, but he had to try. Leif grabbed his cell phone from the bedside table with his free hand and sent a text to the coven group chat. A response came through from Quintin: *I need to talk to Octavia about something first.*

Moments later, a knock sounded on the bedroom door.

"Come on in," Leif called.

Quintin had always been a quiet person, but now, as he entered the room, his quiet was different, expectant and demanding. He didn't even need to speak to get Octavia's attention. Her head turned to him as he closed the door behind him. He used only one arm; the other arm was concealing something behind his back.

The only sign of Quintin's surprise was a slight hitch in an eyebrow as he met Octavia's eyes, and he registered what he saw there. How close she was to giving up. Quintin's gaze bounced to Leif's, a question posed in his warm, brown eyes. Leif shrugged, feeling completely defeated. He couldn't help her.

Quintin understood well enough. "How are you doing?" he asked Octavia.

Her tight smile didn't reach her eyes.

"I figured," Quintin said, shifting on his feet.

"What's that behind your back?" Leif asked.

"Ah," Quintin began, revealing Octavia's dagger. "Jocasta, Granddad, and I had an idea." He moved to the edge of the bed, sitting next to the footboard. He twirled the dagger between his fingers several times before continuing. "We want to try imbuing this with your light magic, Leif. Not a ton, just enough to hopefully keep Octavia's darkness in check. Then she'd be able to keep this on her person at all times so you two don't have to . . . you know."

Leif looked at Octavia. Her features were hesitant, uncertain. Perhaps there was even fear there, but she returned his gaze after a moment, her eyes glinting in the soft sunlight.

"It's up to you," Leif said. "Do you want to try it?"

She nodded.

"Tripp's containment spell is ready to go," Quintin said to Leif. "All you have to do is touch it and instruct your magic to flow between you and the dagger. You'll know when it's full. It'll feel like your magic is pushing against a wall."

"All right." Leif placed his free hand on the dagger and closed his eyes, concentrating. First, he called to the magic in his cells, coaxing the light awake. It hummed a happy greeting. Then, he focused on sending the light into his hand. His skin warmed instantly against the cool steel of the dagger.

Insistently, he thrust the light from his hand into the steel. At first his magic hesitated, confused by his silent command. But the dagger began absorbing the light, and his magic relented, happy to obey its master.

The dagger drank and drank and drank, until finally, Leif's light hit the wall Quintin had forewarned him about. He released the dagger, his brow slick with sweat, and loosed a sigh. The humming in his cells died down to a calm, gentle simmer.

"Let's try it," Quintin said, handing Octavia the dagger.

She took it, holding it across her lap with both hands.

"Now you," Quintin said to Leif, instructing him to remove his hand from Octavia's knee with a bob of his head.

Leif locked gazes with Octavia before he made any attempt to move. "You sure?"

"Yes."

Leif moved his hand and immediately hated the absence of her.

Octavia's breathing hitched, but absolutely nothing happened. No darkness, no smoke, no earthquakes. Just the woman he loved sitting next to him, who was now staring appreciatively at Quintin. Leif's throat tightened at the fresh tears he saw rimming her eyes.

"Thank you," she croaked.

"Anything for you, Tavi," Quintin replied with a bright smile. "I'm just grateful as shit it worked." He released a heavy breath.

Quintin pulled the dagger's sheath from his back pocket and handed that over too. "Keep this on you at all times, and make sure to keep it tight enough against your thigh that the hilt is always touching your skin. Don't take it off, even to shower—at least for now, until we can learn more about this."

Octavia nodded, staring down at the dagger in her lap.

"None of this is your fault," Quintin murmured, his voice surprisingly authoritative.

Octavia chuckled hoarsely. "Really? How exactly is it not my fault, Quin?"

"You didn't ask for any of this. It's not like you chose to be born early, or chose to be hexed, or chose to be given a magical force so great it's almost impossible to control. You didn't choose any of this for yourself. These things just *happened* to you." Quintin's voice rose an octave with every passing word. "So, how are you going to choose to deal with it? Are you going to shut down and push everyone away like you've always done, or are you going to *rise to the challenge?*"

Those last four words echoed in the air around them. It was as good as a dare—a dare between the oldest and closest of friends.

Octavia glared at Quintin. "What does my being born early have anything to do with this?" She raised a hand to gesture toward herself, her magic. "Besides ruining the whole 'magical seven babies experiment' thing?"

"That's the same question I had, so I asked Jocasta and Granddad about it," Quintin explained. "They think you being born eighth threw the magical balance of power off-kilter. Granddad did some research last night and found some interesting hypotheses. Some sources have postulated that the magical prowess bestowed upon the seven would've been evenly split among them. Our grandparents' theory is an imbalance occurred when you were born, causing you to get said unimaginable magical power instead—power that was originally meant to be shared among the seven of us."

"But we don't really know that for sure?" Leif asked.

"No. We don't," Quintin relented. "But you don't know our grandparents as well as we do, so trust me when I say they won't let this question go unanswered. Jocasta has already sent a message to consult two of the closest covens."

"I'm sorry," Octavia cut in, her jaw slack. "What?"

Quintin chuckled.

"Are you telling me there are other covens around here?" she asked incredulously.

"If it makes you feel better, I didn't know about them either before this morning. And they're not from around here; Charleston and New Orleans, I think. I guess our grandparents know how to keep their secrets well hidden."

"Why have they never told us?" Octavia demanded.

"Apparently contacting other covens is risky. It risks exposing our location, numbers, magical specialties. Any strengths or weaknesses we want to remain hidden. Remember what Jocasta told us? Witches have been tortured and wielded by witch hunters before." Quintin sighed. "There's a chance the other covens won't even respond to us."

"So they could know something about this birth order thing?" Leif asked.

"Maybe."

"So, what now?" Octavia asked. "Do we just sit around and

wait for their replies—if they even decide to reply at all?"

"Of course not," Quintin countered.

Octavia raised a brow in silent question.

"We plan and we prepare."

Leif frowned. "Prepare for what?"

Quintin crossed his arms. "For battle."

"Battle with who?" Octavia asked.

"The witch hunters." Quintin set his jaw determinedly.

Leif's stomach flipped. "Why? Garren escaped before—"

"Octavia caused a city-wide six-point-zero magnitude earthquake. Garren will know she reconnected with her magic. He'll view her as a threat and rally as many of the witch hunters as he can."

Leif and Octavia gaped at him. Suddenly, Leif felt foolish for agreeing to test out the dagger theory. If they'd been wrong...

"We have to learn how to control Tavi's magic, and hopefully how to wield it, before they come for her. We have to get stronger if we want to stand any chance of surviving."

"Okay," Leif agreed easily. "Let's do it."

"Tavi?" Quintin asked as casually as if he were asking her about the weather. But the weight of the question hung in the air as heavy as an anvil. Quintin wasn't asking if she was on board with the plan; he was asking if she'd accept his dare.

Several emotions flashed across Octavia's face before Leif could pin them down. After a moment, one settled and stayed, an emotion he'd seen on her face countless times before—an emotion he hadn't realized how much he'd missed until now: steely determination.

She was in.

He almost fell back against the bed in relief.

"I have one condition," she said.

"You're negotiating now?" Quintin chuckled.

Octavia shot him an impatient look. "We go back home to train."

"We are home," Quintin reminded her, worry etched in the lines of his face.

"I don't mean here in Boston. I mean Salem. We go back home to Salem, or no dice."

Leif straightened, leaning forward to get a better view of Octavia's face. He knew Salem was important to her and her family, but he'd never heard Octavia refer to the city as her home before.

Quintin's eyebrows lowered. "Why?"

"I don't know, but I have this feeling that we need to go back. Like my magic is calling to it. I think if we go back, my magic might behave. And the magic of the land—of our ancestors—will be there to help us." Quintin and Leif locked gazes, both equally unsure. "If the witch hunters are already coming for us, then what's keeping us here anyway? There's nothing to fear from Salem anymore. There's only history, family, and magic."

Silence draped around them for a moment as Octavia's gaze returned to the window. "I want to go home."

"I'll talk to Jocasta and Granddad," Quintin acquiesced as he stood.

"Quin." Octavia grabbed Quintin's hand. He didn't so much as flinch at her ice-cold skin. "Thank you."

Quintin bent over and pecked a single, chaste kiss on her cheek before he turned to leave. As the door latched behind him, Octavia's fingers lingered over the spot her friend's lips had touched. She smiled softly to herself.

The ache in Leif's chest ebbed at the sight of it. That smile. A smile that rarely blessed his waking hours but haunted his dreams. He hoped to see that smile every day from now on, making his dreams a reality.

CHAPTER 46
OCTAVIA

The red wine Octavia sipped settled in her stomach, graciously warming her perpetually cold core. That was a not-so-pleasant side effect of her dark magic. No matter how many layers she wore or how closely she sat to a roaring fire, she was always cold. The only two things that seemed to help were alcohol and Leif's light magic. But since Leif was busy packing up his old apartment, the wine would have to do the trick.

As it turned out, Quintin hadn't had to do much to convince Jocasta and Thaddeus to move the coven to Salem. In fact, they'd already considered the idea themselves. By dinner that evening, Jocasta and Thaddeus had jetted off to Salem to tour their potential new home. They were truly lucky Octavia's grandmother still had such great connections in their hometown.

They'd probably be hearing from the grandparents soon, but for the time being, Octavia and her friends were packing up their loft. Cardboard boxes and half-empty bottles of wine were strewn about haphazardly while music blared from Sage's stereo. The Times Square Ball Drop played on the muted TV.

But despite the cheery atmosphere in the loft, after the disaster of the day before, it was impossible for Octavia to get in the holiday spirit. She'd never really been a fan of New Year's Eve anyway, even before.

Octavia scoffed at the thought. *Before*. She felt like she'd been preaching that word over and over her entire life. *Before I lost my magic. Before my parents died. Before we met the witch hunters. Before my dark magic almost destroyed everything.*

Octavia's grip tightened around her wine glass as she shoved the intrusive thoughts away. No more *before*. No more living life looking through the rearview mirror. She couldn't change what had happened in the past, but she could—and *would*—try her hardest to give her coven a better future. That was her goal now.

Octavia's attention was lassoed back into the moment by the sound of a large crash behind her. As per usual, June and Quintin were the only two truly getting anything done, while Sage and Octavia had been lounging on the living room floor, drinking and recounting the stories that accompanied every single object they owned.

She noted Sage's fervently pleased face as they stood over the garbage bin, a large ceramic lamp, now very broken, sticking out the top. "I always hated that ugly hunk of junk," they said as they reclaimed their spot on the floor.

"Then why did you keep it for so long?" Octavia asked as she sat up.

"Because I'm a sentimental bastard, of course. I mean, come on, look at this!" Sage lifted up a chunky piece of blown glass that poorly resembled the Pokémon Bulbasaur, then bounded headfirst into the story of when they'd purchased it: their first weed pipe. They were still laughing as they walked it over to Quintin, who graciously wrapped it for packing.

"Jiro and Tripp watch anime, don't they?" June asked, blowing a tuft of red hair out of her eyes. "I bet they'll love that."

"You're probably right," Sage agreed, tossing the wrapped pipe in a box.

Quintin was in the kitchen tackling all the breakable dinnerware. Rightly, he didn't trust any of them enough to let them pack anything fragile. "You're killing me, Sage. Can't you at least act like you care about your shit?"

They stuck their tongue out at him. "Oh, shut it, number five."

Quintin laughed deeply. "You don't have to call me 'number five,' you know. That is what my name means, after all."

"What?" June asked, popping her head out of the box she was digging around in. Octavia's ears perked up too.

"You guys didn't notice?"

Octavia, June, and Sage shared looks of confusion.

"Nope," Sage said as they turned back to Quintin.

"Yeah, Quintin is a diminutive form of Quintus, which means 'the fifth.' But it's not just me, you know."

June nodded, looking to Octavia. "Well, Octavia's name is obvious, but . . ."

Octavia laughed. *That's embarrassingly true. I get questions about my name from strangers all the time.*

Quintin said, "Well, June is the sixth month of the year, and Sage, your namesake was probably the Seven Sages of Greece. You should ask your mom about it."

"Seven Sages?" Sage asked as a wide grin spread across their face. "Sick!"

"What about the others?" Octavia asked.

"Well, Delta is the fourth letter in the Greek alphabet."

"And Tripp is used as a nickname for 'the third,' right?" June asked Quintin.

"Mhm, and Jiro means 'second son' in Japanese."

"What about Leif?" Octavia asked, failing to figure out the riddle herself.

"Now, that one I'm not sure about," Quintin admitted, pausing to type something into his phone. "Leif means 'first descendant.' It seems like our parents really didn't leave anything to chance. Did they?"

"That's some crazy shit," Sage murmured, turning back to their glass of wine. "I'm going to have to learn more about those sages, though; that's for sure."

Quintin laughed into his own glass of wine before he taped up a box with the last of their dinnerware.

"How much time do we have left?" June asked as she finished packing the box in front of her.

"Only twenty minutes," Sage replied, checking the time on the television screen.

"Think we can finish before then?" Quintin asked, eyeing Octavia accusingly.

"All right, fine," she groaned. "I'll actually get to work now."

Octavia left the group in the living room, returning to her room to finish packing up. She'd finished three boxes worth, but still had a ton to pack away. Earlier that afternoon, they'd made a deal with each other that they would diligently pack all their crap until midnight, so that they could party their asses off until morning.

Octavia had broken a sweat by the time she taped her last box shut. She'd done a terrible job, but hey, she'd gotten it done. She returned to the kitchen, uncorked a fresh bottle of wine, and practically skipped her way to the couch. Thanks to the dagger sheathed against the skin of her right thigh, she didn't have to think about her magic right now, nor the craziness that had been the last two days of her life. No, tonight she could be plain old Octavia, a magicless witch in a coven of witches.

Octavia snorted at the thought. *The grass is always greener, right?*

"What's so funny?" a familiar voice asked from behind, causing her to flinch and almost spill her drink.

"Don't sneak up on me like that!" Octavia batted her free hand at Leif. "I didn't hear you come in."

He laughed merrily as he leaned against the back of the couch, all hints of the fear and worry from earlier stripped away.

"Did you finish packing too?" she asked.

"Yup," Leif said before grabbing Octavia's wine glass and stealing a sip.

"I'll help you portal everything to the Brookline house tomorrow morning," Quintin called over Tripp's shoulder from where they stood chatting with June in the kitchen.

"Thanks!" Leif called back, returning his attention to Octavia. But Octavia was hung up on their conversation with June. The way June batted her lashes. The way Tripp's muscles were flexing. The way Quintin shifted uncomfortably from foot to foot. *What is—?*

"It's rude to stare, you know," Leif whispered in her ear.

"But—"

"But nothing, nosy."

"Fine," Octavia relented with a dramatic roll of her eyes.

As she took another sip from her glass, Jiro and Sage flopped onto the couch on either side of her. She shoved her drink into Leif's empty hands, still hanging over the back of the couch, as she threw her arms around Jiro's shoulders and squeezed. She buried her face deep into his neck to keep her tears from falling. This was the first time she'd seen Jiro since she—well, since her magic had almost killed him. Him and everyone else for that matter.

"I missed you too, Tavi." Jiro laughed in her ear.

"How come you don't hate me right now?" she asked, pushing away from him to look him in the eye.

"Because I'm fine, and I know you weren't trying to do that to us." He wiped a tear that had fallen without her permission from her cheek. "Are you okay?"

"I honestly don't know," she replied, the buzz from the wine coaxing the truth out of her. "But I think I will be, eventually."

"Good." Jiro smiled wide as he accepted a beer from Leif.

Octavia watched from the couch as Leif listened to Jiro and Sage's conversation, only occasionally jumping in. She had no idea what they were talking about. There was only one thing on her mind at the moment.

After Jiro and Sage got up to grab fresh drinks, Leif caught her observing him. "What are you thinking about?" he asked.

She smiled, the curve of her mouth teasing and playful. "You. All the time. Sometimes clothed. Sometimes not." She shrugged innocently. "It depends."

Leif leaned farther over the backrest of the couch, his face an inch from hers. "And what about right now?" A challenge glinted in his light eyes.

Octavia's cheeks burned, warm as embers. "Wouldn't you like to know?"

Leif's gaze dropped to her lips and her breath caught. Her face gravitated toward his, no thought, just instinct.

"Sixty seconds!" Tripp bellowed over the music and chatter.

Octavia stilled, her lips a breath from Leif's. Their eyes met. He smiled. "Guess we're going to have to wait a minute to finish what we started."

Octavia laughed as she pulled back and turned around to find the boxes pushed to the edges of the room, making space for the eight of them at the center. With a minute to go until midnight, the group gathered around the television, drinks in hands. They chatted amongst themselves quietly, waiting for the final countdown.

Finally, the sparkly ball on the television screen began to fall.

Ten.

Nine.

"Eight," Octavia said, barely loud enough to hear over the music.

But Sage had been standing near and heard. "Seven," they said.

June smiled wide as she continued the countdown. "Six!"

Quintin murmured, "Five," as he shook his head good-naturedly.

Delta rolled her eyes but appeased them by uttering, "Four."

Tripp waggled his eyebrows joyfully as he said, "Three."

"Two!" Jiro cried, throwing an arm over Sage's shoulder.

"One." As Leif said it, he was staring down at Octavia, white shards of light glistening in his blue eyes. Her heart ached at the love she saw in them. Love for her. She couldn't get her lips to his fast enough.

"Happy New Year!" they all bellowed—everyone but Octavia and Leif. They were too busy finishing what they'd started.

Hugging, kissing, and fervent drinking ensued, as the eight of them got to partying. The loft had never felt happier nor fuller despite its contents being packed away. Octavia honestly couldn't remember the last time she'd had so much fun.

So, she rose to the challenge, as Quintin had said she should, and soaked in every single laugh, smile, and good feeling. Somehow, deep inside, she knew that light, love, and happiness were the only weapons she had against the darkness within.

For her family, she would rise.

Acknowledgments

I would like to start by expressing my sincerest gratitude to the entire team at Wildling Press for reading the original (very rough) draft of this novel and seeing its potential. These characters wouldn't have come to life without you, and for that, you have my eternal thanks. In particular, I would like to thank my editor, Christina Kann, for her unwavering dedication and meticulous attention to detail; my proofreaders, Mary-Peyton Crook and Grace Ball, for their sharp eye; as well as my designer, Michael Hardison, for capturing the essence of this story with such a stunning cover and internal design.

To the readers: thank you for picking up this book and sticking through to the end. I'm immensely grateful for the time you've spent in this world I've created, getting to know the characters I treasure so much. I sincerely hope it was time well spent, and you're looking forward to the sequel! I cannot thank you enough for your support.

An extra special thanks goes out to the small army of supporters that have gotten me this far: to my first and favorite beta reader, MJ; my critique partner, Allyson; my best friends, Amy, Caroline, Laura G., and Laura T.; my BookTok, Bookstagram, and Writer Twitter friends (I can't fit all of your names here, but please know I truly appreciate every single one of you); my mother- and father-in-law, Anne and Chris; my wonderful parents, Fred and Kathleen; and Mandy, my little sister and beloved partner-in-crime. Whether you read bits and pieces of the many iterations of this book or whether you let me to talk your ear off for hours about writing and publishing, your support means the world to me. I fervently hope I can repay the favor someday.

And last but not least, thanks to Dom, for encouraging me to chase after my childhood dreams. Without you, I never would have found the confidence to pick up the craft again. I doubt I can ever properly thank you for all the tremendous ways you've impacted my life, but refusing to grow up right alongside me, that's been my personal favorite. So, as I write this, I raise a glass in your honor. To the best listener, alpha reader, friend, and life partner this world has ever known. Cheers to you, my love.

ABOUT THE AUTHOR

KARA BADALAMENTI is the author of *Cursed Coven*, the first book in the Cursed Coven series. She lives in St. Louis with her partner and two naughty cats. When she's not reading, writing, or listening to music, she enjoys frequenting museums and art galleries, as well as tending to her garden. She invites you to visit her on Instagram and TikTok @authorkarabadalamenti or on her website, karabadalamenti.com.